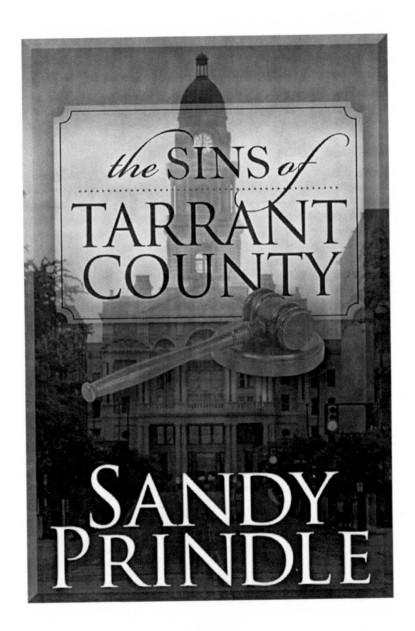

the SINS of
TARRANT
COUNTY

SANDY
PRINDLE

New York

The Sins of Tarrant County

Disclaimer: The Publisher and the Author make no representations or warranties with respect to the accuracy or completeness of the contents of this work and specifically disclaim all warranties, including without limitation warranties of fitness for a particular purpose. No warranty may be created or extended by sales or promotional materials. The advice and strategies contained herein may not be suitable for every situation. This work is sold with the understanding that the Publisher is not engaged in rendering legal, accounting, or other professional services. If professional assistance is required, the services of a competent professional person should be sought. Neither the Publisher nor the Author shall be liable for damages arising herefrom. The fact that an organization or website is referred to in this work as a citation and/or a potential source of further information does not mean that the Author or the Publisher endorses the information the organization or website may provide or recommendations it may make. Further, readers should be aware that internet websites listed in this work may have changed or disappeared between when this work was written and when it is read.

This book is a work of fiction. Names, characters, and events are products of the author's imagination or are used fictitiously. Any resembalance to actual events or persons, living or dead, is entirely coincidental. Readers should not infer that individuals or policies exist in Tarrant county government that could or would lead to circumstances or events that occur in this book. Readers can take comfort in the fact that the author worked twenty four years for this county and in his opinion, Tarrant County has the best government in the state.

ISBN 978-1-60037-543-9

Library of Congress Control Number: 2008941335

MORGAN · JAMES
THE ENTREPRENEURIAL PUBLISHER

Morgan James Publishing, LLC
1225 Franklin Ave., STE 325
Garden City, NY 11530-1693
Toll Free 800-485-4943
www.MorganJamesPublishing.com

In an effort to support local communities, raise awareness and funds, Morgan James Publishing donates one percent of all book sales for the life of each book to Habitat for Humanity. Get involved today, visit **www.HelpHabitatForHumanity.org**.

Prologue

It was in the early afternoon of May 24, 1841, when the group of well-armed horsemen ascended the steep hill. As the weary horses caught their wind, the lead rider advanced a few steps, peering anxiously to the north at the Indian huts across the creek. Behind him, two villages lay in smoldering ruins, as smoke from the fires rose in the cloudless sky.

Disguising his inferior numbers with surprise and audacity, he had ordered precision charges from three directions on the first unsuspecting village. Fortunately, most of the braves were away on a hunting trip. The horsemen had been unaware of the second village when they charged the first. Their momentum carried them through the second village as they chased terrified refugees. Now they faced a third village, larger than the other two combined, and the element of surprise was gone. Caution showed on the leader's face as he counted over two hundred huts on the creek below. The Ripley family massacre was avenged. There was no point in risking his seventy-man militia command in charging that third village.

The leader was a large man, with strong features and a bold mustache, his face protected by a wide-brimmed black hat. The man's gaze was piercing and his skin was dark, tempered by years in the sun. His dark blue tunic had straps from the shoulder to the neck. On each strap was a single gold star. The man was General Edward Tarrant.

The general reached into his saddle bag, pulled out his marine glass, and polished the lens. Extending it, he brought it to his right eye and scanned the landscape from left to right, looking past the Indian village below to a beautiful valley beyond. It stretched for two miles before rising up to another group of hills on the other side. Some of the hills were bluffs with sheer drops to the valley floor. Three waterfalls cascaded down those bluffs and united somewhere out of sight, forming the stream—later to be known as Big Bear Creek—that was running toward them. Timber covered the hills on both sides of the valley, and several deer were grazing contentedly there.

A wide smile softened the general's tough visage. This place had it all: timber, water, wildlife, grassland, and an unobstructed approach to a fort they could build. The general, who had a keen sense of destiny, gazed beyond the beautiful landscape and into the future. *Is this a momentous beginning? Will this raid scare the savages into leaving? Will this area open itself to settlers? If I put an outpost here in this beautiful valley, will it be the beginning of a new*

1

settlement? What will it be like in fifty, a hundred, or even a hundred and fifty years? What will it become?

The general masked his enthusiasm with a modest poker face. His companions wouldn't understand. *This valley will be the center of everything. There will be more people than I can imagine. Good people and bad. Maybe a few will be great. There will be triumphs and failures. There will be prosperous times—this is obviously fertile soil, and like everywhere else, there will be times of terrible trouble.*

General Tarrant was wrong about the valley. Within twenty years, "the center of everything" would move fifteen miles west to Fort Worth. One hundred and fifty years later, the valley would be the largest garbage dump in the county. Ironically, he would be right about everything else. There would be over one million people in the county named after him, and that was more than he could have imagined. There would be scientific advances beyond his comprehension. Tarrant County would have an ample share of honest, hardworking people, along with a few community giants, but it would have to endure miscreants, too. There would be dizzying successes and heartbreaking failures. There would be good times and times of terrible trouble. Tragically, the miscreants would commit many sins.

Chapter One

The slender, dark-complexioned, middle-aged man gripped the steering wheel, his eyes narrowing with concern. The couple exited the swank Stein Ericksen Lodge and walked briskly toward the man's rental car only a few feet away. Well-made plans had just gone to hell. The target's brake lines were already cut. If he didn't do something quick, the woman would die, along with the target, in a fiery crash on the steep winding road below. Buck Reed had shadowed the man for three days without seeing him talk to a soul. *Where had this woman come from?* As he reached underneath the seat for the knife, he quickly calculated the distance. If the target escorted the woman to her side of the car, he could just make it. But if he went to the driver's side and opened her door by releasing a power lock, she had to die. Bending low and moving quickly, Reed opened his door as the couple passed behind his car. The target was a true gentleman. The couple's laughter filtered through the fog as he opened her door. On returning to the back of the car, the target's eyes widened in surprise as he saw Reed appear, literally out of the mist.

There was no time to cry or yell—people can't cry out when their throat is cut. The man slipped slowly down the trunk of the car, desperately fighting for a breath, his eyes drawn to the bright light in the distant sky, a light coming at him with awesome speed. His companion's shrill screams sounded miles away as she appeared above him. Her frantic face dimmed more and more as the light drew nearer and brighter, nearer and brighter ... brighter ... brighter.

Less than an hour later, the slender man, now dressed in more expensive clothing, dialed the pin numbers from a prepaid telephone card into a pay phone at the busy Salt Lake airport.

"Hello?"

"Reed?"

"No names, remember? The job's done."

"Good! Did you make it look like an accident?"

"No. I couldn't. I made it look like a holdup."

The voice turned hard on the other end of the line. "You told me you could make it look like a car wreck."

"I know. I had his brake lines cut. He left the hotel with a woman. I couldn't see it coming."

"So what? Your reputation says that you don't jeopardize your clients. Why didn't you let them both die?"

"Because I don't work that way. I don't hit bystanders."

"I don't like it. Nobody pays attention to an accident. Who knows where a murder investigation stops. Did the woman see you?"

"I don't think so. They'll think it was an amateur holdup. What's the big deal? We're a long way from South Carolina."

"The big deal is that asshole had our client killed last year. If the police find a link to that, they'll be up my ass in no time."

"Our client? I thought you were my client."

"No. Your client is dead. I'm his agent, just as you are."

"Then why was I hired to hit the guy?"

The gruff voice softened a little. "He was my friend. That sorry bastard had him hit over a routine labor dispute. Besides, my friend made a provision in his will that if he died by violent means, money would be set aside to get even."

The hit man smiled a little. *Revenge from the grave.* It had a nice ring to it. "Don't worry. You can rest easy tonight. Townsend is dead, and the police won't look past the holdup. It didn't look professional."

"The police aren't that stupid. They'll find the cut brake lines."

"Hopefully not. I called the rental car people and told them to pick up the car. I told them I was from the hotel and the police authorized the removal. I mentioned the brakes didn't work. I'm counting on Avis and the cops not communicating in the confusion."

"It better work out that way. How did that bastard die?"

"A quick knife to the throat. He was dead in seconds."

"That's too bad. I wanted him to suffer."

"Sorry. It wasn't in the contract. You owe me the balance, another twelve five."

"You'll get it after I'm sure we are safe."

"That wasn't the deal. You'll send it now."

"I don't have to pay you a damn thing, Reed. You don't even know who I am."

Reed chuckled. "I had one other client tell me that. May he rest in peace."

"Don't try to bluff me, asshole."

"I'm not bluffing. I'm the last man you want to piss off."

"I don't buy it."

"Then don't buy it. Make me happy."

"You ain't that good, Reed. You wouldn't know how to find me."

Reed laughed. "You gave me your beeper number, stupid. I could find you in an hour."

"The joke's on you. I stole this beeper. I'm smarter than you think. You can't find me, so screw you. You want to get mean, I'll pay you nothing. There's nothing you can do about it."

Reed grinned. *Could I find this guy? Should I kill him?* "You better think real hard before you take that position."

"You don't scare me, hired killer. I'm going to have a great vacation on your money. I'm not sending you a postcard, either."

Reed hung up the receiver and strolled back to his gate as he checked his squawking beeper. After looking around, he returned to the bank of phones. There was a message in his call notes box. Reed listened to the message and, using his calling card, returned the call.

"This is 555-3139."

"This is Reed, returning your call."

The voice changed from cold to respectful. "Yes, sir. Thank you for returning my call."

"Who am I speaking with?"

"I'm sorry. I can't disclose that."

"I see. What can I do for you?"

"I need your services."

"Who is the recipient?"

The voice chuckled. "Recipient. That's good, Reed. I'm sure that he will be grateful for your charitable attention."

"Who is it?"

"I'm not at liberty to give you a name just now."

Reed frowned. Another game player. But if they were cautious, they were usually serious. "I can't work in the dark. If you can't give me a name, at least tell me what he does and why he needs my attention."

"I can tell you this. He's a judge. I can't tell you the reason."

Reed laughed. "What did he do? Rule against you?"

"Hardly. It's much more involved than that."

"I'm sorry. I don't do contracts on elected officials. There's too much heat, not only for me, but for you as well."

"You don't need to babysit us. Our heat is our problem."

5

Reed paused. *Who the hell is "us"?* "Worrying about my clients is always my problem. If they're caught, they'll rat on me to save themselves. I have survived by keeping suspicion away from them."

"We would keep you confidential. We do need your services, Mr. Reed. We are serious about this."

"I'm sorry. I can't help you right now. I have another job to finish up, and I still won't target an elected official."

"Is that your final answer?"

"I'm afraid so. It just isn't safe enough for me."

"I guess we will have to pay all that money to someone else."

"That's okay. I won't miss it, but thank you for calling." Reed disconnected the phone and returned to the ticket counter to change his destination to Charleston. A date with his client awaited him. Reed didn't know who he was, but that probably would be remedied. Did he want revenge more than the money? That one he would play by ear.

Reed had to wait an extra hour for the flight to Atlanta. A baseball game in the lounge helped pass the time, but he drank only a Diet Coke. Alcohol was a habit a hit man could ill afford. The soft drink was enough for him as he kept an eye on the ball game and enjoyed imagining his next victim squirming. Squirming, begging, and praying. Reed was still smiling at the thought when he boarded the Atlanta flight. As he sat down, he noticed an attractive woman sitting across the aisle. The woman started to smile back, then her expression became confused, and her eyes slowly turned cold with recognition. *Who is she,* wondered Reed as he buckled in, taking care to close his eyes and tilt his head back in the seat to feign fatigue and indifference. The face was only vaguely familiar, but it teased his memory. The answer still eluded him as he felt the plane lift off the runway minutes later.

Ten minutes later, it hit him hard as she spoke to the flight attendant. It was the Denver job. How could she remember him after thirty years? It had been dark, and he had been outside her bedroom window. If she'd seen him at all, it would have been only a glimpse. *I'll be damned! The doctor's mistress! Yes, if she saw me, she would remember. I cost her plenty. She was going to blackmail him. Will she blow the whistle? What a time for a coincidence.* There was nowhere to run.

Chapter Two

Justice of the Peace Ray Sterrett exited his driveway in his old, but maintained, Porsche and pointed the car toward his courthouse office in Mansfield, seven miles away. The route was so well established after eleven years that the car almost found the old subcourthouse by itself. Ray could seldom remember the drive; he used the time to think and plan.

It was the only quiet time he had. His mind drifted back to the problems at home.

I have to get the kids' minds off of Doris. After two years they should be getting better. My grief must be showing again. The kids pick that up so fast, and it increases their bitterness. One more outburst at Anita, and she'll be the fourth housekeeper I've had to replace. How do you convince an eight-year-old son and six-year-old daughter that life must go on when you don't believe it yourself?

The pain of his wife's death in a plane crash swept over him again as he unconsciously clenched the steering wheel. "Get a grip on yourself," he said out loud. "You have a busy day ahead of you." *Maybe Anita was right. Perhaps the pictures of Doris should be put away. It would help the whole family go on.* Robbie's response this morning had Anita crying, and the boy's anger had surprised even his father.

"Those pictures are all we have left of Mommy," he had screamed at Anita. "We can do without you a lot easier than her pictures. You must be tired of dusting them."

When Anita started crying, little Jan followed suit, and breakfast had become another emotional disaster.

I'd better diffuse this situation tonight. I can't go out of town leaving this behind. I'll take the kids to the Rangers game. Robbie and I both like to laugh at the Rangers' pitching staff, and I'll persuade him to stop taking his frustrations out on the housekeeper until I get back.

It happened without warning as Ray came over a hill. He saw an old Ford pickup run the red light and then broadside a little Toyota sedan. The sedan was knocked to the right and wrapped around a telephone pole. The pickup stayed in the intersection, its radiator boiling over. The passenger, thrown from the cab, was lying on the street. Ray skidded to a stop, ran back up the hill, and flagged down the next car, to keep it from running over the man lying in the street.

"Do you have a car phone?" he yelled.

"No," answered the man behind the wheel. "What's going on?"

"There's an accident just over the hill. Anyone coming over this hill will run right into the victims."

"What do you want me to do?"

"Are you a doctor by any chance?"

"No," returned the driver.

"Then flag down the cars behind you and reroute the traffic by turning them around. I'll call for help. This intersection is going to be tied up for at least forty-five minutes."

"I'll take care of it."

Ray ran back to the car and dialed the Arlington police dispatcher. "Wanda, this is Judge Sterrett. We have an accident at the intersection of Green Oaks and Little Road. It's blocking the intersection. There are three, possibly four, serious injuries. We'll need to use the power scissors on one of the vehicles. We'll need at least three traffic units as well as the officers handling the accident."

"By 'power scissors,' do you mean the Jaws of Life?"

"Come on. I'm no fireman, Wanda."

"All right, Judge. Do we need the large or small unit?"

"The small one. There's a Toyota wrapped around a telephone pole."

"Ten-four, Judge. I'll have everything there pronto."

"Thanks, Wanda. See you soon."

Ray hung up the mobile phone and ran toward the accident. The Toyota was leaking gasoline, so he ran back to his car and retrieved a fire extinguisher. An elderly gentleman was checking the victims. He backed away as Ray raced up to the Toyota and applied a generous blast from the fire extinguisher to the rear of the car. The judge approached the pickup's driver, who was wandering around his prone friend. "Are you hurt?"

"No, but Charlie looks real bad. I'm gonna get him off this road."

"No! Don't move him. Help's on the way. You have a big goose egg on your head. Sit on that curb over there till the ambulances get here."

"I'm okay, I tell you."

"What's Charlie's last name?" asked Ray as he gently led the man out of the street.

"Finley," answered the driver. "Let go of me."

"Just sit still on the curb here. What's your name?"

"Bob Wall."

"Bob, can you tell me what happened?"

"My brakes failed. I don't remember anything after that."

"Just sit here. I'll be back in a minute."

Noticing that the man in the street was turning purple, Ray opened his mouth and discovered a loose denture plate blocking his air passage. Ray called to an onlooker. "Hold his jaws open for me. Put this fountain pen against his molars. I don't want him biting my finger off."

"Aren't you Judge Sterrett?" asked the man as he complied.

"Yes. Get a firm grip on his upper and lower plates."

Ray inserted his index finger in Charlie's mouth and wrestled the half-swallowed denture out of his throat. There was still no breathing. "Do you know CPR?" Ray asked his helper.

"Yes."

"Then give this one mouth-to-mouth. I'm afraid to roll him over."

Ray checked with the elderly man, who was now leaning into the driver's window of the Toyota. "What's the situation here?"

The old man slowly backed out of the window, his stomach bleeding from broken glass. "The driver's vital signs are okay, but she's out. I'm worried about the other one. The telephone pole got her. Her legs look crushed. I'm afraid they'll have to cut her out."

"The equipment is on the way. Are you a doctor?"

"No, I'm a retired hospital administrator."

"I'm glad you're here. Is the passenger breathing?"

"Yes, she's breathing."

Ray called out to the man giving CPR, "Any response yet?"

"Not much. He's not breathing on his own."

"Keep at it," called Ray as he headed back to his car. The sounds of sirens wailed softly from the east. Ray grabbed the mobile phone and redialed the dispatcher. "Wanda, this is Ray again. Please advise the first ambulance that they'll need to give oxygen to one of the victims."

"Is his airway clear?"

"It is now. He tried to swallow his false teeth, and he's purple."

"That sounds like respiratory arrest. I'll tell the first unit to have their Ambu bag ready. The first PD units are about sixty seconds away. Two ambulance units are about two minutes behind them."

"I hear them, Wanda. Thanks."

Ray watched the first blue-and-white slide into the intersection, lights flashing and sirens wailing. The driver jumped out and immediately started moving the gathering crowd back. Ray wrinkled his nose in distaste at Trooper Agnew—Arlington PD's answer to the Gestapo. Agnew approached the man doing CPR and gazed at the victim. As Agnew directed the first-aid man away from the scene, Ray ran over to intercede. "Trooper, why are you running that man off?"

"Don't call me trooper. I'm a sergeant. You see these stripes?"

"I don't think that's important right now. Call that man back over. The victim isn't breathing."

"Look, Judge, I don't take orders from you. What're you doing here?"

"I saw the accident. I took charge until a unit got here."

"Well, I'm here now, so buzz off."

"What are you going to do about the guy lying in the street?"

Sergeant Agnew sauntered over to Charlie, stooped over, and took his pulse as two other squad cars arrived. Agnew left the victim and began issuing orders to the three officers as they got out of the cars, while Ray went over to the man who had been doing CPR. "Was he responding any to the mouth-to-mouth?" he asked.

"I was getting air into his lungs, but he can't breathe on his own."

"If you want to continue the CPR, you can do so on my authority."

"No thanks. I've dealt with that prick Agnew before."

Two of the newly arrived police officers went to assist the women in the Toyota, and the other officer approached Ray and the CPR man.

"I need your names and addresses, please."

The CPR man spoke first. "My name is Walter Simmons, 1130 Benoit Bend, Fort Worth, Texas, 76112. Officer, if that man in the street doesn't get some oxygen pretty soon, he's gonna die."

The officer ignored the remark. "And you, sir?"

"Ray Sterrett, 4327 Paloma Place, Arlington, Texas, 76017."

"Judge Ray Sterrett?"

"Yes."

"I'm happy to meet you, sir. I'm Jerry Willet. My son was one of your karate students three years ago. He speaks very highly of you."

"Is that Tommy Willet?"

"Yeah, that's right."

"Your boy's a good kid. Officer, I want to second the concerns of Mr. Simmons. Agnew made us cease CPR on that man out in the street."

"Sergeant Agnew told me the man's already dead."

"I wish you would verify that."

"No way. You haven't seen Agnew get mad."

"Yes, I have. I know what you're talking about."

"Did you see the accident?"

"Yes, I did. The pickup ran the red light and T-boned the Toyota. The driver is the one sitting on the curb. He said the brakes failed."

"Very good. Did you see the accident, Mr. Simmons?"

"No. I came up right afterwards."

Officer Willet went over to the driver as the first ambulance pulled up. Sergeant Agnew directed the paramedics to the Toyota.

"Who needs the Ambu bag?" called out the driver.

"No one," returned Agnew. "That high and mighty judge over there called for it. He don't know what the hell he's talking about."

The fire truck arrived, and the crew began the serious and delicate task of extricating the women from the Toyota. Three minutes later, the second ambulance arrived. Ray came forward and directed it to Charlie. As the paramedics were examining him, Agnew came running up.

"You don't need to bother with him. He's dead."

"Almost," replied the paramedic who was kneeling over Charlie. "Ted, get me the Ambu bag. We can save him if he hasn't gone too long without oxygen."

Ray glared at Agnew, who averted his eyes, doing a slow burn. "You'd better pray that he lives, Agnew," Ray growled as he fought to control his indignation.

Ray approached the officer who was issuing the traffic citations to the pickup driver. "Officer Willet, do me a favor. Call my office and update me on that man's medical condition," he said pointing to Charlie.

"I thought he was dead."

"Only in Agnew's mind."

"Sure, I'll call."

"Thanks. I'll be at the office if you need me for a further statement. I'm going out of town tomorrow for the rest of the week."

"Okay, Judge. Thanks for your help today. Some of the people here told me what all you did."

"What a way to start off the week," muttered Ray as he drove away. "There must be a full moon."

Ray nodded to his staff as he walked past the usual Monday morning pandemonium in the cramped outer office. A service counter divided the public from his four court clerks, who were squeezed into eighty square feet of space. The work area included desks, chairs, telephones, old docket books, computers, printers, and four busy, harassed court clerks. The work area was a mess. The whole building was a joke. The old metal building had been leased on a temporary basis until the new county subcourthouse could be built. The project never made it to the priority list. The building was poorly insulated, and the wiring was worse. The roof leaked in six places when it rained in the next county. The building housed the justice court, and the constable's office was behind the courtroom, which in the kindest terms could be described as unpretentious. There was no jury box. The judge's bench was raised only thirty inches. When seated, the judge had to look up at the litigants. There were two counselor tables and about twenty folding chairs placed behind them. When there was a jury trial, six chairs were moved over to the far wall.

Every attorney in the county was embarrassed to come here. In addition, most attorneys officed in Fort Worth, over twenty miles away. Judge Sterrett's fairness and knowledge of the law had slowly won him their respect over the years, but there was no money to be made at this level, and it was hard for them to convince their clients that enforceable judgments could come out of such a dumpy facility.

Judge Sterrett and Constable Harvey Walling had campaigned for years to build a new subcourthouse on the I-20. They could agree on little else. Constable Walling liked his police powers county wide. He had secured grants to structure a DWI task force and to monitor illegal dumping. These project agendas often conflicted with the municipal police duties. Serving civil process papers for the justice court became an afterthought instead of the primary responsibility. That was where the clash with Judge Sterrett began.

Ray strolled into his chambers and sat in his recliner desk chair, the only modern equipment in the subcourthouse. His head clerk, Cassandra Strange, breezed in right behind him.

"You're running late, Judge. I hope you had a good weekend."

"Good morning, Cass. You look happy and chipper as always. The weekend was the same as all the others. Work is still a lot better than home. A prospective buyer came to look at the karate studio, though. Maybe I'll get lucky this time. You wouldn't believe the gruesome wreck that happened right in front of me this morning. That's why I'm late. Be alert for a phone call from an Arlington officer by the name of Willet. I want to know the medical status on a man named Charlie Finley. By the way, how was your weekend?"

"Well, the new boyfriend flaked out on me again."

"Cass, you keep looking for love in all the wrong places," laughed Ray, admiring her long auburn hair and hourglass figure. If she would just move in better circles, she could find a good man in no time. "Stay out of the bars and go to church. You'll have them standing in line."

"Yeah, right. I tried the Christians once. It was the married ones who lined up. I don't need that grief. There's no good men left."

"Is there anything hot out there this morning?"

"No. Just the usual Monday morning stuff—mostly eviction cases and a couple of the usual peace bond applications that get filed after child visitations. Rachael Frank called. She sounded really pissed off."

"Yeah. That's about a memo I sent last week outlining my plan for petty cash reserves. It's ridiculous to pay double prices for our office supplies. I bet my request for a commissioners' court investigation got her jacked up. I'll call her later. What's on the menu for today?"

"The Billy Earl Stewart peace bond hearing is set for nine o'clock. I didn't schedule any thing else this morning. This afternoon, you've got eight evictions and three civil cases. The post judgment contempt hearing has an agreed pass. Maybe the parties are going to settle."

"I hope so. My patience is running out on that defendant. All he has to do is answer the interrogatories."

"Come on, Judge. When he discloses his assets, he'll have to pay the judgment, or the assets will be seized. He won't answer those interrogatories until he's on the way to jail. You know how stubborn he is. The press is here on the peace bond hearing. I've had two calls already this morning. One was from your admirer at the *Star-Telegram*."

Marilyn Shaw, mused Ray with a half smile. It had been three months since he'd seen her. The judge recalled the humiliation when he brought Marilyn home to meet the kids. His careful coaching of Robbie had gone for naught. As promised, there had been no rudeness, but his son had sat quietly, looking down at his shoes, saying nothing as his tears had flowed freely. Marilyn's attempts at conversation with him were met with rebuking silence. Marilyn, never married, couldn't understand.

"Mother-in-laws aren't this bad," she had commented on her way out. Ray never worked up the nerve to call her again, even with an apology.

"Everybody's here for that peace bond hearing," said Cass. "I finally got the constable to provide a bailiff. But he sent his cousin Sid just to aggravate you." Sid Walling was the constable's chief deputy.

Ray scowled in distaste. If he disliked anyone more than Constable Walling, it was his cousin Sid, known throughout the county for his Gestapo tactics and crazy schemes.

"Cass, please be a dear and confirm my flight to Corpus Christi for the JP school tomorrow and try to find a visiting judge to hear my eviction cases later this week."

"I'm way ahead of you, Judge," replied Cass proudly. "Judge Chavez is coming in Thursday morning. I have him loaded up with twenty-three cases. You won't have to double up when you get back next Monday."

"Thanks," replied Ray. "You're efficient as always. Anything else?" he asked as he headed for the courtroom.

"Nothing that can't wait," she replied as she watched the tall dark-haired judge disappear through the door. Her smile faded into wistfulness. *Why does the only good man left in the county have to be my boss? If I transferred out, would he call me? If he did, could I compete with a ghost?*

Chapter Three

"All rise please. This honorable court is now in session. Judge Ray Sterrett presiding," called Deputy Constable Sid Walling. As Ray passed the deputy constable without so much as a glance, he wondered where Walling learned to say all that. And how did he remember it? The judge assumed the bench and quickly surveyed the courtroom.

There was Terry Sutherland, the prosecutor, dressed as sloppily as ever. *If anyone has a more messed up personal life than me, it's Sutherland,* thought Ray. Next to him sat the petitioner for this proceeding, Shirley Lemons. Shirley was about twenty-eight, reasonably attractive, dressed in green, looking intimidated as hell. Behind them stood a man and woman dressed in Arlington police uniforms, looking at ease. To their right stood Marilyn Shaw, the *Star-Telegram* reporter, and a male reporter Ray had never seen before. Marilyn was staring back at him with an expression that was not pleasant. It took a lot of effort for that beautiful face to look unpleasant. To their right, directly behind the defendant, stood an elderly lady.

The defendant, Billy Earl Stewart, stood in front of the counselor's table in his Sunday best: a pair of sweat-stained khakis with the Arlington Water Department emblem above his heart. He was ignoring the judge and fixing a scowl on Shirley Lemons. If he could intimidate her with dirty looks, this would be a very short trial. Next to Stewart stood his attorney, Leonard Torrey. The attorney, pushing sixty, had a wrinkled face, with dark eyes in contrast to his pale complexion. Torrey was dressed in a Western outfit, complete with black hat. The clothes might have been cleaned twice this year. Sterrett recalled what he had heard about him. Torrey had as poor a reputation in Tarrant County as an attorney could get. A year's paying clients could be counted on one hand. Occasionally, a county criminal court judge would pity Torrey and appoint him public defender. Without that income, he'd starve. Torrey was a former fireman in Fort Worth who'd been fired for reasons known only to his chief. He had returned to school, obtained his law degree with a loan he'd never repaid, and then entered the justice system with a vengeance. Torrey delighted in representing government employees, never missing a chance to embarrass management.

"Please be seated," said Ray quietly, with a slight smile. Sometimes a smile and a soft voice diffused emotional hearings. After the seating noise subsided, Ray began. "We will come to order to hear case number PB026. Is the petitioner Shirley Lemons present and ready?"

Sutherland rose slowly, glancing at the defendant before turning toward the judge. "If it may please the court, the petitioner Shirley Lemons is present and ready." His bored expression and flat tone suggested that he had better things to do.

"Does the petitioner have any witnesses other than herself?"

"Yes, Your Honor. She has two Arlington police officers, Officers Dan Smith and Patricia West. There may be a rebuttal witness later."

"Thank you Mr. Sutherland. Is the defendant Billy Earl Stewart present and ready?"

Leonard Torrey stood up, shuffled his paperwork, and slowly looked at the judge. "Your Honor, Mr. Stewart is present. I respectfully move that this action be dismissed. It's a flagrant example of res judicata. The State knows that charges are pending in another court. As you probably know, Article 7.13 of the Code of Criminal Procedure clearly states, and I'll read this verbatim, 'If it appears from the evidence that the defendant has committed a criminal offense, the same proceedings shall be had as in other cases where parties are charged with crime.' Your Honor, this statute means just what it says."

Ray leaned back in his chair, knowing it was going to be one of those days. He nodded to the prosecutor, "Mr. Sutherland, any response?"

Sutherland got up a little faster and with more enthusiasm this time. "Your Honor, I don't believe that's the meaning of the statute. But before we split hairs on the interpretation, may I bring a case to your attention? It is ex parte Whatley. In that 1939 case, the defendant was out on bail, as this defendant is, and the peace bond was upheld. Miss Lemons is here seeking a civil remedy to ensure that the defendant does not harm her during the interim. There's no double jeopardy here."

Leonard Torrey rose even faster. "Your Honor, if you place a peace bond against my client, and he can't raise the money to meet the bond, he goes to jail. Would you please ask the distinguished prosecutor to explain how in the hell this is a civil remedy if my client stands in jeopardy of going to jail?"

Ray rapped his gavel lightly, maintaining his easy smile and soft voice. "Thank you, Mr. Torrey. Please be seated and kindly remove your hat in this courtroom."

Torrey sat down and put his hat on the floor by the table, exposing his shiny balding head. His eyes showed anger at the reprimand and resentment at having to expose his glossy dome to onlookers.

Ray continued. "As both counselors know, a peace bond has the characteristics of both a civil and a criminal proceeding. The statutory law in Article 7 of the Code of Criminal Procedure gives few rules and standards for this hearing, and the case law behind it is pretty scant. However, the case law Mr. Sutherland has cited is correct and on point. Mr. Torrey's motion for dismissal is denied. Both sides have a right to know my rules on peace bonds. While the remedies may be civil in nature, as Mr. Torrey points out, the ultimate remedy is jail. So, the rules of criminal evidence will apply and the burden of proof will be proof beyond reasonable doubt. Mr. Torrey, does the defense intend to present any witnesses?"

"I have a question, Your Honor."

"Yes, Mr. Torrey?"

"Can my client be required to testify at this hearing? Can the State call him as an adverse witness?"

"No, Mr. Torrey, they cannot."

"In that case, Your Honor, the defense reserves the right to call the respondent's grandmother, Gladys Stewart"—Torrey paused for dramatic effect—"if necessary."

"Thank you. Does either counsel wish to invoke the witness rule?"

Sutherland did not bother to rise. "No, Your Honor, there aren't that many witnesses. It's obviously not necessary."

Torrey bounded to his feet. Maybe he had a chance after all. This judge might not be so bad. "I wish to invoke the witness rule, Your Honor. The State has three witnesses. That's enough for them to feed off each other."

"Very well, Mr. Torrey. The rule will be invoked. Would all persons who intend to testify, please stand and raise your right hands?"

Billy Earl Stewart rose along with the rest of the witnesses, but Torrey raised his right arm and pulled him back down, shaking his head no.

"Do each of you solemnly swear or affirm that the testimony you give at this proceeding shall be the truth, the whole truth, and nothing but the truth, so help you God?"

"I do," echoed the witnesses.

The judge recited the rules for sequestered witnesses. "All of the witnesses, except Miss Lemons, will now retire. Thank you."

As the witnesses left the courtroom, Stewart leaned over to Torrey and whispered, "I need to talk to you now."

Torrey thought and whispered back, "It's too early to recess. We haven't even started yet. I'll try to get a recess after the opening statements. Nothing will happen until then anyway."

Ray looked at the prosecutor, "Does the State's counsel wish to make an opening statement?"

"Yes, Your Honor. Our evidence will show that the defendant, Billy Earl Stewart, at one time was romantically involved with Miss Lemons. The love affair went sour. After many violent arguments, Miss Lemons terminated the relationship. The evidence will show that the defendant continually harassed and threatened Miss Lemons with death if she refused to re-establish the relationship. The evidence will further show that on August 14th of this year, the defendant, Billy Earl Stewart, broke into Miss Lemons' apartment with intent to carry out his threats. The evidence will show that he was arrested there red-handed with weapons. After he made bail, he disobeyed the court order, given at the arraignment, to leave her alone. Your Honor, Miss Lemons is entitled to relief under Chapter 7 of the Code of Criminal Procedure. Thank you."

As Sutherland sat down, Leonard Torrey rose slowly and studied the judge, looking for his reaction to the prosecutor's opening statement but seeing nothing except that slight easy smile. *Damn him! He sits there so easy and relaxed with no movement except his eyes. I can't gauge him unless there's body language. I'll never play poker with this bastard.* "Your Honor, I'd suggest that these allegations belong in the 236th District Court. But if we must try them here, I submit that our evidence will show Miss Lemons is using this court to harass my client. She's bent on revenge because my client was unfaithful to her. This woman has pulled the ultimate woman-scorned trick by making up this whole sordid story. Thank you, Your Honor, and may we have a brief recess? I need to confer with my client again on an important detail."

"Any objections, Mr. Sutherland?"

"None, Your Honor, if it is brief."

"Very well. We'll reconvene in ten minutes. We stand in recess."

Leonard Torrey led his client into the only conference room available, a small room about eight feet square, with bookshelves built to the ceiling on two sides. The third wall had a small window. A credenza sat below the window and extended to the bookshelves on either side. To the right, hung a photo of a younger Judge Sterrett, dressed in a white karate suit, holding a large trophy and sporting a huge grin on his face. The caption at the bottom of the picture read, "Ray Sterrett US Karate Champion 1977." The bookshelves and floor were stacked with old docket books. No chairs were in the room.

"What do you need to talk to me about, Billy Earl?"

"Mr. Torrey, what's this bullshit about me cheating on Shirley?"

"I made it up. You want a chance to get out of this don't you?"

"That's another thing. I don't understand what this is all about. You never told me that I could go back to jail before my trial."

"Look, Billy, I didn't know she'd go this route. Are you sure you didn't go around her after you made bail?"

Stewart hesitated. "I just went by once right after I got out of jail. I wanted to talk to her. I parked two blocks away and waited for her to come by, but she never did."

"Did anyone else see you?"

"No."

"Good! There may be a way out of this."

"Why can't I testify?"

"Too risky. Whatever you say here can be used against you in the trial for attempted murder. You can maintain silence here and there."

"Yeah. That silence could send me straight to jail. I want to testify. I won't admit anything."

"That's easier said than done."

"Ain't there a way for me to defend myself?"

"Yes. I can attack their witnesses. If you testify, the prosecutor can go after you. I know you don't understand the legal system, but this hearing is a break for us. The State has to show their cards."

"This may be a game to you, but it's not to me. When it's my turn to testify, I'm going to, whether you like it or not. I'm not going back to that stinkin' jail. It's a horrible place."

"All right. If you're that determined. Just tell the judge you got caught running around on her after the fighting began. She got upset, then threw you out, told you she'd put you in jail over it. Tell the judge she called you over the night you were arrested and you didn't notice the knives. Tell him that she set you up with the perfect frame."

"That's pretty good, Mr. Torrey, but can we get away with it?"

"Why not?" Torrey knew no boundaries. "Did you bring my money?"

"Yeah. My grandmother's got it. She'll give it to you after the trial. I'm really stretched tight. How much money is that damned judge going to require for a bond if we lose this case?"

"I don't know. How much have you got?"

"Not much, other than my share of my grandfather's trust."

"How much is that?"

"Five thousand dollars."

"You're gonna need that and more on the main trial. If you lose this, I'll get you out on a writ of habeas corpus in a couple of days."

"Are you sure you can do that?"

"I think so. I know a judge with a weakness."

"What's the weakness?"

"Money."

"How much?"

"Probably five hundred. Wait here a minute. I'll see if they're ready to begin."

Stewart gazed out the window, wondering how he could be prosecuted so much for one incident. He knew one thing for sure. That bitch was dead. Anyone that tried to stop him would find out what dead feels like, he mused as he rested his hands on the window latches. Mischievously, he opened them.

Chapter Four

"You may call your first witness, Mr. Sutherland."

"Thank you, Your Honor. I wish to call Miss Shirley Lemons."

Shirley Lemons rose, made her way to the witness stand to the judge's left, and sat down with shaking hands. Clasping them together, she rested them on the ledge in front of her to hide the shaking. She glanced once at Stewart, and then fixed her gaze squarely on Sutherland.

"Would you state your name, please," drawled Sutherland.

"Shirley Lemons."

"Are you nervous, Shirley?"

"Yes, very."

"That's all right. Most witnesses are. Just try to relax, listen to the questions carefully, and answer them as best as you can, okay?"

"Yes sir."

"Do you live in the City of Arlington?"

"Yes sir."

"What's your address?"

"1241 M Street, Apartment 56."

"How long have you lived there?"

"Two years."

"How are you employed?"

"I'm a receptionist at the General Motors plant."

"How long have you been employed there."

"About four years."

Sutherland flipped a page. "How long have you known the defendant, Billy Earl Stewart?"

"About two years."

"How did you meet him?"

"He was living in the apartment directly above me. He helped me move in some of my things."

"When did you start dating him?"

"Several months later."

"Did he move in with you at some point?"

"Yes sir."

"Please explain the time and circumstances to the judge."

"About two months after we began dating, his roommate was transferred to Austin. Billy couldn't afford the rent, and I wasn't exactly rich, so we decided to save money by living together."

"So you lived together for how long?"

"About three months."

Sutherland glanced down at his paper. "How would you describe your relationship after he moved in?"

"Billy became very possessive after he moved in. I felt smothered. He was pushing for marriage right away. I wasn't ready for that. He was very jealous of my friends and raised Cain every time they called or if I met them for a drink after work. When we argued, he drank. When he drank, he got mean. We were having problems within a month."

"How and when did the relationship break up?"

"I made him leave right after the fourth of July."

"Did he go willingly?"

"No sir. I had to get the locks changed. Then I called one of his friends and paid him to come get Billy's things."

"Where did Billy move?"

"I don't know."

"Did you hear from Billy after that?"

Shirley grimaced. "Yes sir. Constantly."

"When did you first hear from him after you changed the locks?"

"About two days later."

"What did he want?"

"He wanted to come back."

"What did you tell him?"

"I told him no way, that it was over."

"Were there many conversations like this?"

"Yes sir."

"What was Billy's reaction to all of this?"

"At first he promised that he'd change, sent flowers to my office and would show up every couple of days or so. After about a week, he became more demanding, yelling, cursing, and threatening me."

Sutherland paused for emphasis. "What would he threaten?"

"That if he couldn't have me, no one else would. That if I began seeing anyone else, he'd kill me and the guy, too."

"Did you believe him?"

"Not at first. Only after he started following me around. He was getting more violent by that time."

"What do you mean by violent?"

"One time he tried to force my car off the road with his pickup. Then he became more graphic in describing how he was going to kill me. His tone of voice got angrier as time went on, and he came to my office and caused a scene. We had to call the police. Then he started coming to my door and would kick it several times when I wouldn't open it."

"Let's move to the second week of August. Do you recall that time?"

"Vividly."

"Tell us what happened."

"The beginning of that week he came to my office and got thrown out by the police. That was when he really scared me. His eyes were wild and his face was very red. I could tell he was losing control. The same afternoon, he tried to run me off the road, and then he called me at home that evening. He started screaming that he couldn't take this anymore and for me to enjoy my last hours on earth. Then he hung up. Two days later, when I came home, I saw my living room light on, and I remembered turning it off when I went to work that morning. I was afraid that he was in there, so I went to a neighbor's and called the police."

"What happened then?"

"When the police arrived, I told them what had been happening. I gave Officer West my apartment key. She and the other officer went in first. I didn't see what happened until they had Billy handcuffed. Officer West took me into the bedroom and showed me ..." Shirley's voice broke and she started trembling. Looking up at Ray, she choked out, "Could I have a drink of water, please, sir?"

Ray signaled Sid Walling over. "Would you get her some water?"

Sid nodded and walked briskly out the door to the left, toward the constable's office. He returned shortly with the water. "Here you are."

"Thank you." Shirley held the glass in a trembling hand and sipped, sitting silently for a moment while Ray glanced around the room. Stewart was leaning back in his chair with his arms folded, looking at Shirley. Torrey had turned around and was looking at the reporters, to distract them. The male reporter was scribbling notes on a pad while Marilyn was looking at Ray. Sutherland rose from his chair.

"Your Honor, may we have a five-minute recess?"

"If your witness wants one."

Shirley interjected, "No, I want to get this over with. I'll be all right. Where was I?"

Sutherland spoke up, "You were saying that you went into the bedroom with Officer West."

"Yes, I went into the bedroom with Officer West. She showed me four knives laid out in a row and two ropes about two feet long."

"Did the police take Stewart away then?"

"The male police officer did. Officer West stayed with me until some friends came over. I was in hysterics—I'm scared to death of him."

"Did you hear from Stewart after that?"

"Yes sir. He called me from jail. He said that I had only received a stay of execution. I'd be dead as soon as he got out of jail."

"Did you see him after he got out of jail?"

"No, sir, but the apartment manager told me she did."

"Objection, Your Honor."

"Sustained."

Sutherland rose, "Your Honor, we can call the apartment manager in, if you'd like."

"You may do so if you wish, Mr. Sutherland. But until she's here and sworn in, the objection is sustained. Continue with the witness."

Sutherland nodded. "Can you identify Billy Earl Stewart?"

Shirley pointed a shaking finger at Stewart. Sutherland turned to the judge. "That's all the questions I have for now. Pass the witness."

Ray turned to Torrey, "You may cross-examine."

Torrey stared at Shirley for a long silent moment. "That was quite a performance, Miss Lemons. Have you ever taken acting lessons?"

Sutherland was ready. "Objection, Your Honor. Counsel is badgering the witness."

"Sustained. Mr. Torrey, let's do this in a professional manner."

"Your Honor, may counsel approach the bench?"

"Yes, Mr. Torrey, you may both approach."

"Your Honor," hissed Torrey, "I'd like a conference in chambers?"

"Okay. The witness may stand down. There's a five-minute recess."

Ray and the attorneys filed into his office. Torrey sat in one of the two chairs, plopping his boot on the other, leaving Sutherland no place to sit. "Judge, there's two sides to every story, and a defense attorney is usually given some latitude when his client faces jail. That young woman out there is not nearly so innocent and defenseless as she's putting on, as you'll see shortly."

"Mr. Torrey, I think you should know that people don't put their feet on my chairs. Now remove your boot so Mr. Sutherland can sit down."

"Thank you, Judge. I don't want to sit down."

Torrey took his foot down and continued the attack. "Judge, am I going to get the privilege of cross-examining the State's witnesses, or should I just surrender the case here in chambers and file a complaint with the Judicial Conduct Committee?"

"I don't know where you've been practicing law, but when you're in this court, you'll act in a competent, professional manner. The questions you'll ask will be relevant and free from innuendo. If you want to make a point, do so with the witness and not from sidebar remarks. If you wish to file a complaint, I welcome it. But remember that can go both ways, counselor. Furthermore, this isn't my first day on the bench. Usually when attorneys pull stunts like you did, they are trying to draw attention away from a weak case. Do I make myself clear?"

"I hear you, Judge. Are you're gonna take this out on my client?"

"That's not going to work either, Mr. Torrey. Now let's get back in there and work this case, unless you have something else."

"I guess that's it for now."

The trio headed back for the courtroom, but an anxious Cass caught Ray. "Judge, you might want to call Rachael Frank back. She called again, hopping mad."

"Tell her that I'm in trial. She'll just have to stew."

Stewart caught Torrey on the way back in. "What went on in there, Mr. Torrey?"

"Nothing much. I tried to run a bluff, but I don't think it worked. Did you catch that statement about the apartment manager seeing you around the apartments?"

"Yeah. But that court order only kept me from going on the apartment property. I was two blocks away."

"You don't think the judge is going to buy that, do you?"

"What are we gonna do then?"

"If the apartment manager shows up, I'll just have to see."

Ray surveyed the courtroom. Everyone was in place. "Miss Lemons, you may resume the stand."

As Shirley walked to the witness stand, Leonard Torrey retrieved a yellow legal pad from his briefcase and studied a list of questions for several seconds, purposely making her sweat. Lifting his head, he fixed Shirley with a cold stare for a few seconds before speaking.

"Miss Lemons, did I understand you to say the only reason you let Billy move into your apartment was to save money?"

"That was the main reason."

"Are you telling this court that Billy didn't stay the night with you before he moved in?"

"No, I said that we were dating. I don't remember saying anything about whether he stayed the night or not."

"I suppose I have to be more direct. Did Billy spend the night with you before he moved in?"

"Yes."

"That's better. That wasn't so hard, was it?"

Shirley said nothing but glared at Torrey, smarting under his intimidation.

"Miss Lemons, is it true that you changed the locks on your door before you gave Billy a chance to move out?"

"No. I told him three times that our relationship was not gonna work out and he should move. But he wouldn't do it."

"Three times?"

"At least three times."

"When did these three times occur?"

"Over the July fourth holidays."

"How many days elapsed between the first time and the third time?"

"Two, maybe three days."

"What was Billy's response when you told him to move out?"

"He'd try to talk me out of it, start drinking, and cuss me out."

"Did he ever strike you?"

"No."

"Then you're asking this court to believe that a man, who never displayed any violence toward you whatsoever, threatened you and tried to kill you a month after you threw him out."

Sutherland rose from his chair. "Your Honor, I object to the question. Counsel is putting words in her mouth. She never said the defendant did not display any violence toward her. She simply testified he didn't strike her."

"Objection sustained. Rephrase the question."

"Miss Lemons, enlighten us on what type of violence Billy displayed toward you."

"He yelled and cursed at me all the time."

"Miss Lemons, do you think couples go through life living together without yelling and cursing at each other?"

"Not like that, they don't."

"Miss Lemons, would it be fair to say that Billy was more hurt than angry when you threw him out?"

"You'd have to ask him. He sounded pretty angry to me."

"I'll ask this another way. Did Billy's objections to the breakup intensify after he found out that you were pregnant?"

"That's when the threats to kill began."

"Miss Lemons, you aborted that baby, didn't you? You killed this man's child without even telling him, didn't you?"

Shirley said nothing, her head hanging low. Ray leaned back in his chair, staring in amazement at Torrey. *What a fool he is. It isn't every day that the State leaves out the motive because of sensitivity toward its client, and the defense attorney is dumb enough to provide it. Somehow, I don't see Torrey fitting in with the Right to Life Movement.*

"Miss Lemons," Torrey continued, "You got pretty tired of Billy calling you, wanting to come back, didn't you?"

"Yes."

"You got pretty angry at Billy, too, didn't you?"

"I was getting tired of being pushed around."

"You were so mad, you decided to get even with him, didn't you?"

"I don't know what you mean."

"Let's go back to the day Billy came to your office. He didn't know that child had been aborted until he saw you that day, did he?"

"I don't know how he found out I was pregnant. I didn't tell him."

"You called him over to your office to tell him personally that you aborted his child, didn't you?"

"No. That's not true. I didn't know he was coming to my office."

"Are you saying that Billy didn't know you were pregnant?"

"No. He knew all right. I just wasn't the one who told him. He was trying to use the pregnancy to get back together."

"You told him that you aborted the child when he came to your office. Isn't that right?"

"Yes."

"You invited him there, so you could personally see the pain in his eyes, didn't you? Did it give you satisfaction, Miss Lemons?"

"That's not true. I just wanted to get rid ..."

"Let's go to the night when Billy came to your apartment. You called him and told him to come over, didn't you?"

"No."

Torrey feigned surprise. "What time did you call the police?"

"About 8:30."

"What time do you get home from work?"

"Usually about 6:00. But that night I met my friends after work."

"You called Billy about 6:15 that night to come over, didn't you?"

"No."

"You laid out those kitchen knives in your bedroom, didn't you?"

"No. That's ridiculous."

"When Billy came over about 8:15, you told him to wait in the apartment until you got back from the drugstore, didn't you?"

"No," cried Shirley. "You're just making that up."

"You framed Billy so you could get rid of him, didn't you?"

"No. That's not true."

Torrey stood for dramatic effect. "Then can you tell me how Billy got into your apartment?"

"I don't know."

"Did you give a spare key to Billy after you changed the locks?"

"Certainly not."

"Were any windows broken?'

"No."

"Had the front door been broken into?"

"It didn't appear to be."

"Were there any window latches left open?"

"No."

"Let's see here. Billy had no key. He didn't break a window to get in. The front door wasn't jimmied. I suppose you expect this court to rule that it's more likely for Billy to flow through the walls than it is for you to have let him in, is that it?"

"I told you, I don't know how he got in."

Torrey shook his head in disgust and looked at Ray. "I have no further questions of this witness, Your Honor."

Ray looked at Sutherland. "Any redirect, Mr. Sutherland?"

"No, Your Honor."

"You may call your next witness, then."

"Thank you, Your Honor. I wish to call Officer Dan Smith."

Ray glanced at Sid Walling. "Deputy, call Officer Smith."

Smith entered immediately. Smith was tall, about thirty-five, with close-cropped blond hair, and a piercing gaze that he fixed on Stewart before looking toward the prosecutor. Sutherland turned to a different set of questions. "Please state your name for the court."

"Daniel Webster Smith."

"How are you employed?"

"I'm a police officer for the City of Arlington."

"How long have you been so employed?"

"Five years."

"Please relate to the court the training that you have undergone."

"I have six hundred hours of TECLOSE training, attended numerous seminars, and I'm a certified instructor in pursuit training."

"Were you certified on the fourteenth of August of this year?"

"I was."

"Were you on duty that night?"

"I was."

"Please relate to the court what happened that night."

"I was on routine patrol with Officer Patricia West. We received a call from dispatch at 8:37 that there was a possible intruder at the Castlewinds Apartments. We arrived at 8:44 pm and met the lady out in the courtyard. She explained that she had a problem with a former boyfriend. She was afraid that he or persons unknown were in her apartment, because a light in the living room was on when it shouldn't be. I entered the apartment with Officer West and looked around. When I checked her bedroom closet, I saw the shoes and legs of the defendant behind some clothes. I moved the hangers aside, and there he was."

"Was the defendant armed?"

"He had no weapons on his person, but Officer West found some knives laid out on the other side of the bed."

"Did you see the knives?"

"Yes sir, after Officer West showed them to me, along with two lengths of cord "

"Is the occupant of that apartment in this courtroom today?"

"Yes sir, the lady seated directly to your left."

"Where was she while all this was going on?"

"I think she was in the living room, or out in the courtyard."

"Was there any way she could have slipped past you and put the knives and the cord by the bed?"

"Not after Officer West and I arrived on the scene."

"Did it occur to you that she might have planted the knives and the cord on the defendant?"

"No, sir. Her actions spoke otherwise, and so did his."

"What do you mean?"

"I don't think you could fake her reactions to those knives. Her face turned white as a ghost's."

"What about the actions of the defendant?"

"If you're innocent, you won't be hiding in a closet."

"Did you take the defendant into custody then?"

"Yes sir."

"What else did you do?"

"I checked for signs of illegal entry, and tried the suspect's keys in her door lock, with negative results. I left Officer West with the occupant, transported the suspect to jail, and booked him in. Then I returned to the apartment and picked up Officer West."

"Why did you leave Officer West with the occupant?"

"Miss Lemons was pretty distraught. She needed some emotional support, and Officer West is very good at that. I didn't need any help transporting the prisoner. He wasn't giving me any trouble."

"Did he say anything to you?"

"Not much. He remained silent after I read him the Miranda."

"Thank you, Officer Smith. Your Honor, I pass this witness."

Ray looked over at Torrey. "Cross-examine, Mr. Torrey?"

Torrey studied the officer for a moment, not wanting any part of him. "No questions at this time. However, I reserve the right to call this witness later."

Ray turned toward the witness. "Very well. Officer Smith, remember the instructions previously given. We'll call you again, if needed. Mr. Sutherland, do you wish to call further witnesses?"

"Yes, Your Honor. I call Officer Patricia West."

"Officer Smith, please tell Officer West to come in as you leave."

Dan Smith nodded and left the courtroom. Seconds later, Patricia West came in and eased into the witness chair. Sutherland looked her over carefully, not having interviewed her before the trial. She was a composed officer, about twenty-four years old, with a rather plain face, but her uniform was immaculate, and her posture was almost military.

"Please state your name for the court."

"Patricia Ann West."

"How are you employed?"

"I am a patrol officer with Arlington PD."

"How long have you been so employed?"

"Fourteen months."

"Please state your educational background."

"I have a master's degree in psychology and six hundred hours of police training, and I'm currently attending courses in rape counseling."

"Were you a certified police officer on the fourteenth of August?"

"Yes sir."

"Were you on duty that day?"

"Yes sir."

"Please relate what you know about the case before this court."

"Dan Smith and I were on patrol in South Arlington. We received a call to see a woman at the Castlewinds Apartments, regarding an intruder. When we arrived on the scene, I talked to Miss Shirley Lemons. She told us she was afraid her ex-boyfriend was in her apartment. She stated he'd threatened to kill her several times, had caused an altercation at her office, and later that same day had tried to kill her with his vehicle. Dan and I went into the apartment and found the suspect hiding in the bedroom closet. I was backing up Dan and noticed a row of kitchen knives and two pieces of rope lying on the floor between the bed and the back wall, so we arrested the suspect. I stayed with Miss Lemons while Dan took the suspect to jail. I phoned some of Miss Lemons' friends and got two of them to come over and stay with her for a while. I tried to comfort her until the friends arrived. Dan picked me up and we left."

"Does your educational background and training give you the capability to correctly judge the reactions of people?"

"I believe so."

"How did you judge Miss Lemons' reactions during this episode?"

"I felt her reactions were quite normal under the circumstances."

"I'll rephrase the question. Was she surprised at the knives?"

"Yes sir."

"In your professional opinion, was Miss Lemons faking her emotions about the knives or the defendant's presence in her apartment?"

"I don't believe so."

"Why not?"

"People can contrive many things, such as widening of the eyes, trembling, crying, and confusion. Miss Lemons displayed all of these. But she also turned white as a sheet. It's a mild form of shock. She couldn't fake that."

"What were the reactions of the defendant?"

"I really couldn't speak to that. Dan handled the suspect."

"Have you ever taken a false report from a citizen?"

"Sure. We all have."

"Were you able to spot that at the time they made the reports?"

"Yes. There are usually red flags like story inconsistencies, body language, eye expressions, and insincere voice tones, to name a few."

"Were any of these red flags present with Shirley Lemons?"

"No, sir. She was genuinely scared to death."

"Thank you, Miss West. No further questions. Pass the witness."

Ray looked over at Torrey, broadening his smile a little. *You walked right into that one counselor*, he mused. *What are you going to do for an encore?* "Cross-examine, Mr. Torrey?"

"Thank you, Your Honor. Are you married, Officer West?"

"No, sir."

"Is Officer Dan Smith married?"

"Yes sir."

"Do you have a thing for Officer Smith?"

Sutherland rose. "Your Honor, I object to this question. It's improper, and furthermore, completely immaterial and irrelevant."

Ray looked over at Torrey. "Where are you trying to go with this?"

"Your Honor, I'm pursuing this officer's concentration at the time of the incident."

"Do you have any independent evidence to support this?"

"Only the testimony so far."

"Then the objection is sustained. Without supporting evidence, I'm not permitting a fishing expedition to impugn a witness's character."

"Judge, you don't appear to allow the defense any case at all. If I can't challenge the witnesses, what is there? I've seen military tribunals more fair than this."

"Mr. Torrey, you are out of order, sir. You may challenge the witnesses within the limits of decorum."

"Thank you, Your Honor. That's so kind of you, sir," retorted Torrey.

"Mr. Torrey, you are beginning to border on contempt. Please conduct yourself in a professional manner, sir."

Torrey turned away and walked to the far end of the room. He turned slowly, facing the witness, who was now closest to him. "May I continue questioning the witness, or is that grounds for contempt?"

"You may continue. Whether it is grounds for contempt or not depends upon your conduct, sir."

"Miss West, you call your partner by his first name, and he referred to you as Officer West. Why?"

"He's just more formal than I am when testifying in court. This is the first time I've been accused of having something going with someone just because I called him by his first name."

Torrey stayed by the wall. "When did you become Smith's partner?"

Sutherland rose again. "Your Honor, you just sustained my objection to this line of questioning. I repeat my objection."

"Objection overruled."

Officer West turned left to face Torrey. "He's been my partner since I joined the force, except for days off and vacations."

"You must know him pretty well then."

"You have to know your partner well to work as a team. But I don't know him the way you're implying."

"Let's change the subject then. How many reports have you taken since you came on the police force?"

"I don't know. Several hundred."

"Are you telling this court that you haven't been fooled since beginning this job?"

"Not that I know of."

"I guess that you're going to be the first officer in history to never make a mistake."

Silence filled the courtroom as the witness stared at Torrey.

"You don't have an answer for that, Miss West?"

"I didn't hear a question, counselor."

"I'll make it plainer for you then. Are you telling me that you've made no mistakes since you joined the force?"

"No. I said I didn't think anyone fooled me when I was taking their report. I made no statements about whether I made any mistakes."

"Have you made mistakes?'

"A few. I even made one today."

"Oh? Tell us about it."

"I didn't take the trouble to find out about you, counselor."

Ray suppressed a smile, but the male reporter laughed out loud. Torrey turned to his left, glaring at the man. The reporter maintained his grin and stared back until Torrey looked back at the witness. "Miss West, how do you suppose Shirley Lemons knew the suspect, as you call him, was in the apartment before you went in?"

"The living room light was on. She remembered turning it off before going to work that morning."

"Does that mean the suspect was in the apartment?"

"Not in and of itself. The fact that he had threatened to kill her was what made it suspicious."

"Don't you think it was a little too neat having the suspect in the apartment and the knives all laid out? Did it occur to you that maybe Shirley Lemons set the suspect up?"

"No, I don't think it's possible."

"Did those knives come from Shirley's own kitchen?"

"Yes. She said they did."

"Could you tell where the cord came from?"

"No."

"Now, for the most important thing. You seem to have all the right answers. How did the suspect get into the apartment if Shirley Lemons didn't let him in?"

"I don't know the answer to that."

"Neither does anyone else. No further questions," Torrey spit out as he moved back to his seat.

Ray looked over at Sutherland, "Redirect?"

"No further questions of this witness, Your Honor."

"Very well. You may call your next witness then."

"Could you give me just a moment, Your Honor?"

"Sure."

Shirley whispered into Sutherland's ear and he immediately walked out of the courtroom. Seconds later, he returned with a lady that Ray recognized as the apartment manager of the Castlewinds Apartments.

Sutherland nodded at Shirley and turned back to the judge. "May we have a five-minute recess, Your Honor? I have not had an opportunity to confer with this witness."

"Any objections, Mr. Torrey?"

"I don't suppose it'd do any good if I did."

"Very well. We stand in recess."

Ray headed to his office while the others headed to the Coke machines or the bathrooms. Sutherland and the new witness went outside. Ray called for Cass and they went into his office.

"Cass, has Officer Willet called about that traffic injury?"

"No, Judge. I confirmed your flight for tomorrow. I sweet-talked the airline into moving you up to row nine, where you'd have leg room."

"Good. Would you get me three seats to the Rangers game tonight?"

"Sure. How's it going in there?"

"We are zipping through real well. We should be finished before noon. That defense attorney is being a pain."

"I'm not surprised. Nora down at Precinct Five says that all the clerks run and hide whenever he shows up at their office."

"How did that subject come up?"

"I called her this morning to give her Judge Chavez's schedule for Thursday. She asked what was going on today, and Torrey's name came up. He doesn't seem to be on anyone's favored list anywhere. He once—"

"Don't tell me any more right now. He's helping me form an opinion of him enough on his own. Are you still planning a vacation next week?"

"I don't know what to do about that. If I give this boyfriend the gate, I may as well not go anywhere."

"Let me know."

"I will. The sheriff called a few minutes ago. He wants you to come to some get-together at his house Friday night."

"Don't I have a big wedding at the park Friday night?"

"Yes, but you should be through by 8:00."

"Okay, call him back and tell him I'll be there if 8:30 isn't too late. I'm headed back to the courtroom. Hopefully, we'll be through in less than an hour, barring surprises."

When the court reconvened, Ray swore in the new witness. Sutherland had acquired some enthusiasm, was even smiling a little.

"Please give your name for the court."

"Alice Nowling."

"Where do you live, Mrs. Nowling?"

"At the Castlewinds Apartments."

"Are you employed there?"

"Yes, I'm the manager."

"Do you recognize Miss Lemons here?"

"Yes. She's one of my residents."

"Do you also recognize the young man seated at the other table?"

"Yes. Billy Earl Stewart. He was a resident there when I arrived."

"Are you aware of any problems between these two?"

"Yes. Shirley had us change the lock on her apartment when he moved out. I assumed there were problems between them."

"Were you aware that Stewart was arrested in her apartment on August fourteenth?"

"Yes. Shirley told me about it the next day."

"Did she also tell you later there was a restraining order on Stewart, so he could not come on the property?"

"Yes. It was a couple of days later."

"Did you see Billy Earl Stewart after that?"

The manager glanced at the defendant. "Yes."

"Was he on the property?"

"No. He was parked across the street from the complex."

"How far away from Shirley's apartment was that?"

"About two blocks."

"How far away from your complex was that?"

"Just across the street."

"What was he doing?"

"Sitting in his truck."

"When was this?"

"About a week ago."

"No further questions. Pass the witness, Your Honor."

"Cross-examine, Mr. Torrey?"

Torrey rose and walked over to the far wall. When he cross-examined from there, a witness looking at him could not see anyone else in the courtroom. "Your name is Nowland?"

"No. It's Nowling."

"Mrs. Nowling, where were you when you saw Billy in his truck?"

"I was passing by in my car."

"Were you traveling toward the front or the rear of his truck?"

"The front."

"How fast were you going, Mrs. Nowling?"

"About thirty, I guess."

"Did you stop and talk with him?"

Mrs. Nowling scowled. "No."

"You just drove by and saw him?"

"Yes."

"How did you know it was him?"

"I know him, and I recognized his truck. It's distinctive."

"What's distinctive about it?"

"The low running boards."

"What was he wearing?"

"I don't know. I didn't look that close."

"I see. Did you just glance at him when you drove by?"

"Yes."

"What time of the day was this?"

"About 5:30 in the afternoon."

"Did you call the police?"

"No."

"Why not"

"Because he wasn't technically on my property."

"Very good, Mrs. Nowling. Whoever was in that truck was not on your property. That's a public street isn't it?"

"Yes."

"How many feet per second does a car go when it's traveling at thirty miles an hour?"

"I don't know."

"Isn't 5:30 the time people come home from work?"

"Yes."

"How much time can you spare from the road to glance at someone sitting in a car or truck?"

"I don't know. A second or two, I suppose."

"How good are your powers of observation, Mrs. Nowling?"

"As good as the next person's, I guess."

"Mrs. Nowling, please look at me until you finish answering the next few questions and don't look away. All right?"

"Okay."

"You remember answering questions for the prosecutor, don't you?"

"Yes."

"You looked at him as you were talking with him?"

"Yes."

"Mrs. Nowling, what color is his tie?"

"I don't remember looking at his tie. I don't know."

"Thank you, Mrs. Nowling. No further questions."

Ray looked over at the prosecutor with a slight widening of his smile. Score one for the defense. And Torrey didn't even have to get ugly to do it. "Redirect, Mr. Sutherland?"

"I don't believe it's necessary, Your Honor. The prosecution rests."

Chapter Five

Ray looked over to Torrey. "You may call your first witness."
"The defense calls Gladys Stewart."

Ray nodded at Sid Walling. "Would you bring in Gladys Stewart?"

Walling strode importantly from the room and a few seconds later brought in a portly woman. Gladys Stewart had a grim expression as she walked to the witness stand. She was dressed in black, as if attending a funeral. Her faced was lined with years of trouble and hardship. Looking gravely at her grandson, she sat down as Torrey pulled out another set of questions.

"Would you state your name for the court?"

"Gladys Ann Stewart."

"Where do you live, Mrs. Stewart?"

"7611 Center Street, Arlington, Texas."

"Are you employed?"

"Yes. I work for Kinder Care. It's a child care center."

"What's your job there?"

"I prepare meals and provide part of the janitorial services."

"How long have you been employed there?"

"Sixteen years."

"Are you the grandmother of Billy?"

"Yes."

"Where are his parents?"

"They're both dead, killed in a car accident when Billy was nine."

"You took Billy to raise then, Mrs. Stewart?"

"Yes. There was no one else."

"Is your husband living?"

"No. He was killed in the Korean War."

"You had to raise Billy alone?"

"Yes."

"You've certainly had your share of grief and disappointments, haven't you, Mrs. Stewart?"

"It certainly seems that way, Mr. Torrey."

"Is Billy your only grandson?"

"Yes. But I have three granddaughters."

"Do they live in this area?"

"No. They live in South Carolina."

"Do you see them often?"

"No. My son was reported killed in the Vietnam War, and his wife lives near Fort Bragg. She don't bring them to visit very often. I haven't seen them in four years."

"You said your son was reported killed. What do you mean by that?"

"He was either killed or captured. He never was accounted for."

"Are you a woman of means, Mrs. Stewart?"

"Heavens no. I've struggled all my life."

"What kind of boy was Billy when he was growing up?"

"He was a good boy, never got into trouble. Bright, did well in school, but had few friends. Billy always felt out of place because he had no parents and the other kids did. I should've spent more time with him in his teenage years, but it was hard working two jobs."

"When did Billy go out on his own?"

"When he was nineteen. A year after he finished high school."

"Did you remain close to Billy after he moved away?"

"Yes. He's all I have."

"You're familiar with his social life then?"

"Yes. What there is of it."

"What do you mean by that?"

"Billy never had any steady girlfriends. We had no money when he was growing up, so he worked a part-time job in high school. He didn't have time to date much. Besides, he just didn't have the confidence to mix with girls. After graduation, he wasn't socially adjusted. He didn't have the confidence to approach girls or ask them out. When he met Shirley, it was a big deal for him. After she threw him out, he was crushed."

"Was Miss Lemons the first girl he ever went out with?"

"No. He had a few other dates. They generally didn't go well. He would have a date or two, and they were gone."

"Would you say then that Miss Lemons was the first girl he had a serious relationship with?"

"Yes."

"Did you meet Miss Lemons before today?"

"Yes. They came by about a month after they began dating."

"What was your impression of her at the time?"

"She seemed like a nice ordinary girl. A little too mature for Billy, perhaps. But, I was very happy for him."

"Did you see Miss Lemons after that?"

"A couple of times. She didn't seem to want to stay long."

"Did that bother you?"

"Yes. Like I said, Billy's all I have. But I didn't say anything."

"What was your impression of their relationship?"

"Billy seemed to care more for her than she did for him. Billy doted on her, but she seemed a little reserved around him."

"You said earlier Billy was crushed when Miss Lemons threw him out. Can you elaborate on that?"

"Billy came over and we had a long talk when it happened. I've never seen him so upset. He was determined to get her back, but I told him to let her go. I told him you seldom married the first girl you were serious about and to treat it as a learning experience."

"Did he listen to you?"

"No. He acted as if she was the only chance he'd ever have."

"Did he ever tell you Miss Lemons was pregnant?"

"Yes. It was a couple of weeks after they broke up."

"How did he feel about that?"

"He was more determined than ever to get her back. He felt this would be the family that he'd missed."

"Did he tell you at some point Miss Lemons had aborted the child?"

"Yes. About two weeks ago."

Torrey threw a dark glance at Shirley. "What was his reaction?"

"He was very upset. He felt he'd been robbed of a child. Billy was so despondent that I feared for his sanity."

"What do you mean 'feared for his sanity'?"

"I knew what that child meant to him. I was afraid he'd become so depressed, he couldn't come out of it."

"Did he ever threaten to kill Miss Lemons when he was upset?"

"No. It would never cross his mind. She meant too much to him."

"Was he angry at Miss Lemons at this point?"

"Certainly. He felt she'd committed a criminal act, and because of that, she'd broken off any hope of them getting back together."

"But he never threatened her any harm?"

"Gracious no."

"Thank you, Mrs. Stewart. I know this has been very hard on you. Judge, that's all the questions I have for this witness."

Ray looked over at Sutherland, who was leaning over the table on his elbows, studying the witness carefully. "Do you wish to cross-examine this witness, Mr. Sutherland?"

"No, Your Honor. I'm sure everyone feels sympathy for Mrs. Stewart. I don't want to put her through a cross-examination."

Ray looked back to Torrey. "You may call your next witness."

"No further witnesses, Judge. The defense rests."

"Mrs. Stewart, you may step down. No matter what happens today, I wish you well. Mr. Sutherland, any rebuttal witnesses?"

"No, Your Honor."

"Deputy Walling, would you please release all witnesses to this hearing. Mr. Sutherland, do you wish to make a final argument?"

"Just a brief one, Your Honor. I believe the State has proved beyond a reasonable doubt that the defendant, Billy Earl Stewart, repeatedly threatened to kill Miss Lemons. The State has further proved the defendant tried to carry out that threat. There's very little to dispute there. I want to stress the importance of the testimony of Mrs. Nowling. There's uncontested testimony from her that the defendant was in the vicinity of Miss Lemons' apartment shortly after he was released from jail. I believe this action speaks volumes about his malicious intent toward her. The defense's own witness has quoted the defendant as saying, and I quote from memory, 'Billy felt Miss Lemons had committed a criminal act, and Miss Lemons had robbed him of his child.'

"Your Honor, we're not here today to debate the morality of abortion. As you know, there are no laws in Texas against abortion. But I think the evidence supports the fact that it's a criminal act in the defendant's mind, and if there are no remedies at law for him, then he has decided to make his own laws and enforce them. He's decided to become Miss Lemons' judge, jury, and executioner.

"Your Honor, I believe the State has gone beyond its normal burden in establishing the defendant's intent here. I would like to bring your attention to two cases in the annotations that bear this out. In 1969, there was a case known as Walker v. Texas, and there was Bell v. Texas, a 1973 case. Those cases plainly say that intent to kill may be inferred from any, not all, but any facts in evidence, which prove the existence of intent to kill. I respectfully submit that all, not any facts in this case show the intent of the defendant to carry out his threats to kill Shirley Lemons. I further submit that his motives might fall into the category of sudden passion. I suspect the defense is going to try to make an issue of this, so I want to show you a case that deals with it. It's an old case, going all the way back to 1912. Grant v. Texas. That case says sudden passion is not an affirmative defense after passage of time when there is intent to kill.

"In closing, I submit that the petitioner, Miss Lemons, is entitled under the law to all the protection she can get after coming home one night, finding the defendant waiting for her with deadly weapons, then finding out later that he was violating the emergency protective order—at least in spirit—that was issued pursuant to the arraignment. Thank you, Your Honor, that's all."

"Thank you, Mr. Sutherland. Mr. Torrey, your final arguments, sir."

"Judge, my final argument is multipronged. On the first point, I want to emphasize reasonable doubt. When the prosecutor says there's uncontested testimony that my client intended to kill Miss Lemons, he's conveniently overlooking the most important testimony in the case: the fact that no one can explain how Mr. Stewart got into Miss Lemons' apartment. We have testimony that the locks were changed when she threw him out and that she never gave him another key. The only explanation that makes sense is Miss Lemons got tired of Mr. Stewart bothering her and concocted a scheme to frame him. I know that it would seem to be a very heartless thing to do, but I ask you, how heartless is it to kill a man's child without even having the decency to consult him about it? If no explanation exists to the contrary, and there has been none submitted here today, I'm saying that at the very least, it creates reasonable doubt. Article 2.03 of the Texas Penal Code says when a reasonable doubt exists, the defendant must be acquitted as a matter of law.

"In the second prong in the defense, I argue on the following points. One: the prosecutor has stated Mr. Stewart waited in Miss Lemons' apartment with deadly weapons. I'm not gonna let him get away with that, Judge. There was no testimony showing the length of those knives. You know full well the knives have to be five and a half inches long to be considered deadly weapons. Two: there were no wounds inflicted on Miss Lemons. Case law says when no wounds are inflicted, the State must prove that a knife was a deadly weapon by factors such as manner of use, size of the blade, and its capacity to inflict serious bodily injury, to determine whether it was a deadly weapon. That's clearly set forth in *Hicks v. Texas*. Three: Mr. Sutherland said we should stress the importance of Mrs. Nowling's testimony and I agree. Her testimony was that she glanced at Mr. Stewart for a second or two. I think the court remembers how good her observation powers are. And four: I don't believe the emergency protective order is worth the paper it's written on. My client had no attorney when he was arraigned. A mistake was made in this case when the municipal judge placed the protective order on my client without appointing him legal counsel.

"In closing, let me summarize this. The State has no explanation for how Mr. Stewart got into her apartment; the State failed to prove the knives were deadly weapons; the State's witness, Mrs. Nowling, has questionable observation skills at best; and even if her testimony is correct, the restraining order is faulty. Judge, the State's case leaks like a sieve. That's all."

"Mr. Sutherland, any response?"

"Yes, Your Honor. Mr. Torrey failed to shephardize the other cases on this knife issue. First of all, the State does not have to have injuries inflicted on the victim to prove intent. That's clearly stated in Soto v. Texas and Batro v. Texas. Furthermore, the most important case on this point is Patrick v. Texas, which clearly says a threat is enough to establish intent with a knife.

"On the next point, common sense tells me this case is not going to turn on Mrs. Nowling's ability to recall the color of my tie. Defense counsel didn't bother to talk about her recollection of the defendant's unique truck and its low running boards.

"Last—and perhaps most importantly after all we've heard today––Mr. Torrey is asking you to believe that Miss Lemons, after a traumatic confrontation with the defendant at work that day, and after the defendant tried to run her off the road, and after his repeated threats to kill her, would call the defendant on the telephone and invite him over to her apartment to set him up. The idea is ludicrous, and furthermore, the theory is flawed. Miss Lemons would have risked getting killed as soon as he arrived at the apartment. The fact that no one other than the defendant knows how he got into the apartment is not as big a deal as defense counsel wants you to believe. This isn't a case made up of circumstantial evidence, where the State cannot have a broken link in the chain. That doesn't apply here. That's all, Your Honor."

Ray surveyed the anxious faces before him. "I'll call a short recess during deliberations."

Without further ado, he rose and walked out of the courtroom and back to his chambers. Cass, as usual, was right behind him.

"Judge, Officer Willet called. He said the accident victim is alive for now, but even if he lives, he lost too much oxygen to the brain to be anything but a vegetable."

"I think his name is Charlie Finley. Do some digging and see what you can find out about him. I need a few minutes alone to deliberate while you're doing that, so have my calls held."

"Okay, Judge."

Ray reviewed the case law references he had jotted down during the trial. The cases were accurate. Leaning back in his recliner, he focused on the testimony. How could Stewart have gotten into the apartment? Could this be a frame-up? The prosecutor had a point: it would take plenty of courage to set it up if you were scared of the guy.

Ray walked outside and found the pickup. It was a 1991 Ford three-quarter ton, maroon, with fancy Laker exhaust pipes and low running boards with black scuff protectors. He'd never seen one like it.

Returning to his chambers, he reviewed Chapter 2 of the Penal Code. When he looked up, Cass caught his eye.

"Is it okay to talk now, Judge?"

"Sure. I think I'm finished."

"The victim's name is Charles Victor Finley. DOB is 1-24-36. His civil history is minimal. Two cases for unpaid utility bills, both defaults. His driving history isn't good. He's had nine speeding tickets in the last five years. You suspended his license for ninety days three years ago for a breath test refusal. He has two convictions for DWI. His criminal history shows two cases of theft by check, both cases dropped, and one case pending for assault on a police officer."

"What city did the assault case come out of?"

"Arlington, I believe."

"Find out from Arlington who the police officer was. I may want to talk to him."

"Hold on. Amanda, over in records, is a friend of mine."

Two minutes later, Cass was back. "I don't think you want to talk to this guy, boss. It's Chester Agnew."

Ray sat back in his chair, stunned. "I'll be damned," he said. "I'll just be damned."

Chapter Six

As Ray entered the courtroom, everyone scrambled to rise. "Please be seated," he said, moving up the single step to his chair. Everyone was there, including the Arlington police officers. They had waited to hear the decision, which was highly unusual.

Ray wasted no time. "I've reviewed the testimony and the case law cited, and have reached a decision that any doubt created is not reasonable doubt. Mr. Sutherland's statement about the risks to Miss Lemons in undertaking such a scheme makes sense. I find that the case law cited is accurate on both sides and pretty much on point. Therefore, I'm placing a peace bond on the respondent, Billy Earl Stewart, in the amount of $1,750. I've taken the financial condition of Mr. Stewart and his family into consideration. They seem to have a small income and little, if any, savings. I think this is apparent even though there was no direct testimony regarding it. I've weighed that against the seriousness of the matter and the actions of the respondent. That is the amount that I consider to be sufficient to keep Mr. Stewart from committing violent acts against Miss Lemons. Does your client have that sum to place in the registry of the court at this time, Mr. Torrey?"

"You know damn well he doesn't, Judge," exclaimed Torrey.

"Mr. Torrey, I've told you before that I expect you to conduct yourself in a professional manner. Any further profanity or other improper conduct will result in a finding of direct contempt."

"What about your conduct, Judge? You didn't bother to find out how broke my client is before you placed this ridiculous amount on him."

"I'll only say this once more: I gave your client the benefit of being totally destitute when making my decision, and I weighed that against the circumstances."

"It looks to me that you picked this amount to ensure that my client stays in jail. I guess it's time for me to catch one of the kangaroos running loose around here and ride off."

"That's fine, Mr. Torrey, and on your way out you can drop off a fifty-dollar fine with my clerks, for contempt."

"I don't have fifty dollars on me, Judge."

"Then you'd better start acting like it. I'll give you ten days to come up with it. That also corresponds to your appeal time. Deputy Walling, take the respondent into custody. If the bond is not posted in two hours, place him in the county jail. This court stands adjourned."

The people in the courtroom sat riveted in their seats as they watched Walling frisk Stewart and handcuff his hands behind his back. Gladys Stewart began to sob as Ray stood and walked out the door toward his chambers. Marilyn Shaw and the other reporter went to the clerk's area to interview Shirley Lemons. Sutherland gave a contemptuous glance at Torrey, then left without a word. Torrey didn't notice. He gathered his papers and motioned for Mrs. Stewart to follow him. Walling escorted Stewart into the clerks' area and shoved him into a chair. "Don't get up without my saying so, jailbird."

"Can I go to the bathroom, Officer? I've been dying for an hour."

"You'll go to the bathroom when I tell you to." Walling signaled one of the clerks. "Phyllis, I have to leave for a minute. If this guy so much as wiggles, call me in my office." Without waiting for acknowledgment, he turned to his left, heading for the back of the building. When he turned, the answer he got from Phyllis was a Nazi salute.

Ray looked up from his mountain of paperwork as Cass walked in. "Judge, your ladylove wants to know if she can have a minute with you."

"My ladylove? You mean Marilyn?"

"Who else?" giggled Cass.

"If she was my ladylove, she wouldn't have to ask," smiled Ray. "Send her in."

Ray rose politely as Marilyn breezed in. He couldn't help but notice her dark hair and tall shapely build. Dark expressive eyes were her best asset, though. When they beckoned, you became her prisoner of war. The eyes looked friendlier now. She looked like a million dollars, after taxes. "Marilyn you look gorgeous as always."

"Sure. I look so good, you haven't called me in three months."

"I'm sorry about that. I was embarrassed about what happened with the kids. I thought you never wanted to see me again."

"I was mad, but I got over it. You could've called a week later and everything would've been fine. I guess you can't expect children to accept you easily after they've lost their mother."

Ray masked his surprise. "Do you want to go out again?"

"Sure. Just tell me when."

"How about this Saturday night?"

"I'm going to see my folks. How about the next weekend?"

"Okay, the Saturday night after. Dinner at Del Frisco's?"

"That sounds mighty fancy. I'll have to dress up. Sounds like you're trying to make amends."

"Maybe so."

"Now that we have the important stuff out of the way, can we talk about that peace bond trial?"

"Sure. What do you need to know?"

"What about that emergency protective order? Did that municipal judge make an error in procedure?"

"I don't think so. I think the defense attorney was grasping at straws. It is a de facto restraining order that expires in sixty-one days. A TRO can be issued at an ex parte hearing for a period of ten days. The difference is that any magistrate can issue one, and it can last longer. The defense attorney was complaining that no counsel was appointed for Stewart, but it's fairer than a TRO when the defendant isn't there at all."

"I see. What else can you tell me about this law?"

"Senate Bill 129 became effective in 1995 and was amended in 1999. It was just one of several bills designed to reduce family violence and stalking. When someone is arrested for those offenses, the judge, the prosecutor, the victim, or a parent or guardian of the victim can move for a family protective order. It can prohibit the defendant from going near the residence, place of employment, school, or child care facility of the victim, or if the defendant lives in the same residence, prohibit the actor from committing acts of violence against the victim. The order can't be rescinded by the victim, and if the order conflicts with another order, this order controls."

"What are the penalties for violating the order?"

"I think it's a Class A misdemeanor."

"Do you think the DA went easy on Stewart by just asking for a peace bond instead of going after a jail penalty?"

"No. I never saw the protective order, but if you'll remember the testimony, there was a reference made indirectly that the order was about not going on the property. Stewart was not seen on the property, but across the street. I'm guessing that the DA didn't think it would fly."

"If it wouldn't fly in the district court, why did it fly here?"

"It didn't necessarily fly here. I could've issued a peace bond on Stewart the minute he got out of jail, based upon what happened before. A peace bond is designed to make a person put up a sum of money as a guarantee they'll not commit an act of violence once they make a serious threat, and demonstrate that they intend to carry out the threat."

"Oh. I thought it was because he violated the protective order."

"That was what the defense attorney wanted you to believe, but Stewart can get out any time he or his grandmother comes up with the cash. When that happens, he walks."

"Thanks, Ray. I better get going. Deadlines, you know."

"Okay. I'll see you next weekend."

"It's a date," returned Marilyn. "Keep out of trouble, and stay out of the newspapers."

"Listen to that," laughed Ray. "The height of hypocrisy."

Marilyn focused on Stewart as she approached the clerk's foyer. *Should I try to interview him? No. He's in custody. Maybe I'll try to get Torrey later. He looks like a better interview anyway.* With a last glance at Ray, she strolled out.

Stewart watched her go, wondering who she was. He closed his eyes, trying to think of something besides his full bladder. He reminisced about Shirley and the good times they'd had. He remembered the baseball games, the picnic at the park, the trip to the zoo when her seven-year-old niece was visiting, and the child's free and easy laughter at the silly monkeys. He had been so proud of Shirley when he took her to meet his grandmother. Best of all, he liked the closeness he felt when they made love. *How could she throw it away? How come I'm being put back in jail when I'm the victim? How can this frickin' judge in this chickenshit court put me back in jail when I haven't even been found guilty? Is this what my uncle and grandfather fought and died for? This really sucks. I'll get even with that stinkin' judge someday when—*

"Hey, jailbird, wake up. Do you still need to go to the can?"

Stewart opened his eyes and saw Deputy Walling standing over him with a shit-eating grin. "Yeah. That problem don't go away by itself."

"Get up and let's go."

Still handcuffed, Stewart rose awkwardly and followed Walling around the corner, past the judge's chambers. The door was open, and there was the stinkin' judge talking and laughing on the phone.

Walling removed the handcuffs and motioned Stewart toward the open door of the bathroom. Stewart needed no further invitation. When he came out, Walling was ready with the handcuffs.

"Do you have to use those cuffs? I promise I won't go anywhere. They cut off the circulation in my hands."

"Sure. I take promises from jailbirds all the time. They'd never lie to me," Walling laughed.

"Deputy, I suggest that you put leg irons on him while he stays in this office. The court patrons won't be so curious when they come in."

Walling whirled and saw Cass standing there with her arms folded. "Whatever you say, Miss Strange," he retorted. Cuffing Stewart again, Walling led him back to the outer office, and left to get the leg irons.

Cass stayed with the prisoner. "Can I get you a glass of water, Mr. Stewart?"

"Yes ma'am. Thank you."

Cass returned in a minute with a glass of water. "Here. I'll just set it here by your chair. You can drink it when your hands are free."

"Thank you, ma'am. That's very kind of you. I didn't think anyone around here had any compassion. That judge of yours sure don't."

"Now, now. I'm sure the judge figured this was better for you than a jail sentence if you got out of hand."

"Yeah. I need more friends like him, right?"

Cass figured this conversation had lasted long enough. She smiled, turned away, then noticed one of her least favorite litigants had just walked in the door. "Mr. Evans, something we can do for you?"

"I've decided to come in here and pay off this two-bit judgment. That damn plaintiff's lawyer won't leave me alone, and I'm losing money in attorney fees fighting him. I guess I'll chalk this one up to experience and go on. How much is it?"

"I'll figure it up for you, sir."

Cass went to the closest computer and brought up the case, did a few calculations, and returned to the counter. "That totals $5,137.83, Mr. Evans."

"I thought $5,000 was the maximum for this court."

"It is, sir, but post judgment interest runs at ten percent per annum until the judgment is paid."

"All right," sighed Evans, pulling a fat envelope out of his coat and counting out hundred-dollar bills. "I demand a receipt for this."

"Of course, sir. That's customary procedure." With that, Cass took the stack of bills to her office and put it in a file cabinet. Stewart watched from his chair, marveling at the most cash he had ever seen.

"Jailbird, stick your legs out here where I can reach them," said Walling as he walked in. "Then I can uncuff you, so your precious wrists won't hurt."

Stewart complied and rubbed his wrists after the cuffs were removed. He looked up at Walling, seeing nothing but anger.

"Is someone going to bring the money up here for you, Stewart?"

"No. We don't have that much money."

"Then I don't see any need in babysitting you. I'm taking you on."

Ray studied the telephone for a long time, hesitating. Then he did something that should've been done a long time ago. Ray dialed the Arlington police chief on his private line.

"Chief Parker here."

"Chief, this is Ray Sterrett. How are you doing?"

"Fine, Judge. How are you?"

"Fine, sir. I'm calling you with some regret, but I think there's something you need to look into."

"What's that?"

"I'm sorry that I'm the one to have to report this. There was an accident with injuries at Green Oaks and Little Road about 9:00 this morning. Sergeant Agnew was the first officer on the scene, and he ran off a guy who was administering CPR to a victim. Agnew claimed the guy was dead, which he wasn't. The paramedics arrived about five minutes later and started giving him oxygen. The guy may live, but he's suffered irreparable brain damage. I had the first ambulance ready to give him oxygen, but they were diverted to the other victims by Agnew."

Chief Parker broke in, "Judge, I know how you must feel, but it's the officer's responsibility to direct the units to the victims most in need. That's a judgment call on his part."

"I know, Chief, but the other victims were not that critical."

"I'm afraid it's his call, though. If there's nothing else, I don't see a valid complaint."

"But there is something else, and I'm afraid it's the kicker. That victim on the road has a criminal case pending for assaulting Agnew."

"Oh, shit."

"That's right."

"He was the first officer on the scene? Who else was there?"

"Jerry Willet was who I talked to. I didn't notice the others."

"Willet hates Agnew, too. Did any of the other officers see this?"

"I don't think so, but there's a civilian witness, the one who was administering the first aid."

"What's his name?"

"I don't remember off hand. Willet took his name down."

"This is a serious accusation you're making. Can you come over and sign a complaint?"

"I'm afraid not. I have to leave for my legal seminar tomorrow. I won't be available for about a week."

"Okay, I'll look into this."

"Thank you, Chief. I'll talk to you next week."

Ray hung up the phone with a sigh. He wouldn't be a favorite of Chief Parker from now on. Parker didn't like waves, and only God knew why he liked Agnew. Oh well, let the chips fall where they may.

"Get up, jailbird. I've got your paperwork ready. It's time to take you down to the hotel. Your reservation is ready," said Sid Walling, as he held out the handcuffs for Stewart.

Stewart held out his wrists. "Can I call my grandmother first, Officer?"

"You can call her after you get down there. They have phones in the holding cells. You've wasted enough of my time today already."

"I need to go to the bathroom."

"You just went to the can a half hour ago, Stewart."

"I know. But when I wait too long, I have to go again."

"Tough shit, jailbird. It's time to go."

"It'll only take a minute."

"I said no. Now get up and head for the car."

Walling followed Stewart out to the squad car, and without further ceremony, shoved Stewart's head down, pushing him into the back seat. After getting behind the wheel, he looked at Stewart, who was leaning forward. Walling shoved him back into the seat with his right hand. "Unless you want the shit beat out of you, jailbird, you'll stay back in that seat. I don't have a cage in here, so don't make me jumpy."

"You don't have to be ugly. I haven't done anything to you."

"Yes you have, jailbird. I could be humpin' a honey right now if it wasn't for you", he growled as he wheeled out of the parking lot.

"This isn't exactly a good time for me, either. I haven't done anything to deserve this."

"You're confusing me with someone else."

"Who's that?"

"Somebody who gives a shit," chuckled Walling. "I haven't met a jailbird yet who didn't poor-mouth."

"You're no better than that asshole judge. I don't deserve a bad time from you."

"You have the judge pegged. He's an asshole, all right."

"I'll get even with him one of these days."

Walling laughed. "You better bring help, Stewart. He can tear your head off. He can break bricks with the edge of his hand. He was a karate champion years ago. If you go after him, you better be in a tank."

Maybe I won't need a tank with you, surmised Stewart, as the squad car stopped at the sally port of the jail, the door opening toward the top. Walling pulled in and parked to the left in the underground garage. "Sit tight, jailbird. I'll be right back."

Walling strolled over to a line of boxes with keys, put his pistol in one of the boxes, removed the key and put it in his pocket. He walked around to the back of the car and opened the door for Stewart. "Out of the car, jailbird. Lean against the car and spread 'em."

"You already frisked me."

Walling grabbed Stewart, spun him around, and pushed him roughly against the car. Kicking Stewart's right foot to the right, he started his search. "Don't give me any lip, jailbird."

Walling finished the search, grabbed Stewart's right arm with his left hand, and led him through the automatic door. They walked about ten steps, to a door on the right. "Stand with your toes on that line, jailbird." Walling pushed a button on the wall and the door opened. After uncuffing Stewart, he pushed him as hard as he could.

Stewart stumbled forward as the door clanged shut. Turning around, he glared at Walling, who grinned back at him, then returned to his car for the paperwork.

Stewart turned and looked over the holding cell. The walls were painted light green, and the floor was concrete. The room was about eight feet wide and sixteen feet long, with a concrete sitting ledge running the length of the back wall. There were two other prisoners in the cell. One was a young black man, who was sitting on the ledge in a forward position, studying his shoes, paying no attention to Stewart. The other prisoner was an old, poorly dressed, white man, lying on the floor passed out. On the back wall hung a telephone. Stewart walked over, grabbed the receiver, and dialed his grandmother.

When he finished, he hung up the phone and turned around. A police officer was motioning him toward a glassed-in partition with a pass-through drawer. Stewart walked over. "Yes, Officer?"

"I need to check in your valuables. Empty your pockets into the drawer. Then give me your name and date of birth."

Stewart put his keys, change, high school ring, and billfold in the drawer. "My name is Billy Earl Stewart, November 5th, 1969."

The sheriff's deputy, looking bored, wrote down the information. He entered the items on the inventory form, starting with the ring, then counted the keys on the key ring and marked down six keys on the form. Spreading the change out on the counter, he removed the bills from Stewart's wallet and spread them out next to the change. "You have seventy-nine cents in change and fourteen dollars in bills. When you get your receipt, step back to the white line and turn around. Put your hands on your head and stand with your feet apart."

Stewart nodded and watched the deputy finish the form. The deputy tore off the bottom copy of the form and pushed it through the drawer to Stewart.

Stewart checked the information on the form and nodded confirmation to the deputy, then turned around and went over to the white line for another search, which seemed to him to be the order of the day. After the search, he went over to the young black prisoner and sat beside him.

"How long have you been here?"

The prisoner looked up from the floor at Stewart angrily. "Get out of my face, white boy. I didn't invite your ass over here."

"Well, excuse me for trying to be decent," fumed Stewart as he moved away. This just wasn't his day.

It didn't seem to be Rachael Frank's day either. She sat at her desk on the second floor of the county administration building, trying to get her anger and frustration under control. She had just hung up from a nasty chat with Commissioner Bill Campbell.

Rachael Frank had been the purchasing agent for Tarrant County for nineteen years, having succeeded her father, Benjamin, who had held the position for thirty-three years. The Frank family had been active in county politics for three generations, with Rachael enjoying more influence than the rest of her family combined. If an elected official needed an increase in budget, or a new procedure was to be tried, she was always consulted. Any official who failed to do this would have problems when the request went to the commissioners for budget approval. Rachael's knowledge of computers and of how county government worked allowed her to ask very pointed questions at those hearings. Those questions inevitably led to the request being denied.

Everyone in the county knew that if their proposals were to be passed, they would first have to have Rachael Frank's blessing. Everyone but Bill Campbell. He had challenged her influence from the time he had been elected to the commissioners' court three years ago. Now Sterrett had sent him a memo questioning the purchasing process for office supplies, and it was like letting a dog sniff raw meat. Rachael's time would be taken up with this instead of monitoring the rest of county government. She didn't like to play defense. And then there was Sterrett. Rachael had never liked him because he wouldn't play ball. And now the bastard wouldn't even return her phone calls.

"It's time for lunch, Rachael," called Brenda Wilson, Rachael's administrative assistant. Brenda looked younger than her thirty-six years, with honey blonde hair falling just past her shoulders and warm blue eyes that could melt an iceberg. She had a body that could, and often did, stop traffic. Brenda was intensely loyal to Rachael.

Rachael had hired her after she had been replaced in the sheriff's office. Once Lee Sanders had won the last election, he had brought in his own people. Lee Sanders was on Brenda's shitlist, and she never passed up a chance to scheme against him.

Rachael had been a little jealous of Brenda's looks at first, but she had learned how to take advantage of them. If Rachael needed to find out something from a department and couldn't get it, she'd sic Brenda on them. Brenda was an expert at flattering elected officials until she got the information. The official usually didn't even know she wanted the information. Brenda was that good.

"Okay, Brenda. I'll just be a minute," returned Rachael, retiring to her private bathroom to freshen up. As she looked in the mirror, she noticed new gray in her black shiny hair. The wrinkles that were getting more pronounced she touched up with light base. Her hair was thinning too. Bifocals had to be next. "Damn," she muttered. "Only forty-five and I look like a grandmother of ten." Quickly finishing, she gathered up Brenda. "Where should we eat today?"

"Gary and Doug want to meet us at the Fans of Champions sports bar. They called while you were talking to Bill Campbell."

"Great. I could use some relaxation after putting up with that asshole Campbell."

"What did he want?"

"The usual shit. Sticking his nose into everything." Rachael wasn't ready to confide the latest to Brenda.

A few minutes later, they strolled into the noisy sports bar on Camp Bowie Boulevard. It was relatively new and had adopted the winning combination—a great buffet along with taped highlights of local sports teams and good country music. The decor was early Dallas Cowboys. Super Bowl teams, past and present, were featured daily on the big screen. What really made the place thrive was the free valet parking. Businessmen, lawyers, and women wanting to meet Mr. Right, flocked in. One of the private booths was reserved by the law firm representing the Fort Worth *Star-Telegram*. Attorneys from that firm never came, but the *Star-Telegram* reporters did. Here was where the stories were.

It was toward that booth that Rachael and Brenda headed, with every male in the room eyeing Brenda. Rachael extended her hand toward Douglas Harrison, the reporter.

"Doug, thank you for the lunch invitation. I hear it's an honor to just drive by this place, let alone get in for lunch."

Douglas rose, shook hands with both women, and indicated seats to his left. He managed to get Brenda to sit next to him and immediately became the envy of every male in the place.

Brenda smiled at him in amusement, remembering her one date with the lecherous bastard. She had found him to be a scoundrel of the highest order. *He's been trying to get in my pants ever since. I wouldn't get in bed with him if he was the last man in town. The kindest thing I can say about him is that Will Rogers never met him.* "Yeah, thanks for the invite, Doug."

Doug summoned a waitress as if he owned her. "Menus please," he growled. Then he smiled at the women. "I'm having the crawfish hors d'oeuvres. They're really good. May I order some for you?"

Brenda and Rachael made a face and shook their heads. "No thanks," said Rachael. "I heard their buffet is good. I'll have that."

"Me too," chimed Brenda. "Didn't you say Gary was gonna be here?"

"Yeah. He'll be along soon."

"Is anything juicy happening in the county today, Doug?" asked Rachael, always ready for gossip.

"No. Things are pretty quiet. I went over to Jake's court this morning to cover that armed robbery trial, but it looks like the jury selection will take all week. It was boring, so I left. I invited Tim Lindsey to join us for lunch. He's the defense attorney, you know."

"Oh good," said Rachael. "I need to talk to him."

"You're not in trouble are you, Rachael?" laughed Doug.

"No, and screw your newspaper, you hound," laughed Rachael.

That brought laughs all around as Gary Reynolds, the county's facilities administrator, arrived with Tim Lindsey and his sidekick, Leonard Torrey, in tow. "I see you're having a great time with the ladies," boomed Reynolds. "I found these two beggars outside, so I took pity and invited them to our table."

"Beggars, my ass," grinned Lindsey. "You wouldn't have that chickenshit facilities job if it wasn't for me. You all know Leonard."

"Sure," said Doug. "Have a seat."

Rachael and Brenda excused themselves and headed to the buffet. Lindsey watched them go. "Are you getting any of that yet, Doug?"

Douglas Harrison smiled knowingly. "Tim, you know gentlemen never discuss those kinds of things."

"That means no. He's not getting any," Gary chuckled. "If he was, you'd be reading about it on the front page."

"Hey! Come on. That's not fair," retorted Harrison.

"Fair?" bantered Lindsey. "You wouldn't know fair if it bit you on the ass. Gary, did you know that Harrison here wrote the world's shortest book? It's called the Newspaper Reporter's Ethics Guide."

The table erupted, with everyone but Harrison laughing and pounding the table. "Fair, he says," continued Lindsey. "Fair from the reporter who ran

Commissioner Gary Swilling out of office on trumped up sexual harassment articles—he's hollering fair." The loud laughter began to attract the attention of the nearby patrons.

"Come on, you guys. Swilling needed to go and you know it," said Harrison, smiling and raising his hands in mock surrender.

Lindsey wasn't about to let go of a good thing. "Harrison, you're the world's biggest asshole, but I like you. But there again, I get paid to like assholes." The table erupted again, with all of them pounding the table as Rachael and Brenda came back with loaded salad plates.

"Have you boys managed to get drunk while we were gone? It looks like you're entertaining the whole room. Everybody's looking over here," smiled Rachael, as she waited for Brenda to slide in next to Harrison. But Brenda nodded to Rachael to go ahead. Gary Reynolds and Tim Lindsey cast knowing side-glances at each other as the laughter subsided.

"They're ragging me something awful," said Harrison, in feigned indignation. "Something about me writing a book on press ethics."

"It must be a short book," returned Rachael, warming to the mood.

"That's what we said," smirked Lindsey, the laughter rising again.

Later, Rachael looked over at Lindsey. "Tim, I hear you're having trouble seating a jury on that armed robbery trial."

"That's no problem. I get paid by the hour."

"That is a problem. I checked the public defender fund. We've spent eighty percent of the fund as of March, and we still have half the fiscal year to go. I have to ask you not to drag your feet on this one."

"Why should I agree? It's not in my client's best interest."

"Because, dear love, you wouldn't be getting those lucrative cases without my intervention. If you use up that money, it's going to look bad on me for getting you appointed."

"Well, since you put it that way, I'll see what I can do."

"Is your client guilty?"

"Yes. Would it make any difference if he were innocent?"

"Not really."

"Rachael, you're tough, as always," smiled Lindsey. "I guess I'll have to eat cheese and crackers this month, or borrow from Torrey here. He's finally found a paying client."

Rachael looked over at Torrey. "Leonard, how wonderful. I know you've had a tough time lately."

"Yeah, I sure need the money. It doesn't help paying out contempt fines, though. I got one this morning. Can you get it rescinded?"

"Probably. Who's the judge?"

"Ray Sterrett."

"Sorry. I can't do anything with that blankety-blank ..."

"Neither can I. He nailed me and my client to the wall this morning. Really made me look foolish. He put my client in jail and fined me for contempt. I'm pissed off about it."

"He put your client in jail for contempt?"

"No. He put a peace bond on him, and he can't make the bond."

"Sterrett's just a JP. I thought he only heard Class C misdemeanors. Those are just punished by a fine."

"That's what I thought, but apparently he has the authority."

"Well, I'll be damned. I guess you learn something new every day."

Douglas Harrison leaned closer. This story was getting interesting. "Tell me all about this, Leonard."

"Doug, I don't think it's much of a story. Nothing has happened. There's this Joe Six-Pack out in Arlington whose ex-girlfriend claims that he's harassing her. The police found him in her apartment last week and arrested him. My client says she invited him over there and then set him up. Anyway, he had one of those magistrate's protective orders put on him, and the girl's apartment manager said she saw him hanging around after that.

"The DA's office didn't have a strong enough case to file on him for violating the protective order, so they ran this peace bond, and it worked. Sterrett claimed he was going to apply the criminal standard to the case, but I think he used the easier standard of preponderance. I doubt if the stupid idiot knows the difference."

Harrison pondered this. Stories were mighty thin. "Do you want me to run a story on how the justice system has run over your poor client?"

"No, it wouldn't help any. Besides, I think you had a reporter out there covering the trial."

"Who was it?"

"I'm not sure. I've seen her around. I think her name is Mary Lynn, pretty, about thirty-five, with dark hair."

"That sounds like Marilyn Shaw. I heard that she's hot for Sterrett. I bet she volunteered for the assignment."

"Looks like I'm screwed again. I'm gonna get even with that judge, if my client doesn't get him first."

Gary Reynolds broke in. "More power to you. You won't find any Sterrett allies at this table."

Chapter Seven

Buck Reed finally opened his eyes, then smiled flirtatiously at the frightened woman across the aisle. Caught staring at him again, she responded by grabbing a magazine. Undeterred, he decided to give her a chance to live. "How are you tonight, pretty lady?"

Startled, the woman looked at him. "Excuse me?"

"I thought we might as well get acquainted. You have been staring at me the whole flight."

"I have not."

"Suit yourself, ma'am. You don't want to talk?"

"Certainly not. Not to you."

Reed smiled, feigning indifference. "Is something wrong with me?"

The woman didn't smile. "I know you. I saw you once."

Reed's eyes widened in fake surprise. "So? Are you in the farming industry?"

"The farming industry? What are you talking about?"

"I figured you saw me at the trade show."

"The trade show? What trade show?"

"The show in Salt Lake. I was in the John Deere Booth. I sell combines. Is that so bad?" Reed smiled reassuringly. "You act as if I were a train robber."

The woman returned a doubtful look. She wasn't buying it, not yet. "How long have you been selling combines, Mr.—?"

"My name's Wilkerson. Roy Wilkerson. I've been selling farm equipment since I got out of college. What is your name?"

"Bea Maddox."

"Are you in the farming industry, Bea?"

"No. I know nothing about farming. Where did you go to school?"

"Texas A&M. I got a scholarship."

The woman began to show a touch of doubt. After all, it might not be him. After all these years, maybe she was wrong. "You didn't serve in the army? You know, fight in Vietnam?"

Reed laughed. "Hell no. I was a peacenik. Then and now. I was one of those who hid out in Canada. I went up there with my best friend. He died up there, tragically."

The look of doubt deepened. "What happened to him?"

"We were in the mountains and he got sick. There was no doctor. I couldn't help him."

The doubtful look changed to sympathy. "How did you get him home?"

Reed had her. "I didn't. He's better off where he is. People travel from all over to visit the tomb of the unknown draft dodger."

The woman shook with laughter. Now relaxed, she smiled at Reed for the first time. "Where are you traveling to, Mr. Wilkerson?"

Reed relaxed, too. "Miami."

"That's too bad. I was hoping you were going to Myrtle Beach."

"Why Myrtle Beach? Is that where you're headed?"

"Yes, that's where I'm going. I like men who can make me laugh."

"Do you live there?"

"I will be. I'm starting a new job there."

"What are you going to be doing?"

"I'll be events director at one of the golf resorts. Do you play?"

Reed smiled in earnest. "Unfortunately, no."

"Cass, when is the judge returning from lunch? Commissioner Wade's on the phone and wants to talk to him," called Phyllis, another clerk.

"He'll be back by two. The eviction docket is full today."

"Okay, I'll tell him."

Cass wrote a note for Ray and put it on his desk. Thinking her figure could stand it, Cass decided to skip lunch.

Cass had worked for Judge Sterrett six years, measuring every potential suitor against him. So far, they had all failed miserably. Cautious because of a bad early marriage, she developed the habit of running credit and criminal histories on anyone who asked her out. The information was readily available and often the results were startling.

Judge Sterrett had suggested that Cass start going to political meetings and chamber of commerce events, but she shied away from those. Ten years ago, she started out in politics working for a local congressman in his reelection campaign. She had been initially impressed by Congressman Whist. He was polished, sure of himself and of the direction the country needed to go. The congressman noticed her, too. Within two weeks, he made a pass at her when he caught her alone. Cass had to physically fight the leach off. She didn't need a married man. Although she left abruptly, she had enjoyed working on the campaign.

The spirited Cass bounced back, getting involved in a state senator's campaign, and politics got in her blood. The senator got her a job working in a justice court after the election. Attention to detail and a willingness to work long hours moved Cass to the head clerk's position within a year. The judge taught her office procedure and public protocol, and she became one of the best head clerks in the county. When the judge died two years later, Sterrett brought her in on his staff.

Three months ago, she met a man at a sports bar who passed her preliminary tests. Carl Holt seemed like an exciting guy—he owned his own business, CH Construction, and had three crews doing home remodeling. The money was good, his manners were impeccable, and he was fun to be with. Cass learned slowly that he was caught up in himself. Carl's selfishness was causing her to have second thoughts about him. She caught him buying a birthday gift for his former girlfriend's daughter. He shrugged it off by saying he hadn't broken up with the daughter, just her mother. Cass wasn't so sure, and the absences could explain why he would go for several days at a time without calling her.

After he backed out of a promised trip to the Caribbean with her, she wondered if that daughter's birthday fell at the same time.

"Cass, did you hear me? When did Jim Wade call?" asked Ray.

"I'm sorry, Judge. I didn't see you come in. He called about ten minutes ago. I didn't take the call, though, so I'm not sure what he wanted."

"Something must really be wrong for him to stoop low enough to call. See if you can get him on the phone for me."

"Sure, Judge." Cass called the commissioner's office. Jim Wade had stepped out. "He's not there, Judge. He'll call you back."

"Okay. How many eviction cases do I have this afternoon?"

"Eight."

"Then I'd better get started. Anything after that?"

"You have one transfer venue hearing, and some minor plea misdemeanors."

"Okay. I'm headed into the courtroom."

He opened the door into the courtroom and walked briskly to the bench as the litigants scrambled to stand. Ray recognized several landlords and apartment managers from previous cases. The cases rolled on for more than three hours, with Ray finishing up with a difficult eviction involving a family with a trouble-making teenage son. He continued the case for a week and managed to find other housing for the widowed mother because he felt sorry for her.

After finishing up the paperwork, Ray made his way back to his office where an anxious Cass waited. "Judge, Commissioner Wade's called again, insisting he has to talk to you this afternoon." Sighing as he cradled the phone, he dialed Wade's number.

A bright, cheerful voice answered. "Commissioner Wade's office."

"Betty, this is Ray Sterrett. Is the good commissioner there?"

"He sure is, and he's waiting for your call. Hang on a second."

The commissioner came on right away. "Jim Wade here."

"Commissioner, this is Ray Sterrett, returning your call."

"How are you, Judge?"

"Just fine. How are things with you?"

"They were just fine until Chief Parker called. The complaint you've lodged is against one of his favorite officers. He called me to see if I would ask you to reconsider."

"Are you asking me to reconsider?"

"You're damn right, I am. I owe the chief, and besides, you don't need to be meddling in his affairs."

"Did he tell you what happened this morning?"

"No, and frankly, I don't give a damn about what happened."

"Well, Commissioner, I'm sorry to hear you say that. A man is probably going to die over this. This is a renegade police officer running amuck. There's a question of right and wrong here."

"Who are you calling a renegade police officer?"

"Sergeant Agnew, that's who."

"I know Agnew. He's fine people."

"We don't agree on that," said Ray, thinking back to Wade's election. *You like Agnew because he puts up your campaign signs.*

"Look, Sterrett, you're just going to look foolish pursuing a complaint against Agnew. I'd consider it a favor if you'd just drop it."

"Sorry, Commissioner, can't do, won't do."

"Is that your final word on this?"

"Absolutely."

"Then I won't forget this."

"You never do," huffed Ray as he disconnected the dead line.

In Charleston, Jaspar Deveroux entered his Lincoln Town Car in the gathering darkness, turned on the news, and exited the covered garage with tires squealing. It had been a long hard day and the aging attorney was late for dinner with his lover. Deveroux turned the radio up as the news station covered a local story of interest. As fast as traffic permitted, he headed beyond Broad Street, turned right on Meeting, hurried past the major intersection at Wentworth, and then went left on Calhoun, where he mashed on the gas pedal, ignoring the complaining horns. *To hell with them, I've got to go. I'm going to have to work like hell after dinner and in the morning, to get out on the noon flight. I better slow down a little, though. I don't want another damn ticket.* Deveroux's eyes swept ahead for squad cars with a quick glance in the rearview mirror—*Wait a minute! Where's my damned mirror? Oh shit.* Deveroux felt the round hollow barrel press against his neck.

"Don't turn around, asshole. Not unless you're ready to die."

Discovering what real fear is, Deveroux felt his bladder let go. "Is this a holdup?"

Bitter laughter came from the back seat. "You wish. You know why I'm here."

The fear got worse. *Oh my God!* "Reed, I changed my mind. I wired your money to the Caymans yesterday, just like you asked."

The laughter grew. "Deveroux, you're lying. I checked. You get to die a little slower for lying."

"Don't kill me! Please! I'll do anything you ask."

"Anything?"

"Oh God, yes! Anything! What do you want?"

"I want you to beg while you're dying. Turn right here on Ashley."

Deveroux meekly did as he was told. "Please, Reed. I'll pay you extra. I can pay you plenty— in less than an hour, I promise."

The voice hardened. "You promise. Big deal. Keep driving ahead. Pull into Hampton Park."

The frightened attorney followed directions, frantically searching for a way to stay alive. "Reed, you've killed many men. You wouldn't enjoy killing me. Getting more money would be a lot better."

"I don't know about that. I get a bang out of icing someone who says 'Screw you. I'm going to have a vacation on your money.' I think justice is divine. I have plenty of money."

Deveroux needed to keep him talking. "How did you find me so fast?"

"I told you it would be easy. All I had to do was look back in the newspaper to find a businessman who was murdered because of a labor dispute. Then I checked with the probate court to see who the executor of the estate was. It only took about an hour and half."

"It was that easy, huh?"

"It doesn't pay to underestimate me, Deveroux."

"I'll pay now, dammit. Just give me a chance."

"Pay what, Deveroux?"

Hope glimmered. "I've got a hundred grand in my office safe right now. You can have it all. Just let me live."

Reed paused. *A hundred grand. That would make the trip worthwhile. A suitable penalty for Deveroux, too. On the other hand ...* "Pull over and stop about fifty feet from that park bench ahead."

"Please don't kill me. I promise. I've got the money."

"How would you get it here?"

"We could go get it. It's in my safe."

Reed reflected. "No. I wouldn't trust you as far as I can throw an elephant. You have to get someone to bring it here, or it's no go."

"All right, dammit. I'll get my son-in-law to bring it."

"Where is he?"

"At home."

"Where's that?"

"About five minutes from my office. Clarence has a key."

"Does he have your safe combination?"

"No. I'll have to give it to him."

Reed thought of where dangers might lie. Letting him call a friend might be more dangerous than going to the office himself. "Your son-in-law has a cell phone?"

"Yes, of course."

"Then call him at home and have him call you right back on his cell phone. When he's on the way to your office, keep him on the line. If you tell him anything else, I'll have to kill him, too. Got it?"

Deveroux sighed with relief. "Yeah. Thank you." Reaching for his car phone, he dialed a number.

Reed pressed the gun to his neck. "Hang up the receiver and leave it on speaker."

Deveroux complied. A male voice answered. "Hello?"

"Clarence, this is Jaspar."

"Hello, Papa Jaspar, What's going on?"

"Clarence, I need your help right now. It's urgent. Call me back on your mobile phone, right now."

"What the hell's going on, Papa?"

"Don't ask questions. There's no time. Just do it."

"Are you in trouble?"

"Just do as I say, please. And, do it right now."

"Okay. What's your number?"

"It's my car phone, 555-2804."

Reed eased back on the barrel as the line went dead. "When he gets back on the line, keep him talking. Ease his fears. Otherwise, he'll keep asking questions."

Deveroux nodded as his phone rang. "Clarence?"

"Yeah. It's me. Tell me what's going on."

"I need you to go to the office right now. Don't hang up. I'll explain while you're on the way. This is very important."

"Is that where you are?"

"No. Don't worry about me. I'm okay. I have a client that's in danger. Do you have your office key?"

"Yeah. I've got it. What do you want me to do at the office?"

The gun pressed against his neck, to warn him. "I'll tell you when you get there. Where are you now?"

"I'm about two minutes away. Can't you tell me what's going on?"

"Just do as I ask, Clarence. Time is critical."

"I'm moving as fast I can, dammit. I'm in the parking lot."

"Park in my spot. When you get inside, go to my office."

"Okay. I'm on the way. What's next?"

"Go into my office. Under my desk is a button. When you push it, Clara's portrait will move to the right. I ... I have a wall safe behind it. I need you to open it."

"All right. I'm in your office. I found the button. The picture's moving. It's a combination. I don't have the numbers."

"Here's the combination. Turn right three times to forty-one. Turn left twice to thirty-one. Then turn right once to fourteen. Stop it on fourteen and twist the lever down. The safe will open."

"Okay. The safe's open. What now?"

"There's a locked tray on the bottom shelf. Take it out and put it on the desk. There's a key in my middle drawer."

"You have a bunch of keys in this drawer. Which one is it?"

"It's the one with green paint on the top."

"Just a minute. Okay, I found it. I've opened the tray—Jesus Christ! Where did you get all this money?"

"It's not mine. Take four straps ..."

The gun pressed against his neck again. " All of it."

"Take all of it. Clarence, just bring the whole tray."

"The whole tray?"

"Yes. The whole damn tray. Close the safe and take the whole tray back to the car. Don't hang up, though. I'm going to put you on hold a minute." Deveroux clicked a button. "What now, Reed?"

"You were holding out on me, weren't you? You asshole."

"I figured a hundred grand was penalty enough."

"How much is your life worth, Deveroux?"

"All right, you're getting it all. What do you want him to do?"

"Have him bring it right here. There's a trashcan by that park bench. Tell him to drop it in there and go home. If he calls the police, you're both going to die. Now, get him back on the phone."

"Clarence, are you there."

"Yeah. I'm here. Have you been kidnapped?"

"No. I'm with my client."

"You're not in danger?"

"No, dammit. Please stop asking questions. His life could be in danger if you don't do as I say and do it quickly. Bring the tray to Hampton Park. Come in the Ashley entrance, turn left, and go to the first park bench. There's a trashcan there. Put the tray in there."

"Are you going to be there?"

"No. Just leave the tray and go home."

"Can I hang up now?"

"No, but hold on a minute." Deveroux pressed the hold button again. "What now?"

"Drive around behind the fountain. Hide the car under the trees, where we can see the trashcan from beyond the pond. Keep him talking. After he leaves the money, we'll pick it up and drive to the excursion boats at the Cannon Street dock. Now, get your boy back on the line before he spooks."

Deveroux started the car, pulling away as he released the hold button. "Clarence, where are you?"

"I'm on Rutledge, crossing Montague."

"Good boy. You're only three minutes away. Stay on the line. I'll be right back." Deveroux eased under the trees as instructed, shutting off the engine and lights. "I have a favor to ask, Reed."

"You're not in a position to ask favors, asshole."

"It's nothing unreasonable."

"What is it?"

"Please don't kill my son-in-law. I don't want to die, but my daughter would hate me forever if something happened to Clarence."

"I have no reason to kill him if he does what he's told. How much money is in that tray?"

"Six fifty. That's all I have in the world."

Reed suppressed a smile. "This will teach you to pay your bills. But I don't buy your poverty claim. You haven't told me the truth about anything. Why should I believe you now? Besides, you wouldn't keep every dime you had in currency."

Deveroux decided to drop the subject. His son in law pulled up to the trashcan. Reed was smart, no doubt about it. It was time to stop underestimating him. "How long do you want me to keep him on the phone?"

"Till we get to the excursion boat."

Thirty minutes later, Reed approached the airport, only to find squad cars everywhere. What had happened? Could they be waiting for him? Reed had taken all possible precautions with Deveroux. Had he called the police, or was this some other emergency? Reed decided not to find out. He passed the exit and headed to Savannah. He could fly out from there, but he'd have to pay a drop charge for his rental car. Reed laughed. He could afford it. Turning on his cell phone, he checked his call notes box. Another call from Fort Worth. Those people just wouldn't take no for an answer. Should he return the call?

Reed was a careful and thorough man of fifty-five. Reed wasn't his real name. Although notorious for many years, no one in the business knew what his real name was. Criminal insiders knew they could get a professional hit by dialing 1-800-555-Reed.

The FBI had tried to trace him a few years back, after easily finding that the phone number originated in Tulsa, but from there they hit a stone wall. The telephone bill traveled through a maze of mailrooms and forwarding addresses that changed often. The box owners were real enough, but they never met the man who paid them to open the mailboxes. The FBI did find one common denominator: they were all Vietnam vets.

Reed had served in Vietnam in 1965–66, in the Special Forces. As a Green Beret, he learned to kill in many ways. He could imitate different Vietnamese dialects to perfection. With makeup, and by darkening his skin with juices and herbs, his small build and dark hair enabled him to infiltrate enemy villages. His intelligence work made the unit famous for it's success in smashing enemy columns in transit. Reed learned about radios, weapons, chemicals, and could perform minor surgery under fire.

The other enlisted men loved him, but he never got along with the officers, because of his inborn resentment of authority. During his hitch, a gung-ho West-Pointer took command of the unit. Captain Wilbarger had a particular distaste for Reed, who would never prepare for inspections. He dressed sloppily, and his military courtesy was nonexistent. When Wilbarger pieced together a helicopter from spare parts, he ordered Reed to go up with him on a test run. Reed took one look at the chopper and declined, resulting in a bust in grade. The next night, Reed crept to Wilbarger's hooch, lobbed a CS gas grenade inside, and blocked the only exit with a broom handle. Retreating back to his own tent, he listened with amusement to Wilbarger's screams. He lived only six more weeks. A victim of sniper fire, they said.

After his discharge, Reed went to Fairview, Oklahoma, at the invitation of a buddy in the unit, Bill Anderson. Bloody Bill, named by his army buddies after the Civil War outlaw who served with Quantril, earned his nickname with his thirst for action in Nam.

Bloody Bill returned to a thriving family dealing with newfound riches. Their two-section wheat farm sat on the perimeter of a booming new oil field. He was gifted with a new 1967 Corvette and a five-bedroom home. Bill invited other army buddies there, as well as Reed, bankrolling a three-month party where the whiskey and women flowed freely. Anderson eventually got Reed a job as a roughneck and let him live in the house rent-free.

Reed made friends with several families getting rich from the oil. One of the friends was a young man named Wesley Williams. The Williams family felt they had been cheated by a wildcatter named Warren Sibley, who had convinced the family that drilling on their land was so risky that he needed a better deal than the going rate. The Williams family was at first elated then angered when Sibley hit five wells in a row. When they tried to renegotiate, Sibley just smiled and told them they should have shopped around before signing his lease. Reed worked for Sibley on the Williams place. Sibley's arrogance and harsh treatment reminded Reed of Captain Wilbarger, but Sibley didn't live in a hooch, and there were no CS grenades.

Reed listened to the Williams' complaints every time he visited them. Wesley's father said he wished Sibley was dead. When Reed asked how that would help, Williams replied that he could get out of the contract if that happened. A new lease could be written, with Sibley's forged signature. Reed pointed out that the lease was registered with the county, and all parties would receive notices of proposed contract changes. After some thought, Williams agreed that it would have to be filed before Sibley's death. An idea began forming in Reed's mind.

Reed spent the next week looking over the Sibley operation. A weak timber was discovered on the number four rig. Reed worked two nights weakening the timber further and testing its strength. When he was satisfied, he went to old man Williams with a proposition. He had a friend who could arrange Sibley's death for $25,000, guaranteed. No death—no money, and it would look like an accident. Reed wanted ten percent of the difference in the oil income for his part in making contact with the killer. Williams jumped at the chance and arranged to file the forged lease the same day. At midnight, Reed sabotaged the pump on the rig and summoned Sibley to fix it. As he sleepily examined the pump, Reed split his skull with a two-by-four, then collapsed the rig on top of him. After crawling through the debris, Reed rubbed Sibley's hair and blood on the nearest timber. He fixed the damaged pump, then left, taking the two-by-four with him. Later, he cut it up and burned it. The local police ruled it an accident. Williams kept his word about the money and the slice of the oil revenue. Reed retired from the oil fields with more money than he could spend.

Two weeks later, Williams came back to Reed, and told him about a problem his sister was having in Denver. Her doctor husband was cheating on her. He had a hefty insurance policy, and she was the woman scorned. Could Reed get his friend to look into the matter? Reed met the sister in Colorado Springs the next week. He got the details and avoided a contract price until he could check out the deal personally. To Reed's surprise the woman agreed to a $10,000 research fee. From there, he went to Denver, where he followed her husband each morning from his exclusive home in the Crestmoor Park addition. Within three days, Reed had the young girlfriend sighted and learned that she had a young boyfriend. The good doctor visited her every Tuesday night, while Williams' sister played bridge, and on Sunday afternoons, when he was supposed to be playing golf. The boyfriend always left about an hour before the doctor arrived at the girl's home. Reed followed the boyfriend back to his apartment, where he found a pistol hidden under the mattress, next to photographs of the girlfriend and the doctor in some embarrassing positions. *So they were going to blackmail the doctor.* Reed smiled as he replaced the pictures. That was the least of the good doctor's problems.

Now that he had all the information he needed, Reed contacted the sister. His friend was ready. The price was $50,000, in addition to the research fee. When the woman reluctantly agreed, Reed learned the top rate for a contract hit. The sister arranged for a trip to Vegas with a friend. The day after they left, Reed pilfered the boyfriend's pistol, careful not to smudge the existing prints, and ditched the dirty pictures. After dark, he went to the girlfriend's house and found the doctor and the girl in a love scene that would make the devil blush. As the girl was slipping into the bathroom, Reed broke the bedroom window and shot the doctor through the head. As the girl looked at him in horror, he dropped the pistol and retreated over the back fence, leaving the police with a murder case that was easy to solve. Reed went back to Oklahoma with $60,000.

Six months later, Williams had a friend in Kansas City with a problem. Could Reed send his friend to handle a labor problem? Reed made a connection there who referred him to five more jobs.

By 1972, Reed had established himself as the perfect hit man, one who could do the job with no suspicion ever falling on the boss. With notoriety came caution. Putting the word out that the killer's real name was Buck Reed, he announced that he—the messenger—was stepping out of the business. At first, go-betweens and surrogates were set up, and Reed was contacted through them. Later, he set up his 1-800 number. Technology eventually allowed him to use call notes, complete with an access code to keep the cops out. Reed was always careful to verify his callers before making contact.

Reed bought a seven-hundred-acre farm in his own name in Bixby, Oklahoma. It was a beautiful place on the river, only an hour from Tulsa. Hired staff worked the place, and it was profitable in two years. Laundered cash from the jobs repaid the veteran's loan.

Reed vacationed in the Caribbean, where he learned to transfer his illicit funds into untraceable accounts. By 1975, he was a millionaire. The jobs kept coming, his reputation growing each year. No one knew him, but everyone knew who he was. Being dark-complexioned, he could change his looks whenever he wanted, and he kept drivers' licenses from several states, always under assumed names taken from persons who were dead. He learned that if someone died young, states never cross-indexed their birth and death certificates. As a philanthropist, Reed funded several rehab clinics for Vietnam vets. He visited many clinics, making contacts for mail drops through his new and unsuspecting friends. In 1990, he bought an adjacent thousand-acre spread with irrigation rights, and his crops increased in yield. By the late nineties, he was ready to step down from his contract work. Reed was getting old, and his reflexes weren't what they used to be. Besides, he had more money than he could spend. The jobs were cut back, and he took them only when the clinics needed more money. A plan was slowly forming in his mind: he would retire on his own island and find a woman who could put up with his independence. Eight million dollars awaited him in the Caymans. Kings could make it on less than that.

Reed always worked by telephone. Anonymity required it. Never arrested, no mug shots or prints on file, Reed was truly an invisible man.

There was one more aspect to his reputation: Buck Reed had never failed.

Chapter Eight

It was 7:35 am Tuesday morning, and Stewart, just returning from breakfast, eyed the clean-cut prisoner approaching his pod. When the door slid open, he realized that he would have a private cell no longer. As the door slid shut, a dark-haired man in his thirties offered his hand. "My name's Larry Atwood. Sorry to see you."

Stewart slowly extended his hand. "Billy Stewart."

"What are you in for, Stewart?"

"I think it's called a peace bond."

"You must be trying to kick somebody's ass."

"Something like that."

"Somebody did you wrong?"

"Yeah. What are you in for?"

"Hot checks."

"Is this your first time? You don't look like you belong here."

"I've been in several times, I'm afraid."

"All on hot checks?"

"Some were forged or stolen checks. I'm in real trouble this time."

Stewart eyed this guy with caution. "Why do it, then? You look like you could get a regular job."

Atwood leaned back against the wall with a dreamy smile. "Beats working, and it pays the rent. It pays for nice clothes and the shiniest sports car you ever saw. I travel all over, play with the honeys all night, and it supports my gambling habit. It's a good life, really."

Stewart leaned back and relaxed. "Where do you get your checks?"

"The underground. I have contacts that can get me anything."

Stewart's eyes widened. "Anything?"

70

"Just about. As long as the money's right."

"Could they get some stuff for me?"

"What kind of stuff?"

"Like a gun."

"You gonna kill somebody?"

"Maybe."

"My boys don't handle that. That's the Blade's territory"

"Who's that?"

"The best fixer in the county. Who are you going to shoot?"

"My ex-girlfriend. I'm going to kill the bitch." Stewart propped his feet up and told his newfound friend the whole story.

Atwood asked an occasional question but was mostly silent. Finishing, Stewart leaned back, watching Atwood, who returned a wicked grin. "You're out on bond and put back in jail for the same thing?"

"Yeah. That's what my attorney said."

"You ought to kill the frickin' judge while you're at it."

Stewart's eyes widened with shock. "I couldn't do that."

"Why not? The penalty's the same if you get caught."

"I would get caught doing something like that. I wouldn't know what to do."

"I know what to do."

"Why would you help me do this?"

"Cause I hate judges. I can talk to the Blade for you and get you a plan."

"How can I talk to him?"

"He's here in jail, up in maximum security. He goes to the infirmary twice a day for his arthritis. I'll go up there this morning and lay the groundwork for you. You can talk to him this afternoon. All you need is a kite."

"A kite?"

"Yeah. A sick slip. Just complain to the guard about a stiff elbow. You'll get the Blade's doc. Now tell me more about this judge."

Stewart walked to the elevator, pushed the button and waited. Security seemed lax here, he noticed as the door opened. When he got in the elevator, he looked up and saw the closed-circuit TV monitor. When he moved back, the monitor followed him. The ride to the fifth floor was quick and uneventful. A new camera picked him up when he left the elevator. When he approached the infirmary, the drawer opened, and he put the kite in as the drawer closed. Seeing no one, he looked up and saw another TV camera, then turned into the waiting area. There were seven prisoners inside. Everyone was silent, and no one looked like the Blade. *What the hell do I do now?* Finally, he sat across from the roughest-looking customer in the room. The prisoner shuddered as he emitted a chest-rattling cough.

"That sounds like a bad cough."

"Bad enough, son. I'm gonna die in here, and nobody gives a shit."

"Don't they give you some medicine for it?"

"Yeah, but it's not helping."

"How long have you been in here?"

"About a month."

"What are you in for?"

"None of your damn business."

"Sorry. I was just trying to be friendly."

"That ain't how to do it, boy."

"Can the guards overhear us in here?"

"No. That camera is visual only."

"I need to find the Blade. Do you know him?"

"Sure. Everybody does."

"How can I reach him?"

"Just sit tight. He'll be along directly."

"Thanks."

Stewart looked around. His conversation was generating several others among the prisoners. A few minutes later, as the room filled, a graying, older man with a scar on his right forearm walked in and sat in the corner. The rail-thin, seventy-year-old man had stooping shoulders and walked and sat as if it was painful for him to move. Stewart looked at the prisoner across the aisle, and the prisoner nodded just a little. Stewart walked casually over to the water fountain, and on returning, sat next to the old man. Stewart spoke without looking directly at him.

"My name's Stewart, and I need to talk to you."

"Are you the one Atwood told me about?"

"Yes sir."

"If your attorney is Torrey, I know you're okay. What do you want?"

"I need a gun and a place to hide."

"What kind of gun and how long do you need to hide?"

"An automatic, I guess. I'm not sure how long I'll need to hide."

"Are you going to have a lot of heat on you."

"Probably."

"Do you know anything about automatics?"

"Not really."

"You better stick with a revolver then. Automatics can jamb on you pretty easy. If you need more ammunition, you can use a speed clip."

"How much is this gonna cost me."

"I don't know. I need to know what you're up to."

"Why?"

"Without that information, I don't know what kind of gun you need or what kind of safe house to put you in. I have to know what kind of heat's coming. The more the heat, the more it costs."

Stewart shifted in the chair. He didn't like spilling his guts. "I'm gonna kill my ex-girlfriend and maybe some other people."

"What other people?"

"A judge, maybe. I might have to shoot my way out of a courtroom."

"That sounds like a lot of heat."

"Could be."

"Have you planned all this out?"

"Pretty much."

"Pretty much will get you caught. You better forget about this, son. You may not live very long."

"That's not as important to me as killing the bitch."

"I can hide you if you kill the girl, unless she's somebody important. The judge is another matter. The price goes way up then."

"If I go out, I'm going with a bang. Can you help me or not?"

"I can get you a untraceable revolver for about $350. I'd have to put you in our best safe house though and that costs $1,000 a week."

"Here in Tarrant County?"

"No. That's why it's the best one available."

"Where is it?"

"You won't know till you're headed there. We don't pass out that information. The house wouldn't be safe if we did. How long do you want to stay there?"

"I don't know. What do you think?"

"Two weeks minimum. After that, get out of Texas, change your identity, and never come back. Does this mean enough to you to do that?"

"Yes."

"Do you have enough money for all this?"

"I'll have it within twenty-four hours after I get out of jail. Come to think of it, I might need a lockpick. Can you get me one?"

"All right, son. I'll throw that in for twenty-five dollars, but don't call us until you have the money. Memorize this phone number: 555-5557."

Stewart recited the number back three times. The Blade rose, murmuring as he walked away, "When you call, ask for Angel."

Ray opened the newspaper as the American Airlines MD-80 raced down the runway. He was no longer active in the statewide Justice of the Peace and

Constables Association that supervised the education courses. The association's training center was located in Austin and sponsored by Southwest Texas State University. Ray had mixed emotions about going to the mandated courses. The classes were generally informative, and he enjoyed visiting with the other judges around the state, exchanging ideas and information, but since Doris died, it was hard for him to be away for three days. The kids usually picked that time to make problems for the housekeeper. Ray had wrenched a solemn promise from Robbie at the ball game last night that he and his sister would be nice to Anita this trip. After he read the sports section, he found Marilyn's article on the peace bond hearing. Ray surmised that most of the article had been trimmed. Although the article was only fourteen sentences and contained nothing about the new restraining orders, there were kudos for Ray from Shirley Lemons, but there was no response from the defense attorney. He found nothing about Agnew and wasn't surprised. Laying the newspaper aside, he studied the training outline that the training center had provided. *Damn*, he thought. *I never got back to Rachael Frank yesterday. She'll be mad when she finds out that I left town without returning her call.*

Rachael Frank was more than mad when she finished talking to Cass. Her empty coffee cup sailed across the room and shattered against the wall. Brenda charged into the office to see what was wrong.

"That no-good son of a bitch. He's not going to have enough money in his budget next year to buy paper clips when I get through with him."

"Who are you talking about?" asked Brenda.

"Ray Sterrett, that's who," fumed Rachael.

"Do you want me to compromise that boy and swing him your way?"

"No. You'd probably have to throw up on him while you were at it."

Brenda laughed. "What's he done?"

"The prick's too arrogant to return my phone calls."

"I can drive out there and talk to him if you like."

"No thanks," replied Rachael, thinking her assistant sounded way too eager. She picked up the ringing phone. "Rachael Frank speaking."

"This is Bill Campbell."

"Yes, Commissioner?" said Rachael through clenched teeth.

"I just received a memo from Judge Sterrett on these office supplies we were discussing. He's thinking along the same lines. I want you to get the office supply figures for every office in the county."

"Commissioner Campbell, that could take some time. How about just the subcourthouse offices? The agencies downtown could still use my purchasing office. It's still closer to them than any office supply."

"Maybe you weren't listening to me, Miss Frank. I said every agency, and I want it today. I know what your computer capabilities are."

"You must think it's my fault the prices are not in line. I can't make these discount houses bid on these items, and the law requires bids. If you try to circumvent this, you'll be breaking the law."

"Miss Frank, you know as well as I do that bids have to go out on any expenditure over $5,000. If these offices use less than that, we can let them buy their own supplies at cheaper prices than we're paying now."

"If that happens, I'd have to lay off at least two employees."

"Good!"

"All right, Commissioner. I'll get the figures to you."

"And Miss Frank, I want those figures today. I'll send my AA for them about 3:00."

Rachael grimaced. "I'm going to fight you on this one." Campbell didn't hear it. The phone line was dead. "That miserable bastard," hissed Rachael. "I've got to get him focused on something else."

"Cass, Carl Holt is on line four for you." called Phyllis.

Cass frowned a little as she picked up the phone. "Hello, Carl."

"Hi, babe. What's going on?"

"You need to send me some money."

"What for?"

"I couldn't get a refund on that trip cancellation next week. They would only refund the plane tickets. Nothing else."

"How much is that?"

"Eight hundred and twenty dollars."

"Damn. I wish you'd waited until I gave you the go-ahead before you committed us on that trip."

"We've already been through this. You were out of town, the travel agency had a deadline to meet, and you hadn't given me any indication you couldn't go. You didn't complain after you got back until yesterday."

"I'll do what's fair. I'll give you my half."

"Carl, I didn't cancel this trip. You did."

"That's the best I can do, honey."

Cass sat for a long moment. "I'll tell you what you can do. You can kiss my you-know-what. Don't bother calling me again." She ran to the restroom so no one in the office could see her tears.

Chapter Nine

J udge Jake Eaves studied his silver hair in the office bathroom mirror. For several years, he'd dyed it, until he could no longer fool the voters. Satisfied with his appearance, he brushed an imaginary speck of lint from his impeccable Botany 500 suit and returned to his desk. He'd been a judge in the 41st Criminal District Court for twenty-two years and was the last Democratic countywide office holder. The Republicans had begun an onslaught on the criminal courts in the mid eighties, capturing every other court in the county. Jake had held on by squeezing the defense attorneys for large contributions to finance his highly visible campaigns. Every four years, he'd spend over $100,000 to tell the voters how he'd championed the death penalty all his life. The defense attorneys snickered at his hypocrisy but gave with gusto.

Jake trumpeted every jury death verdict as his own, but the attorneys knew that in cases that weren't heavily publicized, Jake would help them when he could. If you needed a writ of habeas corpus in the middle of the night for a drug-bust client with big bucks, Jake was there. When you could bluff the DA's office and get a lenient plea bargain, Eaves was there to rubber-stamp it.

As a senior judge, Jake had one of the biggest chambers in the county, and he had decorated it lavishly. His proudest possession was the tiger skin rug in front of the desk. Trophies of all kinds, from deer to mountain lions, were displayed on the walls. An avid hunter, Jake had shot every trophy in the room but the mountain lion. Luck had awarded him that bargain, discovered at an auction in Austin many years ago, but he and his second wife were the only ones who knew that secret. The story of his narrow escape from the lion took over an hour to tell to anyone foolish enough to ask. No one asked much anymore.

Jake came from an old Fort Worth family dating back before the Civil War. A picture of a Confederate cavalry captain graced the far wall; a caption in gold underneath the portrait read: Captain Harry Eaves Terry's Texas Rangers 1864. Encased in glass beside it was a very rare Leach and Rigdon cavalry pistol. Jake had found it at another auction, but had to pay dearly for it. His new bride at the time had raised holy hell with him for spending $5,000 "for that old gun." But Jake had the last laugh on that one. The pistol had tripled in value in only seven years. The treasure was better than anything in his stock portfolio. To interested parties, Jake claimed it was his great-grandfather's.

Jake also had a penchant for the ladies. It had already cost him two wives and a large fortune. He had slowed down some, but another shining trophy sat at his court coordinator's desk. Carol was a twenty-eight-year old beauty Jake had found in Hurst. He had romanced her shamefully for over a month before they wound up in bed. A genius for finding a weakness, he found Carol's to be jewelry and Super Bowl tickets. That's how he had got her. He'd coughed up some big judicial favors to an attorney for those tickets. Now he remembered with a smile his special thanks from Carol. All you had to do was ask at the right time.

A month later, he'd framed his court coordinator, claimed she'd made a blunder, fired her, and brought in Carol. Some of his lunch hours were pure delight, and his wife never suspected a thing. Carol's fancy car and apartment were leased in the name of one of his closest campaign contributors. Jake's sexual prowess was extraordinary for a man of sixty-six. Viagra was a wonderful thing. Those pleasant memories were cut short by the phone buzzer. With anticipation, Eaves picked up the phone.

"Yes?"

"Don't forget today is Wednesday. You're giving a speech at the Fort Worth Lion's Club. Tim Lindsey and Mr. Torrey are here to see you."

"Thanks darlin'. Send them right in. I forgot about that speech. I wanted to spend lunch with you."

"Not today," returned Carol with a sullen frown. *Just a little more money and I'm gone. I won't need anymore of your lecherous ass.*

Lindsey and Torrey strolled into the office and sat down in two cushy chairs, after extending their hands for the traditional shake. Lindsey took the lead. "How are you today, you corrupt old rascal?"

"Please, Tim, voters may be listening."

That got guffaws all around, breaking the ice. Jake looked at the prey with his broadest smile. Lindsey was his largest contributor. "What can I do for you boys today?"

Lindsey leaned back, put his hands over his crossed knees, and smiled back at the judge. "A couple of things, Judge. First, Rachael Frank asked me to hurry this case along for county budget reasons. Being the patriotic citizen that I am, I've complied with her wishes."

A smile crossed Jake's lips. "Are you withdrawing your request for a continuance in the voir dire?"

"Yes, Judge."

"Okay. We'll start back in the morning. And the other?"

"Leonard here has a motion for a writ of habeas corpus. I'll let him tell you about that."

Jake understood. Torrey had no money, which translated into no campaign contributions. Torrey needed Lindsey for an introduction. Looking at the shabbily dressed Torrey, Jake smiled. "Yes, Leonard?"

"Judge, I've got a client languishing in jail on nothing, really. He's in on some chicken shit peace bond where an ex-girlfriend trumped up a charge that he violated a protective order. The case was so weak, the DA's office didn't even try to prosecute it on a revocation order. Instead, they went to a JP court and got a peace bond. Judge, I swear to you, he didn't lay a hand on this girl. I put some additional details in this motion." Torrey handed the paperwork over.

Jake looked over the crudely drawn motion and saw why Torrey didn't make any money. Looking up at Torrey, he asked, "What kind of criminal history does your client have?"

"Absolutely clean, Judge. Saint Francis has a worse record."

"Who was the JP?"

"Sterrett."

"I see. Doesn't some violence have to happen before some magistrate issues a protective order?"

"Apparently not."

"Is this guy one of your pro bono clients, or is he paying you?"

"He's a paying client, Your Honor, employed for six years."

Jake looked at Lindsey, who nodded back in understanding. Twenty-five percent of the fee would go into Jake's campaign account. "All right, Leonard, I'll sign this." Signing his name with a flourish, he handed it back to Torrey with a smug smile.

"Thanks, Judge," returned Torrey as he got up to leave. He'd just made a fast $500, or so he thought.

Stewart was napping on his bunk when his cellmate shook him, pointing to the guard outside the open door. The screw looked as bored as ever, but his news sure wasn't boring. "Get up, Stewart. You're outta here. There's a nice writ of habeas corpus waiting for you down stairs."

Stewart got an exit slip and followed the guard to the elevator. Following directions, he carried his belongings into the exit room. On the wall was a phone. Stewart grabbed it, dialed his grandmother, but got no answer. Quickly, he dialed Jerry.

"Hey, Jerry, it's Billy. Can you come get me, man? I'm down at the county jail, and I don't have a way home."

"I don't know, man. I'm broke. You'd have to give me gas money."

"No problem. When can you get here?"

"Thirty or forty minutes, I guess. Where are you exactly?"

Stewart looked around and spotted a sign with instructions for prisoner pickup. "I'll be at the northwest corner of Weatherford and Houston. Can you find it?"

"Yeah, I think so."

"Come as soon as you can, then. I'll be waiting." Stewart hung up, changed clothes, dropped his jail duds in a basket, and hit the door. Fresh air and freedom were waiting.

Jerry Chandler picked him up right on schedule in his Oldsmobile. Stewart was glad to see him. "Thanks for picking me up, old buddy."

"Don't mention it. What are you doing in jail? Harlan told me you got out last week."

"It's a long story. Something about violating a court order."

"Do you want to go to your apartment? That's where your truck is."

"Yeah. But take me by the bank first. I need to get some cash."

"For my gas money?"

"No. Here's ten dollars for that. But that's all I have. By the way, I need you to loan me your car for a day or two."

"Sure if I can drive your truck while you have it."

"No. I'll need the truck, too."

"Sorry man. I ain't walkin'."

"Look, there's a hundred bucks in it for you. But I can't bring the car back to you. You'll have to get it yourself."

"I could use the hundred dollars. I'm really scramblin' since I lost my job. Where do I pick up the car?"

"Don't know yet. I'll call you and tell you where it is."

"Why don't you just rent a damn car? That's cheaper."

"Because I want yours. Anyway, I need you to drop it off at a certain place for me, then I'll take you home."

"Okay. What are you up to anyway?"

"Don't get nosy. I'll tell you about it later. Here's the bank. Turn in here." Jerry pulled into the bank parking lot and started to get out of the car, but Stewart stopped him. "Just wait right here. I'll be back in a jiff." With that, he got out and sauntered into the bank, returning shortly with his life savings, $739.00. He handed Jerry one hundred dollars and stuffed the rest of the money in his pocket. "Take me home."

When they arrived, Stewart directed Jerry to be back with the car at 5:30 sharp, got out, and walked into his hot apartment. As he turned on the air conditioner, he saw an eviction notice taped inside his door. "Vacate in three days," it read at the bottom.

Stewart laughed and wadded up the notice. *I'm way ahead of you, bitch.* He pulled out his two suitcases and opened them on the bed. He packed the big one with three changes of clothes, leaving one of his water department uniforms on top, along with some tennis shoes. Toilet articles were put into the smaller one, along with a plastic garbage bag. Stewart put on his favorite Western outfit, his cowboy boots, and his fancy Resistol hat. After loading the large case under two blankets in the back of his Club Cab pickup, he drove to Shirley's apartment and slowly circled it twice. Neither the apartment manager's or Shirley's car was there. After parking two blocks away, he donned his hat and sunglasses. No one would recognize him in that outfit. He walked to the flowerbed at the back of Shirley's apartment and found the master key under her bedroom window, thrown out when he had seen Shirley returning with the police. Sticking the key in his pocket, he walked away, turning around after several yards and surveying the scene. No one had noticed him.

The next stop was a hardware store, where he purchased some duct tape, a flashlight with batteries, and a large and a small screwdriver. After buying a stamped envelope at the post office, Stewart drove south to Mansfield on Highway 157. Turning right on Debbie Lane, he slowly drove to the subcourthouse. Things looked quiet, and the judge's parking place was empty. Continuing south, he found just what he was looking for—an old vacant house on the right, just past the curve. Parking his pickup in the driveway, he walked to the backyard and looked back toward the subcourthouse. What he saw wasn't good. Someone had built a self-storage facility in that huge pasture nearby, and part of it appeared to be near the drainage pipe. The manhole cover he was looking for was only thirty yards from where he stood. "Everything would work out just the same", he told himself. Remembering some other items he would need, he drove back to his apartment. After picking up a denim jacket, he sat down at the table to write his grandmother a letter. Stewart was crying when he finished it.

His watch read 2:30 pm when he went to a pawnshop and bought a used briefcase for ten dollars. Stewart browsed through the pistols to see how bad the Blade was screwing him. Not bad as it turned out. There was one detail that he had forgotten. Ammunition hadn't been discussed, and he didn't know what caliber to buy. Going to a public phone, he dialed the number, which was answered quickly. "I need to speak to Angel."

"This is Angel. Who's this?"

"My name is Stewart. The Blade gave me this number."

"Yeah. He told me you might call. Got the money?"

"Not all of it. I'll have the rest by tonight. I need the pistol and lockpick now, or at least to know what type of ammunition to get."

"It comes with ammunition."

"How many rounds?"

"It's got six in the piece and six in the speed loader."

"What kind is it?"

"Smith and Wesson .357 Magnum. It's a nice piece."

"Can I pick it up now?"

"No. I'll bring it to you when you have the money."

"I've got it."

"Where are you?"

"In Arlington."

"Okay. I'll meet you at the Mobil station on the corner of Arkansas Lane and Collins in twenty minutes."

"How will I know you?"

"You won't. You tell me what you're driving."

"A maroon Club Cab Ford pickup with running boards and Laker pipes. You can't miss it."

"I'll be there in twenty minutes. Be there." Angel hung up.

A trip back to the pawnshop yielded Stewart a box of ammunition. Proceeding to the service station, he waited almost an hour for Angel. Finally a Lincoln Town Car drove up. A man got out of the back seat and jumped in the truck with Stewart. He was a swarthy man, about thirty-five, with a balding head, and looked Stewart over with an unfriendly stare. Stewart decided to break the ice. "Where have you been? You said twenty minutes. It's been an hour."

"I've been across the street, boy. Checking you out."

"The Blade already checked me out. You're wasting your time and mine. Where's the gun and the pick?"

"Where's the money?"

Stewart handed over the money, and Angel made a show of counting it. Stewart did a slow burn, beginning to dislike Angel. "Hey man, do you think I'd cheat you when I need you tomorrow for a safe house?"

"I wasn't put on this earth to trust you, kid. For all I know, you won't even call for the safe house. Did you say tomorrow?"

"Yeah. Sometime between 8:30 and 10:00."

"You better have $2,000 for me then."

"Where's the damn gun?"

Angel pulled the pistol and lockpick from under his jacket, placing them next to Stewart. Picking up the pistol, he broke the cylinder. There were no bullets. Angel pulled out the speed loader. No bullets were in the loader either.

"What about the ammo?"

"My driver will put them out on the pavement before we leave."

"Why are you acting like such an asshole?"

Angel smiled a little. "That's why people call me Angel."

"I've got one last request."

"What's that?"

"I want to meet at a certain place tomorrow for the getaway."

"That sounds dangerous. I'm not part of what you're doing."

"It won't be dangerous. If anyone's pursuing me, I'll drive on."

"It'll cost you extra."

"How much extra?"

"Two hundred."

"How 'bout a hundred? You have to pick me up anyway."

"All right, kid. Where do I meet you?"

"The Walnut Creek Country Club in Mansfield. Wait in the parking lot. When you see a 1989 blue Oldsmobile coming from the west, with it's lights flashing, start the car and pop the trunk latch. I have to put two suitcases in there, and you'd better get me the hell out of there without playing anymore of your damn games."

"How far away is the country club from your action?"

"About two miles. Anyone at the site will never see my car, though. It's all worked out."

"I want the hundred in advance."

"What!"

"Come on, kid. What if something happens, and you never show up?"

"All right, man. Here's the hundred." Angel got out of the truck and nodded to his driver. As the driver started the Lincoln, he opened his door and leaned over. When Angel got in, the two sped away. Stewart retrieved the ammunition from the pavement and checked his watch. He barely had time to go to the shooting range before Jerry picked him up.

Jerry rang the doorbell at exactly 5:30, getting no answer. Getting back in his car, he waited until Stewart drove up beside him, three minutes later.

"Are you ready?"

"Yeah."

"Follow me, and if we get separated, we'll meet at Highway 157 and Debbie Lane in Mansfield."

"Okay." Stewart sped off, with Jerry following. Stewart drove back to the vacant house on Russell. He stopped at the side of the road and motioned Jerry to pull into the driveway.

"Park here and wait," ordered Stewart as he walked behind the house. Jerry couldn't tell what he was doing. After a while, Stewart returned. "Lock up your car, give me your keys, and let's go."

Jerry got into the truck, and Stewart turned back north on Russell.

"What in the hell are you up to, Billy?"

Stewart ignored the question. He turned left at the next corner and drove about a hundred feet. After carefully checking the buildings to his right, he pulled off the road and into the subcourthouse parking lot. Climbing out of the truck, he crossed the street and walked behind another house. Stewart was gone for about ten minutes, then came back with a huge grin. Jerry couldn't stand it any longer.

"Billy, tell me what's going on, or the deal's off. You can find another car. You're acting weird, man."

Stewart laughed. "It's no big deal, Jerry. I'm just checking some work that we did out here. The boss asked me to do it, but I never got the chance before I got thrown in jail."

After studying the buildings to his right again, he drove Jerry back to his house and dropped him off.

"Is that where my car will be when I pick it up?" asked Jerry as he got out of the truck.

"It will be if I don't use it. Otherwise it'll be at the Walnut Creek Country Club in the parking lot. Get Harlan or somebody to take you out to get it between 10:30 and 11:00 in the morning. Don't come any earlier. I won't have it there till then. I'm afraid they might tow the car if you wait past 11:00."

"Are you gonna tell me what this is all about?"

"I will tomorrow. I have to run now. I'll call you tomorrow."

Stewart drove to the HyperMart on Highway 157 in Arlington and stole a set of file cabinet keys, then returned to his apartment and took a nap.

He awoke with a start when the alarm went off. He bathed, shaved, repacked his toilet articles in the small case, and put it in the truck. Famished, he found a waffle shop and stuffed himself. Thinking as he ate, Stewart carefully went over every detail of his plan. It seemed fool proof to him. There was only one problem: his life here would be over. *Was it worth it?*, he wondered, remembering how empty his life had been before Shirley and how different it had been when he met her. *Can I find another girl someday? Probably not with a police record. This life I'm giving up isn't worth jack shit.*

Quietly, he paid his bill, drove back to Mansfield, dropped the letter to his grandmother in a mailbox, and drove past the subcourthouse three times. There appeared to be no one in sight, and everything was quiet. After driving around to the vacant house on Russell, he packed the briefcase with the lockpick, pistol, ammo, speed loader, duct tape, screwdrivers, and file cabinet keys. Then he took the flashlight, a change of clothes, his tennis shoes, a plastic garbage bag, and walked behind the house to the field behind it, where he found the drainage culvert with the flashlight.

Three years ago, Stewart's boss had loaned him to the City of Mansfield for this very project. Mansfield had a very small water department and a big drainage problem. This field was a watershed, dumping flood water onto Russell Road. The only solution was to divert the water under Russell Road into the huge eight-foot sewer drain that ran just east of the road. The project had entailed putting a sixty-inch drainage pipe from just east of a pickle factory that fronted Debbie Lane to the eight-foot drainage pipe on Russell Road. The five-foot drainage culvert ran over six hundred yards and had work openings every hundred yards, complete with junction boxes, drainage grates, and access ladders. The ladder openings were covered with unlocked twenty-four-inch manhole covers. The Mansfield city council had elected to rent the equipment and personnel from the city of Arlington rather than buy it themselves. Stewart had worked on this project from start to finish and knew every detail of the job, never dreaming of the dividend it would later pay.

Raising the manhole cover, Stewart went down the access ladder and put the garbage bag, now holding his tennis shoes and clothes, on the third rung from the top. The bottom of the work opening was dry, courtesy of the August weather. Not wanting wet clothes in the morning, he decided to leave them on the ladder, just in case. He climbed up the ladder, leaving the manhole cover off, returned to his truck and locked his two suitcases in the trunk of Jerry's car. Leaving his hat and sunglasses in the truck, Stewart walked casually back in the field, carrying his flashlight and briefcase, then walked along the line of the culvert to junction box number two. After making sure there were no blockages in the drainage culvert, he quietly crossed the street to the subcourthouse. After circling around to the back to make sure no one was around, he checked his watch: 12:30. No traffic on the roads to the east, which allowed him to walk to the window that he had unlocked Monday morning. It was still open. Raising it, he dropped his briefcase inside, followed it, closed the window, and looked around.

There was no burglar alarm, as he suspected. As he moved to Cass's office to his left, everything looked normal. He flicked the flashlight toward the file cabinet where he had watched her put up the money and couldn't believe his eyes. The file cabinet was closed but unlocked. The top drawer yielded five zippered bank bags in the back. Three of them felt full. *What luck,* he thought. Taking the bags down the hall to the windowless bathroom, he closed the door and switched on his flashlight. He rifled eagerly through the bags. Most of it was court paperwork. That was a disappointment. Carefully, he removed the money from each bag. It looked like slim pickings until he searched the last bag, which contained several hundred-dollar bills. He counted carefully. *If there isn't $2,000 here, I'm in deep shit,* he thought as he kept counting: $1,000, $1,500, $1,800. He was almost finished. "Jackpot," he exclaimed. Sandwiched between some five-dollar bills were several twenties and six hundred-dollar bills. When he finished, Stewart totaled $2,840. He had hoped for more, but this would do.

After stuffing the money into his pocket, Stewart replaced the bank bags, smiling as he pushed in the lock, thinking of the confusion in the morning. He then drove to the country club, making sure there were no detour signs. On the trip back to Arlington, he drove past Shirley's apartment and confirmed that her car was there. Checking his watch again, he realized he was two hours ahead of schedule, even after allowing himself time to break into the file cabinet. The drive back to his apartment was made to get some rest. Sleep didn't come. His heart was racing too fast, so he contented himself with walking around the apartment for the last time and packing a few small sentimental items.

Chapter Ten

It was 3:45 am when Stewart left his apartment. Shaking with excitement, he drove to Shirley's apartment complex and pulled into the parking area closest to her front door. A car occupied the space he wanted on the end, thirty feet from her door. Slowly, his vehicle jumped the curb and pulled up near Shirley's door. The Laker pipes scraped on the concrete curb, causing Stewart to grit his teeth. First shoving the pistol into the back of his belt, he fished the large screwdriver and duct tape out of the briefcase. After taking a quick look around, he strode to Shirley's front door and eased the master key into her lock. Taking pains to be quiet, he took twenty seconds to open the door, but the safety latch stopped it. Undaunted, he pried off the latch with the screwdriver. The task took over three minutes, but Stewart didn't make a sound.

Shirley Lemons awoke in terror as a hand covered her mouth with force. Her frightened eyes looked into a face that she couldn't make out. She vaguely made out a large cowboy hat. Although she screamed with all her might, no sound escaped the strong hand. A fierce struggle ensued, until she saw a gun come out and rest against her temple. The terrified woman lay there shaking for thirty seconds while the shadowy man kept the pressure on her mouth. A familiar voice came out of the dark.

"Shirley, calm down. It's just me."

Shirley's eyes widened in terror. *Oh God! It's Billy! How did he get out of jail and in here?* After another struggle, the hand pushed down harder on her mouth. The click from the cocked gun forced Shirley into submission.

"Baby, if you calm down and cooperate, you'll live through this. Otherwise, I'm gonna have to kill you, and I don't want to do that."

Shirley lay frozen in fear, wondering if she would survive. *Why wasn't I called when they let this animal out of jail?*

"Baby, I'm gonna take my hand off your mouth and put some tape over it, so you can breathe. Nod your head up and down if you promise to cooperate. If you scream, I'll have to shoot you. Understand?"

Shirley's head bobbed up and down in compliance. The hand came off slowly. "Billy, please don't …"

"Now sit up and put your hands behind your back. This is just to keep you from doing something foolish till we can talk, okay?"

Shirley nodded again, rose to a sitting position, and put her hands backward as the sheet fell, exposing her bare breasts. She felt her hands being tightly bound with more tape. Billy went around and around with the tape. Shirley's spirits fell with every revolution. Done, Billy stepped away and turned on the bedside lamp. Shirley could see him fully for the first time. *He looks pale and nervous, too. Maybe I can live through this. But if he didn't come to kill me, what does he want?* Gazing at her bare breasts for a moment, Stewart put the gun in his belt and sat down beside his captive.

"Baby, I've got it all worked out. You and me are going to take a trip and make a fresh start. I know you'll give me another chance once I explain, and I can, once we are on the road. If you don't agree to take this trip, then we're both gonna die together right here. Nod your head and tell me what you want to do."

Shirley lowered her head and pretended to think. *Is he really that crazy, or does he have something else up his sleeve? On the other hand, what other chance do I have?* Slowly, she nodded her head. *If I can just get this tape off my mouth, maybe I can talk my way out of this mess.* Shirley began making sounds through the tape to signal that she wanted to talk.

"Sorry, baby. That tape can't come off now. We'll talk later."

The muffled sounds continued.

Stewart stared at her in distrust as he pulled the pistol back out. "All right. I'll take the tape off for a minute, but if you scream, it's all over. Understand?"

Shirley's head moved up and down. Stewart reached over and ripped off the tape in one quick motion. "Sorry, baby. What is it?"

"I have to go to the bathroom real bad. You just about scared the pee out of me."

Stewart mulled over the request. The window in the bathroom made up his mind. "The only way you can go in there is with me."

"Like hell. I can't go anywhere with my hands tied. You know I have to have privacy. If you want us to have any chance, you better start treating me right." *And please be stupid enough to leave the tape off.*

"Okay, baby, have it your way. But I have to take some precautions." Stewart cut a fresh piece of tape, slapped it over her mouth, and led her into the bathroom. When she got to the toilet, Shirley turned and faced her captor, making more sounds through the tape. Stewart pulled her panties down, pushed her down on the toilet, then backed out, closing the door part way and blocking it with his foot. Shirley couldn't close the door with her head or feet; it could only be locked with inward pressure. If that was what she had up her sleeve, it wouldn't work. After a long wait, he heard the sound of splashing liquid.

Stewart waited a few moments, went back in, flushed the toilet, and stood Shirley up. He stood back to get an eyeful Eyes full of hatred peering back made him rethink his idea. He pulled Shirley's panties up for her and led her back into the bedroom. While her back was turned, he checked his watch. Stewart noted it was 4:15. Dawn would break in about an hour. The complex would start stirring about five. Sitting Shirley back down on the bed, he gazed again at her luscious breasts. It had been a long time. He didn't have anything to lose. On the other hand, he didn't want to deal with her kicking and screaming for the next few hours. Deciding that he'd better not, Stewart went to her closet, found an oversized sweatshirt and, without undoing her hands, pulled it down over her head, then pulled out some jeans and put them on the trembling woman. Shirley was so relieved to escape a sexual assault that she cooperated fully. More sounds came through the duct tape.

"What is it now?"

The sounds continued as Shirley looked toward the closet. Stewart cursed under his breath as he realized she expected to take clothes with her. He hadn't considered that. "You can take two changes of clothes, baby. We don't have room for anything else." Stewart walked to the closet, pulled out some dresses, and held them out to Shirley one by one until she shook her head yes to one of them. He pulled a blouse and another pair of jeans out of a dresser, then got a small suitcase out of the closet and stuffed the clothes into it. More sounds were made as she looked into the bathroom. Billy took the case into the bathroom and had started to put some of her toilet articles into it when he noticed her reflection flash by in the mirror. Dropping the case, he caught her as she was pitifully trying to open the front door with her bound hands. Stewart grabbed her by the hair and dragged her back on the bed, sat her down, then slapped her hard. Tears welled in her accusing eyes as she raised her head in defiance. He'd never struck her before. Stewart looked down at her with similar eyes.

"You promised me you wouldn't do that, baby. Have you changed your mind? Do you want to die?"

Shirley shook her head no and tried to talk through the tape. Stewart wasn't about to pull the tape off again.

"Listen, Shirley, if you try to pull that stunt again, it's all over. I'm gonna beat the hell out of you, and then I'm gonna shoot both of us. Understand?"

Shirley nodded, the left side of her face turning bright red where he hit her.

"You're not the boss anymore. I am. You understand that?"

Her head nodded again.

"Are you going to cooperate and do everything I tell you to?"

Shirley's head bobbed up and down again. "Good," returned a satisfied Stewart. He turned, pulled a pair of loafers out of the closet and pitched them at her bound feet. "Slide into those." Stewart went back to the bathroom and threw a few cosmetics into the small suitcase.

When he returned, Shirley hadn't moved a muscle. Thinking that he wouldn't be in this fix if he had hit her earlier, he took her suitcase to the front door, then went back for Shirley.

"Shirley, listen carefully. We're leaving. You're gonna walk out and get in the back on the floorboard of the truck and lay still. You don't make a sound or move till I tell you to. Understand?"

Still gagged, Shirley nodded. Stewart pulled her off the bed, walked her to the truck, and put her in the back floorboard, with her head facing the passenger side. He walked to the other side of the truck and bound her legs with duct tape. Stewart threw both blankets over her body, but two weren't enough. After getting another one off her bed, he picked up her suitcase on the way out, leaving the screwdriver forgotten on the nightstand. The third blanket did the trick. He then positioned the briefcase on her legs and used her small case to cover her head. If anyone took a casual glance in the back, it would look like a bunch of junk. He drove away slowly, knowing this was not the time to get a traffic ticket.

Shirley lay in the back, her fear mixed with relief. If he had raped her or had not gone back for her suitcase, she knew she would certainly die. Now she wasn't sure. Shirley moved her head a little to work some breathing space under the blankets. Stewart's hand came crashing down on the suitcase, causing her head to hurt like hell. After that, she didn't move.

Heading west on I-30, Stewart noticed that his gas gauge was showing empty. Second thoughts crept to the edges of his mind. *Damn! I should've gassed up before I went over there. What else did I forget to do?* Stewart parked at the island farthest away from inside the Texaco station. He got out of the car, walked around to the passenger side, and watched Shirley. For about thirty seconds, she didn't move. Slowly she started to move her head, throwing off the suitcase as she tried to get up. Stewart opened the passenger door and thrust the seat forward. Grabbing Shirley by the hair, he yanked her head up, slapped her hard, pushed her head back down, and covered her back up. Stewart gassed up the car and quietly walked away to pay the cashier. When he got back in the car, Shirley hadn't moved. He could hear her sobbing as he pulled away. Stewart drove aimlessly on the freeways, taking care to stay at the speed limit and to stay in the middle of the light traffic. Stewart checked his watch as the sun came up. It was 5:46 am. He had three hours to kill.

Cass opened the office at 7:50. After putting the coffee on, she opened the file cabinet to get an early start on yesterday's report. Routinely, she carried the bank bags over to the desk and set them down. Her face blanched when she opened the first one. There was no cash in it. Hurriedly, she opened the others, with the same result. The confused head clerk sat for several moments, totally stunned. When the other clerks came in, she ignored them. Finally, she summoned Phyllis and told her to shut the door. "Phyllis, something's wrong."

"What is it?"

"There's no money in the bank bags."

"That's impossible."

"When you closed up for me yesterday, did you lock the cabinet?"

"Yes, I think so."

"You think so? You're not positive?"

"I'm pretty sure. But I got a phone call right as I was doing that. So it's possible that I didn't. What are we going to do?"

"I don't know. If you did lock it, we have a more serious problem than if you didn't. I'm gonna look for signs of a break-in." Cass wandered around, checking for anything unusual, seeing nothing. Walking back to the constable's office, she found Harvey Walling.

"Harvey, would you look around and see if there are any signs of a break-in? I think something may be wrong."

"What's wrong?"

"I'm not sure. Does anything look out of the ordinary back here?"

"No. Not that I can see."

"Check the whole building immediately, please."

"Yeah sure. What am I supposed to be looking for?"

"I don't know, Harvey. You're the cop. Broken windows, footprints, that sort of thing."

"Okay. I'll get right on it."

Cass went back to her office. "Phyllis, do you remember how much money was here last night?"

"No. I just checked the money against each clerk's receipts. Just like you told me to."

"Did you put all the money in one bag?"

"No. I left it in each bag."

"Did we have a light day yesterday?"

"No. We had a pretty heavy day."

"Shit."

"Am I in trouble?"

"We're all in trouble. Add up the receipts and see how short we are. Do it right now."

"But I have to check in the eviction parties."

"I'll get Clara to do that. Get busy."

Cass looked over the clerks to see if anyone was acting strangely. "Clara, check in the eviction litigants for Phyllis. I've got her on another project." At that point, Judge Chavez pulled up and parked in Ray's spot. Cass, ever the diplomat, met him at the door.

"Good morning, Judge. We appreciate you coming out here to help."

"Good morning, Cass. Think nothing of it. Ray does the same for me. What do we have cooking this morning?"

"Lots of evictions."

"Okay. Can I get out of here by noon?"

"You should be able to. Want some coffee?"

"No thanks. I'm coffied out. I need to use Ray's phone, though."

"Sure. Help yourself."

Judge Joe Chavez walked back to Ray's office. After three years on the job, he was getting his feet on the ground. A virtual legend had been replaced when he had taken office. Judge Carlos Ochoa had stepped down after sixteen years to run for county commissioner, but had been defeated in a close election by Bill Campbell. Judge Chavez had struggled in his first year as many JPs do. He'd gotten crossways with the commissioners' court and Rachael Frank, and consequently faced annual budget battles in retaliation. Many of his early verdicts were questioned openly in the newspapers, and he'd gone too far in dealing with the problem juveniles in his district, trying to keep them in school. Things were beginning to die down, and slowly the other JP's in the county were accepting him. Putting the receiver down after his brief call, he went into Cass's office, where she and Phyllis had their heads together. The judge was always eager to socialize.

"You ladies sure look busy this morning."

Cass looked up without her customary smile. "Busy isn't the half of it, Judge. Can I do something for you?"

Judge Chavez was smart enough to take a hint. "No. Not really. What time do the trials start?"

"8:30."

"I'll be in Ray's office. Let me know when it's time to go in."

"Sure, Judge. I'll let you know." Cass lowered her head, returning to her problem as Judge Chavez left.

"How much, Phyllis?"

"The checks are still here as far as I can tell. The only thing missing is the currency."

"How much is that?"

"The cash receipts total $2,845."

Cass sat down in her chair trying to think. The noisy litigants pouring in through the outer office made it difficult. *I'm going to have to call Judge Sterrett about this before I do anything else. Somebody picked a time when he was out of town to pull this stunt. Who'd be the most likely culprit? It has to be someone with financial problems, but that could be anyone in the building. The only ones with a key to that cabinet are Phyllis and me.*

"Phyllis, concentrate and retrace your steps in your mind. Try to remember whether you locked that cabinet."

Phyllis closed her eyes in an effort to focus her thoughts. When she opened them and looked at Cass, there was fear. "Cass, now that I think about it, I don't think I did. I put the bags in the cabinet when the call came in because I had to check something at my desk. Then another call came in. It was on one of the eviction cases this morning. I completely forgot about the cabinet. I'm so sorry. Will I be fired?"

"I don't know. It's up to the judge. He's responsible for any shortages."

"Oh no. He's gonna strangle me. I know it."

"I'll call him in a few minutes. There'll be a major investigation over this. I don't know who the judge will want me to call to start it. Go back to your desk and say nothing about this until I tell you otherwise. It's 8:30 and I have to get these evictions going."

Cass walked into the judge's office, managing a weak smile. "Okay, Judge. The parties should be ready to go. It's time."

Judge Chavez swung away from the desk and stood up. Looking in the mirror, he adjusted his tie, smoothed his hair, and without a word marched into the courtroom. Despite the disaster, Cass had to smile at his rookie enthusiasm. Returning to her office, she started searching the file cabinet in a futile attempt to find the money.

Stewart drove by the subcourthouse for the third time since 8:00 am. Glancing to the right, he smiled. The judge's parking space was finally occupied.

Continuing south on Russell, he pulled into the driveway of the vacant house behind Jerry's car and exited the truck, removing his license plates and pitching them into the trunk of Jerry's car. Taking the pistol out of his briefcase, he faced away from the truck, checking for movement in the yards nearby, then slipped the gun in his belt at the small of his back. Everything was still as he donned his denim jacket, covering the pistol. He walked out in the backyard and surveyed the huge open expanse. A woman was walking her dog several hundred feet away at the mobile home park. The storage facility looked deserted. Walking back to the truck, he checked on Shirley, lifting up the blanket covering her feet. She was lying still, but her legs stiffened when he looked. Detecting a pungent odor, he raised the blanket again, looking closer. The carpet was wet underneath her. A terrified Shirley had peed in her pants. A spiteful smile crept across his face as he got into the driver's seat, his thoughts drifting back to the child he'd never see. The bitch had it coming.

Turning back north on Russell, Stewart drove cautiously to Debbie Lane and turned left in front of the sub-courthouse. Easing to a stop on the opposite side of the street, just past a house, he studied the parking lot at the sub-courthouse carefully. The parking lot was full, and a police officer was walking around the building. Stewart scowled as he watched. The last thing he needed was an armed man on the outside. A few minutes later, the officer walked into the building through the side entrance. Putting on his sunglasses, Stewart checked the angle of his truck, moved the vehicle forward two feet, and checked it again. *Perfect!* Donning his hat, he strode toward the entrance, but slowed when he noticed a lady approach from the parking lot to his left. Opening the door, he beckoned her in politely. The woman, late for a trial, smiled her thanks and hurried in. Stewart followed her to the courtroom door as if he was with her, but stopped at the door when she opened it. Glancing back around the outer office, he saw the clerks were on the phone or bent over their computer terminals. Opening the door a few inches, he peeked into a crowded courtroom with several people standing at the back. A big fat-ass was standing in front of Sterrett, and a woman stood about two feet to his right. The only open shot at the judge would be if Stewart stepped over people sitting in the chairs. If he stayed by the door very long, the clerks would notice him. There was only one thing to do. Taking a deep breath, he opened the door with his left hand, pulled his gun with his right, and stepped inside.

Squaring around with the gun in both hands, Stewart fired a shot into the fat man, the pistol kicking up like he knew it would. He brought the gun down, instantly aimed at the judge, and fired, the bullet striking the judge in the forehead, forcing his head back in the chair. Stewart stared at him in disbelief. *Who the hell is that?* Swinging in an arc to his right, he checked for opposition, but saw nothing but screaming people hitting the floor. Two steps and he was out of the courtroom, looking toward the head clerk's office. The attractive redhead was standing at her desk, looking at him with horror-filled eyes.

Hearing footsteps running down the hall from the bathroom, he leveled the pistol at the corner and waited. Sid Walling came around the corner, trying to dig his revolver out of the holster. "Merry Christmas from a jailbird," muttered Stewart as he shot Walling square in the face from three feet away. "An unexpected bonus," he whispered as he turned to his right and checked the clerks again, who were standing there wide-eyed and shaking.

Stewart exited the office and bolted into a run to his truck, knowing this was his most vulnerable moment. Reaching his truck, he turned toward the building, using his cab for a shield. A man with a gun was poking his head out of the door. Stewart sent a shot in his general direction and the man ducked back. Opening his truck door, he threw back his seat and yanked back the blankets and suitcase covering Shirley's head, leveled the pistol at her head and fired. Blood and brain matter sprayed everywhere as Stewart backed out of the cab, putting his hat over the headrest on his driver's seat.

He changed the speed load and fired another round into the front door of the subcourthouse. He then crouched and crossed the field on the run, keeping the truck between himself and the subcourthouse entrance. Tucking the gun into his belt, Stewart ran the fifty open yards to the access hole, ducked down the ladder, looking behind him as he closed the manhole cover over him. He had forgotten his flashlight in the excitement and had to run three hundred yards crouching in the dark. Keeping one hand in front of him, he chugged easily down the corridor, knowing he had the jump on the police. Stopping at the base of the ladder, he hurriedly changed into his uniform. After putting his old clothes and boots in the garbage bag, he climbed the ladder until his head cleared the opening. He couldn't believe his luck. No one was in the clearing or at the storage facility, and the only gunfire came from the direction of the subcourthouse, over a hill, behind a house, and out of sight.

After replacing the manhole cover, Stewart walked briskly to Jerry's car and threw the garbage bag in the trunk. As he backed out of the driveway, he heard the first sirens wailing from the south. "Don't speed," he told himself as the first Mansfield patrol car sped by him at over a hundred miles per hour. Two more squad cars went screaming past as he merged onto Business 287. Turning left on Pleasant Ridge, Stewart drove east to the country club. Flashing his lights, he entered the parking lot and headed for the Lincoln Town Car parked at the back of the lot. After loading the suitcases, license plates, and the garbage bag in the back of the Lincoln, Stewart replaced the keys in the ignition. Sweating profusely with excitement, he jumped in beside

Angel. Leaning his head back and relaxing, he noticed for the first time how he was shaking.

"How did it go, kid," asked Angel as the Lincoln eased out of the parking lot and turned right.

"It went like clockwork, except for one thing."

"What was that?"

"I shot the wrong judge."

Angel laughed. "How did that happen, genius?"

"There was someone standing in the line of fire. I couldn't see."

"Damn, kid. How many did you shoot back there?"

"Four for sure. Maybe more."

Angel whistled and looked at Stewart with new respect, then at his driver. "Jerry, turn the radio to KRLD and see what's going on."

Stewart leaned back in the seat with his eyes closed, the enormity of what he had done sinking in. Four people murdered, a burglary, and a kidnapping by a guy who had never committed a crime in his life. A familiar sensation came welling up from the pit of his stomach.

"Kid, you sure are a cool customer. I misjudged you."

"Stop the car a minute. Quick!"

Jerry pulled over just before Stewart opened the door and threw up.

Chapter Eleven

Constable Harvey Walling knelt by the front door, peeking around the corner at the maroon pickup. The top of a man's hat was visible through the back glass, but it hadn't moved in a couple of minutes. Looking around as the door to the courtroom opened, Harvey yelled at the people coming toward him, "Get back inside. Don't come out till I tell you it's safe." The people backed in and closed the door. Walling looked at his cousin's feet, which were quivering like he was in some kind of spasm. After checking again for movement in the truck, he crouched and moved toward Sid. What he saw made him sick to his stomach. Half of Sid's head was gone, and blood was gushing out the back. Struggling to contain his emotions, he glanced at Cass, who was standing at her desk, frozen, with her eyes wide and mouth open.

"Cass, snap out of it. Cass, do you hear me?"

"Huh?"

"Call the Mansfield police and tell them to send every unit, code 10-32. Do it now!" Walling whirled and checked on the other clerks, who were lying on the floor. "Phyllis, get up and use the phone on your far right. Call my office and tell Bailey and Stephens to get up here, now!" Returning to the door, he peeked out again. Nothing was moving around the truck, but he could still see the hat. Hearing movement behind him, he swung around with his pistol pointed to the ceiling as his other deputies arrived. "Crouch down, you damn fools. He's still out there."

Deputy Stephens crouched and looked down at Sid, then back up at his boss. "Is he dead?"

"I'm afraid so. There's nothing we can do for him. Go see what's happened in the courtroom and report back to me. Bailey, take the clerks and courtroom people back to our offices. Then report back to me."

Walling looked back at Cass, who was coming out of her daze. "Cass, call the sheriff's office. Get us some more help out here." As Cass picked up the phone again, Stephens came out of the courtroom and crept over to the door by Harvey Walling. Walling peeked out again, seeing no change. "Is everything okay in the courtroom?"

"Hell no! The judge is dead, and there's a guy in front of the bench wounded real bad. Bailey is moving everybody back like you said. There must be over thirty of them."

"He shot the judge?"

"Yeah. Right between the eyes."

"Go back to Cass's office and tell her to call Mansfield PD back and get us an ambulance out here. Tell her she can go back with the others if she wants to. Then report back. We're going to get that no-good son of a bitch."

As Bailey moved back, Walling peeked quickly out the door again at the immobile hat. Fearing an ambush, he stayed put. Stephens returned quickly. "Cass is talking to Gary Baker at the sheriff's office. They're dispatching an ambulance from there. Seven or eight sheriff's units are headed our way, but it will take several minutes for them to get here."

"I'm not waiting for help any longer. That sorry bastard ain't getting away with killing Sid. I want you to get Bailey and go out the side door. Take cover by the cars. Move up as close as you can to that truck without him seeing you. Radio me when you're ready, and I'll fire a shot through the back glass to distract him. After that, unload on him."

Stephens moved off again but came back when Bailey came out of the courtroom on his own. "We'll be ready when we can get to the back door."

Walling looked at his watch. "Thirty seconds from now ... mark."

"You sorry bastard," Walling muttered as he continued staring at his watch. "You're a dead son of a bitch in one minute." Raising his Glock automatic, with five seconds to go, he took a quick peek out the door.

After firing at the back glass, he ran out the door to his left, ducking behind Judge Chavez's car. Walling unloaded three shots at the hat, then moved to the back of the car for a better angle as gunfire exploded from the parking lot. The glass in the truck shattered, but the hat didn't move. Unloading three more rounds into the cab, he ran across the street to a tree, pumping more rounds through the open driver's door. Walling detected no movement as the deputies continued to fire into the truck. The right rear tire sank as a round ricocheted off the rim and buzzed back into the window where the clerks had been standing.

"Cease fire!" Walling yelled. "Cease fire!" Hearing a siren approaching to his left, he ran back into the subcourthouse, not wanting to get shot by the Mansfield police just because he was in plain clothes. After pulling in his deputies, Walling returned to the front door, watching as the first squad car screeched to a stop sideways on the street. The officer riding shotgun jumped out with pistol drawn and crouched behind the hood. The driver exited behind him and took position over the trunk. Walling holstered his pistol and called out, "I'm Constable Walling. He's in the truck. I think we've already got him."

"Okay," yelled the driver, as he reached into the car to use the radio to update the dispatcher on the situation.

Walling and his two deputies came out the door to join the officers behind the squad car. The officer at the hood continued pointing his pistol at the truck, but glanced over at Walling. "Have y'all checked in the truck?"

"No. We heard you coming and we went back inside."

"You're not sure he's down?"

"We put about fifty rounds in that truck. He couldn't have survived even if he was hiding in the back seat," responded Stephens.

"Okay. Let's mosey up there real slow and take a look."

The five of them spread out and slowly approached the truck from both sides. When Stephens got to the driver's door, he let out a whoop. "I got him, boss. The back's covered with blood." The officers opened the doors and flung back the blankets gazing in stunned silence at Shirley's bullet-riddled body. Stephens staggered into the garden and vomited.

The Mansfield sergeant looked at Walling. "Where did he go?"

Walling couldn't stop staring at Shirley, seeing his political future turning sour before his eyes. The Mansfield officer persisted. "Constable Walling, where could he have gone?"

"I don't know, dammit. I saw him open the door, and I thought he got inside."

"Were you watching the truck the whole time?"

"No. I went back to check on my cousin. He's laying inside dead on the floor."

"Do you know who this asshole is?"

"No. I didn't get a good at look at him."

"What did he look like?"

"Male, Caucasian, medium build, wearing brown boots, jeans with a hat, and sunglasses. That's all I saw."

"What color was his shirt?"

"Black and red, I think."

The second and third units came flying up with lights flashing and sirens wailing. Police Chief Harry Hawkins stepped out and approached the group, looking at his sergeant. "What do we have here, Bill?"

"Chief, we have a lone gunman apparently escaping on foot. Direction unknown. A Caucasian male dressed in jeans and boots with a black and red shirt. We've got a dead deputy inside, and it looks like our heroes here shot a hostage by mistake."

Chief Hawkins was a fifty-eight-year-old pro and a police chief in cities around Texas since he was thirty-four. He had been the chief in Mansfield for ten years and intended to retire there. Mansfield treated him well, and he had responded by whipping the force into shape.

With a sad look, he raised the blanket. Shaking his head, he walked around the truck. Missing license plates were no surprise. After taking a long look at the scene, Hawkins finally looked at the constable. "Do you know why he killed your deputy, Walling?"

"Chief, it's worse than you think. The judge is dead and there's another man seriously wounded. I think my cousin got killed responding to the shots."

The chief whistled. "Sterrett's dead?"

"No, sir. Sterrett's out of town. We had a visiting judge today."

"I better call an ambulance for the wounded man."

"That's already done, Chief."

Hawkins nodded. "How long has it been since you saw the gunman?"

"Twelve to fifteen minutes."

"We better call in some sheriff's units and start a manhunt. Did you call my dispatcher before or after you last saw the gunman?"

"About a minute after. There's several sheriff's units en route."

The chief nodded again as the ambulance pulled up. He motioned them inside, headed back to his patrol car and got on the radio. "Dispatch, this is unit one. Emergency! Over."

"Unit one, this is dispatch. Go ahead."

"What time did you receive the call to the subcourthouse?"

"Eight fifty-three, sir."

Chief Hawkins checked his watch. Fourteen minutes ago. "I've got units two and seven with me. How many units are behind us?"

"Just one, sir. Unit five is two minutes away. Units three and four are working an accident at Main and Heritage."

"Any injuries or fatalities?"

"One minor injury, sir."

"Tell unit five to go to highway 1187 and Business 157. Pull unit three off the accident and send it to the intersection of Russell and Business 157. We're searching for a Caucasian male, medium build, boots and jeans, red and black shirt, age unknown, armed and dangerous. Repeat, armed and dangerous."

"Roger. Over and out."

The chief walked back to the group and looked at his sergeant. "Bill, drive up to the mobile home park. Have Gene canvas the park to find out if anyone saw this guy, and you start checking back this way. Take your portable radio with you when you leave the car." Chief Hawkins signaled over his other unit. "Harold, go look beyond Grimsley Cemetery. Get Joe to canvass the pickle factory. Walling, would you mind taking one of your deputies and go over the big field south of here? See if you can come up with anything."

"Yes sir."

"Send your other deputy with me. I'm gonna look inside."

Walling nodded and grabbed Bailey, taking off on the run.

"Walling!"

Walling stopped. "Yes, Chief?"

"Go slow. Just look for boot prints or anything else laying on the ground. You're not going to catch him. He's been gone fifteen minutes."

"Yes sir." Walling and Bailey turned dejectedly, walking away with their heads down.

The chief led Stephens inside the subcourthouse, took a quick look at Sid, and entered the courtroom. Cass and a man were watching the paramedics tending to the wounded man. Walking past them, Hawkins looked at the judge lying behind the bench, noting the huge hole in the back of his head. Returning to Cass, he took her hand. Recognizing him, she threw her arms around him. "Oh, Chief. I'm so glad to see you. I was so scared, I about died."

Hawkins patted her shoulder, then kneeled down and examined the wounded man. The well-dressed unconscious man was heavy-set and breathing with difficulty. Hawkins slipped his hand under the man and extracted his wallet from his pants. Opening his wallet to his driver's license, he read: "Eric Peagram, 6914 Thornbird, Arlington, Texas." The chief looked back at Cass. "Do you know this man?"

"No. I don't think so."

The chief checked in the man's shirt pocket and extracted a business card reading "Eric Peagram, Attorney-at-Law," with a business address and a phone number. He handed it to Cass. "Please call his office and tell them the bad news. Have them call his family and tell them he will be at"—he looked up to the paramedic for confirmation—"Arlington Memorial Hospital. Come find me when you get through."

Cass nodded and headed back to her office as Hawkins questioned the paramedic on the man's condition. The wound was on the right side of the chest, so he might make it. The frowning chief extracted the wallet of the slain judge, taking it back to Cass's office and opening it as Cass was talking to Peagram's law office. When she hung up, Hawkins tossed the wallets on the desk. "Did you see the gunman?"

"Yes sir. He shot Sid right in front of me."

"Did he see you?"

"Yes. He looked right at me."

"Did he try to shoot you?"

"No. Thank God."

"Did you know him?"

"No. I don't think so. There was something familiar about him, though. He had a hat and sunglasses on, but what I looked at most was that huge gun."

"What did the gun look like?"

"Big."

Hawkins suppressed a smile. This wasn't funny. "Did the gun have a shiny barrel?"

"Yes."

"Was it an automatic or revolver?"

"I don't know."

He pulled out his pistol and laid it on his lap. "Did it have cylinders like these?"

"Yes."

"Could he have been here for a case this morning?"

"Could have been. I don't know."

"Was there anyone else in the courtroom when this happened?"

"God, yes. The room was full."

"Where are all of those people?"

"They're back in Walling's office, I think."

"Would you call back there and make sure none of them leave before I talk to them?"

"Sure."

Chief Hawkins went back outside to check on his manhunt. His assistant was sending two sheriff's units off to the west as he walked up. "Do we have anything yet, Herb?"

"Not a sign of him yet, Chief."

"How many sheriff's units are on the scene?"

"Four so far."

"Where have you sent them?"

"I sent two south on Russell and spread them out to the west. I sent the other two out to Business 287, checking for hitchhikers."

"Good thinking, Herb. Spread the next units out west of Business 287 and check the woods over there. Send a unit west on highway 1187 and check for him hitchhiking over there. He could be going north on Business 287 toward Fort Worth as well. What I don't understand is why he didn't drive off in his truck."

"I don't think he ever intended to, Chief."

"How do you figure that?"

"Come over to the truck. I want to show you something."

Herb led the way over to the truck and showed the chief the hat still resting on the headrest. "He really slicked them, Chief, pinning them down with this hat. He used this truck for a shield. With the running boards and exhaust pipes, you can't see underneath. I figure he took off in the direction of the pickle factory."

"Has Joe reported back?"

"Yes, but he's not through. There's about thirty employees there."

Hawkins looked back at the bullet-riddled hat. "Maybe this guy planned this pretty well. If he had a getaway car close by, we've lost him. Do you think this could be a professional hit?"

Herb scratched his chin thoughtfully. "The hostage doesn't figure."

"Sure she does if the gunman carjacked her. The truck is going to be stolen. There's no license plates."

"Yeah. I see what you mean. But it takes time to find a truck with running boards. If that's the case, he would have shot the wrong judge. Did he shoot him first?"

"Yeah. Cass says that the shots were fired in the courtroom before the deputy was killed."

"For this guy to stalk a truck and know that the visiting judge was going to be out here kinda stretches the imagination. It would be easier to kill him closer to home."

"Maybe he didn't care which judge he killed."

"No. There's too much planning here. Somebody had a grudge."

"You figure Sterrett was the target?"

"Yes, unless we get lucky and find some disoriented dumb shit in the next few minutes."

"I better go back inside and talk to Cass. When the next unit comes in, send them in the direction that you showed me behind the truck, unless Walling gets back first."

"Yeah. I sure would hate to be in those bastards' shoes."

"It looks like they screwed up big time," said Hawkins as he turned back to the office. Cass was scooping up paperwork and stuffing it into bank bags. After she put them into the filing cabinet, she turned to Hawkins.

"Two tragedies in one day. I don't think I can take much more."

"Two tragedies?"

"Can you keep something under your hat for a day or two?"

"Sure, if it doesn't have anything to do with this case."

"Somebody stole over $2,800 out of this cabinet some time after we closed yesterday afternoon."

Hawkins mulled this over. "Okay. It's probably not connected. We have more serious things to deal with now anyway. I need to explore some other areas with you."

"What do you mean?"

"Have there been any volatile cases here lately, where somebody got really mad at the judge?"

"Sure. It happens every day. He has to rule against people."

"I want you to get one of the clerks to review his schedule for the last week and prioritize the nasty cases."

A look of understanding came on Cass's face. "You think this guy meant to shoot Judge Sterrett?"

"A lot of signs point that way. The more we dig, the better planned it looks. Planning takes time. Didn't you say that something was vaguely familiar about this guy?"

"Yeah, but I can't put my finger on it. It might have been his face under the sunglasses, or his voice, or both."

"I didn't know he said anything to you."

"He didn't speak to me. He muttered something to Sid just before he shot him. I couldn't hear what it was, but the voice sounded familiar."

"Let me know if something comes to you." He decided to try a long shot. "Come outside with me for a second. I want to show you something." Leading her outside, Hawkins pointed at the truck. "Have you seen that truck before?"

"Yes. It was here a few days ago."

Hawkins snapped to attention. "When?"

"I don't know. Let me think a minute."

Hawkins took her back inside. "While you think, I'm going back to talk to the witnesses. Come see me if you remember." Walking back to Walling's office, he entered a room full of turmoil. Walling's secretary was trying to keep them there against vociferous objections. Hawkins raised his voice. "Be quiet, everybody. Hey, I said listen up!" he yelled. The room quieted immediately. "I'm Chief Hawkins of the Mansfield PD. Would all of you please find a spot against the wall. The lady will take your names and phone numbers, and you'll be able to leave shortly. If there's anyone in this room who knows the gunman, please raise your hand." No one did. "I need to talk to whoever was

closest to the gunman when he came in. Would you raise your hand, please."
A man in the corner slowly raised his hand.

"What is your name, sir?"

"Leo Greene."

"Mr. Greene, would you come with me, please?"

"Where?"

"Just into the courtroom, Mr. Greene. I need your help with something."

"Do I have to go back in there?"

Hawkins smiled reassuringly. "Come on, Mr. Greene. You'll be all right."
He turned and walked into the courtroom. Greene followed with something less than enthusiasm.

"Are those dead people still in here?"

"It's okay, Mr. Greene. Nothing in here can hurt you. Can you show me where you were when the gunman came in?"

"I was sitting in a chair right by the door."

"Please show me. Take one of the chairs and sit right where you were sitting."

As Greene complied, Chief Deputy Sheriff Gary Baker walked in, nodded to Hawkins, and walked back behind the bench, studying the dead judge. Hawkins continued with Greene. "Mr. Greene, did you see the gunman walk in the room?"

"Yeah. I glanced up at him."

"Did you see the gun?"

"No. "

"Could you see both of his hands?"

"No. Just his left one."

"Where was his right hand?"

"Behind him."

"What was his left hand doing?"

"Closing the door."

"Did you get a good look at his face?"

"No, sir. I just noticed he had sunglasses on."

"How long was he in the room before he started shooting?"

"No more than two or three seconds."

Chief Deputy Baker quietly walked up to them, listening. Hawkins continued. "Where was he standing when he started shooting?"

"Right where you are."

"Did he shoot the judge first?"

"No. He shot the big guy. He was in the way."

"In the way of what?"

"He was standing right in front of the judge."

"Mr. Greene, you're saying that he came in to kill the judge and the big guy just got in the way?"

"That's the way I saw it."

"Can you show me where the big guy was standing when he got shot?"

Greene walked up to the bench and looked over the top at the dead judge. Shuddering visibly, he turned around. "Can't you move this poor man out of here?"

"Not yet. The crime lab has to photo him first. Show me where he was standing."

Greene moved over to his right, blocking out the center of the bench perfectly. Hawkins motioned for him to come back by the door. "What did you do when he started firing, Mr. Greene?"

"I froze. It happened so fast, it was a complete shock."

"Did you see him leave the room?"

"Yes sir."

"How long did he stay in the room after he fired the gun?"

"About five seconds, I guess."

"What did he do in those five seconds?"

"At first he stared at the judge. Then he looked around at everyone in the room, then ducked out the door."

"Did he close the door?"

"Not completely."

"Could you see him through the opening?"

"A little."

"What happened then?"

"He turned to his left and waited … about three or four seconds, then fired again. He looked around behind him and then back through the door at me. He turned around after that and left."

"Did you ever hear him speak?"

"Yeah, I did. I forgot about that. Just before he fired, outside the door I mean, he spoke to the one he fired at. He said something like 'Merry Christmas, jailbird.' He didn't say it very loud, though."

"Thank you, Mr. Greene. You've been a big help." Hawkins looked over to Gary Baker, who was studying Greene and listening intently. "Gary, do you have any questions for Mr. Greene?" Baker looked around the room and up at the bench, then back at Greene.

"Mr. Greene, did the man fire only two shots?"

"I believe so."

"He used one shot for each man?"

"Yes."

"How did he hold the gun?"

"He held it with both hands."

"Were you ever in the military, Mr. Greene?"

"No. "

"Okay. Did the man look pretty cool while this was going on?"

"I wouldn't say cool."

"Was he excited?"

"No."

"How would you describe his demeanor, then?"

"He looked methodical, but not cool."

Baker looked back at Hawkins. "That's all I can think of."

Hawkins smiled at Greene. "Thanks again, sir. As soon as you give your name, address, and phone number to the secretary, you can go."

Greene nodded and exited the room as fast as he could. Hawkins looked at Baker. "Did you get the story outside from my assistant?"

"Yeah. Herb filled me in. This is a mess. I better get on the phone and get the medical examiner out here and make sure the crime lab boys are en route."

Without further comment, Hawkins went back to Cass, who was putting down the phone when he came in. All of the other lines were blinking. Cass looked at him with fearful eyes. "I remembered when and where I saw that truck. It was here Monday morning while that peace bond trial was going on. The judge put a guy in jail on a peace bond for trying to kill his ex-girlfriend. When I put a cowboy hat and sunglasses on the defendant, he looks like the shooter. I wouldn't have been surprised if he had shot his ex-girlfriend. But not the judge."

"Cass, I suspect that's his ex-girlfriend laying out in the back of his truck."

"Oh no! No one told me about her."

"Do you remember their names?"

"His name is Billy Earl Stewart. Hers is—was—Shirley Lemons."

"Where's Ray?"

"South Padre Island. In JP school."

"It looks like that school saved his life. You better get his family away from his house. Who knows what this bozo will do next."

"I just did that a couple of minutes ago. I told Anita, his housekeeper, to get them out of school and take them to my apartment. Now that I think about it, I have to call my apartment manager and tell her to let them in." She picked up the phone and Hawkins went back to find Baker, who was using the phone in the clerk's area. Hawkins signaled and Baker put his hand over the phone, looking up at Hawkins.

"Got something?"

"Yeah. I think so. Cass thinks she knows the shooter."

Baker spoke back in the phone. "Hold on, Tom. Don't leave the line." He looked back at Hawkins. "Who is it?"

"The perp's name may be Billy Earl Stewart. The girl's name would be Shirley Lemons."

"Thanks. I'll get right on it."

Hawkins stuck his head out the door and motioned Herb to come over. "Herb, tell dispatch the gunman's name is probably Billy Earl Stewart. I'll have more information in a minute." Running back to Walling's office and pushing through the loud impatient crowd, he caught Phyllis's attention and motioned her to follow him. "Phyllis, can you get me the peace bond file on Billy Earl Stewart?"

"Is he the one who did this?"

"Possibly. Hurry, will you?" He returned to Baker, who was just getting off the phone. "Gary, would you call airport security? He could be flying out of here by now."

"Do we have a good description yet?"

"I'm working on it. Cass said Sterrett put him in jail. You may have fingerprints and mug shots there."

"I'm working on that. Have one of the staff get me the fax number out here."

"Will do. Phyllis, have you found it yet?"

"Yes sir. Here it is."

Hawkins studied the names and addresses in the file. There was a copy of an arrest report from Arlington PD that had everything he was looking for. He handed it to Phyllis. "Would you make me three copies of this, and hurry please." Phyllis dashed off, and Hawkins caught a clear line and dialed the Arlington PD. On request, he got through quickly to Chief Parker. "Hello, Chief. This is Harry Hawkins down in Mansfield."

"Hello, Harry. I just heard there was a shooting down at the subcourthouse. Is that where you are?"

"I'm afraid so."

"What happened down there?"

"We have a real mess on our hands. We've got a dead judge, a dead deputy constable, and an unidentified dead female. Her name may be Shirley Lemons. She lives in your city, Chief. That's why I'm calling."

"Sterrett's dead?"

"No. He had a stand-in. Ray's out of town."

"That's right. I forgot. What's this girl's address?"

"It says in this file that her address is 1241 M Street. Apartment 56. I'd appreciate it if you'd send your crime lab over there."

"You said may be her. You're not sure?"

"Not yet. We can't find any ID."

"Do you know where she works?"

"Let me check the file. It's not in here, but I'm having one of your arrest reports copied as we speak. I think it's in there. Hang on and I'll go check." Phyllis came back with the copies and Hawkins smiled his thanks. "Chief, the last known POB is the General Motors plant. The phone number there is 555-4900."

"What's the file number on that arrest report?"

"0816990214."

"I've got it. I'll get back to you as soon as I can. Should I go through your dispatcher?"

"Yes. The phone lines here are limited. One other thing. Could you send a unit out to Sterrett's house and make sure everything is okay? There shouldn't be anyone there."

"Okay, Chief. I'll get back to you." Parker hung up.

Hawkins went back outside to Herb. "Turned up anything?"

"Not much. Gene found a lady in the mobile home park who thinks she saw a guy fitting that description between 8:00 and 8:15."

"Where was he?"

"Over behind an old house on Russell Street. She's on her way over there with Gene."

"Anything else?"

"One of the sheriff's deputies walked that area we talked about toward the pickle factory. He found a couple of boot prints and a spot where he must have changed direction while he was running. He turned back southeast apparently."

"Probably back toward that house that Gene's going to."

"Probably. I moved the manhunt over to the east a couple of minutes ago. They didn't turn up anything on the west side."

"Good thinking, Herb. You're a good man. It looks like you're ready for your own city pretty soon."

Herb smiled as he reached in to the squad car and picked up the radio receiver. "This is unit one. Go ahead."

"Herb, this is Gene. We've located the house. It's vacant. Do you want us to enter? Over."

"Negative. Any signs of anything on the outside?"

"No. We found one boot print, facing the wrong way. Over."

"Don't touch it. Take the lady back to the mobile home park and report back here. Over and out."

Hawkins looked at his watch, which showed 9:40. "Herb, cancel the dragnet. We've missed him. Notify the highway patrol to be on the lookout for him. Tell them the sheriff's department will be faxing a full description in a few minutes."

Walling and Bailey came walking back from the pasture. Hawkins signaled them over. "Find anything, boys?"

"No, nothing," replied Walling. "He couldn't have escaped there."

Herb and Hawkins exchanged glances; then Hawkins looked back at Walling. "Y'all come on inside. Get your other deputy, too. I need to talk to all of you."

Walling and Bailey exchanged glances as they followed him back to Walling's office, where Stephens joined them. "Boys, I need your weapons. Put each one in a plastic bag with your name on the outside."

Bailey was too new to understand. "Chief, you don't have the authority to suspend us."

"I'm not suspending you. I need the weapons for ballistics."

"For the girl?"

"That's right." Hawkins left them to it and went back to Cass, who was on the phone talking to the press. When he slid his finger across his throat, she nodded and terminated the conversation. "Cass, have you called Ray?"

"No. I will as soon as I get confirmation that his kids are okay. I'm not looking forward to it, though. He won't take this well."

Hawkins looked serious. "I wouldn't either if I was him. That son of a bitch is still loose."

Chapter Twelve

J udge Sterrett smiled as he checked his schedule for the ten o'clock lecture. After a morning of tedium, Ray would get to hear Judge Terry Callahan from San Antonio, a crackerjack judge who knew his stuff. Maybe he could stay awake until lunch.

Judge Terry Callahan nodded to Ray as he and the class coordinator walked briskly to the front of the room. The coordinator picked up the microphone to address the seventy-person class.

"Judges, let me have your attention. It's my pleasure to introduce the next speaker. I know most of you know him, so I'll be brief. This is Judge Terry Callahan from Bexar County. Judge Callahan has been a justice of the peace for nineteen years and has served in a number of positions for the state association, including president. As most of you know, he was our legislative chairman in the last session. He was instrumental in passing most of our legislative agenda and in fighting off the bills that would have adversely affected all of us. I need not remind you how we are all deeply indebted to him for the many hundreds of hours that he spent on our behalf in Austin. He's speaking to you today on distress warrants and writs of sequestration, which are some of the most intricate procedures that you have to deal with. Please give a warm welcome to Judge Terry Callahan!"

The class applauded as Judge Callahan took the mike and faced the group with a smile, glancing down at his notes as the applause subsided. Looking up, Callahan walked away from the podium, without his notes, toward the center of the seated group.

"Thank you, Judges, for that nice reception. That's sure a more friendly response than I receive from the losing litigants in my courtroom." There was some polite laughter. "It's certainly a pleasure to be here. My trials are getting so intense at home, this is a welcome relief, so I am truly glad to be here. The litigants are sure glad that I'm here." There was a little more laughter. "My staff is thankful that I'm here." There was louder laughter. "My wife is sure enough glad I'm here." This time there was a lot of laughter. "Speaking of my wife, I just want to take a minute and brag on her for putting up with me and my many absences last year. She's really a trooper. We have one of those really rare perfect marriages. We agreed in the beginning, that she would make the minor decisions in our household and that I would make the big ones. For example, she decides what I do for a living, what clothes I wear, the kind of car I drive, where the kids go to school, and what kind of house we live in; but I get to make the big decisions, deciding who we will vote for in the presidential elections and our position on the Middle East peace accords." The laughter became loud and general as the crowd loosened up.

"Judges, what we're going to study this morning is some of the case law that restructured our rules on distress warrants and sequestration writs. In addition, we'll review the steps in issuing these writs. How many of you have never issued either a distress warrant or a writ of sequestration?" Half of the hands in the audience went up. "How many of you never want to issue one again?" All of the hands went up and the laughter began again. Callahan had them where he wanted them, in good spirits and paying attention.

"Judges, it may be hard to believe but only about thirty years ago the rules were either very lax or nonexistent on these procedures. In 1972, the U.S. Supreme Court handed down a landmark decision in Fuentes v. Shevin. You can find this case in 407 US 67. Mrs. Fuentes was a consumer in Florida who purchased an ordinary appliance on credit from a nationwide chain store. About a year later, while she was current on her payments, she purchased a stereo on the same revolving account. A few months later, problems arose with the appliance, and she called the store for a routine warranty repair. The repair was not satisfactory, so she ceased making her payments on both products.

"The department store went to the magistrate in her area and received from the court clerk what was then called a writ of replevin, and pursuant to that writ, seized the appliance and stereo.

"Mrs. Fuentes sued the store on four specific grounds. One: the language in the writ application did not allege that she was delinquent. Two: there was no language in the application alleging that she intended to secrete or harm the merchandise. Three: there was no provision in Florida law for her to replevy the merchandise or even to request a hearing to get her merchandise back. Four: most importantly, there was no judicial review, and therefore her Fourteenth Amendment rights were violated in that her property was seized without due process of law. Remember, Florida law at the time allowed the court clerk to issue these writs.

"Mrs. Fuentes lost her case and appeals in the Florida courts, but pursued her claim through the federal court system. Mr. Shevin was the attorney general of Florida at the time and became the defendant when the appeal was transferred to the federal courts. When the suit came before the Supreme Court, it was joined with three companion cases. The most noteworthy of these cases came from Pennsylvania. In that case, a deputy sheriff, being familiar with the system, seized his minor son's furniture from the child's mother during a divorce action.

"The Supreme Court held that Mrs. Fuentes' Fourteenth Amendment rights were violated. They handed down some specific instructions to the lower courts that one: there must be judicial review in the form of an ex-parte hearing before a seizure order can be signed. Two: the seizure order must be signed by a judge. Three: the application for a seizure writ must allege that there is a default and that the plaintiff believes that the defendant will secrete or harm the merchandise. Four: there must be procedures established where the defendant may recover the merchandise pending a trial on the merits. Five: there must be a suit filed before or simultaneously with an application for a seizure writ.

"Two years later another case came before the Court. It was a Louisiana case, known as Mitchell v. W. T. Grant. That case is found in 416 US 600. At first glance, it would seem that the Court reversed itself in this decision because the Court ruled for the seizing party. However, the Louisiana court procedures were far more modern. In that case, there was judicial review and provisions in the law allowing the defendant to replevy the merchandise. When you look closely at this case you will see that the Court's decision was, in fact, consistent with the guidelines that the Court set two years before in the Fuentes case—"

As Ray was turning to the handout provided a hand tapped him on the shoulder. A grim-faced class coordinator looked down at him. "Ray, you need to come with me. You have an emergency phone call."

Ray jumped out of his chair and followed the coordinator down the hallway. "Curt, what's wrong? Who's calling?"

"It's your office. Apparently something's happened up there."

"What's happened?"

"I'd better let them tell you. Here, take the call in the manager's office. I managed to get you a little privacy."

Ray sat down as Curt was closing the door. Not liking the looks of this, he punched in the blinking button. "Hello?"

"Judge?"

"Cass?"

"Judge, it's just awful up here." Cass was sobbing.

"Cass, calm down and tell me what the hell's going on."

"Judge, some man in a Western outfit walked in here this morning and killed Judge Chavez, and Sid Walling, too. They just hauled some wounded attorney out of here. I don't know if he is going to live or not, and there's a dead girl laying out there in a pickup truck."

Ray leaned back in the chair in shock and confusion. "Cass, was anyone on our staff hurt? Are you all right?"

"I'm okay. The girls are all right. Judge, he killed Sid right in front of me. It was awful."

"Why did this happen, for God's sake? Did some trial go haywire?"

"Judge, it gets worse. We think the gunman was that Stewart guy you jailed Monday. The police think he was coming after you."

Ray turned white. The kids! "Cass, have they caught him?"

"No. It looks like he got away clean."

"My God, Cass. He might go after my kids!"

"He won't be able to find them. I had Anita take them to my place. I just got off the phone with her before I called you. They're okay."

A wave of relief swept over Ray. "Thanks, Cass. I really appreciate that. I don't know what I'd do without you. Give me more details now that I know Robbie and Jan are okay."

"Judge, there's something else, too. When I came in this morning, I found all the cash missing out of the bags with the reports. We're about $2,850 short."

"Damn, Cass. How did that happen?"

"I don't know. The cabinet was locked when I came in. Phyllis closed up yesterday, and she thinks she left the cabinet unlocked."

"Let's deal with that later. Tell me more about the shooting."

"Let me close my door first. I've got police and press crawling around everywhere."

Ray got up and opened the manager's door. Curt was waiting outside. "Curt, I've got dead people all over my courthouse. I'm going to catch the next plane out. Would you get me a reservation? Also, could you have someone pack my things? I'm in room 507."

"I've got people doing that all ready. I should have some flight information for you in about five minutes."

"Thanks, Curt. I'm glad somebody can think straight."

Ray rushed back to the phone. "Cass, are you there?"

"Yes, Judge. I'm still here."

"Did you recognize Stewart?"

"Not exactly."

"Then what makes you think it was him?"

"His pickup truck is outside with a dead girl in it."

"Where's the truck?"

"It's parked across the street."

"Describe it to me."

"It's a maroon truck with some kind of a low attachment on it."

"Does it have exhaust pipes underneath that low attachment?"

"I don't remember."

"Look out the door and see."

"Okay." Cass put the phone down and walked outside, but men swarming around the truck were blocking her view. Walking closer, she squirmed in among the police to get a better look. The pipes were there. Chief Hawkins was holding the passenger seat forward while a photographer was shooting something on the back floorboard. Cass looked in to see what was going on and instantly got sick at her stomach. Turning, she ran back to the office, making it halfway before she threw up and gagged for over a minute. Some kind lady handed her a handkerchief. Cass wiped her pale sweating face, nodding her thanks. "Thank you. I think I'm about to faint. Would you see if you can find me a Coke or Seven-Up?"

"Sure. Were you here when this happened?"

"Yes. I'm afraid so. I work here."

"What's your name?"

"Cass Strange."

"Can you tell me what happened?"

"Not now. Please. I have to get back to the phone. I have Judge Sterrett on the line waiting for me. If you will bring me that Coke, I'll talk to you after I get through with him."

"I thought it was Sterrett that got killed in the courtroom."

"No. He's out of town. Judge Joe Chavez was here standing in for him. Let me go, please. I'll tell you about it in a few minutes."

The lady hurried back to her news truck with this important information as Cass returned to the telephone. "Judge, are you there?"

"Yes, Cass. I'm here. Tell me about the pipes."

"The pipes are there underneath, just like you said."

"Then it's Stewart all right. That's his truck. Did you say that there was some girl dead in the truck?"

"Yes, Judge. I just got a look at her. It's awful."

"I'm sure it is. Now tell me exactly what happened."

As Cass relayed the story, the lady returned with a soft drink. The woman started taking copious notes as Cass continued. Ray finally broke in.

"Cass, think back to Monday when we were holding that peace bond hearing. I recessed that hearing early to let Stewart and his attorney talk. Do you remember where they went?"

"Let me see. Yes, they went into the storeroom."

"Go in there and see if there's a broken window."

"Okay." Cass left the reporter and walked into the storeroom. The window looked okay. *No! Wait a minute!* The two latches were unlocked. Cass rushed back to the phone. "Judge?"

"Yes?"

"The window's not broken, but the two latches are open."

"That's probably what happened to the money. Have Hawkins check that window for prints both inside and out."

"Yes sir. Judge, do you think that Stewart will come back here?"

"No. Not with the police all over the place. You'll be okay until I get there. Is the sheriff there? I want to talk to him if he is."

"No. I think he's out of town but Gary Baker's here. Do you want to speak to him?"

"No. I'll wait till I get there. Write this flight number down. American Eagle, number 3812. It arrives at 1:30. Get me a couple of hotel rooms under an assumed name, and pick me up with the kids. I only have a couple of minutes before I leave for the airport. Ask Baker to provide some protection for my kids at the hotel. And Cass—"

"Yes, Judge?"

"I can't thank you enough for getting my kids to a safe place. As bad as this is, it could be a lot worse. I know my kids and staff are safe. Have Phyllis close the office when things quiet down. Hawkins and Baker will probably secure the building anyway. Okay, love?"

"I'll handle everything, Judge. I'll see you in three hours."

Cass put the phone down and smiled at the reporter. "I need to do one more thing, and then I'll talk to you. Okay?"

"Sure. I'll be right here."

Cass went back outside and found Gary Baker. Hawkins was still busy around the truck, supervising the removal of the body. Cass shuddered, not wanting to go back over there. "Gary, I just talked to Judge Sterrett. He wanted you to do a couple of things."

"Sure, Cass. Just tell me what you need."

"The judge wants fingerprints taken around the window in the storeroom, inside and out. He also would appreciate a protection unit for his family. He wants to make sure they're not in danger."

"Will do, Cass. In fact, I have a safe house over in west Fort Worth I can put him and the kids in for a few days. No one will get near them."

"That's great, Gary. Get back with me and let me have the address and directions. Is it all right if I talk to the press?"

"Sure. We're busy and they're all over us. See if you can pull them into your office."

Cass managed her best smile at Gary. Returning to her office, she gave a brief advance story to her soft drink benefactor. The reporter from Channel 5 news raced back to her news truck and shook out her minicam operator for the first detailed on-site report. Cass went back outside and notified the rest of the press that she had a statement to make. They all rushed in, eager for the inside scoop. Cass waited patiently for them to set up the cameras and jostle for space. As they were settling down, Marilyn Shaw came rushing in. With a worried look, she motioned Cass to come outside, and Cass excused herself from the grumbling group.

"Yes, Marilyn. What is it?"

"Was that Ray that was killed?"

"No. Ray's still out of town."

"Thank God! The reports were still sketchy on the way out here."

"I can't give you the whole story in front of these other guys. I thought they were going to string me up just for coming out here."

"I understand. Can I see you afterwards for some other questions?"

"Okay. I'm sure Judge Sterrett would approve that, but I may not have much time." Cass turned and went back inside and stood in front of the group, waiting a few moments for them to settle down after they grabbed pads and turned on cameras. Cass was suddenly nervous, never having done this before. Remembering Judge Sterrett's advice, she ignored the cameras, pretending they weren't there. With voice shaking, she recounted the sordid story. Finished, she breathed a sigh. "Any questions?"

Everyone started shouting at once. Cass nodded to a man in front of a minicam with a big number eight on it. "What is your name, ma'am, and are you an employee here?"

"Yes. I'm sorry. My name is Cassandra Strange, and I'm the head clerk for Judge Ray Sterrett." Cass nodded to a man in the front row with a pad and a tape recorder.

"Mrs. Strange, are there any suspects yet?"

"Yes. There is a good chance that the gunman is named Billy Stewart. It's too early in the investigation to say for sure." Cass looked at Marilyn, whose eyes got wide, but she remained silent.

The questions flew fast for several minutes. The group started to get up and disperse; the story was too hot to wait any longer. As they left, Marilyn closed the door and sat down before Cass.

"Cass, is that Shirley Lemons out there in that truck?"

Cass nodded. "Probably. I didn't get a good look at her Monday."

"How did Stewart get out of jail?"

"He either made his bond or got a writ of habeas corpus."

"How does that work?"

"I'm not sure. We don't have jurisdiction to handle those, so I don't know what the procedure is."

"Can your computer show when he got out?"

"Sure." Cass booted up the criminal hard drive and pecked in the necessary codes. "He got out yesterday about noon."

"Is there a release reference number?"

"Yeah. 09040091."

Marilyn wrote it down. "Does your computer say how he got out?"

"No."

"Okay. Does your case file have a work number for Shirley Lemons?"

"It should. I think Baker has it." She rose to get it.

"Can I use your phone while you're looking for it?"

"Sure."

Marilyn dialed in a friend at the sheriff's office. "Harry, this is Marilyn, and I need a favor real fast."

"What do you need, beautiful?"

"There's a release file on a Billy Earl Stewart, released yesterday. The reference number is 09040091. I need to know if he made his bond or if he got out on a writ of habeas corpus. If he got out on a writ, I need to know who the judge was and when the hearing was held."

"Okay. I'll call you back as soon as I get it. Where are you?"

"Harry, if it's all right, I'll just hold."

Marilyn looked up at Cass who was thumbing through the peace bond file. "Did you find a phone number?"

"Yes. Here it is. She works for General Motors. Here's the number."

"I'm on hold. Would you call the number and see if she's there?"

"Sure." *I should have thought of this myself,* thought Cass as she dialed the number.

"General Motors, Arlington division. This is Andrea McKnight. How may I help you?"

"I need to speak to Shirley Lemons, please."

"Miss Lemons is not here today. May someone else help you?"

"Did she call in sick today?"

"Could you hold on please? I'll connect you to her supervisor."

"This is Evelyn Strong. May I help you please?"

"Yes ma'am. My name is Cassandra Strange and I work for Judge Ray Sterrett. I was wondering if you had heard from Shirley Lemons today?"

"No, as a matter of fact, I haven't. You're the second person who has called this morning. Could you tell me what's going on?"

"Mrs. Strong, we've had a shooting out here at our court this morning. Her ex-boyfriend may be involved. Would you be kind enough to tell me who her relatives are?"

"Good God! Is Shirley dead?"

"We're not sure yet, Mrs. Strong. There's a dead girl in his pickup truck, but we don't know who she is."

"What does she look like?"

"You don't want to know, Mrs. Strong."

"Oh God. How awful. Hang on. I'll get her parents' phone number."

Cass looked at Marilyn, who was hanging up her line. "Shirley's not there. The supervisor is getting me her parents' phone number."

"When's Ray coming back?"

"He'll be here at 1:30. Do you want to go with us to the airport?"

"By 'us', do you mean his children?"

"Yes. A deputy sheriff is going with us, too."

Marilyn pondered this. "No. I don't think so. I have too much work to do. Ask him to call me later. Here's the number where I'll be. Thanks for your help, Cass."

Cass nodded and went back to her call, to write down the phone number of Shirley's parents. When she finished, she found Gary Baker in the courtroom with an army of investigators. There was a fingerprint specialist dusting the courtroom door. In the chaos she'd forgotten what the judge had asked her to do. "Gary, did your fingerprint man get the window in the storeroom?"

"Not yet. What's with the window? He came in the front door."

"We had some money missing this morning. The judge wanted to see if there's a connection."

"Okay. Show him the window."

"Thanks, Gary. Could you send someone with me to get Ray at the airport? I don't know where this house is."

"Sure. How soon are you leaving?"

"About fifteen minutes. I have to lock up some things. Are you going to secure the building?"

"Either Hawkins or I will. We've got a long way to go before we're finished. All of my people are busy here. I'll dispatch a unit and have them meet you at the airport. What's the flight number?"

"Is it possible for them to meet me at my apartment? The judge wants protection for the kids, not himself."

"Sure. How soon do you want them there?"

Cass checked her watch. It was 11 am. "An hour from now will be fine. Judge Sterrett doesn't get in until 1:30. Here's the address. Could you send plainclothes officers?"

"Okay. I'll tend to it. I'll send Fred Walker."

"Thanks. Gary, he intended to kill Judge Sterrett, didn't he?"

"I'm sure of it. If we don't catch him, he may try again."

"What can we do?"

"Just lay low till we catch him."

"What if it takes a long time?"

"It won't. I have someone at the office working on a reward plan. If it works out, someone will turn him in within a few days."

"Thanks, Gary. You're a sweetheart. I better get cracking. I've got a lot to do."

Marilyn Shaw approached Judge Jake Eave's attractive secretary, who was sitting at her workstation, talking on the phone. It was a personal call, and the secretary ignored Marilyn's rising temperature until she finished, about three minutes later. Finally hanging up, she looked at Marilyn with a look of annoyance. "Yes?"

"I need to see Judge Eaves."

"Who are you?"

"My name is Marilyn Shaw. I'm a reporter from the *Star-Telegram*."

The secretary brightened and turned professional. "I'll see what I can do. May I tell him what this is concerning?"

"I would like his reaction to the murders at the Mansfield courthouse this morning."

"Wasn't that terrible? I just heard about it. I think Judge Eaves is in trial at the moment, but I'll check and see if he'll recess for a minute. He always has time for the press, you know." Returning in two minutes, she flashed her best professional smile. "Judge Eaves can see you now. This way please."

Marilyn followed her into the judge's private office. The judge rose from behind his desk. "Mrs. Shaw, I'm delighted to meet you. Are you new on this beat? I don't recall seeing you before."

"It's Miss Shaw. I work in the Arlington section. I don't get to downtown Fort Worth very often."

"I can't believe a beautiful woman like you could be single. The young men of your generation must all be blind."

"Judge Eaves, I'd like your reaction to the shooting at the Mansfield subcourthouse this morning."

"Miss Shaw, I find all crime intolerable. But shooting a judge is a flagrant example of where our society is heading. I've spent my whole life fighting for a better legal system, where these criminals are kept locked up or, even better, executed."

"Judge, could you explain how a writ of habeas corpus works?"

"Certainly, honey. This is a protection for our citizens, so they are not incarcerated without charges being filed. This right goes all the way back to colonial times."

"Are judges careful not to release someone with violent tendencies on these writs?"

"Of course. That goes without saying."

"What safeguards are taken? Are hearings held?"

"Most of the time, but not always. What does this have to do with the shootings, anyway?"

"The prime suspect in this case was released on one of these writs."

A warning light flashed in Eaves mind. "Who is this suspect?"

"A man by the name of Billy Earl Stewart."

"That name doesn't ring any bells with me."

"Well it should, Judge. You released him on a writ yesterday."

"That's impossible. I don't remember that."

"Maybe you don't remember because you held no hearing. I checked your docket before I came up here. I have a copy of the writ with your signature on it. Would you like to see it?"

Judge Eaves turned pale as he groped for an answer. *That damned Torrey! I'll have his ass for this.* "Now that you mention it, I did sign that writ. I had the assurance of Leonard Torrey that his client was completely innocent and was being held on a trumped-up charge."

"You didn't check beyond the defense attorney?"

"No. I didn't see any need to. His case didn't seem any different than any other."

"Do you mean other cases where you signed a writ without a hearing?"

"Look, Miss Shaw, I don't like the tone of that question."

"I think you're going to like the tone of my article even less, Judge. My information is that you didn't even check with Judge Sterrett's court before signing that writ. There are three dead people out there because of you."

"That's ridiculous. I can't be held responsible for that. There was no way for me to know that he would do that."

"Not unless you bothered to check first. I attended that hearing, so I know what was involved. I would think that you'd have more confidence in Judge Sterrett than to just ignore one of his rulings."

"Miss Shaw, be reasonable. You're just trying to make me look bad on this. I assure you, I have an impeccable record on crime. You should check before you smear me all over your newspaper."

Marilyn rose and put her pad back in her brief case. "Don't worry, Judge. Your record is going to be checked out real close. Good-bye."

Judge Eaves watched her leave, his trepidation growing as he buzzed his secretary. "Carol, come in here right now. I need you."

Carol came running in with her notepad. Eaves would have laughed if he wasn't in so much trouble. His dog could take a letter better than Carol. That wasn't the dictation she was good at. "You don't need your pad. Tell the bailiff to announce that the case is continued. An emergency has come up. Tell Tim Lindsey I need to see him on another matter. Right now!" Carol went scurrying, and Lindsey was there in a matter of seconds.

"What's going on, Judge?"

"That partner of yours has got me in deep shit, that's what. Do you remember that writ you and Torrey had me sign yesterday?"

"Yeah. What about it?"

"Apparently that's the asshole that shot up the Mansfield subcourthouse. The press is all over my ass for signing that writ."

"Holy shit! What can we do for damage control?"

"You better call the paper and see if Harrison can pull some strings on this bitch Marilyn Shaw. She's about to crucify my ass."

"I don't think he has the power to pull that off, Judge."

"Call him, dammit. You don't know what he can do until he tries."

"All right, Judge. I'll call him." Lindsey dashed out and headed toward his office, needing to find Torrey fast.

Marilyn was heading out of the downtown courthouse when she saw a group of people crowded around a television set by the entrance. Deciding to see if there were any further developments, she moved to the far right of the crowd and saw the well-known face of Jessica Jones on the screen. Jessica's face was somber, and there was a picture of Judge Joe Chavez behind her. Marilyn strained to hear the words.

"—at the Mansfield subcourthouse this morning just before 9:00 am. Cassandra Strange, the head clerk for justice of the peace Ray Sterrett, and Chief Harry Hawkins of the Mansfield police department, confirmed that three people are dead and one man is in critical condition—" Marilyn's thoughts returned to her assignment as the news bulletin went on. "Sources say that preliminary evidence shows that this hostage was killed by return fire from Constable Harvey Walling and his deputies, who were not aware of the hostage—" Marilyn turned as she realized that this was only the initial report being played again. "For an on-the-scene report, let's go to Betty Anderson."

The scene changed to a lady with stunning looks and blonde hair, with an appropriately serious look on her face. The subcourthouse was in the background, with police roaming around. "Jessica, the investigation is ongoing. I just finished talking to Deputy Sheriff Gary Baker. Deputy Baker tells me that the truck in question belongs to a Billy Earl Stewart, according to the VIN number. There were no license plates ...”

Marilyn turned back to the district clerk's office for something she hadn't checked. Walking into the large outer office, she got the attention of one of the clerks. “Could you tell me how I can find out how many writs of habeas corpus have been issued in the last two years?”

“No, I can't. The computers don't record those that way. That information would be with each individual case that had one issued.”

“Would the computer be able to tell me how many writs that a particular judge issued in a given period of time?”

“No. The same principle applies.”

“Okay. Would the individual cases indicate whether a writ was issued without a hearing?”

“I don't know. I've never looked at it that way before.”

“Would you check for me, please?”

“I wouldn't know where to begin. Do you have a case where you know a writ was issued?”

“Yes. I do, but I already have that information.” Marilyn closed her eyes and thought a minute. “How long would it take to review Judge Eaves cases and see how many writs he has issued for the last year?”

The clerk changed screens and laughed. “It would take a long time. He's handled over eight hundred cases in the last year. On top of that, a writ can be issued in a case that's pending in another court. I don't know how you'd dig that out.”

“Can you print out cases by the defense attorney?”

“No.”

“I see. Thank you. You've been very helpful.” Marilyn turned and grabbed a phone to call her friend at the sheriff's office. “Harry, if I sent in a news team, could you provide the computer to allow them to dig out the history of writs that have been issued in the last year?”

“Gee. I don't know. I'd have to get authorization for that.”

“I think I can swing that. Is it possible to dig it out?”

“Yeah. It's possible, but it would be a bitch of a job.”

“I'll get back to you on this. Thanks, Harry.”

Marilyn hung up and dialed Leonard Torrey's office. She didn't have to wait long.

“Hello?”

“Mr. Torrey?”

“Yes. Who's this?”

“This is Marilyn Shaw with the *Star-Telegram*.”

“What do you want? Are you the reporter that was at the hearing?”

"Yes. I wanted to know if you wanted to make a statement about the shooting this morning."

"I'm confident that my client is innocent on that. The only proof I've heard that they have is that his truck is parked out front."

"Mr. Torrey, was there a hearing held on that writ of habeas corpus that was issued on your client yesterday?"

"No. Not a formal hearing. I just took the application in to a judge and he signed it."

"You didn't see any signs that your client intended any harm?"

"None whatsoever."

"Have you heard from your client today, Mr. Torrey?"

"No."

"If your client calls, could I talk to him?"

"I would advise him not to."

"Thanks again, Mr. Torrey. Good-bye."

Torrey hung up the phone, and it rang as he put it down. Damn place was getting busy for a change. "Hello?"

"Torrey?"

"Yeah. Who's this?"

"Never mind who this is. Let's just say you have an anonymous client. Would you like to make $2,500?"

"Probably. What do I have to do?"

The muffled voice hesitated. "I want you to find Buck Reed and hire him to do a job for me."

"You must be crazy. Buck Reed is a known killer. I couldn't hire him for $2,500 if I wanted to."

"I didn't say the $2,500 was for him. It's for you."

"I don't do that sort of thing. I'm an attorney."

The muffled voice chuckled. "Yes. A very broke attorney."

"You could be the police for all I know. Trying to entrap me."

"But I'm not. You and my client have a mutual enemy. That's why I called you."

"Who is that?"

"Ray Sterrett."

"Is that who you want hit?"

"Yes. Are you interested?"

"Maybe. Why does your client want him hit?"

"That doesn't matter. Let's just say the timing is right."

"What do you mean?"

"I mean that if Sterrett's killed right now, your other client's going to get blamed for it."

Chapter Thirteen

County Commissioner Jim Wade put the phone down, leaned back in his office recliner, and closed his eyes. Thirty-eight was young for a commissioner. The voters had welcomed his boyish freckled face, red hair, and ready smile when given a chance to oust Gary Swilling at the last election. Swilling had come under a cloud from a sexual harassment suit shortly after the filing deadline. Wade had put his name on the ballot, with no intention to win until that had happened, only wanting to obtain name recognition for a future state representative's race. Wade had been smart enough to take advantage of the political windfall and put together a coalition headed up by the Arlington police chief. Since then, he had abandoned aspirations for the legislature. This job was too good, paying $98,000 a year. His staff handled most of the details, unless an emergency came up. This was one of those days.

The subcourthouse shooting had put the county offices in an uproar. There was an emergency commissioners' court session scheduled in the morning, and the five members were calling back and forth for ideas to put on the agenda. Several had suggested putting airport-type security in all county buildings that didn't already have it. Scurrying around to get bids and estimates, Wade had to smile at this reactive political body. The cost would be about $200,000, to look good and to act like an effective court to stop this from happening again. Wade wouldn't oppose it, though. He wouldn't dare. It was a damn shame this idiot didn't kill the right judge. All of Wade's political problems would be solved if he had. Sterrett had been one of the few who had not jumped on Wade's bandwagon during the election. His reasons didn't matter to Wade. That's where the problems had begun. Sterrett continued to this day to claim that Swilling had been framed on that sexual harassment suit. Wade figured that Sterrett blamed him for the suit because of the timing of it, although they had never discussed it, or anything else unless necessity demanded it, maintaining a distance that the whole district noticed. Sterrett was popular in the district, and his supporters shunned Wade as well. Wade knew Sterrett would run against him in the next election. What was worse, Sterrett could probably beat him.

His telephone intercom buzzed. "Yes?"

"Commissioner, Sergeant Agnew is on line three."

"I'll take the call." He punched the button and leaned back in the chair. "How's it going, Chester?"

"It's not going worth a shit. The chief put me on suspension."

"I was afraid he'd have to. I tried to get Sterrett to drop it, but he won't. I guess you'll have to ride it out and hope for the best."

"That's easy for you to say. It's my ass on the line here."

"Chief Parker said you let a man die in the street because he assaulted you last year. Is that true?"

"No. The asshole isn't dead. He's alive as we speak."

"Is he in a coma?"

"According to the chief, he is."

"Did you recognize him at the accident scene?"

"Yeah, but so what? He's nothing but a drunken bum anyway. Nobody gives a shit if he dies."

"Nobody but Sterrett."

"That miserable bastard. It's too bad he didn't get killed out there in Mansfield. My two-bit problem would go away if he had."

"I know what you mean. It would've solved most of my problems, too."

"Maybe we'll get lucky. That guy could come back and finish the job."

"I doubt it. Security will be pretty tight for a while. He'll probably get caught before the security eases."

Agnew paused on the other end of the line. "Maybe he could use a little help."

"What do you mean?"

"I mean that if something terrible happened to Sterrett, this clown would get all the credit."

"I don't think I want to hear this."

"You better hear it. I found out that Sterrett is nosing around your bail bond contacts. He's coming after you. You better hope for a godsend."

"Are you telling me that you can arrange that?"

"Maybe. What do you think about it?"

"I don't want to think about it. But if something happens, it's fine with me."

"That's almost good enough. I need some minimal assistance, though."

"What kind of assistance?"

"Money and information."

"How much?"

"I'm not sure, but I think $1,000 would get the job done."

"That wouldn't be a problem if it couldn't be traced back to me. What kind of information would you need?"

"If the security is too tight at the courthouse, I need to know where Sterrett is or where he will be at some given time."

"Why don't you just check his house? It should be in the phone book."

"I wouldn't go there if I were him."

"I'll see what I can do about that. When do you need to know?"

"As soon as possible. This won't work after that redneck is caught."

"Yeah. You're right. I'll see what I can do tomorrow. I don't think anyone's over there right now. Sterrett's out of town anyway. See my brother for the money. I'll tell him it's just a loan while you're suspended. And Chester?"

"Yeah?"

"This conversation never happened, right?"

"You got it."

Wade hung up the phone and leaned back in his chair. He had been around politics all of his life but never thought he would see anything like this. Starting as a campaign worker for a sheriff almost ten years ago, he moved on to Austin and latched onto a state senator from southeast Texas. Working on his staff for six years, he learned every legislative trick in the book from the senator and the lobbyists who worked in the capitol. Wade had made more enemies than friends with those tricks. When the senator retired four years ago, he moved back to Tarrant County and caught on with a bail bondsman. Spending many nights at the county jail, Wade earned fees for his former boss, and for himself on the side when he thought he could get away with it. His cronies laughed at Wade when he filed for office, but they weren't laughing now. Still pulling commissions in from bail bonds, he made contacts inside the jail. For a few bucks, he passed referrals to his former boss and other bail bondsmen, making thousands on the side. That was his biggest secret. His name didn't appear on anything. It was an easy-money deal that Wade didn't want Sterrett snooping around.

It was high time he visited the crime scene. After all, it was in his district and maybe the press was still there. He turned on KRLD, the news radio station, as he headed toward Mansfield.

"Sheriff Sanders also announced that reward money is pouring in from several sources. He mentioned the Tarrant County Automobile Association, the Texas Apartment Association, the Texas Association of Justices of the Peace and Constables, Crimestoppers, and Citizens for Better Government. Sanders estimated that the fund reached over $35,000 in the first hour. The sheriff pledged that his department would make maximum effort until the killer is caught. From News 1080, this is Harry Jenkins on the scene at the subcourthouse."

Ray hurried through Gate One at DFW airport. To his left, he saw Cass holding the hands of Robbie and Jan. Right behind her were two plainclothes deputies and Sheriff Sanders himself. Beyond them were several uniformed deputies, who were scanning the crowds and watching the doors. The children broke away from Cass and ran to their father, who hugged them both and led them back to Cass and the sheriff.

"Sheriff, thanks for coming."

"It's the least I could do, Ray. Hand Childers your baggage tickets. He can catch up to us. The less time spent here the better. Follow me."

Ray grabbed the kids and followed him to a squad car and three unmarked units outside. More deputies opened the car doors, ushered them in, and slammed the doors with military efficiency. In less than five seconds the vehicles were rolling. The squad car led the way with lights and sirens going, with Ray and the sheriff following in the back seat of the next unit. Cass and the kids were next, and the last unit had three deputies, who were armed to the teeth. A helicopter flew overhead. Ray leaned back and relaxed. "Sheriff, aren't you overdoing it a bit with this cavalcade?"

"Probably. But it doesn't hurt to be safe."

"Where are we going?"

"I have a friend who's going to be out of town for a few weeks. The house is in West Fort Worth, and we can secure it without bringing attention to ourselves. He's graciously invited you to stay there until he gets back from Europe."

"Aren't we publicizing our location with this convoy?"

"No. If anyone asks, I'll tell them I escorted a visiting U.S. senator around. When we get to the west side, I'll have the lights and sirens cut off. Until then, I don't feel safe. We have no idea where this asshole is."

"Have you called Joe Chavez's family?"

"No. The county judge is handling that."

"I want to call Maria."

"Who?"

"His wife."

"You'd better wait until tomorrow. I hear she's pretty upset."

"I can imagine. It's my fault that he's dead."

"No, it's not. You can point a few fingers around, but no one's blaming you."

"Who is getting blamed?"

"Judge Eaves, for one. Constable Walling is in trouble. His return fire killed the hostage in Stewart's truck. The press may eat him alive over that. Plus, he let Stewart vanish right in front of his eyes."

"How could Walling know the hostage was in the truck?"

"I know, I know—but you know the press."

"Since we have time, tell me the details that you know so far."

As they sped toward West Fort Worth, Sanders filled him in. Ray leaned back and closed his eyes as he listened to the bone-chilling story.

Deputy Sheriff Fred Walker and his partner Bob Scroggins left Gladys Stewart's house on Center Street in Arlington armed with names, addresses, and phone numbers of Stewart's friends. Walker, forty-two, was a twelve-year veteran of the sheriff's department. Languishing for eight years in patrol, he rose only to lieutenant before transferring to criminal investigations. There he had flourished with his keen mind and drive. His father had been killed in an armed robbery attempt that was never solved, when Walker was fourteen. By the end of high school, he had resolved to be a cop, and if he couldn't get the perps who killed his father, he'd get some others. Relentless on any case that involved robbery or murder, he often worked sixteen-hour days to bring criminals to justice. This schedule had left a marriage with two children by the wayside. Fred didn't care and never burdened anyone with his true motive. Once he had escaped patrol, his real marriage was the job. When Lee Sanders took office, he promoted Walker to captain in one of his first personnel moves, and the division quickly rose to the top of the department in efficiency ratings. Walker had outstanding organizational skills as well as dedication and surrounded himself with officers who didn't worry about time clocks. The eight-to-fivers quit or transferred out. Walker replaced them with crack investigators from all over the state, choosing many of them because they had had a family member killed or maimed by criminals, and they shared his driven dedication. Walker was a short five feet six but weighed two hundred pounds, and there wasn't an ounce of fat on him. Any criminal who underestimated him acquired a rough lesson in physical combat. That was Walker's favorite part of the job. His staff loved him and would follow him anywhere, proud that they were the best investigation unit in the state.

Walker and Scroggins headed west on Pioneer Parkway to the Heaven's Rest Apartments. Circling around to the back of the complex, they found Harlan Wells' apartment. Parking two units away, they watched the apartment for several minutes. There was no sign of movement and no cars in front. Scroggins checked his watch.

"It's 4:55, Captain. We don't have much time before the six o'clock meeting."

"To hell with the meeting. Stewart could be hiding in there. Harlan Wells is his best friend. Where else would you go if you were in trouble?"

"It would be the last place I'd go."

"Yeah. But you're not an idiot like this one."

"He can't be an idiot to get away as clean as he did. He's probably in Kansas by now."

"Maybe so, but you don't want to go blundering in there. If Wells is working today, he'll be home shortly. We'll go in right behind him."

"We don't have a search warrant, do we?"

"No. We won't need one if he's not in there. If Wells demands a search warrant, we'll stake his place out until the troops arrive. Hang on. That looks like his car pulling in. Remember Stewart's arrest report. Check the closets first."

A boyish-looking man with blond hair and glasses drove up and parked in front of the apartment; he was in a gray four-year-old sedan. When he got out of the car, he turned and walked right into Scroggins before he saw him. He didn't see Walker at all, who had slipped in behind him.

"Excuse me, I didn't see you."

"Are you Harlan Wells?" asked Scroggins, whipping out his badge.

"Yes. Who're you?"

"Detective Scroggins with the sheriff's department. Have you seen Billy Stewart today?"

"No, sir. I haven't seen him in over a week."

"Is there any chance he's in your apartment?"

"No. He doesn't have a key."

"Do you mind if I take a look?"

"No. Go ahead."

"Give me your apartment key and stay outside until we tell you to come in," said Walker in a low voice.

A startled Wells whirled around and faced Walker, slowly fishing his keys out. Walker looked down at a key ring with several keys on it. "Which one is the apartment key?"

"That one."

"Do you live alone?"

"Yes sir."

"Wait here," growled Walker as he and Scroggins hurried to the front door, entering military-style with their pistols at high port. Scroggins headed for the bedroom and threw open the closet door, crouching low, with his automatic pointed into the closet. Walker checked behind the curtains and looked behind the sofa. Running to the bathroom, he looked behind the shower curtain. As small as the apartment was, there was no other place to look. Walker went back to the front door and motioned Wells inside, pointing to the recliner. Wells sat down and looked up at Walker expectantly. Walker sat on the couch while Scroggins moved back in from the bedroom and scowled at Wells.

"You know where Stewart is, don't you?"

"No."

"If you're so innocent, why haven't you asked what this is all about?"

"I heard about it on the radio coming home."

"Did you know he was going to do this?"

"Hell no. I knew he was crazy over the girl, but I never dreamed he'd kill anybody."

"How long have you known Stewart?"

"We went to high school together. Ever since then."

"How long has he had that gun?"

"I didn't know he had a gun. He wasn't interested in them. I don't even think he knew how to use one. Are you sure he's the one who did this?"

"It sure looks like it. Did he ever go hunting?"

"No. He never was interested in that kind of thing."

"What was he interested in? What did you two do together?"

"Nothing much. We just drank a little beer and shot pool. Played football games on Play Station. That kind of stuff."

"Did he try to call you after he got out of jail yesterday?"

"No. He called Jerry. I was at work."

Walker glanced at Scroggins. "Where is Jerry?"

"At his place, I guess."

"Where's that?"

"It's just a couple of blocks from here."

"How do you know he called Jerry?"

"He told me at lunch. I had to take him to Mansfield to pick up his car. Stewart had borrowed it last night."

"Where was the car?"

"It was at some golf course."

"Where exactly?"

"It's on a road that's just this side of Highway 287."

"What's Jerry's last name?"

"Chandler."

"Will you show us where he lives?"

"Sure. If you want me to, I could just call him."

"No. Stewart could be over there."

"I don't think so. Jerry would've said something about it."

"Let's go. We can talk about it in the car."

The three hurried to the squad car and Scroggins put Wells in the back seat. As Walker got the car rolling, Scroggins picked up the radio mike. "Dispatch, this is unit eleven. Over."

"Unit eleven, this is dispatch. Go ahead."

"Can you patch me through to the sheriff?"

"Roger. He's coming back from Mansfield. I'm routing you now."

"This is unit one. Over."

"Sheriff, this is Scroggins. We have information that Stewart had a second car. It was picked up about noon at some golf course in Mansfield by some friends of his."

"What does the car look like and who's it registered to?"

"We believe that it's registered to a Jerry Chandler. We're only a block away from his apartment now. If he's home, I'll have a complete description in a couple of minutes."

"Okay. I'll call Chief Hawkins and get a unit over there. Secure the car when you find it. Over and out."

Scroggins put the receiver back as Walker headed into another apartment complex. The parking lot was different in this complex, with the cars parked in a central parking area. Wells led them right to the car. Walker followed Wells to the apartment door while Scroggins radioed the license number and description of the car to the sheriff. When he arrived at the apartment, Walker had already searched the unit. Walker was seated with Wells and a very scared-looking kid, who was receiving the grilling of his life.

Sheriff Lee Sanders strolled into his outer office, nodded to his secretary, and headed into his private office. Taking a quick glance at his two dozen messages, he slowly shook his head. I have to teach this staff how to prioritize these calls, he thought, reaching for the police radio mike.

"Dispatch, this is unit one. Over."

"Go ahead, unit one."

"Are all units headed back for the 6:00 pm meeting?"

"Most of them, sir. Unit eleven will be about ten minutes late. They're interviewing a witness. Baker in unit two just left the Mansfield scene and should arrive about 6:05. Unit fifteen went to the country club with the Mansfield P D. Their arrival time is unknown. Everyone else should be there as far as I know."

"Tell Blair and Carter in unit fifteen to break off and come to the meeting now. They can go back in the morning to question the people at the country club. They'll need the full picture just like everyone else."

"Roger. Over and out."

Sanders checked his watch to see if he had time for a short breather. It was 5:45. Grabbing a Coke out of his refrigerator, he leaned back in his chair to relax and reflect. This was his third year in office. Sanders was a veteran law officer of eighteen years. His face, a road map of wrinkles, looked much older than his forty-two years.

Starting out as the police chief in Taos, New Mexico, with a small staff of five, he had moved to chief deputy sheriff in Amarillo, Texas, when he was thirty. Getting lucky three years later, he foiled a bank robbery with quick thinking and bravado. Walking into it unaware, he disarmed the lookout at the front door before the lookout realized what was going on. The two other robbers were in the vault, scooping the loot, and he simply closed the vault door, trapping them. One of the trapped robbers was on the FBI's most wanted list. Sanders was the cover boy on law enforcement magazines for the next year. This landed him a job as the second-in-command in the Fort Worth police department a year later, where he made a name for himself as an effective administrator by taking a proactive approach to crime and organizing all the crime-watch groups in the city. He raised money for each neighborhood-watch group to buy a portable police radio. Taking the citizen drug fighting forces known as DARE to new frontiers in fighting drugs in the schools, he expanded citizen school patrols to discourage outside drug dealers. His fame made him one of the darlings of the Tarrant County Republican Party, who recruited him to run for sheriff, and he had won easily.

Now, three years later, he was in a mess. Reviewing his notes on the shootings, he checked his watch again. It was 6:10 and time to go. Going down one floor, he entered a large meeting room with a platform and podium, with his officers seated in folding chairs in front of the platform. All conversation ceased as he mounted the platform and moved to the podium, glancing about the room. The officers he expected to be late were there, except for Scroggins and Walker. A civilian was leaning against the wall to his left. That would be the representative from the medical examiner's office. Sanders motioned the middle-aged man over.

"Are you from the ME's office?"

"Yes, Sheriff. My name is Herman Fielding."

"Dr. Fielding, what do you have for us? Did you do the autopsies?"

"I did the one on the girl. Dr. Tompkins did the work on the judge and the deputy."

"Do you have Tompkin's report?"

"Yes sir."

"Good. I'll let you go first if you want. You're probably the only one in the room that doesn't need to stay for the whole meeting."

"Thanks, Sheriff. I'd really appreciate that."

"Give me just a minute and you'll be up." Sanders turned back to a group that was swelling every minute. Many other members of the department were crowding the back of the room, curious about what was going on. The room seated about fifty, but there were more than double that in the room. Sanders looked around carefully. "Are there any members of the press in the room? If there are, please identify yourselves." No one moved or spoke. Sanders continued.

"Staff members, all of you know what happened this morning, so I won't take your time reviewing what you've already heard on the news. The purpose of this meeting is to fully apprise everyone involved in the investigation with all known details. You know already that you could come upon a piece of information that would seem to you insignificant but could be vital to some one else on the investigation team. Until further notice, we'll hold one of these meetings at 6:00 pm each day. I want each of you to refrain from speaking to the press. That must be channeled through me or the public information officer. We'll begin the briefing with Dr. Herman Fielding from the ME's office." He signaled to Dr. Fielding.

Dr. Fielding walked to the podium, laid out his notes, and looked up at the group. "Thank you, Sheriff, for allowing me to go first. I performed an autopsy on a white female in her late twenties. She was five feet four inches tall, with a body weight of one hundred twenty-four pounds, medium blonde hair, with no distinguishing marks except for an appendectomy scar on her lower right abdomen. The body received three bullet wounds, with the primary wound at the back of the head from a large-caliber weapon. I estimate that the distance was less than four and a half feet, based upon the powder burns to the lower left part of the skull, which remained intact. The bullet traveled from the back lower left of her skull and exited the right center of the skull on the top. The skull has a piece missing from the entry wound to the exit wound measuring four and one-eighth inches long by two and three-quarter inches wide. There was a significant loss of brain matter and blood from this wound. There's a bullet entry to the forehead and another to the cheekbone. I won't go into detail on these because the wounds occurred after death.

"The body had marks around the wrists and ankles, indicating binding. The absence of hair in these areas indicates that the body was bound by some type of heavy-duty tape.

"Absence of blood in the extremities suggests to me that the body was bound some three to four hours before death. There were general bruises on both sides of the face, indicating blows received before death. There were no signs of sexual activity, violent or otherwise.

"Before going to the next autopsy report, are there any questions?"

Deputy Larry Blair raised his hand. "Doctor, was there any foreign matter found under the fingernails?"

"No, sir. The nails were clean, and I found no foreign hairs unconnected with the body either. Any thing else?" The room stayed silent.

"I have the autopsy reports from Dr. Tompkins on the other two. The first is on Judge Chavez. I will dispense with the description of the body since the identity is known. The judge sustained a bullet wound from a large-caliber weapon in the center of the forehead, about one inch above the eyebrows. The bullet traveled through the brain and exited the back of the skull, seven-eighths of an inch to the left of the spinal connection. This wound caused instant death. There were no powder marks on the body.

"The second report is on a body identified as Sid Walling. This body received a single bullet wound, also to the forehead. The entry wound is the same size as Judge Chavez's, located about one and three-quarters of an inch above the center of the body's right eyebrow. The bullet traveled on a straight line through the right side of the brain and exited through the back right of the skull. There's a piece of skull missing from the exit wound. There is a heavy residue of powder marks about the right side of the face, indicating that the victim was shot at point-blank range. Are there any questions on Dr. Tompkins reports?"

Larry Blair raised his hand again. "Dr. Fielding, if you don't mind, I would like to go back to the girl. I want to make sure of what you're saying. Are you saying the girl was killed from a shot behind and above her, and the shots to the face did not cause death?"

"I don't know what you mean by 'above her'. However the shots to the face did not cause death."

"What I mean by 'above' is that she was found face down behind the seat in a Club Cab pickup. If the primary wound came from behind and traveled in an upward path, her death may have been caused by the same person who shot the other two."

"I am not privy to the position of the body at the time of death. I can demonstrate the path of the bullet for you." Fielding walked over to a blackboard at the side of the room and drew a skull. He then drew a straight line through the skull, then returned to the podium. "Any further questions?" There were none.

Sheriff Sanders walked back to the podium. "Thank you, Doctor. We'll call you if we have any further questions." Not seeing Walker and Scroggins, he went to the next speaker. "Chief Deputy Baker spent most of the day at the scene. He'll have the most comprehensive report."

Nodding to the sheriff, Gary Baker rose from the front row, strode to the podium, with two legal pads full of notes. Looking out over the audience as

Walker and Scroggins walked in, Gary nodded to a deputy to his left, who started up the center aisle distributing a handout.

"You're receiving the prime suspect's book-in photo and fingerprints. Starting on the second page, you will find photographs taken at the scene this morning. The caption below each picture will explain its significance. On the sixth page you'll see a map of the subcourthouse with the crime areas. On the same page you'll see a map of the area surrounding the subcourthouse. The numbers on the maps signify the events in estimated time order. The letters A, B, C, et cetera, indicate either the location of the victims or the known location of the witnesses during the crime. The dotted line shows the estimated travel lines of the perpetrator. The legend for the numbers and letters is at the bottom of the page. Officer Wilkes did a great job in putting this handout together." Baker took the next twenty minutes to review every detail with the staff. At the end, Baker nodded to the Sheriff and stepped back. Sanders looked over the audience. "Any questions?"

Frances Mendez raised her hand. She had recently joined Walker's department. "Gary, is anyone contacting the motels for anyone ordering room service and hiding from the maids?"

"No. That's a great idea. He could have checked into a motel before the shootings, under an alias."

The sheriff looked over the girl, not remembering seeing her before. Who was she? There were brains to go along with the beauty. Blair was looking at her, too. *Could she be single?* Sanders looked back at the audience. "Anyone else?" No one moved. They were all studying the handouts. Sanders nodded to Gary Baker. "Thank you Gary. Captain Walker, do you have anything to report?"

From the back of the room, Walker nodded that he did and walked briskly up to the podium. Most of the officers were still bent over the handout, so he cleared his throat to get their attention. The next ten minutes were spent updating the staff on Stewart's two friends and Chandler's car.

When he finished, Sanders checked his watch as he moved back to the podium. It was 7:15. "Does anyone else need to report? Okay. Blair, take four units back to Mansfield. See if you can get some help from Chief Hawkins and canvass all of the homes near that golf course. He could still be hiding around there, holding a family hostage. Also, find the golf pro and get the list of golfers who played there this morning. I want anyone who drove up in that parking lot from 8:45 on interviewed. We want to know if they saw Stewart driving up or anyone who was just sitting in the lot.

"Captain Walker, I want you to run down the rest of Stewart's friends on that list. See if anyone knows his whereabouts. Check for out-of-town relatives with his grandmother. Check with his employer in the morning and see if he was working on any projects in Mansfield. Check his co-workers for his whereabouts. Take two teams with you.

"Gary, I want you to ask the police chiefs in the Dallas-Fort Worth area to canvas their motels to see if he's hiding there. Make sure they have Stewart's picture. Keeping watch for someone maintaining a low profile is a good idea, too. Anyone who uncovers anything significant, contact me right away. Are there any more questions before we adjourn?"

Captain Blevins of patrol raised his hand. "Sheriff, how much force should we use if we locate him?"

Sanders looked down for a moment and stroked his chin. "I want him alive if possible. But if he endangers you, or any one else, or if it's likely that he'll escape, take him out."

Chapter Fourteen

Ray kissed his children good night after tucking them in. Excited about the mansion, they had little comprehension of the crisis at hand. As he returned downstairs, Ray smiled, remembering their glee at jumping into the big swimming pool that afternoon, oblivious to the stern-faced guards who remained in the background. Crossing to the large heavily draped window, Ray looked out over the grounds to the front gate, counting seven deputies in plain clothes. In the back, there was a guard just outside the door, watching three canine patrols; two were patrolling the back fence, with one in reserve.

Checking his watch, Ray noticed it was time for the 10:00 pm news. When he joined Cass in the very small media room—with five comfy recliners and a huge TV screen—he became engulfed by surround sound. After the obligatory commercials, the screen showed the two familiar anchors grimly facing the cameras, with a picture of Judge Chavez in the background. When the music faded, Jessica Jones began the sordid story. Ray listened in vain for something new as the broadcast waded through the witnesses. At the end, a serious looking Commissioner Wade came on the screen. Ray increased the volume.

"—is a terrible tragedy. I will support increased security at all county facilities to prevent this from happening again. I have information that the commissioners' court will convene tomorrow to expedite the implementation of this plan. The citizens of this county deserve safety whenever they conduct business at one of our facilities. On behalf of the court, I want to extend sympathies to the victim's families and our support in the apprehension of the suspect. I pledge to our citizens that the utmost effort will be made to catch and punish the animal who did this."

Wade's picture faded and a portion of Sheriff Sanders' interview came on. Ray lowered the volume and turned to Cass. "Thank you for staying with me today. You've been great with the children. It's a big help not having to look after them while I'm setting everything up. I know this has been a terrible day for you."

"That's okay, Judge. I'm glad I was busy." Her voice quivered as she continued. "It took my mind off—" She stopped talking and leaned back in the recliner. Ray stood up and took her hand, pulling her up and holding her close. Cass started sobbing, buried her head in his shoulder, put her arms around his neck, and cried for a long time. Ray said nothing as he held her close. Finally the crying subsided, but she continued to hold him close. "Judge?"

"Yes?"

"It's my fault that Sid is dead."

"Why do you say that?"

"I heard him coming up the hall and didn't warn him. He turned the corner and walked right into that bullet. If I had called out, it wouldn't have happened."

"How much time did you have to warn him?"

"A couple of seconds."

"Did you think about warning him?"

"No. There wasn't time. That gun was pointed at me and I just froze."

"It wasn't your fault. If you had yelled, he would've shot you."

"But he didn't shoot me. He could've after he shot Sid and he didn't."

"You couldn't have known that at the time. Don't be so hard on yourself. No one expects you to react like a police officer. You're not trained for that. You were standing there unarmed, with a gun pointed at you. Most police officers would freeze under those circumstances. There's only one person to blame for this and that's Stewart."

"Do you think he'll come back?"

"I doubt it. Security will be pretty tight for a while."

"I don't want to go back there tomorrow."

"You won't have to. You couldn't get in if you tried. They still have it cordoned off."

"When will we open again?"

"I don't know, maybe Monday. They might have Stewart by then."

"How long can you and the children stay here?"

"A couple of weeks. I'd like you to stay here, too. The children need you. I'm amazed at how they have taken to you. I need you, too."

Cass lifted her head off his shoulder and looked at him. "You need me? Why?"

"I don't know. I just feel better having you here."

Cass started backing away from his embrace. "I'm sorry for hanging on to you."

Ray gently pulled her back. "Don't be. I need to hold you, too." They stood for a long time in a warm embrace. Cass felt him stir in that familiar place. Raising her head, she kissed him with a long, slow, searching kiss. Ray stayed passive for a time and then responded in kind. Embarrassed, he started to back away. Cass pulled him close again and put her head back on his shoulder.

Neither his embarrassment nor his erection went away. "Cass?"

"Yeah?"

"I can't hold you like this. It's been too long for me."

"Don't worry. It doesn't bother me. I need to hold you." She reached up and kissed him again. Ray's hands drifted down to her shapely rear and pressed her to him, returning her kiss with ardor. It was Cass who finally broke away, taking his hand and leading him to a bedroom on the same floor. Guiding him to the bed, she gently stripped him to his shorts and rolled him over on his stomach. "Don't move. I'll be right back," she whispered in his ear. Rolling off the bed, she vanished into an adjoining bathroom and returned in a few seconds with a bottle of body lotion. Warming some of it in her hands, she spread it on his muscular shoulders. Rising up on her knees and pushing down with her arms for maximum leverage, she rubbed the lotion into his skin with circular motions. She warmed some more lotion and started with the bottom of his feet, rubbing his entire body while he moaned in pleasure.

Finally, he rolled over on his back, pulled her to him, and kissed her gently. His body was more relaxed but ached in a way he had long forgotten. Cass responded again with that soft searching kiss. Rising to a sitting position, she pulled her sweater over her long, silky auburn hair. Reaching behind her, she unsnapped her bra, exposing two of the most gorgeous breasts he had ever seen. They were liberally sprinkled with freckles, and her nipples stood out at rigid attention. "I feel silly with all these clothes on," she whispered with a slight giggle.

"Well, it looks like you found the solution."

Cass removed her skirt and pantyhose, slipping down beside him. Ray pulled her on top of him and buried his face in her bountiful bosom. Cass arched her back and put her hands behind his head, pulling gently to signal encouragement as Ray went from one breast to the other. Rolling her over, Ray slid her panties off and kissed her again as his hand probed her. Cass started sighing, reached down, and ripped his briefs away. Then she rolled him over to where she was on top and gently guided him into a warm wet world that was pure heaven.

Leonard Torrey walked into the dive on Jacksboro Highway known as the Stagger Inn. It was a typical small country lounge with a long bar and cheap stools. A few tables in an adjoining room were separated from the bar by support columns and a two-step stairway. Between the columns was a Formica-topped area where patrons could sip drinks while standing. The room was three feet higher than the bar, and people wanting to converse found their way to this area. Torrey looked through the smoke and found the county government crowd that he hoped to find. Two tables had been joined together, and the group around it numbered about ten. He saw Doug Harrison holding court, as usual, and trying to put the make on Brenda. Next to her sat Rachael Frank and Gary Reynolds in earnest conversation. On the other side of the table were some people he didn't know. One was a stunning blonde, who was leaning over the railing and talking to some man in a suit, standing below. Leonard had seen her before but couldn't remember where. Walking casually up the stairs, he tapped Rachael Frank on the shoulder. "Fancy meeting you here."

"Hello, Leonard. Pull up a chair and make yourself homely."

Grabbing an empty chair, Torrey slipped between Brenda and Rachael. Reynolds introduced him to two more reporters from the *Star-Telegram*, Ralph Tiner and Cynthia Ware. Next to them was Rachael's brother, Benjamin. Torrey had heard of him, a stock broker of some renown. Tim had once told Torrey he could reduce your fortune for a smaller fee than his competition. Next to him was the stunning blonde. Her name was Carol Watson, the court coordinator for Judge Eaves. Torrey remembered her now; he'd caught a glimpse of her Wednesday morning. If Benjamin was her escort, she was making a point of ignoring him. After briefly acknowledging Torrey, she turned and resumed her conversation with the man in the expensive suit. Next to her sat Gary Reynold's assistant, Harvey Ford, and his girlfriend, Betty Blankenship. Harvey was dressed in a maintenance uniform and Betty wasn't dressed much better. Harvey, however, was impressed with the new arrival.

"Aren't you the attorney for that Stewart guy who blew away those people out in Mansfield?"

"Not for that charge. I'm representing him on some other matters."

"What's he like?"

"He's just an ordinary Joe who never has been in trouble before."

"Ordinary Joes don't blow away judges."

"Don't jump to conclusions. He hasn't been convicted of anything."

"You don't think he's innocent, do you?"

"I believe everybody's innocent till they're proven guilty."

"Isn't the evidence overwhelming?"

"I don't think so. No one has put him at the scene of the crime. That crime was too well planned, in my opinion, for Stewart to have done it. He has no criminal experience to pull off something like this. I think somebody had a beef with the judge and set up my guy to be the patsy."

"You think someone killed Stewart's ex-girlfriend just to set him up. Who would be that mad at him?"

"They wouldn't be mad at him. They would've been mad at Sterrett."

"They would've killed an innocent girl to set Stewart up as the patsy? That would be really cold. Who could be that mad at the judge?"

"Almost anybody. He makes lots of enemies."

"Enemy enough to kill him and a lot of other people as well?"

"It makes more sense to me than what they are trying to sell on TV. Stewart isn't smart enough to rob a lemonade stand, let alone plan something this big and get away clean. This was a professional hit. Somebody paid a lot of money to kill Sterrett. Consider how cool that shooter was. It's apparent to me that he didn't know what Sterrett looked like. That's why this happened."

All conversation around the table had stopped during this discourse. Even Carol had turned around after dismissing her suitor. "Mr. Torrey, how can you, in good conscience, say that guy is innocent? That trial happened Monday and Stewart just got out of jail. How could someone set up Stewart in less than twenty-four hours?"

"I don't have all the answers. I'm saying this doesn't add up."

Rachael Frank chimed in. "Leonard, I think you're full of shit. He's got to be the killer. Maybe he's smarter than you give him credit for."

"Then why did he shoot the wrong judge?"

"I don't know. You're the one who knows the asshole. Maybe he didn't care which judge he killed. Maybe he was just making a statement against the justice system."

Torrey threw it right back at her. "If that was the case, he could have simply left without firing a shot and come back another time. I'm telling you that the events point to the fact that the shooter didn't know what the judge looked like. I think he intended to kill Sterrett, and frankly, I wish that's what had happened. Don't you, Rachael?"

Rachael stared at him in surprise. "No, I don't. Why would you say that?"

"Because you were cussing Sterrett yourself at lunch Monday."

"Maybe so. But that doesn't mean I want him dead. You don't kill somebody just because you have a beef with him."

Benjamin had listened to all this in silence. "Rachael's right. We can't condone this type of behavior even if we did have a dispute. We'd regress back to the days of the Old West, if not worse."

"Hear-hear," echoed Gary Reynolds, lifting his beer. "Anarchy is not acceptable for any reason."

Most of the group echoed the thought as they joined in the toast. Gary Reynolds drained his glass and looked at Torrey. "Maybe he killed the girl himself and hired a hit man to go in and kill the judge."

Torrey laughed. "Hired him with what? The guy's broke."

"What does it cost to hire a hit man? A few hundred dollars?"

Torrey laughed again. "You can't hire a hit man to kill a judge for a few hundred dollars. You're living in a dream world."

"Maybe so. Since you deal with the criminal element, perhaps you can explain to me how someone else would go to the trouble to hire a hit man for Sterrett and not give him a physical description. How could a professional hit man confuse a Hispanic for Sterrett?"

"Because I think the hit man had instructions to kill the judge. I don't think the person who hired him thought of the possibility of a visiting judge."

As the debate continued, Torrey eased out of the conversation. Listening for clues to the phone call that afternoon, it dawned on him that the only person at the table not participating was the reporter, Doug Harrison. Torrey's gaze drifted to Harrison and their eyes met, Harrison's expression revealing nothing. *Is he the one who called me? I don't know what his motive would be. He doesn't even know Sterrett, probably just playing newspaperman. I'll throw him some bait.* "Doug, You're sure quiet."

Harrison put his drink down with a sigh. "The bottom line on this, from my perspective, is that it's a black eye for our community, and I think you're going to look damn foolish trying to sell that hired hit man theory, my friend."

Torrey nodded slowly. This was not the group he was looking for. But he was determined to keep digging until he found it.

Pablo and Jose Cruz sat in another club in Arlington, a gentlemen's club called Boomers. No one had to ask what Boomers stood for. Pablo was the oldest at twenty-six. Known around Arlington as a rough customer, he had even rougher connections. He was a short five feet six, had a pirate's mustache, weighed one hundred and fifty pounds, with no visible muscles, a product of soft living. Those who knew Pablo avoided messing with him. There were whispers that Pablo's enemies were rewarded with a one-way trip to the undertaker.

Jose, his brother, was larger, carried a switchblade, and knew how to use it. Pablo's girlfriend Maria worked here as a dancer, and Jose was hustling another of the girls. They never acknowledged the girls during working hours unless some redneck got out of hand. It was bad for business. Pablo's girl,

Maria, could make $300 a night by flirting with the customers. Pablo had semiretired. With his golden goose out of sight, they were eyeballing a new dancer who was a knockout except for the tattoos. The dancer gyrated above two drunken gringos who couldn't wait to stuff five-dollar bills down her G-string. Glancing often at Jose, she ran the gringos out of money and came over to his table. To the beat of rap music, she stooped over Jose and pulled his face into her oversized tasseled bosom. Jose smiled as he backed his head away, shaking his head no, not needing Tanya to get jealous. Giving your money to another girl was a sin in her eyes. As the girl danced away, he saw Tanya on the other side of the room, watching him through the smoke and smiling when their eyes met. Knowing he had passed her test, he looked forward to having a shot at her when the club closed. Jose's smile faded when he looked past her to the front door. In sauntered Sergeant Agnew, his least favorite cop. He leaned over to Pablo. "The heat's here."

"Who is it?"

"It's that prick Agnew."

"I wonder what he wants, he's not vice."

"Just hang loose. He's probably looking for somebody. It can't be us. We haven't done anything lately."

Jose's eyes stayed on Agnew, who went to the bar and ordered a beer. Surveying the room, Agnew's eyes met Jose's and he came toward their seats. "Pablo, he's coming over here. He's looking for us."

"Just be cool. Let me handle him." Pablo slowly turned around and looked into Agnew's humorless face. "Hello, heat. What do you want?"

"I want to talk to you boys outside."

"Why? We haven't done anything."

"Are you coming easy or hard? It makes no difference to me."

"Are we under arrest?"

"Did I say you were under arrest, asshole?"

"No."

"Then you're not under arrest. At least not yet. Come on, I don't have all night."

They followed him to the side of the building where it was semidark. Agnew turned to them and looked Pablo square in the eye. "I had an interesting talk with Jesus this afternoon. I found four stolen stereos in his garage. He said that he got them from you."

"Then Jesus is lying. I don't have to steal stereos to make a living."

"If Jesus is lying, that's your problem. Not mine. What do you know about those stereos?"

"Nothing, man. I swear."

Agnew laughed. "Sure. You two are as pure as the driven snow. That's why you have such impeccable reputations."

"I'm telling you, I don't know shit about any friggin' stereos."

"Well, that's too bad. I guess you'll have to be my guests at the jail till you remember."

"That's not fair, man. Jesus is just trying to save his own ass. If he finked on his real source, he'd probably end up dead. Can't you see that, man?"

"Maybe. Maybe I can let you off the hook if you tell me who blew away those people in Mansfield. I know damn well that murder is in your line."

"You're crazy, man. I don't know anybody that goes around blowing away judges."

"If somebody hired a hit around here, you'd know about it."

"I might hear about it if it happened, but I didn't. Besides, they already know who did it. They said so on the radio. You're blowing smoke up my ass, man."

"If someone did hire a hit on a judge, what would it take?"

"I don't know. Fifteen hundred, maybe. It would take a lot."

"Could a thousand get it done?"

"I doubt it. Nobody wants that kind of heat."

"What if it was a thousand and other considerations?"

"I don't know what you mean."

"I'm talking about a thousand and staying out of jail."

"I still don't know what you're getting at. Are you saying that you want me to find out if a hit was ordered?"

"No, dumb shit. I'm saying that an acquaintance of mine asked me to tell you that if you hit this judge, he would pay you a thousand and keep you out of jail on the other charge."

"Is he a cop?"

"Yeah."

"I still don't get it, man. That judge is already dead."

"The wrong one got shot."

"You mean that deal in Mansfield was a professional hit?"

"Could be. I don't know. I'm just the messenger."

"Wow, man. That's really heavy. Who were they supposed to get?"

"Ray Sterrett."

"Why?"

"I don't know. Like I said, I'm just the messenger."

"I didn't know you were involved in this kind of shit, man."

"I'm not involved, Cruz. The one who sent me is. What about it? Do you take the deal, or do you go to jail?"

"I don't know, man. That stereo rap is a frame. But it's easier than a murder charge."

"You won't get caught on this one. My friend can steer the investigation away from you if the hit's here in Arlington."

Pablo looked at his brother. "What do you think, Jose?"

"If it's safe, I can go with it. I could use the money. Besides, Sterrett is the one who suspended my license last year. It would be sweet revenge."

Pablo mulled this over. This might be a golden opportunity. He had never had anything on a cop before. He finally looked up at Agnew. "No deal, man. That's not enough for icing a judge. I'd have to have more."

"There's no more money, kid. That's all there is."

"Then you'd have to give something else. Like keeping the heat off me and Jose for other stuff."

"What other stuff?"

"Anything, man."

"All right, kid. For as long as I'm on this force. We have a deal?"

"Yeah. We have a deal. When do you want this done?"

"As soon as possible. In the next couple of days."

"I can't go in that courthouse and do this, man. They probably have heat all over the place."

"That's cool. That place isn't in Arlington anyway."

"I don't know where else to find him, man."

"Leave that to my friend."

"You can find out where he'll be?"

"Yeah. I'll call you. I need a cell number where I can reach you day or night. You may not have much time after I call."

"Call me on my mobile, man. 555-5559."

Agnew turned to go. "All right. I'll call you."

"Ain't you forgetting something, man?"

"What?"

"The money, man. The $1,000."

"Oh. Here's $500. You get the rest when you finish the job."

Tim Carter and Larry Blair headed north from Mansfield toward Arlington after initiating a fruitless house-to-house canvas around the golf course. After reporting in, they traveled east on Division, driving slowly as they looked for a favorite snitch. After an hour of searching the boulevard, they spotted him selling dime bags a half block off Division. Not surprisingly, his nickname was Rascal. They let him finish his transaction and pulled up beside him. Rascal was not thrilled to see them, but that was normal. Blair stuck his head out the window and playfully slapped Rascal on top of his head. "Get in the back seat, Rascal. We need to talk."

Rascal looked around to make sure no one saw him and ducked in the back of the unit. Carter sped away as he slammed the door. "What do you guys want?"

Blair hid his distaste by flashing a smile. "Information, boy."

"I'm lucky if I can find out anything with you guys hanging around, let alone conduct business."

"You better keep coming with the information, Rascal. That keeps you out of jail. What've you heard about the shooter down in Mansfield?"

"I ain't heard nothin'. That just happened today."

"Start diggin'. We want to know something fast."

"Like what? Y'all know who he is."

"We want to know where he's hiding."

"How am I going to find that out? I never heard of this asshole before today."

"He could be in the underground. If he wasn't, we'd have him by now."

"What's it worth to you?"

"You mean over and above staying out of jail?"

"Yeah. I mean money, you cheapskates. Something this big is going to cost you. The underground ain't talking for free. If that's where he is, I'm gonna have to dig. Diggin' ain't cheap."

"I don't know, Rascal. That has to come from the top. I'll see. I know you can do it. You got us that sleezeball child-killer last month."

"Yeah. You cheapskates didn't pay me a cent for that. I spent a whole week findin' that prick."

"You got paid plenty. I got your possession charge dropped. Do you know how hard it is to get a judge to dismiss charges on a dope dealer? That saved you several thousand dollars in legal fees alone. That don't take into account a year in jail. Quit bitchin'. You got paid plenty."

"Yeah, yeah. I know. But I'm small-time anyway. It couldn't have been that hard."

"It was hard. Trust me."

"Trust you guys? Now I've got Arlington PD all over my ass, pressuring me to snitch for them."

"Life's tough all over, Rascal."

"Well, I don't have charges pending now. You cheap pricks are going to have to spring for some cash. I'm broke and have to move on soon. I snitched on some guys last week and they have to have figured out by now who did it. That's going to cost me."

"How much do you have to have, Rascal?"

"Five hundred at least. Maybe more."

"Bullshit. We haven't ever paid out that much. You've probably got that much in your pocket anyway. We saw you score back there."

"I wish. I'm having to work consignment. The money ain't even mine. I'm not makin' shit. Consignment only pays ten percent."

"How did that happen?"

"I got rolled last week for a grand. On top of that, some friggin' sergeant over here shook me down for $300. I tried to make it up by playin' the Rangers last Sunday night and they folded on me. I tell you, I don't have a pot to piss in."

Carter couldn't restrain his laughter. "Rascal, you'll never learn to leave the bookies alone. You can't gamble worth shit and you know it. Who's shaking you down over here?"

"Some bastard named Agnew. He caught me sellin' last week and grabbed my whole roll."

"Well, I can put a stop to that."

"No. Leave it alone, man. Agnew's mean. My ass is grass if I squeal on him for that. Do you know him?"

"No. I don't think so."

"There's only one thing worse than an Agnew."

"What is that?"

"Two of him."

The two deputies broke out in laughter again. When Rascal got on a roll, he was a natural comedian. Blair's laughter finally subsided and he nodded to Carter, who reversed his path, heading back to Rascal's location. Blair looked back to the snitch. "I'll check on the money and let you know first thing in the morning. Where will you be?"

"I'll be at the Sunrise Coffee Shop around 10:00. If you pull in, just circle the building and go down Bowen about half a block. Don't come inside. I've got sources in there. I'll be down in five minutes."

"Okay. Find out what you can tonight."

"No can do. There's only a couple people I can talk to about this, and they won't be around till morning." Without speaking another word, Rascal dashed away from the car and headed down an alley.

Carter turned south. "Larry, we've got one more tree to shake."

"Whiskers?"

"Yeah."

"Let's do it. He should be easier to squeeze. He was arrested last week for burglary. We won't have to pay that asshole anything."

"He's a better snitch than Rascal anyway."

"He used to be. We've wore him out, though. I've heard his sources are getting suspicious. If we're not careful, he could catch it."

"To hell with him. This case is too big to overlook him. If he gets it, it would be a small price to pay."

"Tim, I've got a gut feeling about this case. This one's so nasty, I think somebody will get it before this is over."

Chapter Fifteen

Ray awoke gradually as the sun filtered through the fancy sheer drapes. Opening his eyes slowly, he let them travel the unfamiliar luxurious bedroom as the memories returned of how he came to be there. Turning slightly to his left, Ray watched Cass sleeping soundly beside him, lying on her stomach with her left hand slipped under his pillow. Her rich auburn hair covered the left side of her face, which was highlighted with a soft smile of contentment. The rose satin sheet covered her all the way to the neck. Conflicting feelings rolled over Ray in waves as he admired her beauty. Getting involved with an employee was a recipe for disaster. His guilt increased as he thought of Doris, wondering if she was up above watching him. If she somehow knew, would she understand? Would she expect him to remain celibate for the rest of his life? Would she want a replacement mother for her children? Those were things that they had never discussed. Women in their late thirties never expected to die unless they had a terminal disease. Would Doris be sympathetic to the emptiness that she had left with Ray and the children? Ray couldn't know, nor had he given it much thought until now. The children's rejection of Marilyn had prevented, or at least postponed, these dilemmas of semiguilt. Why do the children respond to Cass? Does she have a magical touch with them? Or was yesterday an exception because of the traumatic events? Ray didn't know that either, but he could find out. *But, do I want her?* He remembered first her passion, and then her instincts for protecting his children when her whole world was exploding around her. He liked her instincts—and yes, her passion, too.

What about Marilyn? He couldn't help but compare the two. Marilyn was a classy lady with looks that were as good as Cass's, if not better. Ray admired her cool poise and inquisitive mind. *Marilyn would go far, with him or without him. Why had Marilyn never married?* Ray figured she'd been burned when she was younger. Marilyn had told him that she had sized him up a year before she'd made her move. Her personality was easy going, and she had maneuvered Ray into taking her out without him feeling awkward at all. Her constant rejection of men made them feel that she was cold and detached. That barrier had shown itself when the kids had not responded to her.

Cass didn't have her social poise, but she was warmer and cozier. She seemed to have a natural chemistry with children that perhaps Marilyn would never have. Cass was a natural mother and just never had the opportunity before now. Marilyn wasn't natural with children at all; she moved in adult circles and had been an only child. Cass had two brothers and a sister in a close family. *What am I going to do?*

Cass stirred and opened her eyes. Ray was the first thing she saw. Smiling as her hand came out from underneath the pillow and putting her arm around his neck, she snuggled close with her warm body and fell back into a light snooze. Ray held her, lightly breathed into her ear, and kissed her on the neck. Cass's embrace tightened. "Ummh. Good morning."

"Good morning. Did you sleep well?"

"What do you think?"

"I think yes."

"I think you're right. How did you sleep?"

"I slept pretty well. You made certain of that."

Cass opened her eyes and drew back a little. "Any regrets?"

"I don't think so," he lied.

"Are you sure?"

"A lot of things have happened awfully fast. That's all. My psyche hasn't caught up. I didn't know you were going to drag me in here and rape me last night."

Cass giggled and snuggled close. "You didn't fight very hard."

"I guess not."

"Besides. You're the one who got all turned on. You just swept me right off my feet."

"Yeah. Look at you. As sweet and innocent as a newborn vulture."

"That's not fair. I didn't plan that."

"I know. I'm only kidding."

"What do we do about this? Do I have to transfer?"

"I don't know. I haven't had time to think about that. We have a crisis to get through first. After that, we can decide."

"Do you want me to sleep in another room tonight?"

"No. I think I could get used to sleeping with you real fast. I've really missed that."

"In front of the children?"

"Not exactly. They're upstairs. They won't know."

"You're not going to tell them?"

"Not yet. I will when the time is right."

"What do you think their reaction will be?"

"I don't know. Let them get used to us being together. I know one thing, though."

"What's that?"

"They took to you yesterday. They don't usually do that. I brought Marilyn home one time. They ran her out of the house in ten minutes."

"You never told me about that."

"There wasn't any reason to until now."

"What are you going to do about her?"

"Now, now. Don't get jealous. She doesn't have any hold on me. We haven't even gone out in three months."

"Oh. I thought you were seeing her more often than that."

"No. It's been pretty casual."

"What do you mean by pretty casual?"

"I don't know. Just pretty casual."

"Do you promise not to get mad if I ask you a personal question?"

"I'll try not to. I guess that you're entitled to ask personal questions now that we're lying naked in bed together."

"Okay. Is she as good as me in bed?"

Ray had to laugh. "I don't know the answer to that. I guess that was what I meant by pretty casual."

"You mean you never slept with her? After all this time?"

"Not even once."

"Why not?"

"I don't know. We just weren't ready. We only went out three times."

"Oh. I knew you took her out almost six months ago and that she was still interested. I assumed you were seeing her more often. I didn't know."

"Well, now you know. Are you satisfied?"

Cass smiled and snuggled up again. After a long silence, she giggled softly. "I can't believe you came to bed with me after Marilyn has been trying for six months. If she knew that, she'd die."

"That's what rape will do for you."

Cass swatted at him playfully. "Stop it. You're making me feel like a wanton woman."

Ray bantered back. "You better stay a wanton woman if you want to keep me around."

"Okay. How about some more? Right now."

"Not now, angel. The kids will wake up any minute. Save it for tonight. Let's get up and get cracking. We need to feed the kids and I have a bunch of calls to make."

Jim Wade drove up to the crime scene at 8:05 am. The place was a beehive of activity, with press units milling around in front of the area cordoned off by the yellow crime scene tape. Inside the area were police and firemen. Chief Hawkins was leading a citizens' group around to the back of the building to search for slugs. Sheriff's deputies were going over the pickup truck. Wade parked, ducked under the tape, and approached Gary Baker, who exited the car to meet Wade.

"Hello, Commissioner. What can we do for you?"

"I'm considering putting security gates in here. I wanted to see if you thought something like that could work out here."

"Where do you intend to put them, Commissioner?"

"I don't know. I wanted your input on that."

"I see. There's no room for a security gate once you're inside. I don't know if it's feasible to put one in out here."

"Is it okay to look inside?"

"I guess so. Just don't touch anything."

"Okay. Is Sterrett here."

"No."

"How can I get in touch with him? I need his thoughts on this."

"He's incommunicado right now."

"Why?"

"Because the sheriff has concerns for his safety."

"I see. How long will he be under protection?"

"I don't know. Probably until Stewart is caught."

"Damn! You mean there'll be no court until Stewart's caught?"

"I don't know about that. Is there a problem?"

"Sure. We can't shut down the government. I'll get complaint calls day and night if that happens. It could be weeks before you catch him."

"I doubt if it will take that long, Commissioner."

"Why? Have you got some leads?"

"Nothing yet."

Wade lowered his head and marched into the clerk's outer office. Looking around, he saw two officers talking to Phyllis, who appeared to be the only clerk there. Wade caught her eye and nodded toward Cass's office. Phyllis broke off the conversation and approached him, looking tired and haggard but managing a professional smile. "Yes, sir?"

"Hi, Phyllis. I wanted to say how sorry I am about this awful thing and see if there's anything I can do?"

"Thank you, sir. That's very kind."

"Where is Judge Sterrett? Is he here?"

"No, sir. I just talked to him but he didn't say where he was."

"Did he leave you a phone number?"

"No, sir."

"Is he going to call back later in the day?"

"He didn't say."

"Is he coming out here today?"

"I don't think so. He didn't talk like it."

"What did he say when he called?"

"He just wanted to make sure that I was all right and to get some information on a wedding that he's doing tonight."

"He's doing a wedding tonight? Is that safe?"

"He seemed to think so."

"Where is it?"

"Just a minute. I'll have to look." Phyllis pulled out his wedding folder. "It's at River Legacy Park."

"What time?"

"Seven thirty. Why do you want to know this?"

"I just want to make sure he's safe. That's all."

"Okay. Is there anything else I can do for you, sir?"

"I'm just looking for a place to put up security gates. Do you have any ideas on that?"

"No, sir. This outer office is too small for one."

"Thank you, Phyllis. Is there anything I can do for you?"

Phyllis hesitated. "Yes sir. Now that you mention it, there is. I need a transfer. Could you help me out there?"

"You're not happy here?"

"No, sir. Not after yesterday."

"Oh. I see. Are you afraid that guy might come back?"

"Well, no. I just need to leave."

"Why?"

"I really hate to say."

"I have to know if I ask other supervisors to hire you on."

Phyllis blurted it out. "There's some money missing and I think I'll get blamed for it."

Wade smiled his most reassuring smile. "I'm sure no one would blame you for such a thing, Phyllis. Tell me all about it."

"There was some money missing when we came in yesterday morning. I closed up the night before and forgot to lock the cabinet."

"How much is missing?"

"Over $2,800."

"Who all knows about this?"

"Cass and I guess the judge. I don't know who Cass told."

Wade smiled again. "I'll do what I can, Phyllis. But I need something from you."

"What's that?"

"Keep me posted on everything that goes on out here. Understand?"

"Yes sir. What do you want to know?"

"I want to know how the investigation is going and anything else. Tell me everything."

"Should I leave word at your office if I find something out?"

"No. Don't call me there. Here's my cell number. Call me on that and, by the way, don't tell anyone about our calls. Okay?"

"Yes sir. Are you going to find me another job?"

"I told you I'd do my best. I'll have to find you a job where you don't handle money, though."

"You don't trust me?"

Wade smiled at her again and patted her on the shoulder as he turned to leave. "No. It's not that. If you left here under suspicion, it would just be easier to find you one like that."

"Oh. I see."

"Keep in touch, Phyllis. Call me at least twice a day."

Wade walked back to Baker, who was outside looking at a spent bullet with Chief Hawkins. "Thank you, Deputy, for your help."

"Did you find a place to put that security gate, Commissioner?"

"Yes. I'm going to build an entranceway extending out in the parking lot. Sort of an entrance to an entrance."

"That makes sense, sir. Are you leaving now?"

"Yes. I got what I came for."

"Have a good day, sir," called Baker although Wade was already getting in his car.

Wade turned north on Highway 157, heading toward Fort Worth. Pulling out Agnew's number, he dialed it on his mobile.

"Hello?"

"Chester, this is Wade. Did you set up that deal?"

"I'm just waiting on you to deliver, Commissioner."

"I'm delivering. Our boy's performing a wedding tonight at 7:30 at River Legacy Park. Will that work?"

"Probably."

"All right then. I look forward to reading the paper in the morning."

"There's one more little problem."

"Yeah?"

"The package ran more than I expected. I need another $500 to accept delivery."

"All right, dammit. I'll call my brother and arrange it. You can catch him at his construction office about 5:00 this afternoon." Wade clicked off his mobile and headed to the commissioners' court.

Captain Walker and Scroggins left the Arlington water department office, pulling away as Scroggins picked up the radio. "Unit eleven to unit two. Over."

"This is unit two."

"Who is this?"

"This is Baker. Who's this?"

"This is Scroggins. Go back in that pasture where Stewart escaped and find a drainage pipe. There are ladders below the manhole covers. Go down that ladder and see what you can find. Stewart helped build that pipe three years ago."

"Roger. Over and out."

Ray was impressed with Cass as she bustled the kids to the table and presented them with their favorite breakfast. After wheedling out of Robbie that they loved pancakes, she labored over the griddle until she had fixed enough pancakes to feed Ray, the kids, the deputies, and half the homeless in Fort Worth. The kids looked at that stack of pancakes like they had just ascended to heaven. Cass was busy making friends for life. Ray smiled with amusement as he finished and reached for the morning paper. The front page was predictable, showing pictures of Judge Chavez, Sid Walling, Shirley Lemons, and the wounded attorney. Below the four pictures were two larger pictures of Stewart, with book-in numbers underneath. Above the pictures was the headline **mansfield massacre**. Ray scanned the front page and found an index of companion stories. Marilyn's byline, under the headline **killer set free without hearing,** caught his eye. Underneath the headline was a picture of Judge Jake Eaves. Adroitly using his own words against him, Marilyn minced no words in blasting Eaves for releasing Stewart. Quotes from Shirley Lemons' father and Judge Chavez's brother further scalded the judge. After mentioning Cass twice in the article, she closed by promising an exposé on Eave's record on writs of habeas corpus.

Ray laid aside the newspaper to finish his coffee, looking at Cass and nodding to the newspaper. "It looks like Marilyn's after Judge Eaves on that writ of habeas corpus. You're mentioned in her article."

"I want to read it then. By the way, she told me yesterday that she wanted to talk to you."

Ray smiled a knowing smile. "Did you forget until now?"

Cass smiled with a slight blush. "Yeah. I guess I did. Are you going to call her?"

"I think so. She deserves an interview."

Robbie had been busy putting away the pancakes, trying for the world's record. "Can I have some more pancakes, Cass?"

"Yes. You can have two more. If you eat any more you'll get sick and won't get to go swimming."

Jan cleaned her plate and looked up at Cass. "Is this your house?"

"No. It would be nice if it was. Do you like it here, Jan?"

"Yes ma'am. It's pretty. How long can we stay here, Daddy?"

"A few days, maybe."

"Can we go feed the ducks after breakfast, Daddy?"

"Where are the ducks, Jan?"

"In the back yard."

Ray looked at Cass. "What's back there?"

"There's a pond behind the bath house with ducks and geese in it. I can take them back there. It's secluded."

"Yes. You and Robbie can go feed the ducks if Cass takes you."

"Oh boy. Will you come with us, Daddy?"

"I can't right now. I'll come out later if I can."

The phone rang in the next room. Ray rose and answered it. "Hello?"

"Hold on please. I'll put you through to the sheriff."

Ray turned to Cass at the table. "It's the sheriff. I'll catch up to you and the kids later."

"Ray, are you there?"

"Yes, Sheriff. I'm here. What's going on?"

"I just thought I'd check in with you and make sure you're comfortable out there."

"Yes, thank you. This place is magnificent. I do need to handle some things later, though. I need a car."

"I don't want you leaving there, Ray. It's not safe. What do you need? The guards can handle it."

"I need some extra clothes for the kids. I also have a wedding to perform tonight."

"I'll handle the kid's clothes. You'll have to scratch the wedding."

"Can the guards take Cass and the kids to the mall?"

"I guess that would be all right, as long as they stay on the west side. I don't have any reason to think Stewart's over there."

"I can't scratch that wedding. The groom is Harry Fletcher's boy. Harry's my biggest contributor. Yours, too, if I recall correctly."

"Damn. Where is it?"

"River Legacy Park."

"In Arlington?"

"Yes."

"You can't do it, Ray. I'll call Harry and explain."

"You know Fletcher better than that. He'll be really mad if I screw up his kid's wedding. We'll both be punished for it."

"Surely, he'll understand. He'll accept someone else."

"I don't think so, Sheriff. He'll get mad if we even approach him with it. Stewart can't know my schedule."

"All right, dammit. Just be careful. Get one of the guards to take you. Get right back to the house after the ceremony."

"What about your party tonight. Is that still going on?"

"Yeah. But everyone will understand if you can't make it. Call me when you get back, so I'll know you're safe."

"Okay. What's happening this morning? Any leads?"

"Nothing definite. We found out how Stewart vanished into thin air."

"How?"

The sheriff disclosed the information on how Stewart escaped. As Sanders relayed the story, Ray did his best to picture the escape in his mind. "I just can't believe that this joker's that slick. Anything else?"

"Hawkins found a large-caliber slug behind the courthouse. We think it's the one that killed the girl. It's too damaged to test, though."

"What about the golf course?"

"Nothing so far. We've checked all the houses and the employees at the country club. No one noticed a thing. It may take several days to catch all the golfers that played there yesterday morning."

"What about Stewart's friends?"

"We're coming up with zeros. His co-workers, too."

"Does he have any friends out of town?"

"None that we can find. He don't have many friends, period."

"I remember from the testimony in the case that his apartment roommate moved to Austin about six months ago."

"What's his name?"

"I don't know. It never came into testimony. Check with the manager of the Castle Winds Apartments in Arlington."

"I'll check it out."

"You told me you were checking to see if he escaped in the Arlington underground. Have you turned up anything there?"

"It's too early for that. Snitches don't get up early."

"Do you have a gut feeling about where this joker could be?"

"Not really. I have a hunch someone picked him up at the golf course. I think there's someone else involved. I'm hoping we can shake them loose with the reward."

"How much has that risen to?"

"It's leveled off at $73,000."

"Will that be enough?"

"It should be. People turn in their own mothers for $5,000."

"How long does it usually take for that to work?"

"The time varies. One more thing and then I've got to go. You haven't given anyone your phone number, have you?"

"No. Your guards cautioned me about that last night."

"Good! I'll call you back if something develops." Sanders hung up and picked up a waiting call. "Sanders here."

"Sheriff, this is Frances Mendez. You probably don't remember me. I just joined Captain Walker's staff about a month ago."

"Sure, Frances, I remember you from the meeting last night. Have you got something?"

"I don't know. Maybe. There's no one here in the office, and I have something on tape that I need someone to look at."

"Where are you?"

"I'm down in jail security."

"What do you want me to look at?"

"I didn't learn much about Stewart's movements here at the jail. He didn't circulate at all, but he did go to the infirmary."

"Yeah? Go ahead. I'm listening."

"He had a couple of conversations with some other prisoners in the waiting room. Since I'm new to the department, I don't know who they are."

"Okay. I'll be right down." Sanders headed to the elevator, dodging a contingent of reporters waiting in his outer office. Descending to the second floor, he saw Frances waiting for him in the hall. Sanders couldn't help noticing that she was a knockout— long black hair and she filled out her black sheriff's uniform like a poster girl, with a beautiful face showing no lines or blemishes. He couldn't guess her age, but she had captivating brown eyes. He knew Walker was divorced and wondered if he might have hired her for some other reason.

"Let's see what you have, Frances."

They walked inside jail security, where two deputies were staring at rows of TV monitors, ignoring Sanders and Frances. Walking over to the monitor closest to the far wall, Frances grabbed a remote control and the picture started moving backwards at a fast clip. Frances slowed it down and finally pushed the forward button, showing Stewart, in jail garb, walking up to the check-in area. They watched him slide the kite in the drawer and sit down across from a prisoner. Sanders fought impatience until Stewart's lips started moving, but he couldn't tell who he was talking to. Several minutes went by before the man sitting across from him moved his head slightly just before Stewart got up and walked away. Stewart went out of the camera's range, then reappeared thirty seconds later, sitting down by another prisoner, who was an older man with a familiar face that Sanders couldn't quite place. After the conversation ended, the older man got up and walked out of range of the camera. "Frances, back the tape up and let's see how long they talked."

"I've already done that, Sheriff. It was thirty-eight seconds."

"Get Captain Willoughby, the head jailer, up here. I want to know who that old man is."

"Yes sir." Frances picked up the phone and summoned Willoughby, who arrived within sixty seconds.

"Willoughby, I want you to tell me who a prisoner is."

"Sure thing, Sheriff. If he's been here more than a week, I'll recognize him," drawled the captain as the tape rolled backward. He watched intently as the tape rolled forward for a few seconds; then he held up his hand. "Sheriff, that old man to the left is Blade Hawkins. I don't know who the younger man is."

"We already know who he is. Who's Blade Hawkins?"

"He's in here for fencing stolen merchandise. He also has a reputation as a fixer."

"Oh? What can he fix?"

"You name it and he can fix it. He has contacts everywhere."

"How long is his sentence?"

"He got the max on a Class A misdemeanor. I think he's been in about three months."

"Has he qualified for good time?"

"Yes sir. He don't cause trouble."

"Will he talk?"

"I doubt it."

"Can a lip-reader get me the gist of their conversation?"

"I don't think it will work, sir. The angle's not right. We can barely see the right corners of their mouths."

"If that younger man walked in cold off the street and wanted to fix something, who would send him to Hawkins?"

"Almost anybody."

"He must be well known."

"He is. As far as I know, he's the best fixer in the county."

"Would he have contacts in Arlington?"

"Probably a half dozen of them."

"See what you can do. Let me know as soon as you get something." Sanders turned to Frances with a smile. "Good work, Frances."

Frances brightened and started to respond, but Sanders was headed out the door.

Ray dialed the Arlington division of the *Star-Telegram* and was told that Marilyn Shaw had been transferred that morning to the main Fort Worth office. He got the number and dialed there.

"News section."

"May I speak to Marilyn Shaw, please?"

"Sorry, she's not here right now. If you'll leave your name and number, I'll ask her to get back to ya."

"Who am I speaking with, please?"

"This is Bryan."

"Bryan, this is Judge Ray Sterrett. She wants to talk to me and I can't leave my number. Does she have a beeper?"

"Yeah, probably. But I don't know what it is. She just transferred in here this morning."

"All right. Can you find her?"

"Yeah, I think so. Aren't you the judge out in Mansfield?"

"Yes, I am."

"Let me ask you some questions. Are you afraid this guy is coming after you?"

"No dice, Bryan. I'll call back in fifteen minutes. Please have her there or have a phone number where I can call her." Ray hung the phone up, remembering why he couldn't stand the downtown reporters.

Lee Sanders hung up the phone after talking to Captain Willoughby. They had no luck in lip-reading Stewart's conversation with the Blade. After a moment's thought, he picked up the phone and dialed again.

"This is Detective Mendez speaking."

"Frances, this is the sheriff. No luck on the lip-reading. Would you bring up this Blade Hawkins up to an interrogation room? I'll meet you there in ten minutes."

"Sure thing, Sheriff."

"Thanks. I'll see you then." Sanders put the phone down and picked up the radio mike. "Dispatch, this is unit one. Over."

"Go ahead unit one."

"Patch me through to unit eleven."

"Roger. Over and out."

"This is unit eleven."

"This is unit one. Is Walker with you, Scroggins? Over."

"Yes sir."

"Good. I want you to visit the manager of the Castlewinds Apartments there in Arlington. Stewart had a roommate who transferred to Austin about six months ago. Find out who he is and all available data the apartment complex has on him, and get it back to me. Understood?"

"Roger. Is that where you think he is?"

"Possibly. I may know more in a few minutes. It looks like Stewart made contact with the criminal elements while he was here in jail. That may be our hottest lead for now."

"Can you tell us about it?"

"Frances Mendez found a video of him having a conversation with Blade Hawkins in the infirmary. Do you know this guy?"

Walker looked at Scroggins and smiled. "Yeah. We're familiar with that clown."

"Do you think he will talk?"

"Not very likely. He never has."

"Do you know who his contacts are in Arlington?"

"An easier question would be who his contacts aren't."

"That many, huh?"

"I'm afraid so."

"Is it likely that he could hide Stewart?"

"Anything's possible with the Blade."

"Do you know of any weakness that might make him talk?"

"Negative."

"Okay. I'll take him on anyway. Over and out." Sanders headed over to the old jail and found Frances waiting outside the interrogation room. Nodding to her, he looked through the one-way mirror and saw a slender old man sitting at the table, calmly smoking a cigarette. Frances handed Sanders the prisoner's criminal history as they walked inside. Sanders sat down across the table from the old man and studied the rap sheet. Liking to make prisoners sweat, he ignored Hawkins. Hawkins had a long history, but no felonies. After a few moments, he looked up abruptly and stared at the old man. Hawkins looked back as if he had all the inner peace in the world. "I'm Sheriff Sanders. Are you Bennie Hawkins?"

"That's right."

"You've never been in this much trouble before, have you?"

"Trouble? I don't know what you're talking about, Sheriff."

"I'm talking about accessory to capital murder."

"I sure enough don't know what you're talking about."

"We've got you on video tape talking to the guy who murdered those people in Mansfield. You have him hid out and we want to know where."

"You don't know that or we wouldn't be having this conversation."

"What makes you think that?"

"Because if you did, you would be running out your Miranda warning before we started. You're on a fishing expedition here."

While he collected his wits, Sanders sat back and stared at Hawkins like he was crazy. This guy knew the score. "Yes. You're right about the warning. I wanted to give you the opportunity to come clean first. If you tell us where he is, I probably won't file charges against you."

"That's mighty nice of you, Sheriff. There's just one problem. I still don't know who you're talking about."

"I'll spell it out for you. Tuesday morning you had a short conversation with Stewart in the infirmary. We have it on video tape and lip-reading experts are reviewing it now."

Hawkins leaned back and laughed. "Are you talking about that young punk who approached me in the waiting room?"

"That's the one."

"Then you sure enough don't have anything on me. He came up to me and asked me to find him a gun on the outside. I told him to hit the road and got up and left. I didn't talk to him more than thirty seconds."

Frances Mendez broke in. "Thirty-eight seconds to be exact. It doesn't take that long to tell some punk to hit the road."

Hawkins looked her over before he answered. "Lady, that tape will show that I got up and left him right after he sat down by me."

Sanders cut back in. "Don't shit me Hawkins. That kid didn't know enough about crime to snatch a grandmother's purse before you talked to him. After that, he murders three people and vanishes into thin air. Do you really think we're that stupid?"

The Blade lit another cigarette and chuckled as he blew smoke to the side. "You're telling me I teach this kid to be a career criminal in thirty-eight seconds? Wait till I tell the boys back in the cell about this one. They'll laugh almost as hard as the jury."

Sanders smarted after that one. Hawkins was right. That was pretty lame. He tried again. "All you had to give him was a phone number. That's pretty easy in thirty-eight seconds."

"Did I bust him out of jail, too?"

"Don't get cute, Hawkins. I know all about your capabilities."

"All right, Sheriff. I'll be serious. Do you really think that I would help some asshole who walks up to me that I don't even know? I'm not that stupid. He could have been a plant for all I knew."

"He didn't talk to anyone else in jail that could have helped him that way. Only you."

"Sheriff, be reasonable. I never saw that kid before in my life. If you were me, would you trust some stranger in here enough to risk that kind of trouble?"

Sanders decided to try another approach. He couldn't beat the old man's logic. "What exactly did he say to you?"

"I don't remember exactly. He just sat down beside me and asked me if I could get him a gun. I asked him who he was, and he said his name was Billy or Willy. I asked who sent him to me, and he answered with some general name that I don't even remember. I told him that he was mistaking me for somebody else. I got up and left. That's all I remember."

"Did you send him to someone else?"

"No."

Sanders rose to leave. This was a tougher nut than he could crack. "I'll be talking to you again as soon as the lip-readers get through. If you're not telling me the truth, I'll be back with that Miranda warning you know so well." He motioned Frances to follow him outside and they closed the door. "Frances, what do you think?"

"He's lying through his teeth."

"Why do you think that?"

"Because he wouldn't have remembered the kid if that conversation was that insignificant. He didn't need much prompting to recall him."

Sanders nodded. "Keep working on him for a while and see what you can do." He walked away with admiration for this new detective. Walker didn't hire her for his bimbo after all. Frances Mendez was going far.

"Sheriff's office bond desk. This is Linda White. May I help you?"

"Yes. Is Marilyn Shaw with the *Star-Telegram* over there? This is Judge Sterrett calling."

"Yes sir. One moment and I'll transfer you."

"Hello?"

"Hi, Marilyn."

"Ray, is that you?"

"Yes, it's me. I understand that congratulations are in order. I hear you've been transferred downtown."

"Thank you. God, I've been worried about you. Are you all right?"

"I'm fine."

"Where are you?"

"I can't say. It's a state secret."

"Oh baloney. I want to see you. You can search me to make sure that I have no weapons."

"I'm sorry, Marilyn. I'm on strict orders from the sheriff. I can't even give out a number, let alone receive visitors. You're doing a great job on your story. Those writs have been a burr in my saddle for years."

"Ray, I don't want to talk business now. I'm worried about you. Are your kids with you?"

"Yes, and they're fine."

"Ray, I need to talk to you. Now."

"Okay. I'm here. Let's talk."

"Not like this."

"I'm sorry, Marilyn. Trust me. There's no other way."

"How long are you going to be like this? You know, hidden away?"

"I'm not sure. Hopefully, just a couple of days. What's on your mind?"

"You are. Just a minute and let me close this door where I can have a little privacy. There. Ray, I've done a lot of thinking the last twenty-four hours. When I was driving out to your court yesterday, I thought you had been killed. You have no idea how upset I was. I don't think you have any idea how much you mean to me. Do you know that I haven't gone out with anyone else since I was at your house three months ago?"

"No, I didn't. That's a surprise with all the guys you must know."

"That's just it, Ray. I probably know ten thousand guys and there's only one that I look up to and respect. There's only one that I find attractive and only one that I would ever consider having a serious relationship with. Would you like to know who that is, Ray?"

"I'm getting the picture. Why didn't you tell me this before?"

"I guess I wasn't sure until yesterday. And I sure didn't want to say this over a damn telephone. Ray, when can I see you?"

"Soon. I promise. I'm sorry about all this security, but it's for the best until they find Stewart."

"That could take weeks. I'm not going to play pillow talk with you that long. I want you to figure out how to get me to where you are. I'm leaving for Houston to visit my folks this afternoon. Please have this worked out by Monday, or I'll camp down at Lee Sanders' office until he takes me to you."

"Marilyn, I had no idea you had such passionate thoughts about me. You were always so cool and casual when we were together, I thought I was just another date to you."

"You just work out the details by Monday and I'll show you how passionate I can be. I have to go now. I've borrowed some one's office and they're back. Bye now."

Ray hung up the phone feeling guilt toward both Marilyn and Cass. "I wonder if I can get harems legalized in the next legislature," he mumbled.

"Unit eleven to unit one. Go ahead. Over."

"Walker, you were right about Blade Hawkins. I can't crack him. I've got Frances Mendez working on him."

"Don't feel bad, Sheriff. Nobody's ever cracked him. I doubt if Frances will have any luck with him either."

"Walker, I want to compliment you on her. She's good. She's very perceptive and has good attention to detail. Where did you find her?"

"She was working in civil affairs at Houston PD I ran across her at a TECLOSE training seminar in Austin. She told me she wasn't happy where she was and wanted to work criminal investigations. I came home and checked her out and got rave reviews, so I hired her. She even paid her own moving expenses to come up here."

"She must not have a family if she could do that."

"Her husband was a chief deputy constable down there and he got killed on a drug bust a couple of years ago. They had no children."

"As good as she looks, that won't last long up here. She has a body that speaks eight languages. Are you looking at that, Walker?"

"No. I'm too old for her. I just hired her because she's good. You better watch Larry Blair, though. I've noticed that his eyes light up every time her name is mentioned."

"Frances thinks this Hawkins is lying through his teeth and I'm inclined to agree. You better turn the screws on those snitches in Arlington. I'm beginning to think that's fertile ground."

"We've got a pretty good snitch over here that might turn something but he wants $500. We've never paid out that kind of money before. What do you think?"

"That's a lot of money for a snitch. Can he come across?"

"He has before."

"We didn't have to pay that much before. Why now?"

"That's something you don't want to know."

"All right. But don't pay him until he comes across and it turns out to be accurate. I'll have to pull that out of our drug contraband fund and that committee asks questions every time we use fifteen cents."

"Can we use any of the reward fund for this?"

"Later we can, but there's no cash yet. It's all pledges."

"All right. I'll start turning the screws. I'm not getting anywhere on that Austin lead. Stewart's former roommate moved again last month with no forwarding address. I doubt if Stewart could even find him."

"We can't count on that. Did the apartment complex show any relatives on the guy?"

"Yes. They're right here in Arlington. We just got off the phone with them. They haven't heard from him since he moved to Austin."

"What's this guy's name and date of birth?"

"Randall Allen Hines. DOB is April 28, 1971."

"Have you run a TCIC?"

"Blair's working on that as well as a new address with DPS."

"Okay. Keep me posted. Over and out."

Walker disconnected and patched through to Blair. He checked his watch. It was 9:55.

"This is unit fifteen. Over."

"Blair, this is Walker. You're authorized to pay your snitch the $500 when Stewart's caught and the information has been verified."

"That'll help, Chief. I'm still working on Hines. Nothing yet."

"Are you on the way to see your snitch?"

"Yes. We're pulling through the parking lot right now."

"Good luck and keep me posted. Over and out."

Blair and Carter pulled down Bowen Street, as instructed, and waited. A few minutes later, Rascal jumped in the back seat and they sped away. Carter laughed when he looked in the back seat and beheld Rascal in a big floppy hat drooped over sunglasses. "Rascal, is that supposed to be some kind of disguise?"

"It helps. I can't afford to be seen with you assholes."

"Did you find out anything?"

"What about my money?"

"We can get it for you only after we verify the information and catch the bastard."

"I need some money now, man."

"Sorry. That's the best we can do. What did you find out?"

"Nothing exact. Something big's going down, though. Nobody's saying shit. I get the cold eye whenever I ask a question. When they're that tight lipped, they're hiding something."

"What are they hiding?"

"Everything. Everybody that knows anything won't talk at all. They won't even talk about baseball, man. They just sit there in their little groups and shut up whenever I come around. The last time I saw this happen, that drug dealer got blown away out by Six Flags."

"Are you saying that you're not going to find out anything?"

"No. I'll have to catch them alone to talk. That takes time and has to look natural."

"How long does that take?"

"Usually two or three days."

"Let me ask you this. If you needed to hide, who would you go to?"

"There's four or five guys I could go to."

"Who are they?"

"Let's see. There's Lucky, Shorty, Angel, Bullet, or Mexican Joe."

"What are these guys real names?"

"Questions like that would get me killed, man."

"Are all those guys hanging out back there in the cafe?"

"Some of them."

"Who's there?"

"Angel and Mexican Joe."

"Do they work together?"

"No. Not many of them do."

"Tell me what Angel and Mexican Joe did this morning."

"Nothing really. Like I said, they just shut up when I came by."

"They're not usually like that?"

"No. That's why I think something's going down."

"Who's with them?"

"Angel just has his driver Jerry with him. Mexican Joe was sitting with the Cruz brothers and one of his heavies named Devil."

"Does Mexican Joe usually sit with the Cruz brothers?"

"Sometimes."

"Do these guys work somewhere? Do they have offices?"

"Mexican Joe owns a pawnshop on Division. I don't know that much about Angel except that he's a mean bastard."

"What's the name of this pawnshop on Division?"

"Top Dollar Pawn."

"Does he ever run stolen merchandise out of there?"

"I don't know, man. Not that I know of. The local heat checks them pretty often. They'd be crazy to do something like that."

"What do they usually do?"

"Mexican Joe hides a lot of wetbacks from INS. He's got a cousin who brings them in from Mexico. Mexican Joe finds them jobs, for a percentage."

"What does Angel do?"

"He does a little of everything. He dabbles in stolen merchandise. He has some big connections in Dallas."

"What kind of connections in Dallas?"

"I've heard that he hides people that are wanted over in Dallas."

"What about the other three?"

"Lucky and Shorty work together sometimes, running stolen cars out of state or delivering them to chop shops."

"They don't hide people?"

"Not usually."

"Then why did you say you would contact them if you wanted to hide?"

"Because they'd pay me to drive a stolen car out of state. If I wanted to hide, that's what I'd do."

"What about Bullet?"

"Bullet's a big dog. He can do anything, man. He brings in big shipments of drugs from Columbia. If somebody wanted a hit, they would go to him and he'd get it done. Things like that."

"Why would you pick Bullet to hide?"

"If the heat was really on like it is with your guy, he could send him to South America."

Blair stole a look at Carter and raised his eyebrows. This snitch was in over his head. Maybe they were, too.

Chapter Sixteen

Leonard Torrey hurried through the 2-E parking lot at DFW airport, looking for a parking space. Finding one at the back, he raced toward the terminal. The phone call from Mr. Mysterious hadn't given him much time to get there. Torrey figured that probably was planned. As instructed, there was a men's room opposite Gate Sixteen and he hurried in, checking his watch. It read 3:18 pm, and he was three minutes late. The bathroom was busy, with twenty or more men milling around. Torrey looked vainly for a familiar face. The last stall was hanging ajar, thank God. Closing the door, he sat on the toilet as instructed and slid a business card under the adjoining stall. Five seconds later, a plain white envelope came back to him. Inside was a small stack of old hundred-dollar bills. There were thousand-dollar bank bands around two stacks and five loose bills.

Following directions exactly, Torrey flushed the toilet and left. Spying a newspaper lying on a seat at the gate opposite the busy bathroom, he impulsively grabbed it. Opening the paper to hide his face, he waited and watched. It looked like a lost cause for half an hour, but then a young man exited quickly, turning to his right, with no luggage. Torrey searched his memory for that face. He had seen it before, but where?

The young man was dressed in a tan raincoat over a business suit. Torrey stayed about twenty paces behind as the man ducked into a deserted baggage claim area, grabbed a lone case circling the ramp, and hurried out the nearest exit without a backward glance. Torrey followed him across the street and into the covered parking area. The young man went down two levels and turned left. Torrey waited at the stairs, watching as the man entered a dark green Jaguar. As soon as a van passed, Torrey ducked behind it and dashed down four more flights of stairs. Running almost a hundred yards to his car, he arrived out of breath, fumbling for the keys. As time ticked, he tore out of the parking lot to the main exit road, looking vainly for the Jaguar. Cursing, he turned south for the exit going back to Fort Worth.

When he arrived at the exit tollgate, he gratefully spied the green Jaguar four cars ahead of him in another lane. Carefully, he followed the Jag to Arlington. The young man turned right on Abrams Street, continuing west along the beautiful tree-lined boulevard. After about ten blocks, the Jag pulled into a small parking lot at a business office, and the young man hurried in, without the suitcase. Circling the block, Torrey pulled into the same parking lot, where he wrote down the license number of the Jag.

Three men exited the front door, so Torrey eased out of the lot on the opposite side. Glancing at the three men, he recognized one of them, John Webb, a prominent attorney. Torrey parked in an adjoining lot, facing the building that Webb had left. The three men chatted easily in the parking lot for several minutes, finally departing in separate cars. Torrey's watch showed 4:15. While waiting a few more minutes, he pulled the envelope out of his pocket and counted the money. It was all there.

Impatiently, he left his car and walked across the street, approaching the front door of the building. The sign on the door read Wilson, Williamson, & Webb attorneys at law. Torrey then drove to Fort Worth, reviewing what he remembered about the attorney. John Webb was a prominent attorney who represented oil companies. Webb never bothered with justice courts and had no reason to be involved in something like this. Torrey didn't know anything about Wilson and Williamson, but he intended to find out. How would that law firm know to pick him as a go-between? They or their client must have a pipeline into that justice court.

When he returned to his office, he checked out their ad in the yellow pages. "Oil and Gas Attorneys," it read. Dialing the number, he got lucky. Some secretary was working after hours.

"Wilson, Williamson, and Webb. May I help you?"

"Yes ma'am. My son received a traffic ticket this morning, and I was wondering if some one could help him with it?"

"I'm sorry, sir. Our firm doesn't handle those matters."

"Oh. You don't have a junior attorney who could help me?"

"We do have junior attorneys, sir. But we only handle oil and gas contracts and litigation. I'm sorry. You'll have to contact some one else."

"Thank you anyway. Good-bye."

"Thank you sir. Have a good day."

Torrey hung up and thumbed through his bar directory, checking their junior attorneys. There were six in the firm. Torrey had never heard of any of them. But he didn't deal with oil and gas. He leaned back in his chair and pondered. It had to be one of their clients, and that could be anybody. The client could have got one of the juniors to deliver his money, without anyone else in the firm knowing about it. Possibly, the courier didn't know any details. The envelope had been sealed, and it could have come from anywhere. It was pretty slick. Somebody wanted Sterrett dead, and they were rich enough to hire the most famous hit man in the southwest, had an excellent intelligence network, and were experts at remaining at arm's length. Someone in the oil and gas business. It didn't add up. There was one connection. Buck Reed lived in Tulsa, Oklahoma, and Tulsa was an oil and gas town. Torrey reached for the phone.

Captain Walker and Bob Scroggins shifted impatiently in the outer office of Arlington Police Chief Parker. The chairs were hard, but the treatment was worse. Walker clenched his teeth in frustration. "We've been sitting here thirty-five minutes."

"They could have at least offered us some coffee."

"Maybe the secretary doesn't know any better."

"Bullshit. Listen to her when the phone rings. She's a crackerjack diplomat. This insult isn't an accident. We are persona non grata."

The two watched as the secretary breezed into Parker's office, shutting the door. Coming out a few moments later, she left the door ajar and resumed her place at her workstation, while they heard Parker in his booming voice returning a phone call to some friend and talk fishing. The conversation rolled on and on while Walker's temperature rose. Finally, they heard the chief hang up, and his large imposing frame appeared at his door. With a slight frown, he motioned at them through the window.

"Captain Walker, would you come this way?"

The two men strolled into his imposing office. Parker sat down but did not offer them a seat. Walker swallowed his pride and nodded toward Scroggins. "Chief, this my assistant, Bob Scroggins."

Parker merely nodded at Scroggins. "What do you need, Captain?"

"Chief, early indications are that Stewart had assistance from certain unknown members of the Arlington underground in escaping and hiding. I know this isn't your case, but we could use some help from your department since you know the lay of the land."

"What do you mean by Arlington underground?"

"The criminal element, sir."

"Other than some petty thieves, I think any organized criminal element would come from Fort Worth. I'm not aware of any significant criminal element here in Arlington. You have been misinformed, Captain."

Walker stared at him in surprise, saying nothing for a moment. "Chief, it's possible that I've been misinformed. Like I say, we don't know the lay of the land here. What I'm specifically asking for is you having your officers check with their snitches for any leads they can come up with and passing that information on to us."

"Like you say, Captain, it's not my case. As I'm sure you know, snitches have a limited usage before criminals figure out who they are. I would be jeopardizing my department's effectiveness if I granted your request. I'm afraid that it's out of the question."

Scroggins inhaled, starting to speak, but Walker stepped on his foot. Walker continued. "Chief, this is not only a big case, but one of your citizens has been killed and another one seriously wounded. I think you have a vested interest here."

"It didn't happen in my city, sir. I was able to cooperate with your sheriff yesterday on some of these matters. He hasn't even bothered to call and thank me. He's sent his officers into my city without coordinating it with me. This is not just a violation of protocol, gentlemen. You guys could mess up half of my ongoing investigations while you're kicking over every trashcan in this city. Anything else?"

Walker turned to leave but stopped and turned his reddening face toward the chief. "I was going to share some of the things we've uncovered while we were kicking over those trashcans, like finding out one of your sergeants is dirty. But that might violate one of your precious protocols, so I won't bother. As for the sheriff, I'm sure he'll call you when he can. He hasn't slept since this thing went down and neither have we. It's not my place to respond to the reception we've received here, but you can rest assured it will be reported. In the past, whenever your officers have come to us needing help, we've assisted whenever possible. I wouldn't count on that to continue." Walker stormed out with Scroggins following.

When they were back in their unit, Walker checked his watch. It was 5:30. "Let's get to the meeting, Bob. I want to get out of this damn town before I explode."

Scroggins stroked his chin in thoughtful silence. "Captain, I've been a policeman for twenty years and haven't seen anything like this."

"I know. I'm wondering if anybody will believe us when we announce this at the meeting?"

"I can't believe it and I was standing there. There's something bad wrong here."

"What do you mean?"

"I don't know. Something's wrong. I can't put my finger on it."

Ray opened the front door for Cass and the kids, who were returning from their shopping spree. Little Jan's eyes were shining with excitement as she displayed her new purchases. "Daddy! Daddy! Look what Cass bought for me." Jan held up a fancy matching blouse and scarf.

"That's nice, honey. Take it upstairs and I'll look at it later. What did you get, Robbie?"

"A pair of jeans and two new shirts."

"Do you like them?"

"Yes, Daddy. Cass let me pick them out myself."

Ray returned Cass's smile. "Did you have fun playing mother?"

"I sure did. I'm spoiling them rotten."

"I was just on the way out the door to do that wedding. I'm glad you got back here before I left. I was getting a little worried."

"We were fine. The guards were always close by. Now it's my turn to worry about you. When will you be back?"

"I'll be okay. Stewart has no way of knowing where I'll be."

"How many guards are you taking with you?"

"None. There's no need to."

"You ought to take one with you. There's plenty here."

"He'd just get in the way."

"Ray, you're just being macho. I'd feel better if one went with you. Did you talk to Marilyn today?"

"Yeah. But I barely got a word in edgewise. We couldn't talk long."

"Did you tell her about us?"

"I never had the chance."

"When are you going to tell her?"

"Monday, I guess. She's going out of town this weekend."

"Gee. That's too bad," said Cass with a mischievous smile.

Ray smiled and gave her a hug. "I'll be back before you know it."

Larry Blair found a seat beside Frances, who looked up and smiled. Francis was conscious of his interest, but wasn't sure what she wanted to do about it. An office romance was never a good idea, but he was cute.

"Did you do any good in Arlington today?"

"Not much. I hear you had a good day, though."

"What do you mean?"

"The captain said the sheriff really bragged on you."

"Really? I didn't do much."

"That's not what Walker said."

"What did he say?"

"He said you who uncovered Stewart's contact with the underground."

"It's not airtight by any means."

"No. But it's a start. I'm glad it was you who uncovered it."

"Why's that?"

"I'd like to see you do well here."

"Why?"

"Why, why, why! You sound like my five-year-old niece." They both broke into laughter. Frances's face showed dimples when she laughed. "You look real pretty when you smile."

"Thank you, Larry. You're sweet. If I didn't know better, I'd think you were flirting with me."

"I am flirting with you. How about dinner after the meeting?"

"You're not married, are you?"

"No, sirree."

"Isn't there a policy here about dating in-house?"

"Not that I have seen. Besides, the captain in civil affairs married his secretary last year. He'd be hard put to come down on us."

Frances laughed again. "That would be awkward, wouldn't it?"

"Yeah. How about it?"

"Let me have a rain check and I'll think about it. I don't think I've been here long enough to make waves. Besides, I have work to do, and you look like you could use some rest."

"Does it show that much?"

"I know you're tired. Nobody got much sleep last night."

"Okay. You have a rain check. You'll be comfortable here by next week."

"By next week?"

"As good as you are, you'll be pushing for lieutenant by next week."

"How long have you been in this department?"

"Three months."

"Do you like it?"

"Yeah. The hours are long but I really like busting perps." A throat clearing at the microphone interrupted them. Gary Baker was standing at the podium. The meeting was more lightly attended this evening. It was obvious that there wasn't any earthshaking news.

It was 7:15 when Ray pulled into the parking lot by the wedding gazebo. Since no parking places were left, he pulled back out and proceeded to the next one, which was about eighty yards away. The lot was nearly full, so he had to park on the back row. Dashing between the vehicles, he arrived out of breath at the gazebo to greet the anxious groom and his father. The area was packed with people, and Ray could see some man setting up loud speakers next to a large tape player. There were four people with video cameras jockeying for position inside the gazebo. The grand parents were being seated. There was little time to check the details. As nonchalantly as possible, he sauntered up to the groom. Charlie Fletcher was a young man who looked more nervous than a mass murderer at confession. He was dressed in a black tuxedo with matching patent leather shoes. Sweat pouring off his forehead, he held a lit cigarette in each shaking hand.

"Judge, where have you been? I thought you were going to be here about thirty minutes ago to tell us what we needed to do."

"Everything's fine, Charlie. Just follow my lead. Let me see your marriage license. I have to make sure you aren't going to escape this life sentence on a technicality."

Charlie laughed nervously. "My best man has it. Hey, Darrell! Come over here. The judge needs the license."

"Yes sir. It's right here."

"Good. Do you have the bride's ring?"

"Yes sir. Do you want it now?"

"No. I'll reach for it during the ceremony. Where's the bride?"

"She's over in those dressing rooms with her father."

"Okay. I'm going to take a minute and talk to her. Do you know if they're going to play any music during the ceremony?"

"No. Just before and after."

"I'll be back in a minute." Ray approached the disc jockey. "Do you have a portable mike for me?"

"Yeah. Right here. Just clip it to your belt and attach the mike about a foot below your mouth on your tie."

"Thanks. Need anything from me?"

"I need to know when to turn on the recessional."

"Hit it just as soon as I turn them around and announce them as the new Mr. and Mrs. Fletcher. Also, when Amy comes up with her father, do a four-second fade-out with the music."

"You got it."

Ray nodded and headed to the dressing rooms, where a proud father with his beautiful brunette daughter awaited. The bride had a full-length white gown, complete with train and a two-hundred-dollar bridal bouquet clutched in her shaking hands. Her maid of honor came forward with Ray's boutonniere.

"Hello, Amy. You look really nice. Charlie's a lucky guy."

"Thank you, Judge. I was getting worried about you with all the tragic news."

"I'm okay, and I'm sorry I'm late."

"That's okay. I really expected you to cancel. Thanks for coming. Is there anything I need to know about the ceremony?"

"Not really. When you and your father come in, the music will fade out. I'll ask Ben who gives you away, and he needs to say, 'Her mother and I,' then he puts your hand in Charlie's and sits down. When I reach for the rings, hand your bouquet to your maid of honor. She'll keep the flowers until you and Charlie exit. I'll take care of everything else. Okay?"

"I've got it."

Ray walked briskly back to the gazebo just in time to take his place and march inside with Charlie and Darrell. The crowd of two hundred closed in, leaving a narrow aisle for the maid of honor, the bride, and her father. As Ray took his place, he looked out to his right at the setting sun as the slightly chubby maid of honor slowly walked toward them. When she took her place, Ben Jordan came forward with his daughter, as the immediate family stood to show the traditional respect. Ray waited for the musician to fade the music. He was right on cue.

"Who presents this woman to this man?"

"Her mother and I."

Ray nodded and smiled. "Thank you, Ben." He turned slowly, facing the family. "You may be seated." Ben Jordan took his seat by his ex-wife as the rest of the family sat down. Ray's eyes calmly swept the crowd as he waited for the rustling to stop.

"Friends and family members, we're gathered here for a very glad and joyous occasion: that of witnessing and celebrating the marriage of Charlie Fletcher and Amy Jordan. Although this is a civil ceremony, I would like to remind everyone present that from man's very beginning, marriage has been an institution of God. It has been subject to the direction, sanctions, and protection of God's laws since long before man's laws were ever put into writing. This is confirmed in the scriptures." Ray continued with his traditional ceremony as the sun slowly set to his right. In the gathering darkness, the families shed tears of mixed emotion to the tune of noisy locusts. Fifteen minutes later, as bulbs flashed, the newly married couple faced their families and friends, who were applauding wildly. Amy retrieved her bouquet and placed her left arm in Charlie's. Ray announced to the group, "May I now present Mr. and Mrs. Charlie and Amy Fletcher."

The music kicked in on cue and the couple walked through the center of the crowd to ringing applause. Ray followed along behind the best man and maid of honor as the whole crowd proceeded to a nearby pavilion. A huge wedding cake was displayed next to a punch bowl filled with a champagne cocktail. After several minutes of congratulations and well-wishing, the groom's father pulled Ray aside.

"Ray, I really appreciate you coming tonight. I know this has been a trying week for you." Fletcher took an envelope out of his pocket and presented it to Ray.

"Mr. Fletcher, that's not necessary. I sure don't need any fees after all you have done for the sheriff and me. This is the least I could do."

"No, Ray. You take this. I mean it. I know the sheriff tried to talk you out of coming tonight. You did a great job, and I wouldn't have blamed you if you'd canceled. My wife and I would be disappointed if you didn't take this small token of our appreciation."

Ray reluctantly accepted the envelope and slipped it into his left coat pocket. "Thank you, Mr. Fletcher. I still feel guilty taking this after all you've done. I won't be able to stay long. I've got strict orders from the sheriff to get out of sight."

"I understand. Any progress in catching that asshole?"

"I don't think we have any definite leads yet. If anything works, it will be the reward. If it's all right with you, I'm going to put this fee in the reward fund."

"That's fine, if that's what you want to do. In fact, I'll match it. I'll call Lee in the morning about it."

"Thank you, sir. I'd better be going. Charlie looks pretty busy. Tell him to call me if he and Amy ever need anything."

"I will. You keep your head down until this is over, you hear?"

Ray nodded with a smile and turned away in the fast-falling darkness. He quickly retreated toward the distant parking lot, lost in thought. Should he spend the night again with Cass with the children in the house? It didn't seem quite right. It wasn't fair to her, either, at least until he made up his mind on what to do about Marilyn. Letting Marilyn go would be difficult and he didn't know if he really ... A silhouetted figure dressed in black leaped from behind a van and slashed at Ray with a knife that gleamed in the light from a distant parking lot. By turning to his right, Ray managed to deflect the knife only slightly, from his heart to his left shoulder. Feeling a searing pain, he reflexively sent a crescent kick to the assailant's right hand, sending the knife flying away in the dark. With mounting fury, he aimed a snap kick to his groin, which doubled the man over. As the man cried out in pain, Ray came back with another snap kick to the man's knee and followed through with a roundhouse kick to the chin. The man went down with a scream. Ray glanced down to make sure the knife was not close to the man and noticed that blood was streaming from his own left shoulder and arm. It was starting to hurt like hell. Ray reached down and grabbed the man by his jacket and jerked him to his feet, revealing a young Hispanic who looked vaguely familiar. Ray slammed him back against the van twice. As the screams continued, Ray looked through the window of the van and saw another figure in the rearview mirror, holding a pistol and approaching him from behind the vehicle.

Ray jerked the kid around to his right as the second assailant came around the van, with the gun firing twice. The kid took both bullets, sagging in Ray's hands. The second man stopped in his tracks and stared at the kid in Ray's grasp. Ray closed the five-foot distance between them and launched a crescent kick with his left foot, sending the gun hurtling through the darkness. That sent the man running off through the cars. Ray never got a look at him. Glancing around to make sure there were no more attackers, he eased the wounded boy to the ground. The kid, gasping for air and blood streaming from his mouth, looked at Ray with pleading eyes. Ray opened his jacket and looked for wounds, not finding any in front. Rolling him over halfway, he saw blood streaming from the two holes in the dark jacket. After rolling him back, he staggered to his car and left, deciding not to disturb the wedding party.

Leonard Torrey walked into the Elk's Lodge in Arlington and looked around. The Arlington Bar Association held a reception here every Friday night. The room was crowded with attorneys and a few judges. Each judge was holding court, with a group of attorneys gathered around. Torrey headed to the cash bar and ordered a drink. As he nursed it, one of the lady attorneys eased over. He searched his brain trying to remember her name.

"Hello, Leonard. Long time, no see. My name's Celia Townsend, in case you don't remember. You've been in the newspaper a lot this week."

"Hi, Celia. Sure I remember you. How have you been?"

"Just fine. I just don't lead the adventurous life that you do. It seems that you've picked up an interesting client."

"You mean Stewart?"

"Who else? Do you know where he is?"

"If I did, I couldn't tell you."

Celia threw her head back and laughed, shaking her pretty black hair. "Leonard, don't be so mysterious. Do you or don't you?"

Torrey smiled his best smile. "Can you keep a secret?"

"Sure. I'm dying to know."

"I don't have a clue where he is."

"Leonard, you shit." This time they both laughed. Celia cocked her head at him. "Are you still footloose and fancy-free?"

"Yeah. No self-respecting woman would have me."

"Why is that?"

Torrey eyed her thoughtfully. Celia was probably a clinger. On the other hand, he might be able to wheedle some financial support. "Because I'm a sex maniac."

"Yeah? Is that a promise?"

"Are you interested?"

"Maybe. I've been loose myself for quite a while."

"I thought you were going strong with Earl Leadbetter."

"That's ancient history."

"Oh. How's your practice doing?"

"Hey, boy. Are you only interested in my money? The last time I heard, you weren't doing very well."

Torrey smiled at her and withdrew his billfold, casually flipping the hundred- dollar bills. Celia smiled back. "Is that money from Stewart?"

"No. I hate to disappoint you, but it's not."

"Have you heard from him since yesterday?"

"No. I thought I'd nose around here in Arlington and sniff out where he might be."

"What are you going to do if you find him?"

"I don't know for sure. Try to get his side of this, I guess."

"Are you just curious or do you have a purpose for all this?"

"No. I have a purpose all right. If I defend this clown, I could get a lot of exposure. Win or lose, I could jump several steps up the ladder."

"You said if. Aren't you his attorney?"

"He sure as hell didn't hire me for this. I'm representing him on something else."

"Do you think he did this? Someone quoted you in the paper as saying he was set up."

"I know. If he did do it, I'm surprised he got away. I didn't think he was that smart."

"Where are you going to start?"

"His grandmother."

"Are you going to see her in the morning?"

"No. I'm going over there tonight. She works so much, she's hard to find in the daytime."

"Can I go with you?"

"Sure. She might respond to you more than me."

"What are we doing hanging around here then?"

"I just wanted to mosey around. I haven't seen most of these guys in quite a while. I thought I'd mix a little and see what scuttlebutt was afoot. Is there much going on around here?"

Celia put her arm through his and led him back to the bar for another drink. After obtaining fresh drinks, they networked through the groups, with Torrey enjoying his newfound notoriety. He finally spotted the silver-haired attorney he was looking for.

"Celia, isn't that John Webb over there?"

"Yeah."

"Is he still hot in oil and gas?"

"The hottest around."

"I heard that he's expanded with several new junior attorneys."

"Not really. That firm has stayed the same for years, unless you count his nephew, George Masters. He joined the firm about three years ago."

"How's he doing?"

"Fine, I guess. I don't keep up with him. He hates my guts."

"Why?"

"When he got out of law school, he ran for JP. He got mad at me because I wouldn't support him. That kid couldn't hold a candle to Ray Sterrett and I told him so."

Torrey dropped his drink on the floor. All talking ceased as eyes turned to him. Torrey didn't notice. He was staring at Webb with an open mouth.

Chapter Seventeen

Sheriff Lee Sanders swirled his highball, surveying the crowd as people mixed easily, the hum of voices rising in volume every minute. The party had been advertised as a combination fund-raiser and housewarming party. Sanders counted forty-one people, excluding his wife Delores and the catering crew. With a few people still drifting in, it looked like the party would be a rousing success. Delores caught his eye and smiled as she headed toward one of the car dealers. She was in her element as a hostess.

They had scrimped and saved for this house since they had moved from west Texas. Real estate was a lot higher here. Waiting several years, they had finally found a house in North Richland Hills that was only two years old, but had every thing they had dreamed of. It was a modern two-story with an acre of land. Lee shuddered when he wondered how he would pay the mortgage if he lost the next election. That was the danger of politics.

Lee ambled over to the bar and refreshed his highball. It was time to mix with the crowd. He drifted to the largest group, consisting of the county judge and several business leaders. The county judge looked up with a smile and put his arm around Lee. "Sheriff, how's the investigation?"

"Well, it's early yet. I think that reward will shake something loose. It looks like the underground is hiding him. We're shaking the bushes in Arlington. Nothing yet, though."

The rest of the group grew silent as the sheriff spoke, hoping to get some inside information. One of the bankers spoke up. "Sheriff, how did that jerk get away? I can't believe some numbskull can walk into one of our county facilities, do something like that, and get away clean."

"George, this guy had worked across the street for several months. He knew the area very well. And frankly, I'm as surprised as much as anyone else that he got away. He planned it remarkably well."

"Isn't he just a high school graduate?"

"That's right. But, you can be smart and not go to college. This guy looks pretty smart to me."

"How long did it take to get the first units to the scene?"

"Fourteen minutes. Mansfield PD got there first. But I don't think it would have mattered if they had got there in half the time."

"Why's that?"

"Because I think he used an underground drainage culvert to escape. He would've escaped a net even if we'd set it up in five minutes."

One of the ladies broke in. "Is your department going to honor Judge Chavez at his funeral tomorrow?"

"We'll provide an honor guard, one for Deputy Walling as well."

"Sheriff, how do you know which shots killed that poor girl?"

"The medical examiner's office determined that the lethal wound was caused from a bullet that was fired from the direction opposite from where Constable Walling and his deputies were firing from. There was no blood loss around the face wounds."

"Do you think this Stewart killed her?"

"Probably. But there's no ballistics."

"This Stewart must be a cold-blooded monster."

"That's easy to determine. What isn't easy is to figure out where he is."

"Do you still think he's still in this area?"

"He could be anywhere from here to South America."

"Why South America?"

"Someone in Arlington has the capability to ship him there."

"Is that your best guess?"

"No. It's just one possibility. There are several people in Arlington with the resources to hide him, or move him out of state or out of the country."

The county judge inserted a question. "Wouldn't it take a lot of money for that kid to go to South America?"

"It wouldn't take a lot of money to get there, but it would take a lot to stay there. I don't have a best guess yet, but I think it's more likely he'll stay in this country. He could melt into the background anywhere in the South, working anywhere they pay cash, or he could use a phony social security number. If he did that, he could stay just about anywhere for three months or so before they could catch up with him. I've sent his face and prints to NCIC just in case he left the state."

"Does he have any hiding money?"

"I think he could have a few thousand."

"Did he have an extra car to escape in?"

"Not that we know of. He might have stolen one. We included all license plates in our APB to an eleven-state area, with instructions to contact us if an unlicensed driver is caught with one. In addition, we're concentrating on the Dallas and Austin areas. The police chiefs there are distributing his picture to the patrolmen at shift changes."

The lady got back in the conversation. "You don't think he's still hanging around here to get Judge Sterrett, do you?"

"I don't think so, but precautions are being taken."

"Sheriff, if he was hell-bent enough to do what he did, he could still kill again. He may not care whether he's caught or not."

"That's true. That's why precautions are being taken. If I can just keep Sterrett under wraps, he'll be okay. He's out doing a wedding tonight. I couldn't talk him out of it."

Delores Sanders eased into the group and slipped her arm into her husband's. She smiled at the group and whispered into Lee's ear. "Someone from your office is on the phone. She says it's important."

Lee nodded and headed for the phone in his study. "Hello?"

"Sheriff, this is Frances. I'm sorry to disturb you at home."

"No problem, Frances. What's up?"

"I went back with the lip-reader and reviewed the tape we looked at when Stewart was talking to the other guy in the waiting room. We were able to get most of Stewart's conversation but not the other guy's."

"Good. What did he say?"

"He was definitely asking for Hawkins. He called him the Blade. I found out that's what he goes by here in jail."

"Did he talk to this guy before or after he talked to Hawkins?"

"Before."

"I guess that just proves that he didn't know who Hawkins was. That's not much, I'm afraid. What else did he say to this guy?"

"Not much. But it proves he went on sick call looking for Hawkins. I went back and checked the records. Hawkins goes on sick call every day. He has a mild form of rheumatoid arthritis. Get this: Stewart went on sick call for a tennis elbow. They would see the same doctor."

"Nice work, Frances. Now we need to figure out who sent him to Hawkins."

"That's not so easy. I've reviewed the tapes from book-in when Stewart came in. He was there for four hours and talked to sixteen different prisoners. It could've been any of them. I've interviewed five so far, with no results. Six are no longer in jail."

"Keep working on it. This is all we have for now."

"Sheriff, there's something else, too. I'm not sure it's connected."

"Tell me about it."

"Harry Fletcher called in to dispatch about five minutes ago and said there was a murder about a hundred yards from his son's wedding."

"When did it happen and how?"

"It happened about ten minutes after the ceremony. Somebody got shot. He said it was some Hispanic kid."

"Was Ray Sterrett still with the wedding party?"

"No. Fletcher said he'd just left."

"Was Sterrett gone when this happened?"

"Fletcher wasn't sure. He didn't know where Sterrett was parked. He just said they heard two gunshots in an adjacent parking lot. They investigated and found a dead Hispanic kid laying in the parking lot."

"How many shots did this kid take?"

"They don't know. We dispatched Arlington PD to the scene, and I also sent one of our units. We'll know more in about twenty minutes. Do you want me to keep you advised?"

Sanders thought a minute. "No. There's probably no connection to the wedding. Have our unit make an independent report and have it on my desk in the morning. I'm not sure I can count on Arlington to provide one after what happened to Walker and Scroggins this afternoon."

"Will do, Sheriff. Sorry again for bothering you."

"That's okay, Frances. Don't ever hesitate to call me. Have Scroggins and Walker gone off duty?"

"Yes sir. They're worn out. No one's had any sleep for forty-eight hours. I'm not far behind them. I've alerted the bond desk to call me if any of the remaining prisoners on my list are due to get out. I'll get the rest of them in the morning."

"That's fine, Frances. I'll see you in the morning." Sanders hung up and dialed the security detail for Sterrett. He hung up when he heard screams in his living room. He ran into the foyer and gazed at Ray Sterrett lying on his floor, his blood running on the tile.

Torrey and Celia Townsend stared through the screen door at a careworn Gladys Stewart. It didn't look like she was going to let them in. Torrey put on his warmest smile. "Your grandson's in a lot of trouble. Can't we come in for just a few minutes? It could be important."

Gladys Stewart lowered her head, and opened the door, and led them into a very plain living room. Torrey and Celia Townsend sat together on the weather-beaten sofa, while the saddened grandmother sat in her rocker, directly across from them. "What do you want, Mr. Torrey?"

"Mrs. Stewart, this is my associate, Miss Celia Townsend."

Mrs. Stewart nodded to Celia and looked back at Torrey. "What do you want?"

"Have you heard from Billy?"

"Would you tell the police if I did?"

"Not necessarily. Has he called you?"

"No. I don't think he will either."

"Why not?"

"I got a letter from him today."

"What did the letter say?"

"Good-bye." Mrs. Stewart started crying.

Celia went over to her and held her hand. "Mrs. Stewart, I'm so sorry for the trouble this has brought you. Is there anything I can do for you? Is there anyone you want me to call?"

"No," she sobbed. "I have no family here. That's very kind, though."

Celia moved to the floor, sitting next to Mrs. Stewart and stroked her hand. "Could we see the letter, Mrs. Stewart?"

"No. It's personal."

Torrey watched this with a solemn look. "Mrs. Stewart, did Billy mention the shooting in his letter?"

"Not directly."

"It could be very important that I look at that letter."

"Why?"

"If the police come for that letter, you'll have to give it to them. There might be something that they could use against Billy."

"Then I won't tell them about it."

"You could be committing a criminal offense by lying to them."

"I don't care. I don't want anyone to see that letter."

Celia looked at her while she continued stroking her hand. "Mrs. Stewart, we are his lawyers. Anything we see or hear is attorney-client privilege. It would be against the law for us to divulge that letter's contents to anyone."

Mrs. Stewart started crying again. Celia said nothing as she continued stroking her hand. Torrey excused himself to the restroom. Celia finally looked up at the sobbing grandmother. "There's something in that letter that you're ashamed of, isn't there, Mrs. Stewart?"

Gladys Stewart nodded her head and continued sobbing.

"Mrs. Stewart, you'll have to choose. Do you want the police to see that letter, or would you rather us look at it?"

"It's my letter."

"The police could get a court order to make you surrender it."

"Why?"

"If there's any thing in that letter that indicates that Billy did the shooting, the police are entitled to it under the law. Is there anything in the letter about that?"

"Not exactly."

"What does the letter say?"

"It says I won't ever see him again."

"Mrs. Stewart, can I see the letter? Please?"

Mrs. Stewart extricated her hand and reached over to her Bible and produced the letter. Celia read the letter as Torrey returned from the bathroom. He started to read over her shoulder, but Celia shook her head no. Silently, he returned to the sofa and watched Celia read the three-page letter. As Celia handed it back to Mrs. Stewart, she looked at the envelope. Torrey saw her eyes widen, then she gave the envelope to him. He looked at the envelope and didn't see anything special about it. There was no return address, and it was addressed in a masculine scrawl. Torrey looked up at Celia with a puzzled expression.

"Leonard, that letter was mailed the day before the shooting."

"So?"

"Although the letter doesn't admit anything, he does tell his grandmother that she'll know everything when she gets it. It clearly shows intent."

Torrey nodded. "Mrs. Stewart, you better let us take this letter and hold it for you. If I have it, the police cannot make me turn it over. As his attorney, I don't have to give them information that would incriminate him. If you keep it, you'd have to turn it over. You wouldn't want to help convict him, would you?"

"No."

"Then let me keep it. You can have it back when this is all over."

"Do you promise not to read it?"

"All right. I won't read it. I'll just keep it safe."

Reluctantly, she handed the letter to Celia, who handed it to Torrey. Torrey put the letter into his coat pocket. "Mrs. Stewart, do you have any inkling about where he might be?"

"No. He says that he's hiding with newfound friends and for me not to try to contact him. He says that he'll never be able to come home again."

"Did you give him any money when he got out of jail?"

"No. I didn't have any. I had to borrow the money to pay you "

"Did he have any money?"

"I don't think he had very much."

"Do you think that he's on the run with limited funds?"

"I guess so."

"Then he'll probably call you when he runs out."

"I don't have any more money to give him. What should I do?"

"Have him call me before he does anything."

"What can you do?"

"Probably save his life."

"What do you mean?"

"He will need an intermediary to turn himself in. If the police find him first, they'll kill him."

Cass met Ray and the sheriff at the door. Sanders was supporting Ray, his arm around him as they staggered in. Ray looked pale from the loss of blood. His eyes had a vacant look and he could barely walk. His suit was ruined, with bloodstains running halfway down his trouser leg. Sanders glanced up at Cass. "Is the doctor here yet?"

"Yes. He's waiting in the lower bedroom."

"Good. Let's get him in there. He's pretty weak."

"How serious is this? He looks bad."

"He'll be okay in a few days. We stopped most of the bleeding."

A youngish-looking black doctor awaited them in the bedroom. He was a resident at John Peter Smith Hospital, the county hospital that handled the county jail patients. Ray's doctor was out of town. It was the best Sanders could do on short notice. The young doctor eased Ray to the bed and glanced at Cass. "Would you take his shoes off, please? After that, slide him out of his trousers." The doctor took a large pair of scissors out of his bag and cut the coat and shirt away from the wound with practiced ease. After pausing, he removed a bloody makeshift bandage from the wound by slicing it away from the tape with a small scalpel. The small wound was still seeping blood. The doctor looked up at Sanders. "We need to take him to ER. He has at least one vein severed. I need to retie it. He also needs some blood. I need his medical history for his blood type and to see if he's allergic to anything. This isn't just a patch-up job."

"Doctor, it would be really dangerous to take him there. Somebody's trying to kill him."

"We can admit him under a John Doe."

"That's still dangerous. Is there any way he can be treated here?"

"It's risky. Something could go wrong. All I could do here is tie off the vein."

"Something could go wrong at the hospital, too. You don't know what's involved here."

The doctor fished a small flashlight out of his bag and studied Ray's eyes. "See if he has any medical information in his billfold."

Cass pulled his wallet out and went through the cards. "Yes. Here's something. He has A-positive blood and he is allergic to Vibramiacin."

"Good. I need to use your phone. Sheriff, can you have one of your units bring over a pint of blood and some medical supplies? An ER nurse is needed, too."

"Sure. Can I send one of my units here? My units at the hospital don't know about this hiding place."

"I want to move quickly. This man can go into shock at any time."

The sheriff thought quickly. "I'll have your unit meet mine. Get the nurse and the supplies together. I'll have a unit at the ER door in two minutes. Will that work?"

"I guess so." The doctor left the room and found a phone, returning two minutes later to give Ray an injection in each arm. After sending Cass scurrying to find alcohol and hot water, he gently pressed around the wound. Ray groaned and jumped reflexively.

"That's all right. That shoulder will be dead in a minute. I also gave you a tetanus shot in the other arm. You'll be feeling better in no time." Replacing the ice compress on the wound, he removed the rest of Ray's shirt while Cass brought him some washcloths out of the bathroom.

Lee Sanders returned as the doctor was soaking one of the washcloths in alcohol. He started cleaning around the wound. "Sheriff, are the nurse and supplies on the way?"

"Yes. They left about a minute ago."

"Good. I need some lamps moved over here."

Sanders summoned two of the security men, who started bringing lamps from other rooms, placing them on the bookcase above the bed. The doctor shielded Ray's eyes with a washcloth. He pressed harder on Ray's shoulder, got no response and then removed the ice compress. The bleeding had slowed to a trickle. After directing the sheriff to hold the doctor's small flashlight above the wound, he gently probed the wound. "The knife penetrated all the way to the bone and bruised it. His shoulder's going to be sore for a week. You'll have to keep him still."

"How about the vein?"

"There are two veins damaged, but I can ligate them without too much trouble. He's lucky, though. That knife missed the main artery by a quarter of an inch. I'll give him a pint of blood and put him on an IV for a couple of days. That will fight infection and speed the healing process."

"Thank you, Doctor. I really appreciate you doing this here."

The doctor merely nodded as he checked Ray's blood pressure. Cass moved to the other side of the bed and held Ray's right hand while this was going on. The sheriff watched thoughtfully.

Minutes later, the security team arrived with the nurse. As they were bustling in the equipment and supplies, the sheriff approached his security supervisor, who was drinking coffee in the kitchen. "Charles, why didn't you send a guard with Sterrett?"

"I offered to, but he said no. In the absence of orders, I felt I had to let him go."

"Yeah. You're right. This is my fault. No one was supposed to know about this wedding."

"How bad is he?"

"He'll be all right. The knife missed the artery."

"Was it Stewart that attacked him?"

"There was a dead man at the scene. It wasn't Stewart, but there was somebody else there and we don't know who that was. Sterrett told me the other guy shot at him, and he shielded himself with the kid that got killed. Sterrett didn't get a good look at him but he didn't think it was Stewart."

"How could they have known where Sterrett was?"

"I have no idea. It's possible this incident had nothing to do with the shootings, but my instincts tell me otherwise."

"Do you think Stewart hired these guys to kill Sterrett?"

"Could be. It kind of stretches the imagination, though. If that's what happened, it means that Stewart's still in the area."

"It also means that Stewart is determined to get Sterrett. I can't figure Stewart being resourceful enough to get this kind of information. It doesn't add up."

"Yeah. He'd to have some help on the inside to find out where Sterrett was going to be unless he knows somebody in the wedding party."

"Was there any publicity on the wedding?"

"I don't think so, but I'll check. I'm going to assign three more units out here. I want you to deploy them two blocks away. If anyone comes snooping around, nail their ass. Have them run all license plates of cars who even slow down going by this place."

"Do you think he might be in danger here?"

"I don't know what to think. I know I want Stewart caught. We can't rest until he is. Who's keeping an eye on the kids?"

"Goldstein."

"Are they asleep?"

"Yes."

The sheriff reached for the phone and dialed dispatch. "This is unit one. Which unit investigated the shooting at River Legacy Park?"

"Unit seventeen, sir."

"Who's that?"

"Cunningham, sir."

"Can you patch me through?"

"Yes sir. Routing you now."

"This is unit seventeen. Go ahead. Over."

"This is unit one. Is this Cunningham?"

"Yes sir."

"Cunningham, give me all you have on that shooting."

"Sheriff, the dead man is Jose Cruz. DOB is 9-14-77. Criminal history shows three arrests. Two for Class A theft and one for assault with a deadly weapon. No convictions. Subject was found dead at the scene with two bullet holes in his back. One penetrated his heart. Subject has a brother named Pablo Cruz. Pablo is known to be a minor underworld figure here in Arlington. He has a longer history than Jose. There were no witnesses to the shooting. A thirty-eight Saturday night special was found thirteen feet away. Arlington PD is running prints on it now. A white bone-handled knife was found at the scene, with a seven-inch blade. They're also running it for prints. That's all I have right now, sir."

"Did anyone see a car leave after the shooting?"

"That's a dead end, sir. There was too much traffic for anyone to notice any one particular car."

"What's the estimated time of the shooting?"

"Between 7:45 and 7:50."

"Advise dispatch when they have print results on the pistol."

"Roger."

"Over and out." Sanders dialed Walkers office.

"Criminal investigation. This is Underwood."

"Chris, this is Sanders. Do you have the notes handy from the six o'clock briefing?"

"Yes sir. It'll take a minute to dig them out. Is there anything in particular that you need?"

"Yeah. Larry Blair mentioned some people one of the snitches spoke about. They were people who were in a restaurant this morning. It was a list of suspects who might be hiding Stewart. Run those names by me."

"Yes sir. Coming right up. Here they are. There was an Angel, Jerry, Mexican Joe, Devil, the Cruz brothers, and Rascal. The other ones mentioned were Lucky, Shorty, and Bullet."

"Go back to the Cruz brothers. Who were they with?"

"The report doesn't say, sir."

"Damn. Do you know where Blair is?"

"He's off duty. Probably home asleep. Everybody's tired."

"When did he go off duty?"

"Right after the meeting. Do you want me to call him?"

Sanders pondered this. His men needed rest. "Not yet. Call Arlington PD and see if they will give us information on the hangouts of Pablo Cruz and known associates."

"Do you want me to call you back when I get it, sir?"

"No. I'll call you back in fifteen minutes." Sanders hung up and looked up at Charles. "What's Stewart doing with the Mexican underground?"

The phone rang and Charles picked it up. "Yes? Hold on. It's for you, Sheriff. I think it's your wife."

"Hello?"

"Lee, the press are calling about Ray getting wounded."

"Damn. Did you tell them anything?"

"No. They already had the story."

"How did they find out, Delores?"

"I think someone from the party told them."

"How much do they know?"

"They know he came in here wounded. They also know you took him away to a hidden location. They were asking me where it is."

"Yeah. Fat chance. Who was it that called?"

"One said his name is Bryan Forrester."

"Did he leave a phone number?"

"Yes. 555-8802."

"I'll call him. Thanks. Anything else?"

"What time are you coming home?"

"Late, probably. I'm sorry."

"You're forgiven this time. I understand."

"Thanks, honey. I'll see you later."

Sanders hung up, cursing under his breath as he headed to check on Ray. The doctor and nurse were hooking up the IV. Cass was still holding Ray's hand and keeping the washcloths moist that were shading his eyes. Ray looked like he was asleep. His shoulder had a clean professional bandage on it. After inserting the needle in Ray's arm for the IV, the nurse laid out clean sheets on the other side of the bed. The doctor helped the nurse move him over and then cut away the bloody sheet. There was a blood spot on the mattress. The sheriff winced, thinking of the county's bill for the incidentals. Sanders tapped the doctor on the shoulder. "Doctor, can I talk to you privately?"

"Sure."

"Let's go into the other room." They headed into the kitchen, where the doctor helped himself to the coffee while the sheriff directed the security chief elsewhere. "Doctor, I never did catch your name."

"Pulliam, sir. Rodney Pulliam."

"Doctor Pulliam, you did a fine job in there. Thank you."

"You're welcome, Sheriff. Anytime. All in the line of duty."

"Will he have any damage from you tying off those veins?"

"No. The tissue feeds off of blood vessels, not the veins."

"No vessels were severed?"

"Thankfully, no."

"Is he up to talking tonight?"

"No. He needs rest. I've given him a mild sedative. He'll sleep for about ten hours. When he wakes up, he should be strong enough for talking."

"All right. I'll have to wait. I need to ask one more favor."

"What's that?"

"Don't tell anyone where you were tonight. Don't even make out a medical report for now. Make sure the nurse understands this, too."

"I gathered that there was some secret to this. I can wait to fill out a report, but I will need to make some notes for a later report."

"Can you leave the names and location out of the notes?

"Yes. I can do that."

"Good. Don't mention to anyone that this man was your patient. Not even your supervisor or your wife. The nurse, too, understood?"

"Yes sir. I understand."

"Thanks again. I'll have one of my units take you back to the hospital. Would you be kind enough to leave your phone numbers with Cass?"

"Sure. No problem."

Sanders nodded, returned to the bedroom, motioning Cass to follow him. They headed out to the patio and sat down by the pool. After the security man was motioned away, Sanders pulled out a cigarette.

"Sheriff, I didn't know you smoked."

"I quit years ago but I started back up today."

"Why?"

"The pressure, I guess. It helps calm me down. Is Ray asleep?"

"Yes. He fell asleep while the doctor was working on him."

"Are you satisfied with the doctor?"

"Yes. He was good."

"He's leaving his numbers in case something comes up."

"Good. Can you do something else for me?"

"Of course. What is it?"

"I would like his housekeeper brought out here. I need her help with the kids while I take care of him."

"Is morning soon enough?"

"Yes."

"I'll tend to it. I need to talk to you, and I'll come back in the morning to talk to Ray."

"About what?"

"I need to know several things about your office. Somehow, word got out on where Ray was tonight, and I've got to find out how."

"Do you think somebody in our office gave out that information?"

"It's one possibility."

"That's hard to believe. Phyllis was the only one there today and I don't think she would tell Stewart anything."

"She may have told someone else."

"You mean somebody else wants to kill the judge?"

"Possibly."

"Surely not, Sheriff. Maybe Stewart looked at the wedding schedule when he broke in and stole the money."

"Where are those records kept?"

"I keep a calendar book on my desk with that information. Anybody that was in my office could look at it. It's no big secret."

"How would Stewart know to look in that book?"

"I don't know. Maybe he browsed around while he was in there."

"Is a light kept on in your office at night?"

"Not usually, but sometimes the janitor leaves it on."

"If it was Stewart who broke in, why would he check on where Ray would be Friday night when he intended to kill him on Thursday morning?"

"I see what you mean. Besides, he would've noticed the notations that he would be out of town until then."

"Was that information in the book too?"

"Yeah. If he intended to kill the judge, he wouldn't have come in Thursday at all, not if he knew he would be out of town."

"Who else could have seen that book?"

"There were a lot of news people in there after the shooting. The constable's personnel have access and, of course, the janitor."

"Do you know the janitor's name?"

"No. Do you think there's a connection between him and Stewart?"

"You wouldn't think so, but Stewart's hard to figure."

"Why do you say that?"

"He seems too street-smart to not have a criminal record."

"Maybe you can thank his sleezeball attorney for that."

"Who's his attorney?"

"Leonard Torrey."

Sanders had to laugh. "Leonard Torrey? I don't think so. I don't like him much, but I can't see him getting involved."

"I don't know. His reputation is awful, and he was pretty mad at the judge when he left."

"Why was he mad?"

"The judge found him in contempt when he was in there with Stewart."

"Why?"

"Some remark that Torrey made. The judge fined him fifty dollars."

"That's the Torrey that I know. I don't see him sticking his neck out over something like that. He's been found in contempt by half the judges in this county. It seems like you had a full-moon week out there."

"Yeah! We had a hard week by 3:00 Monday afternoon."

"Did anyone else have a run-in with Ray this week?"

"Not in court that I know of, but there were several flaps going on."

"Tell me about them."

"Well, there was this litigant who paid off a five-thousand-dollar judgment Monday morning. But he wasn't mad at Ray, he was mad at the plaintiff's attorney. He plunked down the money in cash and stormed out cussing out everybody."

"He paid in cash? Was Stewart around when this happened?"

"As a matter of fact, he was. He was waiting to be transported to jail and was sitting in a chair watching all of this."

"That explains the break-in. He probably thought you kept a lot of money there. Could he have seen you put the money up?"

"I suppose so."

"Okay. Tell me what else happened that day."

"The judge got into a flap with the Arlington police chief. He thought a police officer let a man die because he didn't like him."

This perked up the sheriff. "Who was the police officer?"

"Sergeant Agnew."

The sheriff lit another cigarette while he digested that information. "Does Ray know Agnew?"

"Yes, and he hates him."

"How long has that been going on?"

"A long time, I think."

"Did Ray turn in a formal complaint to the chief about this?"

"I don't think he had time before he left town. I know he called the chief and he wasn't happy about it."

"Why not?"

"I don't know."

"Who else got mad at Ray this week?"

"There was a landlord who lost a case, but once I showed him the law, he calmed down. There was another eviction case where the tenants were mad. I don't know what happened in that trial. That's all I can think of."

"Do the names Jose or Pablo Cruz mean anything to you?"

"No."

"Has Ray had any bad disputes with any Hispanics lately?"

"I don't think so."

"How about Judge Chavez?"

"I don't know. You'd have to ask Tameta, his head clerk."

"When was Judge Chavez lined up to work at your office yesterday?"

"Last week."

"Was this the first time he had come out there?"

"No. He was out several times."

"Has Ray been working on any immigration problems lately?"

"No. Our court doesn't handle those type of cases."

Sanders took her back inside, returned to poolside, lit another cigarette, and pondered the situation as his security chief joined him. "Have you got all this figured out, Sheriff?"

"No. Things just don't quite tie together. This isn't going to be easy."

Chapter Eighteen

It was 8:05 Saturday morning when Torrey and Celia drove into the 7-Eleven parking lot on South Cooper in Arlington. Torrey left Celia in the car, strolled up to the pay phone and waited. There was a yellow out-of-order strip of tape across the phone, just as he had been told. From across the street, Buck Reed examined them through binoculars. Finally satisfied, he exited his car and walked to another pay phone next door. Fishing change out, he dialed the number of Torrey's phone.

"Hello?"

"Are you alone?"

"There's nobody where I'm standing. My girlfriend's in the car, but she can't hear our conversation."

"You were told to come alone."

"I spent the night with her last night and couldn't ditch her without a lot of questions?"

"You're being sloppy. Don't disobey my instructions again."

"All right. I don't see what it hurts, though. I have a number for you to call."

"Are these the people who wanted me here?"

"I believe so. I don't even know who they are. They appear to be careful people, just as you are."

"That's how I like to do business. What's the number?"

"555-3139."

Reed paused. Yes, he was still dealing with the same guy who wouldn't take no for an answer. "Is that a pay phone?"

"I'm told that it is."

"Do you know who the target is?"

"Yes. His name's Ray Sterrett. He's a justice of the peace."

"That's the same one that's on the front page this morning?"

"Yeah. The same one."

"Your contact couldn't wait for me to get down here? He had to send two amateurs after him last night and put him on his guard? That's not smart, Torrey."

"You'll have to take that up with him. I didn't know anything about it. It's possible our contact didn't even do that. Some other people are after this guy. That's why I think you've been brought in. Somebody else is going to get the credit for your work."

"I see. Who's going to get the blame?"

"A guy named Billy Stewart."

"Do you know him?"

"Yeah. He's one of my clients."

"If he's going to do the job, why do they need me?"

"I'm not sure. You'll have to ask him."

"Tell me everything you know about this Stewart."

Torrey relayed all the information that he had on his client while Reed listened without comment. When he was finished, Reed was far from satisfied. If Torrey was smart enough to be an attorney, why didn't he have better contacts in the sheriff's department? Reed decided to let it pass. "Okay. Tell me all you know about this Sterrett."

"You already know what he looks like. His picture is in the paper this morning. He's a hard-ass judge in his late forties. I remember something about him being a karate champion."

"Does he have a karate studio?"

"I don't know. Check the phone book."

"Do you know where he lives?"

"No. Maybe our contact can give you that information."

"What else can you tell me about this Sterrett?"

"Not much. I had never been in his court before Monday."

"Does he have a family?"

"I don't even know that."

"I remember the newspaper saying he was being hidden at an undisclosed location."

"I remember that, too."

"How am I supposed to find this guy? This has to happen before they catch Stewart."

"I don't have the answer to that. Ask our contact."

"When can I call our contact?"

"He'll be waiting for your call at 9:00 am."

"How can I find you later?"

"Call me on my pager."

"Okay. When you call me back, use a pay phone."

"I understand." The line went dead, and Torrey returned to the car, where Celia was looking across the street at a dark, slender man getting in his car next to the Mobil station.

Buck Reed watched Torrey's car disappear, making a mental note of the license plate number. He retrieved his newspaper and reread the front-page story on the attack on Sterrett. The article gave no clues as to his whereabouts. The picture helped but gave little insight as to the man himself. The man seemed to have eyes of steel. *Could I take him one-on-one?* he wondered. *Maybe not. I'm not as fast as I used to be. My last job could come this year,* he thought, checking his watch. It was 9:05 am. His contact should be waiting. Reed lit another cigarette and returned to the pay phone. He dialed the number and waited.

"Hello?"

"Who is this?"

"This is 555-3139."

"This is your friend from Tulsa."

"Good! I've been waiting for your call."

"Are you speaking from a pay phone?"

"Yes."

"Will I be able to reach you here in the future if I need to?"

"That can be arranged. I can be here at 7:30 am and 6:00 pm everyday until this is finished. I can wait ten minutes. That will be our only contact possibility."

"That's fine. I need all the information you have on the target, and we must arrange a money exchange. The fee will be $25,000 now and another $25,000 upon completion. In addition, I estimate that there will be $10,000 in expenses. That also is in advance." Reed heard a sharp intake of breath on the other end of the line.

"I'm not prepared for that. I was told your fee was $25,000. Nothing about extra expenses."

"Take it or leave it. The price doubles when elected officials are involved."

"I'm not prepared to do either at this point. I'm just a go-between. Can I get back to you in an hour?"

"I guess so. In the meantime, give me the scoop on this guy. I'll do some casing while you're checking with your source."

"The man is forty-six years old and a widower with two children. His home address is 4327 Paloma Place in Arlington. I don't think he's staying there right now. He's under the protection of the sheriff at an unknown location. He owns a karate studio on Bowen Road in Arlington. The name of it is 'Champions Defense'. He spends a lot of time there on the weekends. His court is in Mansfield. Right now the place is crawling with cops."

"That's good to know. What about a girlfriend? He won't stay away from her very long."

"There's no known steady girlfriend. He's seen occasionally with a reporter from the *Star-Telegram.*"

"What's her name?"

"Marilyn Shaw."

"Where does she live?"

"I don't know."

"You may have to find out. What else can you tell me?"

"I think he got hurt last night. A knife wound maybe."

"Was that your work?"

"No. We think that was Stewart's work. He'll get the credit for your work, too."

"That's perfect with me. Anything else?"

"Yeah. This guy is a past national champion in karate. Don't try to do this close up."

"I figured that out all ready. You must think I'm an amateur."

"Not at all. Your reputation precedes you."

"Where do his children go to school and what are their ages?"

"Their ages are six and eight. I don't know where they go to school."

"You better find that out."

"We don't want them harmed."

"I don't intend to, but I need to know where he's going to show up. I don't do children. By the way, is this guy a Vietnam vet?"

"Why? Are you telling me that you don't do Vietnam vets either?"

"I'm not asking for that reason. Is he?"

"I don't think so. He'd be a little too young. Why?"

"I just thought he might hang out at a VFW hall. Does he hang out at any clubs?"

"Negative. I don't think he's a drinker."

"How about golf or bowling?"

"I'm not aware of any activities in that direction."

"Is he Republican or Democrat?"

"He's a Republican. Do you do Republicans?"

Reed laughed. "Yeah. That's not a problem. What about this Stewart? Is he going to get caught before I can finish this job?"

"I have no idea. The inside word is that the sheriff's office is hunting him hard but they have few clues at the moment. It looks like you'll have time.

With what happened last night, he'd still get the blame if the target got it after he was caught."

"Do you know where he's hiding?"

"No."

"Why do you want this target taken out?"

"You don't need to know that."

"Okay. I'll call you back at this number in one hour. If you don't pick up, I'll consider the deal canceled."

"If it is, we'll still pick up your expenses down here."

"That's fair enough." Reed hung up and drove across the street to the 7-Eleven, and purchased a local Mapsco. Finding Paloma Place, he routed back to where he was. It looked like a twenty-minute drive.

At 9:30 Lee Sanders assembled Walker's team, who looked and sounded much better after a good night's rest. When the team read the police reports no one complained about the weekend. Sanders began speaking as Baker distributed handouts. "You're receiving the mug shots and criminal activities of the Cruz brothers. Jose is the one who was killed last night, and we think his brother Pablo is the one who fired the shots intended for Sterrett. We don't know why they did this, or how they found out where Sterrett was. As soon as this meeting is over, you will disperse and conduct new investigations on Pablo Cruz. If we can find Cruz, we'll probably find Stewart in the same place. Larry, you mentioned last night that the Cruz brothers were with one of the five criminals who might be hiding Stewart. Who was it?"

Larry Blair checked his notes. "A guy named Mexican Joe."

"What do you know about him?"

"According to our snitch, Mexican Joe owns a pawnshop on Division called Top Dollar Pawn. He runs illegals from Mexico and finds them jobs, taking a percentage. The snitch doesn't think he runs any hot merchandise in the pawnshop. He was in a restaurant with a sidekick named Devil, sitting with the Cruz brothers about 10:00 yesterday morning. That's all I know about him."

"Do you know his full name?"

"No. We can check the assumed name register."

"All right. Get someone on it. I want you and Carter to take ten men in unmarked cars and stake out that pawnshop. Follow any Hispanic who leaves there that don't look like a customer. If you find a hideout, call me and we'll assemble the troops for a raid. Gary, I want you to interview Phyllis and find out if she told anybody about that wedding yesterday. If she didn't, find out who may have been snooping around. Fred, I want you and Scroggins to go with me to interview Sterrett. Something don't look right about this. I can't see Stewart hiring hit men to get Sterrett."

Francis spoke up. "Sheriff, I have an idea."

All heads turned her way. Sanders nodded. "Go ahead."

"After Larry and the guys get in place at that pawnshop, I could go talk to this Mexican Joe and see if I can smoke him out. It would save time. If he checked, I still have my driver's license from Houston. I could cook up a story to let me get a look at the illegals."

Larry spoke up. "That could be dangerous, Francis. We don't know what we're dealing with in there. What if you get into trouble in there?"

"I'll wear a wire."

Sanders thoughtfully stroked his chin. It just might work. He nodded his head yes. "It sounds good to me. Francis, go home and put on some street clothes. Be sure to wear loose-fitting clothes for the wire. Draw out a hundred dollars in case you have to pay him. After you change, come back to the office and get fitted out with a wire. Test it with Larry before you go in. Set up code phrases for Stewart and Cruz. Let's plan for her to go in at 1:00 pm. Walker and I will be there by then. Larry, be sure to keep all the surveillance cars out of sight. I don't want to blow this. Does anyone else have anything before we leave?" No one spoke. "Let's move."

Reed drove slowly around Paloma Drive, watching everything. Sterrett lived in a modern, well-kept neighborhood. The house looked deserted, as expected. There was a stockade fence in the back, which pleased him immensely. What pleased him even more was the house across the street with a for sale sign in the front yard. The house looked vacant, but he couldn't be sure since the front drapes were closed. The yard needed mowing. That was a good sign. Sterrett's yard could use a mowing, too. Reed pulled into the driveway of the on-the-market house, and sat for a few moments, looking around and getting his bearings. This house had no stockade fence, so the neighbors behind and on each side could see him breaking into it. Walking to the front door as if he were an interested buyer, he rang the doorbell, getting no answer. Staring through a gap in the drapes, he saw there was no furniture. Turning his gaze to the Sterrett home, he watched a neighbor lady walk over and pick up Sterrett's morning paper and return inside her home. Writing down the name and phone number of the realtor, he drove away.

A convenience store three blocks away had a bank of phones in front. His watch read 10:05.

"Hello?"

"It's your friend from Tulsa. Do we have a deal?"

"We have a deal."

"How soon can you deliver the cash?"

"One hour. Go to terminal E-4 at the airport. That's the Delta terminal. There's a men's room across from Gate Six. Enter the stall farthest from the entrance at exactly 11:10 am. Slide a blank piece of paper with a number four written on it under the wall. The money will be slid back to you. Take it and leave. Don't look back."

"I'll be there." Reed hung up the phone and wondered about his client. He didn't know much about him. He knew that he had an eight-to-five job, by the timing of the schedule for phone calls, and had a contact in the sheriff's office. Was this guy really a go-between? If he was a go-between, he was a close one. He didn't try to deny that he knew the reason for the hit.

Chapter Nineteen

The pawnshop had shown normal activity for the last two hours. It was an older building with two entrances and a back door. Blair and Carter had them all covered with surveillance units. Larry Blair kept his eyes on the pawnshop as he checked his watch again. It was 12:45 pm "It's been an hour and a half since those two punks went in the back. We're going to lose them to lunch if the sheriff don't hurry up."

Carter shifted his binoculars from the counterman to a customer approaching. "Relax, They don't look like they're going anywhere."

"Are you sure that was Mexican Joe and Devil that went in?"

"They match the description and went in the back. What more do you want?"

"That Devil looks like a mean bastard. I bet he has a pistol under that loose-fitting shirt."

"So what? Did you expect him to carry a hymn book?"

"I still don't like this. It's too risky."

"Francis will be okay. She's got plenty of smarts."

"She's dressed too provocatively to suit me. Something could happen to her in there."

Carter grinned at his partner. "If they're looking at tits, they can't see the wire."

"They won't see it anyway. I couldn't see it from two feet away."

Blair flicked on his handheld radio that would broadcast the wire. He nodded to Carter. "Call the van and have Francis get out and walk away in the opposite direction. I want to test it again."

"You've checked it twice already."

"I want to check it again. Do it."

Carter grabbed the radio. "Unit twenty, this is unit fifteen. Over."

"This is unit twenty."

"We want another test moving away."

"Roger. You guys must be nervous."

"Keep your comments to yourself. Get moving."

Francis got out of the van and walked briskly about a block, finding a secluded area with no people. "Hiya, handsome. Do you hear me? I'm now turning around and heading back to the van." She lowered her voice. "This is a lower voice pattern. Give a high sign if you can hear it." She raised her eyes and saw an arm extend out the van window and give the sign. She walked back to the van and got in. "How was that?"

"Just fine." came Blair's voice over the radio. "Let's go over the codes again. Seeing Stewart calls for the word "gringo." Finding Cruz calls for the word "brother." If there's trouble, use the term "fire drill." Got it?"

Francis nodded her head. "For the fourth time, I've got it. Is the sheriff here yet?

"He just pulled up. We're ready to go. Be careful, Francis."

Francis got into her car and drove the two short blocks to the pawnshop. Entering the building, she approached the counterman, who was trying to take his eyes off her breasts and appear casual.

"Can I help you, Miss?"

"I need to see Mexican Joe."

"What about?"

"That's my business."

"What's your name?"

"Francis Mendez."

"Just a minute." The counter man disappeared into a back room and returned after a few seconds. "This way please." Francis followed him into the back room and was ushered into a plush office with a blue shag rug. Behind the desk was a man in his late forties, wearing an expensive tan suit with a striped shirt and a yellow power tie. He was a little heavy, with black oily hair, the locks falling over a wide forehead shading dark eyes that studied Francis. The eyes started at her breasts and worked their way up. The firm mouth slowly turned up at the corners into a half smile.

"What can I do for you, beautiful?"

"I'm looking for my brother."

"What's his name?"

"Guillermo Mendez."

"I'm sorry. I don't know him."

"He's probably using another name."

"What name is that?"

"I don't know."

"Why come to me with this?"

"He wrote me from Mexico to look for him here."

"Where was he in Mexico?"

"I'm not sure. I think he was in Nuevo Laredo."

"Didn't you look at the postmark?"

"Yes, I did, but it was mailed in Laredo. In Texas."

"I see. What does he look like?"

"He's thirty-two years old, dark hair, and a long face. He's five feet six, and the last time I saw him, he weighed one hundred sixty pounds."

Mexican Joe laughed. "There's only about two thousand guys I know that look like that. Why is he going with another name?"

"He told me that he got in trouble down there."

"What kind of trouble?"

"I don't know."

"Do you have a picture of him?"

"No."

A large silent man moved off to the right of Francis, and she turned to face him. He had a swarthy complexion and the meanest eyes she had ever seen. "Who are you, lady?"

"My name is Francis Mendez. Who are you?"

"Diablo. How come I've never seen you before?"

"I live in Houston."

"Let me see some identification."

Francis feigned irritation. "Why?"

"Because you could be INS, that's why. Either you show me something, or I'm going to throw your ass out of here."

Francis made a face as she pulled out her driver's license and handed it to him. He studied it and then looked at her. Silently, he handed the license to Mexican Joe, who glanced at it and handed it back to her. "I'm not INS," she spat. "I'm just looking for my brother."

Mexican Joe smiled. "We just have to be careful, that's all. Where do you work in Houston?"

"I work at the Ramada Inn on Shepard. It's in North Houston."

"I know where it is. Do you know Rueben Alonzo?"

"No."

"Do you know Roberto Delgado?"

"No, but I've heard of him."

"What have you heard about him?"

"He helps wetbacks with jobs and also handles false papers."

Mexican Joe leaned back in his big chair and smiled. "You passed the test, lady. I never heard of Rueben Alonzo either. But I do know Roberto Delgado. He looked at Devil. "I think she's okay."

"What about my brother? Do you know how I can find him?"

"If he came up in my pipeline, I might be able to find him. Does he speak English?"

"Not very well."

"Then I might still have him around here working somewhere."

"Could you help me find him today?"

"What's the rush?"

"Two reasons. I have to get back home, and our mother is sick. She may not make it. She wants to see her son."

"Does she live with you?"

"She lives in Houston but not with me."

"Where does your father live?"

"He lives in Mexico."

"Where?"

"In Linares. It's south of Monterey."

"I know where it is. What does he do there?"

"He owns a taxicab in Monterey and has a small farm in Linares."

"Why did your mother come to the United States?"

"They don't get along. My father has a mistress."

Mexican Joe smiled. "I'll see what I can do. Why don't you come back about six? If he's here, I can find him by then."

Francis thought fast. "Is there any way we can hurry? I really need to start back."

"I'm busy. I won't have time to look for him for about two hours."

"Could you send somebody with me and let me look for him?"

"My people are busy, too."

"I'll make it worth your while."

Devil butted in with an evil smile. "Boss, I could take her around, if she made it worth my while."

Francis handed him a hundred-dollar bill and returned the smile. "That's what I meant by making it worth your while."

Devil frowned as he took the money. "I was thinking of something else."

Casing the realty office, Reed watched three women come out and cross the street toward him. Reed followed them into a Denny's restaurant, tipping the waitress to seat him across from them. After ordering lunch, the women headed for the bathroom. One left her purse under a sweater. Reed waited until the waitress was distracted, then slid into their booth. With practiced ease, he slipped the woman's keys out of her purse and into his left pocket. No one noticed as he slipped quietly out of the restaurant and headed down the street to a convenience store. Checking the yellow pages, Reed found a tool rental company on Pioneer Parkway that closed at 1:00 pm. He'd have to hurry.

The first stop was at a car lot on Division, where he purchased a seven-year-old pickup for $3,300 cash, with the understanding that he could return it within a week for a $2,800 refund. Reed used a phony driver's license to transact the deal. The dealer agreed to hold the paperwork for a week before turning it in. This would be the easiest $500 he ever made. Transferring his briefcase full of cash, Reed sped to the tool rental company. With ten minutes to spare, he rented a lawn mower, edger, and gas can. After piling the goods into the pickup bed, he rented a room in a Holiday Inn on I-20.

After checking in under the name that he used to get his rental car at the airport, he left one change of clothes there. Finding another Holiday Inn closer to Fort Worth, he checked into that one under the name he used to purchase the pickup. After leaving his fake driver's license in the pickup, Reed took a taxi to retrieve his rental car. Using his normal precautions, he put the other driver's license in the glove compartment of the rental car. It was bad business to get caught with more than one license.

Finding a Kmart, he purchased some cheap work clothes and a large screwdriver. Returning to his second motel, he pried off the car dealer's decal from the back of the pickup. After going to his room, Reed put most of his cash in a manila envelope and scrawled the words "real estate papers" on the front. An accommodating hotel clerk put it in the motel safe for him. After changing into his work clothes, he drove across the street to a convenience store with a bank of phones outside. Digging through his wallet, he produced a piece of paper with a long list of phone numbers. The number in Dallas was at the bottom. Poking coins in the phone, he dialed the number.

"Hello?"

"May I speak to Earnest, please?"

"This is Earnest."

"Earnest, we have a mutual friend."

"Yeah? Who's that?"

"Bill Evans in Abilene, Kansas."

"Yeah? How's he doing?"

"Just fine. He said to call you if I ever needed military supplies."

"He did, did he? Who are you?"

"My name is Terry Blevins."

"What kind of supplies do you need, Mr. Blevins?"

"I need a Glock with two clips of soft-point ammo, and I might need something else later. Do you have a Glock?"

"No. But I can get it. I can't sell this to a stranger, though."

"Why don't you call Evans? He'll vouch for me."

"That costs money."

"Just add it on the bill. It's no big deal. When can you get this?"

"I don't know. I'll have to check around."

"I'll call back in an hour." Reed hung up and turned his head toward the inside of the store as a squad car cruised by. He watched the reflection in the glass as the squad car pulled in to the far side of the parking lot. Uniformed patrolmen exited the car and headed inside. Reed fished more coins out of his pocket and dialed a phony number, with his back to them. When they disappeared inside, he got in his car and left.

Reed returned to Sterrett's street and drove into the driveway of the vacant house. The lockbox opened to reveal the key to the front door. Walking inside like he owned the place, Reed carefully cased the house. It was a two-story with all the bedrooms on the second floor. A window in one of the smaller bedrooms provided the perfect view into the Sterrett property. Reed went back to his car and got his binoculars. A further study showed that the Sterrett property backed up to a park, with only the stockade fence separating it. He couldn't see the back door, but a sidewalk led through a gate, then turned ninety degrees to the back of the house. Reed figured that the gate had a lock on it. Closed drapes prevented him from seeing inside. A fireplace chimney to the left of the front door and a smiley-face decal on the other side helped, though.

This looked like a typical quiet neighborhood with little visiting between neighbors. Reed went to the back of the house and studied the rest of the neighborhood in that direction. There was a German shepherd in the house behind the one he was in. If he mowed the back lawn, the dog was sure to bark. There was a small child playing in the yard next to the dog. The house on the other side of the dog had a cyclone fence instead of wood, so Reed had an unobstructed view into the yard and house. There was a woman dressing in her bedroom. Reed watched the show without emotion. When she was finished dressing, Reed walked back downstairs and checked the kitchen. The refrigerator was on, but empty, and the shelves were bare. The house was ready to show at any time. Reed could occupy the house only at night. After replacing the door key, he backed out of the driveway to check the gate on Sterrett's fence. His eyes widened in surprise. There was no lock.

The faces had become a blur to Francis after she went in the first dirty complex. The stench in these dormitories was a shock, and she had to steel herself against the constant lewd suggestions of the men. Most of them were engrossed in dice games. One slovenly man actually undressed in front of her with a wicked grin. Francis had little doubt that she wouldn't have made it out of the first place except for the men's obvious fear of Devil, whose attitude became more surly with each additional inspection. The men had misread his hostile attitude as one of protectiveness of Francis. As they entered a building and climbed the stairs, Devil abruptly turned to face her.

"This is the last one. If he's not here, we don't have him."

"Thank you for going to all this trouble for me."

"I don't mind if you're legit, but if we get raided in the next month, I'm going to come personally to Houston and find you. I promise that you will beg me to kill you quick. I've shown you all we have."

"Don't worry about me. As large as your operation is, I'm surprised that INS doesn't raid you all the time."

"Just don't double-cross me."

They turned left at the top of the stairs and walked into the largest dormitory she had seen. She estimated that there were over a hundred men in the room, with about thirty sleeping in bunks. She hurried past them with a careful glance at each one. There was a huge dice game in the center of the room with cheers and groans heard every few seconds. The noise and game ceased as Devil and Francis approached, and all faces turned apprehensively toward them. Francis looked them over as best she could, but they kept moving around. One grabbed his crotch and reached for her.

"Hey puta, here's what you're looking for."

Francis brushed him aside with a look of disdain, but the man wouldn't quit. When she turned her back, he grabbed her backside with his hand. Instinctively, Francis whirled and planted her foot in his testicles. He fell to the floor with a groan. Francis realized that she had gone into a defensive stance that she had been taught in the training academy. The men backed away from her with a new respect. To avoid any undue suspicion, she relaxed and gave the remaining men a careful glance and turned toward Devil. He was looking at her with growing suspicion.

"Where did you learn to do that?"

"I learned it in karate school. Let's finish this up and get out of here." She whirled and went to the back of the room, where a small group of men were grouped around a poker game. As the men parted, Francis saw Pablo Cruz at the table dealing cards. He had a huge stack of dollar bills in front of him. Devil saw the stare and his suspicion grew.

"Is that him?"

"No. But he sure looks like my brother."

"Come on then. Let's vamoose." He led the way out of the room and down one flight of stairs. Without warning, he opened a door on the second floor and flung Francis inside. She found herself on the floor with Devil's knee on her chest and her arms pinned to the floor. She wondered how long it would take the deputies to close in. She hoped they would pick the right building. She glared back at Devil, hoping to back him off.

"Get off me, animal. Mexican Joe's going to have your ass for this."

"I doubt it. Who are you, bitch? Hotel maids don't have enough money to go to karate school."

"My boyfriend owns a studio. Now get off me before I start yelling."

Devil laughed. "I'm God here. Nobody's going to help you."

"Surely there's someone in building eleven that won't let you rape me!"

Devil laughed again as he ripped off the front of her blouse. His laughter froze in his throat as he saw the wire running from her neck around to her back. "You set us up, you bitch," he yelled as he raised his right hand. He doubled his fist and hit her in the face as hard as he could. As she lay stunned on the floor, Devil rose and pulled out a straight razor. With his left hand he grabbed her hair and forced her head back. With a quick motion he slashed her throat and escaped out the door.

Taking the steps three at a time, he rushed out of the building toward his car that was waiting a block away. As Devil was fishing for his keys, two deputies slammed his face against the car. One of the deputies twisted his left arm up behind him, which caused the razor to fall to the ground. The deputy cuffed him quickly and spun him around.

"What building did you come out of?"

Devil spit in his face. The deputy recoiled, then slapped him hard across the mouth as he heard Larry Blair's anxious voice crack on his radio. "All units, cordon off building eleven. Now! Top priority!" The deputy looked up to see Blair's unit followed by the sheriff's, heading to the parking lot at top speed, with portable lights but no sirens. Deputies were descending on the complex from all directions.

Blair and Carter stopped the car and ran to building eleven with weapons drawn. Four deputies closed in behind them, two with riot guns. Blair led the way up the stairs to the third floor and burst in on the illegals. Instant pandemonium broke loose in the room, as the wetbacks milled around. Blair fired his pistol in the air.

"Everybody freeze or you're dead!"

The illegals froze as the deputies fanned out across the room. The frightened and confused men were shoved against the wall. Carter spied Pablo Cruz and rushed over to cuff him.

Blair looked anxiously around for Francis. She wasn't there. He searched fruitlessly under the bunks and checked the room across the hall. Blair bounded down the steps to the second floor, where he found the sheriff standing outside a door.

"Don't go in there, Larry. You don't want to see it."

Blair thrust Sanders aside and rushed into the room to stare at Francis lying on the floor in a large pool of blood. Sanders pulled him out of the room.

"Go outside and wait, Larry. I'll handle this."

"But Francis …"

"It's too late, Larry. She's gone."

Leonard Torrey sat in his car down the block from George Masters' house in South Arlington. It looked like a wasted afternoon. The junior attorney hadn't left his house all day. He was about to give up, when Masters backed his car out of the garage and pulled away.

Torrey hung back as he followed Masters to west Fort Worth. Closing the gap when Masters turned into the Green Oaks Inn, Torrey got out and managed to get within five paces. He followed him into the lobby and up some stairs to the second floor, where Masters knocked on a door. Masters glanced up nervously at Torrey as he walked past. Torrey kept his head down but glanced up to catch the room number, 227. The door opened and closed before Torrey had walked ten steps. Torrey found his way to the third floor of the opposite wing and counted down seven doors on the inside. Knocking on the door, Torrey waited without an answer. A maid that could speak little English opened the door for him in exchange for a five-dollar tip. Opening the drapes, he looked down one floor across the courtyard. Torrey could see four men in the room, including Masters, sitting around a small table and talking. Carefully, he noted the faces of the other men and went down to the bar.

A corner booth allowed him a good vantage point without being seen. Two drinks later, Torrey saw Masters leave. Ten minutes after that, the other men passed through the lobby, entered a Lincoln sedan and left, with Torrey close behind. Torrey followed the car east to the downtown area. It exited on Cherry Street and made its way to the Worthington Hotel.

The three men parked the car in valet parking and entered the hotel as Torrey scrambled to find a quick parking place. Torrey found them in the restaurant on the second floor, where two more men in suits joined them. The men didn't notice as Torrey plopped himself in the booth across the aisle, ordering a drink as he listened to their conversation.

"Bob, do you think this kid can pull it off?"

"It'll surprise me if he does. I think he's out of his league."

"If he fails, we'll have to answer for it."

"I know. We were crazy to get caught in this mess."

"Does this kid have a backup strategy?"

"He said he did, but he wouldn't tell us about it."

"Why not?"

"He said he had to work out more details."

"I don't like secrets at this stage of the game."

"Neither do I."

A blonde singer about thirty-five cranked up the piano and began crooning for the customers. Torrey couldn't hear over the music. A sour look at the singer only seemed to raise her volume, so Torrey paid his bill and left. He'd heard enough anyway.

Pablo Cruz looked up sullenly at the three stern-faced men hovering over him. The sheriff stood closest, with a lit cigarette between his lips as his eyes bore holes in Cruz.

"You're in big trouble, kid."

"Why? I was just over there playing poker with some friends. I'm not a wetback. I was born in this country."

"You're going to be sorry you were born anywhere."

"What do you think I've done?"

"Oh, nothing much. Just capital murder last night. Today, it's accessory to capital murder. It's nothing the death penalty won't cure."

"I don't know what you're talking about."

"Let me be more formal. You are going to be charged with one count of attempted capital murder, conspiracy to commit capital murder, capital murder on your brother, and one count of accessory to capital murder. You have the right to have an attorney with you during questioning on these matters. You have the right to stop that questioning at any time. You have the right to remain silent. Any statements you make can be used against you in court. If you're too poor to afford a lawyer, you can make an application for a public defender. If you make that application, a hearing will be held to look into your financial condition. If you qualify for a public defender, one will be appointed for you. You have the right of an examining trial until you are indicted. Do you understand those rights, Cruz?"

"Yeah."

"Where were you at 7:30 last night?"

"At prayer meeting."

"Look kid, if you get smart with me, I'll charge you with murdering your brother too. Do you want to explain that to your family?"

"No. But you can't make that stick."

"Yes, I can. There is a little case back in 1973 called Potts v. Texas that convicted a man who shot a bystander when he was aiming at someone else. Look, kid, you don't have to face the death penalty if you talk. You're a small fish. We want the ones who sent you."

"Will you dismiss all the charges?"

"No. I can't do that. I will dismiss the accessory charge on what happened today. I'll go to bat for you with the DA and the judge on the rest, but I can't dismiss them."

"How much time would that be?"

"I don't know for sure. With your record, probably twenty-five years. With good time, you could get out in ten. That's if you cooperate fully."

"I take it that my brother's dead?"

"Yes."

Cruz looked at his shoes and thought. He saw no point in protecting that louse in Arlington. For a few measly bucks, his brother was dead. "What do you want to know?"

The officers visibly relaxed. The sheriff offered him a cigarette, which he gratefully accepted. Walker flipped out a lighter and took over.

"Why did you and your brother go after Judge Sterrett last night?"

"We were hired."

"Hired by who?"

"Some stinkin' cop in Arlington named Agnew."

The three men exchanged glances and Carter left the room. Walker continued. "How did you know where Sterrett was?"

"Agnew told me."

"How did Agnew know?"

"I don't know that, man."

"When did Agnew hire you?"

"Thursday night."

"Did he tell you then where Judge Sterrett was going to be?"

"No. He called me with that yesterday morning."

"What time yesterday morning?"

"I don't know. The prick woke me up. I didn't see what time it was."

"Did he call you at home?"

"Yeah. No, wait. He called me on my cell phone. I forgot to turn it off when I went to bed."

"You remember how early it was when he called you?"

"About 8:30."

"You said he called you on your mobile?"

"That's right."

"What is your mobile number?"

"555-3232."

"How much did Agnew pay you to hit Sterrett?"

"A thousand dollars."

"Did he say why he wanted him dead?"

"No. He said he was just the messenger. His friend wanted him dead."

"Who's this friend?"

"I don't know, man. He said he was a cop, though."

Walker sat back down. "What else did he say about him?"

"Nothing much. He said this guy could keep me out of trouble. He said the guy could steer the investigation away from me and Jose."

"Did he say anything else about him?"

"No."

"When did Agnew contact you Thursday night?"

"About 10:00, I think."

"Where were you?"

"At Boomers."

"Where's that?"

"On West Division, man. It's a titty joint."

"Who was there first? You or Agnew?"

"We were. Agnew came looking for us."

"Who is *we*?"

"Jose and me."

"You're sure he didn't know where Sterrett was going to be when he talked to you Thursday night?"

"I'm sure, man."

"Okay. Tell us what happened last night."

"Me and Jose went out to this park about 7:30. We drove around till we found the wedding. We parked and Sterrett came right to us."

"How did you know which one was Sterrett?"

"My brother knew him. He suspended Jose's license."

"What happened when Sterrett came your way?"

"Jose waited behind a van to get him with a knife. We didn't want to make a lot of noise. Jose couldn't do it, though. I pulled out my gun to shoot him, but my brother got in the way. I think I shot him instead. After that I ran away."

"What about your car?"

"I had to leave it there, man."

"How did you get away?"

"I got to a phone and called Mexican Joe. He sent Devil to get me. He took me to where you found me."

"Did Mexican Joe know you were going to hit Sterrett last night?"

"Yeah. I told him yesterday."

"How about Devil?"

"Him, too."

"Do you know where Billy Earl Stewart is?"

"No."

"Do you know who's hiding him?"

"No."

"Have you heard Mexican Joe or Devil talk about him?"

"No."

"Could Mexican Joe be hiding him?"

"I don't think so."

"Why not?"

"I would've heard about it."

"Would you have heard about it if someone else was hiding him?"

"Not necessarily."

"Who do you think's hiding him?"

"I don't know. Maybe nobody. I never heard of this guy until this week. Maybe his own friends are hiding him."

"Do you know a man named Blade Hawkins?"

"No. But I know of him. Everybody does."

"If Stewart went to him, where would Blade send him?"

"If he used a contact in Arlington, it would be Angel or Shorty."

"What about Bullet?"

"The Blade don't fool with Bullet, man."

"Why not?"

"I heard that the Blade don't fool with drug people."

"What about Lucky?"

"I don't think so. They don't get along."

"How do we find Angel and Shorty?"

"Angel hangs out at the Sunrise Coffee Shop in the mornings. I don't know where he is after that. Shorty owns a body shop named 'Dents and Dings' over on Pioneer Parkway."

"Which of these two would be most likely?"

"I think Angel."

"Why?"

"Angel specializes in hiding people. The only way the Blade would use Shorty would be if Shorty needed to move a stolen car out of state."

"Where would Angel hide him?"

"I don't know, man."

"What do you know about this Angel?"

"Not much. I just see him around."

"Do you know where he lives?"

"No."

"Do you know what his full name is?"

"No."

"What does he like to do? You know, does he chase women or play golf?"

"I don't know him that well, man."

"Okay, Cruz. If this checks out, we'll go to bat for you with the judge." Walker turned to the sheriff. "It looks like I've got work to do."

Walker walked across the street to his office where most of his staff was waiting. Larry Blair was sitting at his desk with his face in his hands. Walker reached down and patted Blair's shoulder.

"I'm sorry, Larry. This wasn't your fault."

Blair looked up at Walker with teary eyes. "I lost her, Captain. I should've gone with her. If I had, this wouldn't have happened."

"That would have blown it. Francis knew the risk she was taking."

"She was going to be really good, sir. It's my fault. I blew it. I should've gone in closer."

"You couldn't, Larry. Don't beat yourself up over this. You did all you could. Go home and take the night off. You're upset."

"No, sir. I'm going to bust this case. I owe it to her."

"Go home, Larry. You're no good to me when you're upset like this. You can't think straight."

"I'll be okay in a few minutes, Captain. I want in. Did you get anything out of Cruz?"

"Yeah. We have a starting point."

"What did he tell you?"

"The sheriff will cover it in the meeting in a few minutes. Tim, get Larry two cups of strong coffee. The meeting's in five minutes."

The team was already assembling as they spoke. The sheriff passed without comment as Walker ran off a *Star-Telegram* reporter who had slipped into the room. He motioned to Baker as he approached the front of the room.

"Gary, were you able to talk to Sterrett's clerk?"

"Yes sir."

"Did she tell anyone about the judge's whereabouts?"

"She says she didn't."

"Is she telling the truth?"

"I guess so."

"Do you have anything to report?"

"Not really."

"This is going to be a late night for us. I'm putting you on a confidential assignment. You're to tell no one about this. Okay?"

"You've got it, Sheriff. What do you want me to do?"

"I want you to check the background on Chief Parker. Find out where he worked before he came to Arlington. Check back ten years and see if he could be involved in any questionable behavior."

Baker pondered this. "Sheriff, if I start asking questions, people are going to start talking. I can't keep something like this quiet."

"I know. Go to Dallas and borrow some undercover officers from Sheriff Culberson. Let them do the asking."

"How soon do you need this?"

"Let's try for seventy-two hours."

"Sheriff, don't get mad, but I have to know something."

"Yes?"

"Is this investigation criminal or political?"

"It's criminal, Gary."

"What am I looking for?"

"I'm not sure. Tendencies for criminal activity. I also want to know if he has shielded dirty officers before."

"Okay, Sheriff. I'll get on it first thing in the morning."

"Get on it first thing tonight."

"Yes sir."

Sanders walked to the podium and paused while the conversations ceased. Sanders looked out over a group of forty officers looking up at him expectantly. "I'm sure you all know by now that we lost one of our own today. Francis Mendez had only been here a short time, and I know that few of you got to know her. I worked with her quite a bit in the last few days, and I can tell you that we lost a good one. I was very impressed with her knowledge, skill, and dedication. The best compliment I can give her is that she would have gone far in this department if she had survived. We've received some breaks in this case that we owe to her. It was her idea to go undercover. Francis gave her life today for these breaks, and let's not waste any time in pursuing them. I'm sending the honor guard to her funeral in Houston, and I'll go personally and speak if I can. I want her friends and family down there to know what her contribution was to this case."

The meeting continued as Sanders brought the team up to speed. At the end, Larry Blair walked to the front and snapped the flag halfway down the mast. After that, the officers silently left the room, leaving the sheriff with Walker and Underwood.

Sanders looked at Underwood. "Who's the judge on duty this weekend?"

Underwood checked his notes. "It's Judge Jake Eaves, Sheriff." An uncomfortable silence followed as Sanders pondered the problem. "Chris, as soon as this meeting is over, see if you can get Judge Jack Rhoads down here. I want an arrest warrant issued for this Agnew. I'm going to arrest that bastard myself. I also want search warrants issued for that body shop. Larry, I want you to get Rhoads to sign a search warrant for the phone records for Pablo Cruz's mobile number. Get Rhoads to expand the warrant to any numbers that the investigation reveals."

Underwood nodded as he wrote down the number. "Do you want me to contact the phone company tonight, Sheriff?"

"I sure do. Fred, I want a minimum of three undercover officers at the Sunrise Coffee Shop by nine in the morning. I want that restaurant covered until noon. I want some surveillance units nearby to follow this Angel if we can find him there."

Sanders summoned Tim Carter and several others. "Tim, take two men and find your snitch. Concentrate on this Angel. See if you can uncover something tonight."

Sanders checked his notes. "Who checked Mexican Joe's full name?"

Bill Blevins raised his hand. "I did, Sheriff. His name is apparently Joe Pasquall."

"Have we got him?"

"No, sir. He disappeared right after we raided his apartment complex. INS is looking for him, too."

"Is he a U.S. citizen?"

"Yes sir."

"Fred, I want his house staked out, if INS isn't doing that. Have someone check on that. Do we have a warrant on him?"

"I don't think so, Sheriff. We haven't had time."

"Get an affidavit worked up for him. We'll get Rhoads to sign it while he's here."

"Can we shake the Blade for information on this Angel?"

"No. It probably wouldn't do any good. I don't want to spook Angel, and that might do it. If we handle this right, we could have Stewart in twenty-four hours."

Chapter Twenty

Buck Reed studied the Sterrett home from the upstairs bedroom across the street. After an hour's study, he'd confirmed that only Sterrett's next-door neighbor paid attention to anything outside her own property. No patrol cars came through the neighborhood. At 8:05 pm, the nosy neighbor and her family backed out of the garage and pulled away. Reed followed them with his field glasses, noticing they were wearing casual clothes. How long would they be gone? As they disappeared, he considered following them. The idea was rejected because the whole family seemed to be in the car, so it was obviously a family outing. Either they were going out to dinner or to a movie. A short trip out for ice cream or to the grocery store wouldn't require the whole family going. Reed figured he had a minimum of an hour.

After collecting his flashlight and lockpick, he casually sauntered across the street and entered the back yard. Darkness hid his activities as he closed the unlocked gate and picked the lock to the back door.

The flashlight revealed an entryway through a utility room with a washer and dryer on one side. A hot water closet was on the other. The next room was the kitchen. Reed checked the refrigerator for food or beverages that only Sterrett would consume. Other than some adult vitamins, there was nothing. Poison wouldn't work.

Reed flashed his light toward the dining room area, and then to the living room beyond. There was nothing there worth the risk of him being seen from the street. An opening to the left led to a hallway that traveled the length of the house. Reed shut off the light and softly walked to the room nearest the front door. A quick flash of light showed this was a bedroom of a small boy. Reed walked into the closet, shut the door, and turned his flashlight back on. There were several changes of clothes for a boy between the age of seven and nine. Reed couldn't tell how many changes of clothes were missing, if any. A shelf above the hangers contained a baseball glove, a bat, and several puzzles. Reed looked vainly for hobbies that would take this little boy away for weekends, such as camping gear or ski equipment.

The next bedroom was different in decor, with a doll resting on the bed pillows. The colors were pink and pastel blue. Reed's attention was drawn to a family picture on the dresser, Sterrett and an attractive brunette woman with two small children. The four were in a park, seated on a carpet of clover and bluebonnets. The smiles hinted at happier times. Reed wondered what happened to the woman. The closet revealed nothing. Where were the schoolbooks? A search turned up nothing in that direction.

Beyond the girl's room and a bathroom was a study with a computer station in one corner and a large bookshelf reaching to the ceiling. Reed passed his flashlight over the books, disclosing the owner's interest in Eastern history and philosophy. There were books on self-defense and American history. Reed noticed several books on the Civil War and the Lincoln assassination. The book in the corner of the third shelf was written by Sterrett himself. Pulling that book down, he took it with him into the next room. A circle with the light showed a large master bedroom with a bathroom and closet opposite the bed. Reed entered the bathroom and closed the door. A quick glance showed that the bathroom window faced out into the back yard. Turning on the light, Reed sat on the commode and perused Sterrett's book. The book showed that Sterrett was an expert in hand-to-hand combat and was a seventh degree black belt. There were pictures showing Sterrett in kickboxing and karate contests. Another showed Sterrett breaking bricks with his right hand. The last picture showed a younger Sterrett holding a large trophy with the caption 1977 US Karate Champion. Reed was impressed as he thumbed through the instruction sections, which disclosed that Sterrett taught offensive tactics while maintaining defensive strategy. The old juices flowed as Reed speculated whether he could take a younger Sterrett one-on-one. Not without the element of surprise, he decided. Besides, he wasn't here for a personal contest, unless there was no other way.

After replacing the book, Reed returned to the master bedroom and carefully searched the dresser. There were no weapons in the room, which was a mild surprise. The nightstands by the king-sized bed yielded an address book, which Reed took into the bathroom for a careful study. It took ten minutes for him to copy the names and phone numbers of Sterrett's friends and contacts. This was Reed's first break, but the book contained few addresses. After replacing the address book, Reed carefully examined Sterrett's closet, taking note of Sterrett's wearing apparel. Reed counted eleven business suits and over twenty dress shirts. Eight fancy sweat suits with stripes were hung neatly in line. The search showed no cowboy boots, only dress and tennis shoes. Reed returned to the bedroom and pointed his flashlight on the phone by the bed. The phone had a normal dial tone when he picked it up. Reed considered inserting a bug but immediately rejected the idea. A discovered bug would alert Sterrett. The flashlight was focused on the headboard of the bed while he considered this. Reed eyed the headboard thoughtfully and then looked behind it. There was a four-inch space between the inch-thick headboard and the wall. Tapping the board, he found it solid, not laminated. Reed raised the bedspread on the sides and ran his hand slowly on the mattress. There was a slight indention on the side nearest the window. That was also the side where the phone was. The other side of the mattress had no indention. Sterrett slept alone.

Reed retraced his steps to the daughter's bedroom and tapped each wall back to Sterrett's bedroom. Counting the bathroom, there were three walls and the bookshelf between Sterrett and his daughter. Reed looked down at the bed thoughtfully and flicked off his flashlight. "I've got you, Sterrett," he murmured without emotion. "You don't have a chance."

Cass quietly set down the decaf coffee on the poolside table beside Ray, who seemed lost in thought. As she was putting in cream, Ray smiled at her, pulled her down beside him, and absently stroked her hair.

"A penny for your thoughts, Ray. You've been quiet ever since the sheriff called. What's going on?"

"Stewart apparently had nothing to do with that attack on me last night. Those punks were hired by Agnew. Can you believe that a policeman could do something like this?"

"That is surprising. How do they know this?"

"They captured the other guy this afternoon and he spilled the beans. Lee told me that they lost a detective when they got him. I'm overwhelmed by the blood spilled this week. I hope it ends soon."

"Who got killed? Did the sheriff tell you his name?"

"It was a she. Francis Mendez."

"I never heard of her."

"She was new. Just transferred up here from Houston last month. I really feel bad for her. She gave her life for me and didn't even know me."

"She probably didn't think that way. She was just doing her duty."

"No. It was more than that. She volunteered to go in under cover to find Pablo Cruz. That's really brave."

Cass laid her head on Ray's shoulder. "That's what I find fascinating about you. You think of others in the middle of the crisis of your life."

"This is a bad time for me. But it isn't the worst time of my life."

"Was that when your wife was killed?"

"Yes."

"Aren't you worried about your safety?"

"Not too much. I'm more worried about the children, and I sure don't want you getting caught in the crossfire."

"Do you think it will be over soon?"

"The sheriff thinks they'll catch Stewart in the next two days."

"I hope so. Maybe then, we can get back to normal."

"Probably. I wonder how Agnew found out I was going to be at that wedding. I may have a enemy I don't know about."

"I don't think so. He could have found that out from anybody. Everyone in Arlington knows who the Fletchers are."

"Yeah. I guess so."

"Do you think Stewart will try anything else?"

"He would be crazy to but maybe he is crazy in a way. The sheriff's not going to let me leave here until he's caught."

"That's all right. I could stay here a month just cozying up to you."

Ray resumed stroking her hair. "It's nice all right. Are you having a good time mothering the kids?"

"Yeah. They like being spoiled, too."

"You're so good with children. Why didn't you ever get married?"

"I did get married when I was too young. It didn't work out. The right guy never came along after that. My standards keep getting higher, too. I would have to find someone who's as good as you."

Ray laughed. "That shouldn't be hard."

"Don't sell yourself short. You have no idea how flaky most single guys are. They're selfish and too set in their ways. The good ones get nabbed in their twenties. Just like you did."

"Doris nabbed me all right."

"When did you start going with her?"

"In my second year of college."

"How long did you go with her before you got married?"

"Three years."

"When did you know that you loved her?"

"It's hard to say. I guess it was when she came with me to New York the first year I competed for the national karate championship. I lost in the third round and I was devastated. I really thought I was good enough to win. She stayed with me and pulled me through when I was down. I guess that's when I knew."

"Did she like you fighting in those championships?"

"Not really, but she knew how important it was to me."

"What got you started in karate, anyway?"

"Oh, I don't know. I think it was back in the sixth grade when I got humiliated by the class bully in front of my friends. I started going to classes to learn how to defend myself. I found out I was good when I got myself into condition and my reflexes got faster. I never told anyone about it, and about a year later, this bully jumped me again and I got great satisfaction in kicking his butt. Nobody ever bothered me after that. I kept going and became friends with the instructor. He was a guy from Korea named Tra Kwan. By the time I got out of high school, I could beat him and everybody else in the school. Tra Kwan sponsored me in a regional event and I shocked both of us by finishing second. After that, I stayed with it and advanced little by little until I thought I was really good.

"I went to the nationals when I was a junior in college. That was when I got my head handed to me. This guy that beat me acted like he was scared of me. It was just an act. He would run away from me and scream with fear. Everybody in the place was laughing their head off. I thought they were laughing at him, but they were laughing at me. I was the only one in the place who didn't know he was setting me up. I got careless when he was running away from me. I got too close and he caught me with a backward kick. He then dropped me with a whirling kick to the head. It was all over and I was embarrassed by all the laughter. It taught me a lesson, though. I was never careless again, and I won the championship the next year. Doris was with me the whole time. I really counted on her. She could take me down a peg when I was too high and build me up when I got low."

"You still miss her a lot, don't you?"

Ray paused, considering his reply. "I'd be lying if I said I didn't."

"Do you think anyone could ever take her place?"

Ray chuckled as he stroked her hair. "Is that a loaded question?"

"What do you think?"

"I think yes. Women are very adept at loaded questions"

"How about an answer? Could anyone ever take her place?"

"I might be able to love again, but that's not the same as someone taking her place."

"Would the children accept another mother?"

"I didn't think so until I saw them with you."

"What are we going to do when this is all over?"

"Let's take it one day at a time, Cass. I haven't talked to the children about this."

"I can't work for you when this is over. You know that, don't you?"

"I know. I'm just not ready to deal with it. I have too much on my mind right now. I hope you can understand."

"I do understand. It's unfair for me to push this. I'm sorry."

Ray put his good arm around her and kissed her softly on the lips. "You're really special, Cass. I don't know how I'd have made it through this without you. Thank you for being so understanding."

Cass did not return the kiss. Her response was to lower her head and maintain silence. Ray pulled back and gazed at her for a long moment. "What's wrong, Cass?"

"You must think I'm a fool for coming onto you the other night."

"No. Not at all." Ray lifted her chin, and Cass looked at him with tears welling in her eyes.

"I assumed too much. You're just not ready for me, are you?"

"That's not it at all. Look at all that's happened. I can't make major decisions on my life with all this going on."

"I just don't understand. If you cared for me, it wouldn't be a hard decision. I guess that's my answer. I just don't measure up to Marilyn."

This time Ray lowered his eyes.

"That's it, isn't it? I'm with you, and you're thinking of Marilyn."

"I don't know what I want to do, and that's the God's truth."

"You told me there was nothing between you."

"What I said was that we had not slept together, which is the truth. I didn't say that I didn't have feelings for her, or her for me. I have feelings for you, too, Cass. Strong feelings."

"So I have to compete with her. Is that it?"

"I didn't say that either."

Cass's tears flowed freely now. "You didn't have to."

"If you did have to compete with her, you'd probably win."

"I'm not even in her class. Look how she dresses and how popular she is. She knows everybody in the county. She'd be a great asset for you."

"That's wrong, Cass. You're as classy as she is, but in a different way. Besides, you have one very important thing that she doesn't have."

"What's that," sniffed Cass.

"Chemistry with the kids. She could never have that."

Cass rose from the lounge chair and turned to face him defiantly. "So you might accept second best for the sake of the kids. I'm sorry, but that isn't good enough for me."

Ray struggled to rise and followed Cass into the house. He caught her and gently turned her around. "Cass, that's not what I meant at all. I only meant that I couldn't turn off my feelings for Marilyn like a light switch. Give me a few days to sort things out and talk to the kids. Okay?"

Cass pulled away from him and started walking upstairs. Halfway up, she turned to face him. "Take all the time you want. But I'm not staying with you while you sort this out. I've made a big enough fool out of myself as it is. You can call me at home if you like."

Buck Reed walked from his car to the phones at the 7-Eleven. As he fished coins out of his pocket, a teenage boy approached, plunked two quarters into the next phone, and began a conversation with a friend. Reed retreated to his rental car, looking again at his notes on Sterrett's phone numbers. The names meant nothing to him, and there were few notations to tell him what their connection to Sterrett was. There was a new number by the name Lee Sanders. Reed remembered from the newspaper that he was the sheriff. There was a note beside the name Cassandra Strange that said "get reports ready." Reed pondered this. Could this be an employee? The teenager chirped on as Reed waited impatiently. Finally he exited the car and dialed the number of Cassandra Strange. The phone rang for a long time, and finally an out-of-breath female voice answered. Reed hung up instantly and purposely backed into the teenager talking at the next phone.

"Hey! Watch out old man."

Reed put on his best imitation of a drunk and stepped on the kid's foot. "Shay, kid. Could you loan me a couple dollars for a long dishtance phone call? It's real important?"

"No. I don't have any money. Get away from me."

"Please, kid. I need shome money." Reed stepped on his foot again.

"Ow! Get away from me, I said." The kid lowered his head and spoke on the phone. "Fred, I've got to go. I'll call you later." Without further ado, the kid ran down the street.

Reed smiled as he watched him go, then put coins in the phone. The operator came on the line. "That will be a dollar forty-five, please."

"Hello?"

"Earnest?"

"Yes."

"This is Blevins. Do you have the Glock for me?"

"Yeah. I got it."

"How much?"

"Six hundred."

"With ammo?"

"That's right."

"Good. I need some more stuff."

"What kind of stuff?"

"I need some flex ex, or a block of M1-12 C-4."

"How much C-4?"

"One block will do. I'll need a military blasting cap, too."

"I can handle that."

"How soon?"

"Three hours at the outside."

"Fine. How much?"

"Two hundred."

"Fair enough. Where can I meet you in three hours?"

"Meet me at the club called Ringo's on Greenville Avenue at midnight."

"How will I know you?"

"I'll be just inside the door with a newspaper in my left hand. I'll wear a red long-sleeve shirt. Be sure and bring the cash."

"I'll see you at midnight." Reed hung up the phone and turned to leave, when he came face to face with the teenager and two of his friends. The friends were football-player size and looked unfriendly.

"Is this the old man that was hassling you, Tommy?"

"Yeah. That's him all right."

The two boys advanced toward Reed, separating to four feet apart. Reed leaned back against the phones, appearing as passive as possible. The bigger of the two looked down on Reed with contempt in his eyes. "Somebody needs to teach you some manners, old man."

"Back off, boys. Nobody got hurt here."

"You're wrong, grandpa. Tommy got his feelings hurt, and he said you cost him fifty cents because he had to hang up. That wasn't very nice."

Reed pulled the top bill off his roll in his pocket and tossed it at the kids. "Here. Keep the change. Like I said, there's no harm done."

The smallest one scooped up the bill. "It's a fifty, Mike."

Mike took another step toward Reed. "What else you got, old man?"

Reed came out of his slouch and straightened his left hand to a rigid position. "That's all there is, boys. Now back off while you still have your health."

Mike edged to his right and laughed. "Listen to him, Hal. Grandpa wants us to believe he's a badass." Mike swung an awkward right at Reed, who sidestepped and caught his arm with both hands, whirled him around two hundred seventy degrees, and flung him into the smaller boy. Both ended up in a heap on the sidewalk. Reed stepped on the smaller kid's wrist and, reaching down, retrieved his fifty-dollar bill. He pulled two quarters out of his pocket and dropped them on the sidewalk. "On second thought, don't keep the change." Three wide-eyed kids watched as he drove away.

It was 4:20 Sunday morning when the phone rang. Sanders withdrew his long legs from his desk and stretched as he picked up the phone.

"Sanders here."

"Sheriff, this is Fred."

"Have you got something?"

"Yeah. It's a bombshell. Are you ready?"

"Give me a minute. I need some more coffee." Sanders ambled into the outer office where an overworked coffeepot awaited. As he poured, he decided not to disturb Baker and two other sleeping deputies. Sipping the coffee, he returned to the phone. "Okay, Fred, where are you?"

"I'm at the phone company with Blair. We've been working on those mobile phone records since 10:00 last night."

"What did you turn up?"

"Agnew called Cruz at 8:37 just like he said. Agnew called him on his mobile phone, so it gets better. Four minutes before that, Agnew got a call on his mobile phone from none other than Commissioner Wade."

"Did Agnew have any other traffic on his phone yesterday morning?"

"No, sir."

Sanders drained his coffee as he sat in stunned silence.

"Sheriff, are you still there?"

"Yeah. I'm here. I just don't know what to say."

"Did you arrest Agnew last night?"

"No. Judge Rhoads wouldn't sign the warrant. He wanted to wait for some confirmation. I guess we have it now and more."

"What do you want me to do now?"

"Wake up Judge Rhoads and get him to sign a warrant for Agnew. When he signs it, I'll go get him."

"What about Commissioner Wade?"

"I'm not sure yet."

"Isn't the phone call proof enough?"

"Maybe. I want verification if I can get it. This is political dynamite, Fred. I better be careful here."

"Are you going to shake down Agnew for the information?"

"I doubt it. I don't want to cut any deals with him. I'll try something else first. I don't want Rhoads having to sign a warrant for Wade anyway. Their offices are next to each other. I'll go to a district judge."

"I read you, Sheriff. Should I call you when the warrant is signed?"

"Yes. Have Rhoads come back down to the office anyway. You and Larry come down and prepare the affidavits for him. I'll meet you here."

"Okay, Sheriff. We'll be there in fifteen minutes."

Sanders hung up the phone and reflected as he poured some more coffee. He shook Baker awake and motioned him to follow him into his office. Baker came in rubbing his eyes. "What's up, boss?"

"Gary, can you find that clerk of Sterrett's that you talked to about somebody finding out where Ray was going to be Friday night?"

"I guess so. What do you need her for?"

"I want you to bring her down here so I can talk to her personally."

"You don't believe her?"

"I don't know. Who did she talk to Friday morning that you know of?"

"I'm not sure. We were wrapping up the crime scene."

"Did you let anyone in to see her?"

"Yeah. Come to think of it I did. Commissioner Wade came out there to look into some extra security arrangements for the building. There was no one else, though. She could have talked to anyone on the phone."

"What time did Wade show up out there?"

"About eight o'clock."

"All right. Go get her."

"Is she under arrest?"

"Not as of now. Just bring her in, and don't tell her anything."

"Okay, boss."

"What's her name, anyway?"

"Phyllis."

"Do you know her last name?"

"No."

"Go get her. I want her here in thirty minutes."

Sanders propped his legs up on his desk as he watched Baker leave. His head was aching as it usually did when he didn't get enough sleep. Questions seeped through the headache. Why would Commissioner Wade get involved in something like this? Would an elected official commit murder just because Sterrett might run against him? Would it be worth the risk? Sanders didn't think so, but he realized that he wasn't Wade. Sanders thought back to the times he had faced Wade in budget hearings. Wade didn't seem that much different from other politicians. If Wade wanted Sterrett dead, why would he pick this time when Sterrett was already under guard?

The sheriff suddenly sat upright in his chair and reached for his coffee cup. The cup was empty. He got up and made some more. As he was flavoring it to suit, Walker and Blair walked in and joined him.

"Fred, something just occurred to me."

"What's that, Sheriff?"

"Stewart has no connection to that Friday night attack on Sterrett. Wade and Agnew went after Sterrett because Stewart would become the fall guy. It's a simple case of opportunity."

"Larry and I came to the same conclusion. Sterrett told us this morning that Wade thought that Sterrett would run against him. If Sterrett got killed, nobody would look past Stewart. Wade would be in the clear."

"That's right."

"There's another possibility, too. Do you think Chief Parker could be involved? It would explain the lack of cooperation."

"Could be. I'm working on that, but at this point we have no proof. I can't come up with a motive either."

"Sterrett told us this morning that there was a common thread between them. It was his impression that Parker called Wade to put pressure on Sterrett to drop the complaint."

"I know. Pablo Cruz said that Agnew told him that another policeman was involved."

"Sheriff, are you going to get a warrant on Wade?"

"Probably. I'll know more in a little while. You guys better get started on that paperwork. Have you got Judge Rhoads coming?"

"He's on the way."

"Did he give you any flap for waking him up?"

"No, sir. He likes Sterrett. Should I name Wade in the affidavit on Agnew? You said that you wanted to go around Rhoads on Wade's warrant."

"You can name him. Just stress to Rhoads how sensitive the information is. You can tell him that I'm getting someone else to sign that warrant for his own good."

"We'll get on it. Can Larry and I go with you when you arrest Agnew?"

"I don't see why not."

"When are you going to arrest him?"

"As soon as Rhoads signs the warrant. We should catch Agnew asleep. I don't want any leaks on this until we have Wade, too."

"We read you, sir. This information won't even go into the staff information system until you say so." Walker and Blair refilled their coffee cups and headed for their own office.

The sheriff took a cup back to his office and tried to go through his messages. There was a reminder call from Austin that he was supposed to speak at a Texas Association of Counties seminar on Tuesday. Sanders wrote a note to his secretary to call back Monday and cancel. Francis Mendez's funeral would probably be that day in Houston. Sanders looked up to see Baker escorting a young lady into his outer office. He waved them in and motioned her to a seat. His gaze fell on a nervous disheveled blonde-headed girl about thirty years of age. The face looked strained and pale with no make up. The girl returned his gaze with unblinking eyes, and she didn't look away much. Sanders liked that. Sanders nodded at Baker who rose and left the office, leaving the sheriff alone with the girl.

"What is your last name, Phyllis?"

"Henderson, sir."

"Phyllis, I wanted to be the first to tell you that you'll be exonerated on the missing money. The evidence looks strong that Stewart took the money. If the file cabinet had been locked, he would've broken into it anyway."

The girl sighed visibly with relief. "Thank you, sir."

"How long have you worked for Judge Sterrett?"

"About three years, sir."

"Do you like working there?"

"I did, but things are getting pretty bad out there."

"What do you mean by pretty bad?"

"The shootings and the missing money. I want to transfer, sir."

"I understand. Do you like Judge Sterrett?"

"Yes sir. I think the world of him."

"You wouldn't do anything to intentionally hurt him, would you?"

"Oh, no sir."

"Phyllis, this is very important. Did you tell anyone about the wedding that Judge Sterrett did Friday night?"

"No, sir, not really."

"Are you sure?"

"I think so. There's been a lot going on, though."

"Who all came into the office Friday morning?"

"Just the sheriff's officers. They still had the office cordoned off. The public couldn't get in."

"I don't mean the public. Did anyone from the government come in Friday morning?"

"Yes sir. Commissioner Wade came in, first thing. I'm sorry. I thought you meant the public."

"What did he want?"

"He said something about improving security there."

"Did you talk to him?"

"Yes, sir."

"What did you talk about?"

"I don't remember much. He was only there for about five minutes. He wanted to know about Judge Sterrett and that he was safe."

"Did he ask where he was?"

"Yes, sir. As a matter of fact, he did."

"What did you tell him?"

"I told him that I didn't know."

"Did he say why he wanted to know where the judge was?"

"No, sir."

"Are you sure that you didn't tell him about the wedding?"

Phyllis hesitated but kept her gaze leveled at the sheriff. "I might have, I don't remember for sure. If I did, I was only trying to help."

Sanders struggled to keep his patience and his voice level casual. "Phyllis, think back and try to remember. It's very important. Judge Sterrett's life could be riding on your answer. Did you mention the wedding to Commissioner Wade?"

"Yes, sir. I think I did. Judge Sterrett had just called for the wedding information before the commissioner came in. When I mentioned the wedding, the commissioner asked me about it. Did I do something wrong?"

"Why did you tell Gary Baker that you told no one about the wedding?"

"I just forgot. I thought he meant did I tell the public about it. I didn't see any reason not to tell the commissioner. Was I wrong?"

"Probably not, Phyllis. You couldn't have known. Did the commissioner tell you to keep the conversation quiet?"

"Yes sir. He did. But I thought he meant keeping quiet about the rest of our conversation."

"What was that all about?"

"About him getting me another job, that's all."

"Did you tell him about the missing money?"

"Yes sir. I thought at the time that I'd be fired over it."

"Why would Wade need to keep that conversation quiet? That doesn't make any sense."

"He wanted me to report the results of the investigation. I think that's what he wanted me to keep quiet about."

"He wanted you to report the results to him?"

"Yes sir."

"Did you?"

"I called him, but I really didn't have much to tell him."

"Did you call him at his office?"

"No sir. He told me not to call him there. He gave me the number of his mobile phone."

Sanders kept his voice level even and casual. "Do you have that number with you?"

"Yes sir. I think so." After rummaging through her purse for a minute, she handed the sheriff a slip of paper. "Here it is, sir."

Sanders looked at the number. "Did Wade write this for you?"

"I wrote it, sir."

Sanders wrote the number down on a slip of paper and handed it back to her. "Phyllis, I want you to write a statement relating all this. Here's some paper. Please do it now."

Phyllis looked back at him. "Will this get the commissioner in trouble?"

"Probably."

"Are you thinking that he told those men who attacked the judge where he was?"

"It looks like he did."

Phyllis looked down at her shoes. "It looks like I screwed up again. I'll lose my job for sure."

"You'll probably be all right. Just fill out that statement and I'll be right back." Sanders scooped up the phone number and headed for Walker's office. Blair was reviewing the affidavits with Judge Rhoads when the sheriff arrived. Walker was nowhere in sight. "Where's Fred?"

"He's in the can, Sheriff. Do you want me to go get him?"

"No. Does this phone number mean anything to you?"

Blair took the number and looked at it. After comparing the number to the affidavit, he looked up and smiled. "It damn sure does, sir. That's the number that called Agnew at 8:33 Friday morning. Where did you get it?"

"I got it from one of Sterrett's clerks. Wade gave it to her to call him with updates on the investigation. We now have independent confirmation." Sanders looked over to Judge Rhoads. "Is this information enough for you to sign a warrant for Agnew, Judge?"

"It looks good to me, Sheriff. Thanks for letting me off the hook on Wade."

The sheriff nodded at the judge and then turned back to Blair. "Call me when the paperwork's ready. I need an extra copy for the other warrant." Without waiting for an answer he strode back to his office, where the girl was finishing her written statement. He leaned over her shoulder and read it with her. It was somewhat disjointed, but it would do. Gary Baker was summoned into the room. The sheriff handed the paper to him.

"Gary, get this notarized and get Judge Nash out of bed. I want a warrant for Wade by the time I get back with Agnew."

"I was hoping to go with you to get Agnew, boss."

"Sorry, Gary. I need that warrant. Fred and Larry are going with me. When you get Judge Nash, ask him to set high bonds on these suspects. I would appreciate it if he would stick around awhile and arraign the prisoners. Get Tim Carter out of bed in an hour or so. I want him to head up the hunt for Stewart in Arlington later this morning like we discussed in the staff meeting."

"Okay, boss. I'm sorry that I didn't do a better job with the clerk."

"Don't worry about it. She misunderstood your questions, but when you questioned her, we weren't thinking about Wade."

Walker and Blair walked into the room. Walker presented the warrant to the sheriff without a word. Sanders glanced at it and handed it back. "Do we have an address?"

"Yes sir. It was easy. He's listed in the phone book."

"Good! Let's go get that no good son of a bitch."

Chapter Twenty-One

It was 5:40 am when the sheriff's unit slipped into Agnew's driveway. Larry Blair shut off the engine, and they exited the car without closing the doors, looking at a rather unpretentious brick home. The grass needed mowing and the flowerbeds grew only weeds. A Sunday-morning newspaper rested in the front yard.

The sheriff walked around to the back with Larry, where they approached an unlocked gate that protected the back yard with a flimsy cyclone fence. The grass in the back yard was even higher than the front. While they were standing at the gate, a black Labrador retriever trotted up, eyeing them suspiciously, but not barking. Larry stuck his hand through the fence, letting the dog sniff his hand, and then stroked his ears. The sheriff pointed to the back of the house. Larry nodded, eased through the gate, and patted the dog once more for good measure. Sanders returned to the front of the house to join Walker as Larry cased the back door. The back porch was a small two-step affair, affording no cover. Larry stood beside it, checked his weapon and handcuffs, leaving his pistol loose. When he heard pounding at the front door, he pressed against the wall and waited.

There was no response inside the house for over two minutes. Larry watched the sun as it peeked above the east horizon. Finally, Larry heard bedsprings creaking and heavy footsteps crossing the house. There was more pounding at the door, and Larry heard the occupant grumbling through the open kitchen window as he approached the front door.

"Who the hell is it?

"It's the sheriff. Open up."

"What do you want?"

"I need to talk to you."

"At this ungodly hour? What the hell for?"

"Open up. Do it now."

Larry heard footsteps coming toward him and he braced further against the wall. The back door flew open, and Agnew ran down the steps and out into the back yard. Using his old linebacker speed, Blair closed and tackled Agnew. Rising to his knees, he cuffed Agnew's left hand with lightning speed. As he pulled the cuffed hand behind Agnew, Blair put a knee on his spine, pulled the right hand around, and snapped the other cuff on. Sanders and Walker ran up as Blair rolled the shirtless Agnew over.

All three broke into convulsive laughter when they looked at Agnew. He had landed face down in a fresh pile of dog dung and was spitting it out as he glared at the officers. Fred Walker continued laughing as he jerked Agnew to his feet. Agnew's anger slowly turned to worry as he looked to his right and recognized the sheriff himself.

"Quit joking around, you bastards, and uncuff me so I can get this dog shit off my face. When I get Chief Parker on the phone, you won't think this is so damn funny. Arlington PD can play jokes, too. You're going to be sorry for this."

Sanders controlled his laughter but maintained his grin as he recited Agnew his rights. "Do you understand your rights?"

"Cut the crap and let me loose. This jokes gone far enough."

"It's no joke, Agnew. Do you understand your rights?"

"Yeah. I know them by heart. I'm a cop, remember?"

"Good. Take him to the car, boys."

"Wait a minute, Sheriff. Let me go inside and clean up. How about a little professional courtesy?"

The sheriff eyed him with the smile widening. "No, I think I like you just the way you are. That dog dung improves your looks. You've got pants on. That's all you need. We have some nice new clothes for you to wear."

"Come on sheriff. At least get this dog shit off my face. A good cop wouldn't treat the worst criminal this way."

"You've treated people far worse than this, Agnew. I've been hearing quite a lot about you in the last few days. You didn't give Sterrett any professional courtesy. You tried to kill him."

Agnew shook his head fiercely and blinked through the dung at Sanders. Shaking his head didn't help much. The smell was getting to him, and that old familiar queasy feeling was coming from the pit of his stomach. More than dog dung was causing that sick feeling. "I don't know what you're talking about, Sheriff."

Sanders nodded at his deputies, and they started leading Agnew toward the car. Agnew resisted the best he could but it was a losing battle. The sheriff roughly pushed his head down as he entered the car. Walker circled around the back of the car and slid in next to Agnew as he leaned forward to try to scrape the dung off his face on the back of the front seat. Walker grabbed him by the hair and pulled him back. His smile widened as he inspected his prisoner, who was sitting there in black jeans. A more pathetic prisoner he had never seen, with a morning growth of beard and tousled hair and a liberal smear of dung reaching from his chin all the way to the top of his forehead. "You really do look like shit, Agnew." This drew more laughter from the occupants in the front seat as the unit rolled out of the driveway and headed east toward Fort Worth.

Agnew made no response for several minutes as the sheriff reported into dispatch. His eyes widened as he heard the sheriff inquiring on the status of an arrest warrant for Commissioner Wade. A fearful understanding began to dawn on him. He was in serious trouble. Perhaps something he couldn't get out of. His embarrassment faded somewhat as he contemplated the fate of a police officer in prison. He hadn't been kind to many that he had sent up. If they were getting Wade, they knew about the whole plan, but how? If Wade had talked, they'd already have him. That only left Pablo Cruz. There had been no news reports that he'd been arrested. Had he turned himself in? That didn't sound like Cruz. Who else could have heard about this? Cruz must have told some snitch about it, but Cruz didn't know about Wade. If all they had was a snitch, they had a weak case unless they could smoke Wade out, or him. Agnew decided to try to smoke the sheriff out.

"Sheriff, would you please tell me what this is all about? This must be some misunderstanding. Maybe if we discussed this, we can clear it up."

"There's no misunderstanding, Agnew. We have good information that you and an elected official hired the Cruz brothers to kill Judge Sterrett Friday night. That led to one man killed on the scene and Judge Sterrett being wounded. That equates to capital murder, in case you need a lesson in law. We had a deputy killed yesterday when we arrested Pablo Cruz. I'll tie you to that if I can."

"What kind of proof do you have of this, Sheriff?"

"You'll know in due time. I don't owe you more than that."

"Sure you do. I'm a cop. I'm entitled to some professional courtesy."

Sanders turned to face his prisoner. "If there's anything I can't stand, it's a cop turned bad. A common criminal I can understand, but I can't tolerate scum like you. Someone who lets a man die on the street because they don't like him, someone who shakes down petty crooks for personal gain, and someone who hires hit men to kill a judge is not entitled to any courtesy at all. Do I make myself clear?"

Agnew said nothing, but glared back at the sheriff. So they had Pablo Cruz and he had squawked. He wondered how they had tied him to Wade. Would a jury believe Cruz? Agnew doubted it without more proof. They had to have information coming from Wade's side as well. It had to be Wade's brother. But Wade's brother didn't know what the money was for. Wade must have told him. That was the only thing that made any sense. Agnew pondered his situation with this information. Could he deal his way out of this at least part way? He didn't know and decided not to admit anything. If he said anything now, it couldn't be retracted. If his lawyer offered, it could.

The silence continued until the car pulled into the sally port of the jail. Few words were spoken as he was processed in. He received stares from prisoners and jailers alike because of the smelly smear on his face. When the sheriff and the deputies vanished, he finally persuaded a jailer to let him go to the bathroom and clean up. An hour later, he watched a dejected-looking Wade being processed in. Wade was put in a holding cell across and one cell down from him. Wade's eyes widened when Agnew caught his attention. Agnew gave him the okay sign and put his index finger to his lips in the old gesture of silence. Wade nodded back.

It was 10:15 am when Buck Reed exited the Home Depot, where he had purchased a Genie garage door kit and other essential supplies. He was dressed in his old work clothes, with a cap and sunglasses for a disguise. Returning to the pickup truck, with the lawn mower in the back, Reed pulled out the remote control, the battery, and the receiver. Driving to a trash can, he threw the rest of the kit away. After inserting the battery in the remote and testing it, he drove slowly toward Sterrett's neighborhood.

When he arrived at the vacant house on La Paloma, he went upstairs and checked out the nosy neighbor's house. There were two cars still parked in the garage, but the newspaper was missing out of their yard as well as out of Sterrett's. Reed went back out to the truck and unloaded the lawn mower. After filling it with gas, he began mowing the front yard of the vacant house. At 10:45, the neighbor and her family pulled out of their driveway, dressed up in their Sunday best. It only took five minutes to finish the yard. He crossed the street and began mowing Sterrett's front yard. There was no activity in the neighborhood and no interest in the yardman. The front yard only took twenty minutes to mow. Reed took the mower to the back yard and closed the gate behind him. Reed studied the neighborhood through the fence to check for anything curious. There was nothing. Crossing the street, he pulled the pickup into Sterrett's driveway, parking in the back. After stuffing the C-4 and the aluminum cone into the Home Depot bag, he put the garage door parts into his pocket. Taking the gas can and a roll of duct tape out of the pickup, he went in the backyard, closing the gate behind him. Once again, he checked the neighborhood. Everything was quiet.

Picking the lock on the back door was much easier in the daylight. Reed headed straight for Sterrett's bedroom and moved the bookcase-bed out from the wall. The indention in the carpet showed him that he could put it back exactly as it was. He pulled out the aluminum cone, full of pellets known in his Vietnam days as a VC hat, and taped it to the back of the headboard, about five inches above the mattress line. Using the C-4, he placed a V-shaped charge behind the cone and attached the blasting cap. Two thin white wires from the cap were attached to the garage door receiver. The bomb was then secured with more duct tape. Reed moved the bed back in place and backed up to the window, making sure that nothing was visible. After picking up the residue in the bedroom, he went back outside and mowed the back yard. Remembering to lock the back door, he loaded up his lawn mower and drove back to his motel.

As he was eating lunch in his room, it dawned on him that Sunday would be a good time to check out Sterrett's friends. He had a phone number for an employee and the girlfriend. Dialing the phone number for Marilyn Shaw got no answer. Perhaps she was with him. A phone listing in the directory showed an address for a Cassandra Strange with a phone prefix matching the one he had. His Mapsco showed that the address couldn't be more than ten minutes away. Was it a waste of time to trail her on a Sunday? What the hell. There was nothing better to do. After showering, he put on fresh clothes and left, leaving his pistol and the garage door Genie in the room.

Driving the rental car to the address, he discovered that it was an apartment complex. Undaunted, he searched the mailboxes until he found her name under Unit 23B. It took only two minutes to find the unit, which was in plain sight of the parking lot. Reed drove to a nearby store and purchased a copy of *Field and Stream* magazine. Returning, he positioned his car where he could see her door and settled in. If nothing else, he would be able to recognize both her and her car tomorrow.

Little Jan brought up the subject as they were eating lunch. "Where is Aunt Cass, Daddy?"

"She's not your aunt, Jan. She left last night. She had a lot of things to do."

"When's she coming back?"

"Do you want her to come back, Jan?"

"Yes, Daddy. I like her."

Ray raised his eyebrows at her. "I thought you didn't want a woman around the family."

Robby put his milk down. "She's different, Dad. I like her, too."

"Do you like having her around, Robbie? You pitched a fit when I brought that other lady around."

"It's not the same, Dad."

"Why is it different?"

"I don't know. She's different. That's all. She's interested in us and looks after us."

"Are you saying that you would like to have Cass look after you?"

Robbie looked back down at his plate. He hadn't thought about it in those terms. Finally he looked back up. "I don't know. I guess so."

"You guess so? You're not sure?"

"You mean like she was our mother?"

"Yes. That's what I mean. What do you think about that?"

"I think I'd like it, Dad. She's really neat."

Ray looked at Jan who was absorbed in a slice of cake. "What about you, Jan? Would you like Cass to come live with us and be a mother to you?"

Jan looked up at her father with a very serious face for a six year old. "Yes, Daddy. I'd like that very much."

Ray looked back at Robbie. "What about that other lady I brought home? You were very upset when I did that."

"That was different, Dad."

"Why was she so much different?"

"Because she was just for you. Cass would be for all of us."

"How do you know about that other lady?"

"I don't know. I just felt it. That's all."

Ray tried to digest this information about the kids' feelings and instincts. The ringing telephone wrenched him from his thoughts. The timing was terrible for a phone call.

"Hello?"

"Ray, this is Lee. I've got some good news."

"Good! Lay it on me. Did you find Stewart?"

"Not yet, but we have Pablo Cruz and the two men who hired him to kill you."

"You mean it wasn't Stewart?"

"No. It was Agnew and Commissioner Wade."

"Damn! I can understand Agnew. That sounds just like him, but Commissioner Wade?"

"They're both under arrest, Ray. There's a $250,000 bond on both of them. We've got them dead to rights by tracing their mobile phone records."

Ray sat in stunned silence as he regrouped his thoughts. "How did they find out where I was Friday night?"

The sheriff relayed the whole story about Phyllis and ended it with a question. "Charlie, my security chief tells me that your head clerk left last night. Why?"

"Let's just say we had a slight disagreement."

"Ray, I can't leave her out there knowing where you are. That's a security risk I can't take."

"Why, Sheriff? Stewart wouldn't even know what her name is."

"Bullshit. Her name was all over the news Thursday, and she's listed in the phone directory. You need to get her back there, or I'll have to put her under guard somewhere else. Which is it going to be?"

"All right, Sheriff. I'll try to get her back here."

"Okay. Have Charlie pick her up. I don't want her coming back alone. And, Ray?"

"Yes?"

"Do it now."

"Okay. I'll do it."

"Thanks Ray. I'm just trying to be careful. This will all be over when we catch Stewart and you can get back to a normal life."

Angel stared through his living room window at the strange car parked a half-block away. With the sheers closed, a small gap in the drapes allowed him to watch without being seen. It was impossible to tell if the two men were watching him or someone else. As he was watching, a light blue sedan pulled up behind it, and the first car drove away. Two men occupied the second car as well.

"Jerry, come here. I want you to see something."

His driver ambled in with a beer. "Yeah, boss. What is it?"

"Look at the car sitting down about a half block. Is that the same car that pulled out of the restaurant when we did this morning?"

Jerry replaced Angel at the window and peered out for several seconds. "Yeah. It's the same one. The guy sitting shotgun is the same, but the driver's different."

Angel didn't like this. "Somebody's watching us then. Who?"

"I don't know, boss. Cops, maybe?"

"Could be." Angel brought out binoculars for a better look, focusing in on two men in casual clothes, both with that clean-cut cop look. As he watched, the man in the passenger seat raised binoculars of his own and stared back at him. "Yeah. It's cops all right. Why are they watching us?"

"Could be for anything, boss."

"How could they have zeroed in on us?"

"I don't know. It could be for Stewart, or it might be the guy that snatched his kids that we're hiding in Grand Prairie."

"Yeah, but which?"

"There's no way of telling, boss."

Angel switched off the football game, his two-hundred-dollar bet no longer important. The Dallas police were turning the city upside down, trying to find the two children that their client had grabbed at school Friday afternoon. The mother was the daughter of a rich businessman in Dallas, and grandpa was sparing no expense in getting those children back. The pending divorce was a nasty one. On the other hand, things had been popping in Fort Worth and Arlington on the Stewart murders, with another attempt on that judge's life Friday night. The sheriff's office had been chasing their tails so far. Angel decided that if the police were after him, it was probably over the Dallas deal. Someone in the Dallas organization must have finked. It was time to check. Angel picked up the phone to call his Dallas contact and quickly put the phone back down. Using his own phone could be a colossal blunder.

"Let's go for a ride, Jerry."

"Where to, boss?"

"Somewhere I can talk on a secure line. Let's go to the Burger King and get some burgers. While you're doing that, I'll call Dallas."

The two men backed the Lincoln out of the driveway and drove past the surveillance car. The occupants appeared to be uninterested as they drove by. Two blocks later, the white sedan that had been there earlier appeared about two blocks behind them, following them to the Burger King. Angel headed for the phone, fished out coins, and called his contact in Dallas.

"Hello?"

"Harvey, this is Angel. What's happening?"

"Just the usual. What's new with you?"

"I'm getting trailed by the heat, that's what. Who all in your group knows about our client?"

"Only three. Terry, Hassan, and me."

"Who set this deal up with the client?"

"Hassan did."

"Who connected the client to Hassan?"

"I don't know."

"Could they have talked to the heat?"

"It's possible, but they wouldn't have known about you. Hassan doesn't even know that you have his client."

"Is anybody watching you?"

"No. I don't think so."

"Who's with you right now?"

"Just Terry."

"Would you have him check outside and see if you're being watched?"

"Sure, I'll check. Hang on for a minute." Angel waited impatiently. Jerry was being waited on at the front of the line. A quick look into the parking lot failed to discover the white sedan, but Angel knew that it would be close by. If they stayed too long in the hamburger joint, the surveillance unit would get suspicious. "Angel, are you there?"

"Yeah. I'm here."

"There's no one snooping around over here. Your problem must be coming from somewhere else."

"Thanks, Harvey. Listen, don't call my place for a few days. The phone may be tapped. I'll check in with you until further notice."

"That's cool, Angel."

"How's Stewart doing?"

"He seems to be fine. He's a little antsy about being cooped up, but they all get like that after a couple days."

"Do you still have him on Swiss Avenue?"

"Yeah. He's still there."

"He doesn't have access to a phone, does he?"

"No, Angel. You know better than that."

"Okay. I'm just a little antsy myself with this tail."

"Thanks for calling. I've got to go now."

Angel hung up the phone as Jerry approached with a sackful of food, and they drove back toward the house. The white sedan was nowhere in sight, but a new tail appeared. It was a van with several antennae. Angel caught Jerry's attention and put his finger to his lips. Jerry nodded in understanding and they drove on in silence. Angel considered the problem. Whoever was trailing him had plenty of units, so they must be powerful.

How long would this go on? Angel didn't have a big enough operation to operate at arm's length. He'd be hurting in a few days. Discomfort would lead to mistakes.

When they reached their turn-off street, Angel motioned Jerry to drive on. They opened the sack of burgers and munched wordlessly as they headed west on Pioneer Parkway. Angel directed Jerry to a multiscreen theater. They parked, walked inside, and purchased two tickets to a movie. Angel turned around and checked the entrance for a tail. There wasn't any yet. After directing Jerry to find them seats in the movie, he headed to a line of public phones in the lobby.

"Tarrant County Sheriff's Office."

"I need to speak to the sheriff, please."

"Who's calling, please?"

"I have some important information for him."

"Who's calling, please?"

"Look, Goddamit! I'm not giving my name. If you don't connect me, it's going to be your ass. Do you understand me? I said I had some important information for him."

"Just a moment. I'll see if I can locate him."

"This is Sheriff Sanders."

"I've got a deal for you."

"Who's this?"

"This is somebody who knows where Stewart is. Are you interested?"

"Go ahead. I'm listening."

"I read that there's a $75,000 reward for him."

"Actually, it's $73,000 and change."

"Whatever. How can I get the money?"

"By telling me where Stewart is. We'll go get him and give you the money. It's that simple."

"No questions asked?"

"I don't know about that. Are you talking immunity?"

"Yeah."

"Immunity for what?"

"Immunity for knowing where he is."

"Actually, it's called harboring a fugitive. There's a big difference in knowing where he is and hiding him yourself. Which is it?"

"What difference does it make?"

"Are you asking for immunity for harboring a fugitive?"

"Could be."

"I might be able to get you the immunity, but probably not the reward, too. Rewards are for people who're not involved in the crime."

"I had nothing to do with those murders."

"I see. Did Stewart set this up with you in advance?"

"Yeah, but I didn't know what he was going to do."

"Did you know Stewart before this happened?"

"No."

"Then how did Stewart know to come to you?"

"Look, Sheriff, I'm not going to go through the third degree here. Do we have a deal or not?"

"Do you want the money or immunity for harboring a fugitive?"

"Both or it's no deal."

"I'll have to get clearance for that. Where can I reach you?"

"You must think I'm stupid. I'll call you back."

"When?"

"You tell me."

"I should know in one hour."

"Okay. I'll call back in one hour."

"One more thing. I need to know if I'm talking to the right person. Where did you pick Stewart up?"

"I picked him up at a golf course in Mansfield. Good enough?"

"That's good enough. If we make a deal, can we get him today?"

"Probably tonight."

"Call me back in one hour."

Sanders hung up and reached for his radio. "Unit fifteen, come in."

"This is unit fifteen. Go ahead, Sheriff."

"Tim, are you trailing that guy Angel?"

"I'm just outside his house but he's not here. Fuqua and Mills have him at a movie theater right now."

"What about this Shorty? What's he doing?"

"He's been home all day. He hasn't moved at all."

"Has Shorty spotted your tail?"

"I don't think so. We haven't trailed him anywhere, and we can watch his house from an adjacent street. We've had to watch Angel on his street, though. The next street over has houses with stockade fences, and we can't see through them."

"Then if somebody spotted your tail, would it be Angel?"

"Probably, sir."

"Is your surveillance unit inside the theater with Angel?"

"They're watching the car, sir. There's too many exits."

"Have one of them go into the theater and find their pay phones. I need to know if one of the phone numbers is 555-1991."

"Roger. I'll get on that right now and report back."

"Over and out."

Sanders put down the radio and picked up the phone. It was a long shot catching the DA home on Sunday. Getting lucky, he was authorized to give limited immunity and a reward negotiable up to $25,000.

As the sheriff hung up the phone, his dispatcher called him on the radio. "Unit one, are you in your office?"

"Yes, I'm here."

"Mills is checking in with some information. Do you want me to patch him through?"

"You bet. Patch him through right now."

"Unit one, this is unit nineteen. Over."

"Go ahead, unit nineteen."

"Sheriff, I went inside the theater and found the number you had. There's a bank of four public phones outside the restrooms."

"Good. Do you know who you're following?"

"No, sir. I think Tim's running that down."

"Give me a description of his car."

"It's a 1997 Lincoln Town Car. The color is pearl gray with license plate number TXX 097."

"We'll run the plate number from here. Is Fuqua with you?"

"Yes sir. He's right here. Do you want to talk to him?"

"No. Are both of you out of uniform?"

"Yes sir."

"Send Fuqua back into the theater with a beeper. Have him put it on vibrate and hang around the phones, but not too close. When Angel calls me, I'll pick up his number on my caller ID. I'll page Fuqua with the number that's calling me. I want him to get a physical description of the caller, complete with what he's wearing. As soon as he gets it, he's to ease out of the theater and report it to you. Then I want him to go back into the theater and stay close to the caller, but not close enough to get spotted. If I beep him again with the number code 7777, he's to arrest him on the spot. If I beep 3333, he's to follow him out of the theater and report his whereabouts to you on his hand held radio. Tell Fuqua to keep that radio off until he needs it. I don't want it squawking while he's tailing the subject."

"I've got it, sir. Anything else?"

"Yes. Radio Tim and tell him to have all his units converge on the theater. Cover the back exits with the backups."

"I've got it, sir. There's another subject with him. Do you want him arrested if the arrest code comes through?"

"Yes, but only if he's with the other subject."

"Yes sir. Anything else?"

"No. That's all. Over and out."

Sanders motioned Gary Baker into his office and handed him the plate number. "Gary, get me a rundown on this plate complete with the registered owner's criminal history. I need it five minutes ago."

Buck Reed's eyes slid over the top of the *Field and Stream* to the uniformed deputy ringing the doorbell of Cass's apartment. The door opened and the deputy stepped inside. A quick glance at the squad car showed exhaust coming out of the tailpipe. Reed put away the magazine, eased out of the lot, and parked farther away. Three minutes later, the deputy exited with a youngish-looking redhead wearing sunglasses.

A quick study through his binoculars revealed an attractive woman in her mid thirties, who was built like a movie star. What Reed found more interesting was the overnight bag she was carrying in addition to her purse. The binoculars swept to the deputy, who looked all business, sweeping the parking lot with his eyes, his hand staying near his pistol. Reed quickly put the binoculars in the glove box and started his car, his assassin's mind calculating quickly. That deputy's on duty. They're not going on a picnic. What's going on?

The squad car exited the parking lot, with the deputy looking in all directions as they left. Reed stayed back about two blocks as the car traveled west on Pioneer Parkway, a busy four-lane divided highway with traffic lights at every main cross street. Reed got delayed by red lights and debated about chucking the tail. Just when he was about to give up, he spied them topping a hill a half mile in front of him. Using all of his skill, Reed tailed the deputy west several miles to downtown Fort Worth. Reed was able to slow down a little because of slow-moving traffic as they traveled over the bridge just south of downtown Fort Worth. The roadway expanded to three lanes, and Reed dropped back to a more comfortable interval. Three miles later, the patrol car put on its turn signal and slowly moved over, exiting on Roaring Springs Road. Reed was forced to close the distance to two blocks.

"Unit thirty-seven to base. Over."

"This is base. Go ahead, thirty-seven."

"I'm about twenty blocks from you, and I have a tail. What do you advise?"

"Hang on a second and I'll get the captain."

"This is Captain Rogers, thirty-seven. What have you got?"

"I've got a male subject in a white two-door sedan tailing me."

"What's your ETA to Westover Drive?"

"Four minutes."

"Go ahead and turn left on Westover Drive. I'll have a reception committee ready. Over and out."

"Units forty and forty-one, this is base. Respond now. Over."

"This is unit forty-one. We're both here and listening."

"Position yourselves in driveways on Westover Drive and intercept the suspect."

"Roger, sir."

"I'll be there in two minutes for backup. Over and out."

Reed slowly turned left on a street leading into a very exclusive neighborhood and watched in surprise as the patrol car in front of him was disappearing at a high rate of speed. He had proceeded only a few feet when another squad car pulled out from a driveway and blocked his path. Another unit slid in just behind him, and he was trapped. Reed kept his cool and remained motionless as one of the officers approached, with the other remaining at the back of his car.

"May I see your driver's license, please?"

"What's going on, Officer?"

"May I see your driver's license, sir?"

"Did I do something wrong, Officer?"

The deputy opened the driver's door. "Get out of the car and don't ask any more questions. Do it now."

Reed slowly got out of the car and was immediately shoved against the car. "Spread your legs and put both hands on top of the car. Do it now." Reed felt the cuffs slapped on his right wrist and his right arm pulled behind him. "Keep your face on the car and put your left hand behind you." Reed complied and as soon as he was cuffed was spun around to face a stern-faced deputy who looked huge. The guy must have spent his whole life lifting weights. Reed glanced over his right shoulder as another unit sped up and screeched the brakes. A plainclothes officer stepped out of the vehicle and approached.

"What do we have here, Hugh?"

"Don't know yet, Captain."

"Check his ID and see who he is."

Mr. Muscles patted Reed down. "He don't have anything on him, Captain."

Reed spoke without moving. "It's in the glove compartment."

"What's it doing there?"

"I don't like to keep it in my back pocket. It bothers me there."

Mr. Muscles found Reed's wallet and thumbed through the contents. "What we have here is a Mr. William R. Wilson of Joplin Missouri."

The plainclothes captain looked at Reed with searching eyes. He saw a smallish man in his mid fifties, dressed in work pants and a white T-shirt. He glanced into the car and saw a plaid short-sleeved shirt. His questioning stare returned to the man. The eyes that met his were just as searching. There was no fear in those eyes, and there should be if he was just an innocent citizen who was being rousted by the police. "What are you doing here, Mr. Wilson?"

"I just wanted to look at these ritzy houses. I had no idea that it was a guarded neighborhood. I thought this was a public street. I'm sorry."

"What are you doing in Fort Worth, Mr. Wilson?"

"Just sightseeing mostly. I came down on a business matter yesterday morning. The business deal didn't work out, but I decided to stay down here and look around. Is that a crime?"

"What kind of business are you in, Mr. Wilson?"

"I sell life insurance. Universal life policies, mostly."

"You come all the way down here from Joplin just to sell a life insurance policy?"

"It's unusual, but yes I did."

"Why?"

"One of my policy holders in Joplin has a brother down here. He sounded interested on the phone, so I came down. The Kansas City Royals are in town, so I decided to take in a ballgame or two."

"Where are you staying?"

"In Arlington. At the Holiday Inn on Park Springs Road."

"This isn't Arlington. This isn't even close. Are you telling me that you drove all the way over here just to look at these houses?"

"Yes sir. That's right."

"How did you know these houses were over here?"

"Some guy told me about them."

"What guy?"

"Just some guy I met in the restaurant. We got to talking about houses, and he said these were some of the nicest houses in the county."

"So you jumped in the car and drove twenty-five miles over here on his say-so?"

"That's right. I didn't have anything better to do. The ball game doesn't start till 7:30 tonight. How about uncuffing me, Officer. I haven't done anything wrong. I don't see any no-trespassing signs."

"Do you have anything embarrassing in that car?"

"No."

"Do you mind if we take a look?"

"Go ahead. Help yourself."

Captain Rogers nodded at the two deputies and they started a systematic search of the car. Reed was thankful that he had left his pistol in the hotel room. He decided to take the offensive, as any irate citizen would do. "If I'm not under arrest for some perceived complaint, how about uncuffing me, so I can talk to you like I belong in this country?"

Rogers ignored him and looked at Hugh, who was handing him a pair of binoculars. The other deputy was closing the trunk lid and shaking his head no. "The only thing in the car is these field glasses, Captain. There's a magazine and a Mapsco in the back seat. Nothing else."

Rogers swept the neighborhood with the field glasses. They were expensive 10 × 50s. "What are you doing with these glasses, Mr. Wilson?"

"I take them to the ball games. Something wrong with that?"

Rogers looked him in the eye. "Could be, if you came over here to spy on somebody. You certainly have the tool for it."

"That's bullshit, Officer. There's no law against having binoculars. If you don't take these cuffs off, my governor's going to hear about this, and you guys will have a lot of explaining to do."

Rogers smiled a little at that one. "Hold your water, Mr. Wilson. I'll be right back." Without another word he walked back to his unit and got inside. "Unit thirty-five to base. Over."

"This is base. Go ahead, Captain."

"Get Harry on the radio. I need to talk to him."

"Roger, sir. He's in the kitchen."

Rogers glanced through the windshield at the suspect. Mr. Wilson was leaning back against the car and watching him. The deputies were checking underneath his car with mirrors. Mr. Wilson ignored them. It was obvious that nothing was going to be found in the car.

"This is Harry, Captain. Did you need to talk to me?"

"Yes, Harry. Give me the details on this tail."

"Captain, I first saw him on Pioneer Parkway about two miles from I-820. He knew that I spotted him and turned into a liquor store, but he never got out of the car. He got back on the road and tailed me all the way here. He's a damn good tail and made all the right moves, hiding behind trucks and keeping just the right distance most of the time. He even changed shirts in the car, just to look different. That's all."

"Harry, is there any chance you made a mistake here? Could he be just an out of town sightseer?"

"I don't think so, sir. I just attended a TECLOSE seminar on this a couple of months ago. This guy did all the things that the instructor told us to do when we're trailing a suspect solo."

"What else did he do that was suspicious?"

"Just little things. Like he stayed in the proper lanes and never maintained eye contact when I looked at him in the rearview mirror."

"Harry, how would this guy pick you up on Pioneer Parkway and know to follow you all the way out here?"

"I think he picked us up at the girl's apartment."

"Did you see him there?"

"Negative. He didn't come out of the parking lot, or I would have spotted him right off."

"How long had you been on the road from the apartment complex before you spotted him?"

"No more than two minutes."

"Were you looking for a tail when you left the apartment?"

"Yes sir. I didn't see him then, but the traffic was pretty heavy. I was looking at all the cars."

"Thanks, Harry. Over and out."

Rogers replaced the radio receiver and stroked his chin while he studied the suspect. He could never put a charge on this guy that would stick. Should he let him go? Not on his own authority, he wouldn't. He exited the unit and approached the subject again. "Mr. Wilson, did you change your shirt while you were driving over here?"

"I just took my outer shirt off. I was a little warm."

"Why didn't you turn on the air conditioner?"

"Is it a crime to drive with just a T-shirt on?"

"Don't get cute with me, Mr. Wilson."

"I'm not getting cute, Officer. I demand an explanation for this. I've never been treated like this before in my life."

"All I can tell you is that this a serious security matter. You've followed a car over here carrying a security sensitive passenger. Perhaps it was just a coincidence, perhaps not."

"Well, I wasn't following anyone. Are you going to let me go or not?"

"I don't know. Who were you were going to sell a policy to?"

"Paul Smith."

"Where does he live?"

"I don't know. We met by appointment at a restaurant."

Rogers eyed him with renewed suspicion. "That's a terrific answer. Do you have a business card on you?"

"No. I didn't think I would need one to view nice homes."

Without another word, Rogers took Mr. Wilson's driver's license from Hugh, retraced his steps to his unit, and picked up the radio.

"Unit thirty-five to dispatch. Over."

"This is dispatch. Go ahead unit thirty-five."

"I need the sheriff. Can you find him for me?"

"I sure can. He's in the office today. I will route you now."

After a few seconds the sheriff's voice crackled over the radio. "Charles, what have you got?"

"I picked up the girl in Arlington as you ordered. On the way back my man says that he picked up a tail. We apprehended the suspect, but he looks clean as a whistle, except for a pair of binoculars. He has a plausible explanation for everything I can throw at him, but the deputy swears that he was tailing him. I trust this deputy on these matters, but I don't have anything to arrest the suspect on. What do you advise?"

"Who's the suspect?"

"A Caucasian male by the name of William R. Wilson, DOB 09-06-49. Address is 1349 Cedar Ridge, Joplin, Missouri. DL number 0421840."

"Hang on a minute and I'll have him run on NCIC while we talk." Sanders handed the note to Baker. "Charles, Are you still there?"

"I'm here. The guy claims to be an insurance salesman who came down here to sell a policy to a Paul Smith, address unknown. He claims that he stayed over to see some baseball games between the Rangers and Royals. That's his explanation for the field glasses. He said that some man he met in a restaurant told him about the fancy houses out here, and he just drove over here to look at them since he didn't have anything else to do."

"How does he look and act?"

"He looks and acts okay. He's holding his cool pretty well."

The sheriff scanned the NCIC sheet. "Charles, this man has no criminal history. I'll have somebody call his home to verify who he is. What does your man say about the way he tailed him?"

"He said that he was as good as they come."

"Have one of your units bring him in and book him. I want to run his fingerprints. Maybe we'll find somebody else."

"What do I charge him with?"

"Suspicion."

"Suspicion of what?"

"Suspicion of anything. We can hold him twenty-four hours on that. After that we'll have to release him. One more thing, get the judge out of that neighborhood within one hour. Take them to the backup security location that we discussed Friday."

"We'll have to bring in more security, sir."

"Do it. Over and out."

Chapter Twenty-Two

Gary Baker brought in the paperwork to the sheriff and handed it to him. Lee Sanders scanned the rap sheet without taking his feet off the desk. "Clean as a whistle, huh?"

"I'm afraid so. I called information in Joplin. The phone is in the name of Cynthia Wilson and it's unlisted."

"Call back up there and get Joplin PD. Tell them what's going on and have them get the number. See if they know this guy. It's not a big town."

"Okay, boss."

"We've got twenty-four hours unless the fingerprints tell us that he's not who he says he is."

The phone rang and Sanders picked it up. He snapped his fingers to Baker to stop him. "Our informant is coming on the line. Hold up on that other detail."

Baker nodded and passed off whispered instructions to another deputy, who left abruptly. Baker quickly flipped on the recording machine. After reading the phone number on the caller ID screen, he dialed the number to Fuqua's beeper and set the ball rolling.

"This is Sheriff Sanders."

"Hello, Sheriff. Are we going to do business?"

"Are you the one I talked to about Stewart?"

"That's me. Do we have a deal?"

"Maybe. There's something that I need to make clear first."

"What's that?"

"First of all, there's only immunity for harboring a fugitive. If we uncover evidence that you were involved with the murders, then all immunity is off. Is that clearly understood?"

"Yeah. I got it. No problem."

"Second, Stewart has to be taken alive. Can you guarantee that?"

"I think so."

"Is he still armed?"

"As far as I know he is."

"Can you disarm him before we move in?"

"I can try. I'll think of something."

"If we walk into a gun battle, the deal's off. Understand?"

A telephone with a red light instead of a ringer started blinking. Baker picked it up without speaking and started writing down notes. He hung it up without uttering a word and handed the note to Sanders. The sheriff looked at it and nodded.

"I understand. I can arrange that."

"What time did you pick Stewart up at the golf course that morning?"

"About 9:30. Why?"

"I'm just trying to verify that I have the right informant. The next thing is the money." Sanders checked the second hand on his watch. Fuqua should be in position right about now. "It's against county policy to give reward money to people who are involved the crime. However, the DA authorized me to give you $5,000 in addition to the immunity."

On the other end of the line, Angel squinted his eyes shut in anger. "You can kiss my ass, Sheriff. You need Stewart worse than I need five thousand measly bucks. I can hang up and you're back to square one. You don't even know who I am, and I'm the only one who knows where he is. If you don't have me, you've got nothing."

Sanders smiled. Time to drop the bomb. "But I do have you, Angel."

Angel almost dropped the phone. "What did you call me?"

"Maybe I should call you Angelino Ocasio. Perhaps you answer to your full name better. Let me lay it out for you. I can arrest you and charge you whether you cooperate or not. Once I get you down here, I may change my mind about the $5,000."

Angel spun around and looked over the theater hallway. There was no one in sight. "You're going to have to find me first. I'll teach you about double-crossing people. I know how to hide. It's my business. Then I'll call the press and tell them how you screwed this deal up. How do you think that will play in the newspapers, Sheriff?"

"You don't catch on very fast, Angel. I'll give you some more clues. You're in the UA Cinema on Pioneer Parkway, talking from a public phone, wearing tan slacks and an olive green golf shirt. How are you going to get out of the theater, let alone hide? I can sweat your partner for the information that I need, and I've got your confession on tape. Would you like for me to play some of it back for you?"

Angel jerked around and checked the hallway again. His searching eyes betrayed his rising fear. There was still no one in sight. Angel dropped the telephone receiver down without hanging it up and bolted for Jerry. Tapping his assistant on the shoulder in passing, he hurried out the exit with Jerry close behind. They walked outside to bright sunlight, their eyes adjusting slowly. The exit door burst open with a plainclothes officer holding a pistol at the ready, gripped with both hands. Angel turned again as he heard racing engines from the other direction heading his way.

"Freeze! Both of you! Police officers! You're under arrest!"

Angel and Jerry were forced to the ground and frisked military style. "They're both clean, Tim."" Angel was jerked to his feet to come nose to nose with a big uniformed deputy.

"It's a pleasure to meet you Mr. Ocasio. You're both under arrest for harboring a fugitive. That's a first-degree felony under the circumstances. You have a right to counsel during questioning and the right to remain silent. Any statements you make can be used against you in court. If you're too poor to afford counsel, one will be appointed for you. Do you understand your rights?"

Angel hung his head for a moment and then looked Carter in the eyes defiantly. "I understand my rights. Do you understand your wrongs?"

Carter looked puzzled. "What the hell are you talking about?"

"You just missed your chance to get Stewart, asshole."

Carter nodded to his team. "Take them away, boys." The prisoners were loaded in separate units and whisked away.

Captain Charles Rogers walked into the sheriff's office and plopped a full clear plastic bag front of him. "Here's his personal effects that were booked in, sir."

Sanders dumped out a wallet, a Seiko watch, car keys, two hotel card keys, and some change out on his desk. The wallet was the first order of business. Inside were two credit cards, two pictures of young children, and eleven hundred forty-three dollars in cash. Sanders held each credit card up to the light and examined them closely. "Charles, these cards are brand-new. They've never been used."

"Their issuance dates shows they were issued over a year ago."

"I know. This wallet looks new as well."

"What are you saying, Sheriff?"

"I don't know. What's this?" Sanders pulled a piece of paper out of a hidden compartment behind the area where the bills were kept. As the paper unfolded, his eyes rested on a list of ten phone numbers with area codes from all over. Rogers took the paper and studied it.

"I don't know, Sheriff. It could be anything. He sure was carrying a lot of money."

"Not really. If he doesn't use his credit cards and he's traveling out of town."

"Do you think he's legit?"

"I don't know yet. I can't get a thing out of the Joplin police department. They picked today to have the department picnic, and I can't reach anybody." Sanders picked up the hotel key cards and glanced at them. "Where does this guy say he's staying?"

"At the Holiday Inn in Arlington."

"Which one?"

"It's on I-20 and Park Springs Boulevard."

"Did you verify that?"

"Yes sir. I had the security base call out there. He checked in yesterday afternoon. Do you want me to get a search warrant?"

"No. We'd never get one. We don't have jack for probable cause."

"Maybe he'd give us permission."

"Well, he might and then again, he might not. How mad was he when you booked him in?"

"He was cool as hell most of the time. There wasn't a lot of talk on the way in. He asked me what the charge was. I told him that he was being arrested for suspicion and he just smiled and shook his head."

"Is that all?"

"Pretty much. When he found out he was being taken in, he clammed up. Did you get any hits on your end?"

"Nothing so far, but we've just started working on it. Where did he say he worked?"

"He said he sells life insurance."

"Who for?"

"He didn't say."

Sanders returned Mr. Wilson's property to the pouch and handed it back to Charles. "Put this back and put him in one of the interrogation rooms. I want to talk to him. Call me as soon as you get him situated. Are you moving Sterrett and his family?"

"They're en route now. I activated three more security units."

"Okay. If I'm not up here when you call, I'll be in one of the other interrogation rooms. Tim arrested some suspects that are hiding Stewart."

"That's great, Sheriff. Good work!"

"Not really, Charles. I hope I didn't botch it. I had him talking on the phone, but he spooked. If they clam up, we're back to square one."

"Well, good luck on that one, sir. If we can catch Stewart, we can coast downhill on the rest of it."

"Maybe. I wonder. If your guy's legit, that might be the case."

"Yes sir. I'll get going. I'm going to the new base after I set you up with the suspect." Rogers turned and left the sheriff staring vacantly over his boots into space. The sheriff reviewed the situation for several minutes until Fred Walker and Larry Blair strolled in.

"Boss, Tim's got the two prisoners waiting for you."

"They're not in the same room, are they?"

"No, sir. Tim knows better than that. He has them separated, two rooms apart. Their criminal histories are there waiting for you also."

"Who's the other guy?"

"His name is Jerry Terrance."

"Will he cooperate?"

"I'm not sure, Sheriff. Tim said he was quiet on the way in."

"Is he hostile?"

"No, sir. I don't think so."

"What's his temperature?"

"Nervous for sure. Other than that, I don't know."

"Does he have a criminal history?"

"Nothing serious. I don't have the details, though."

"Well, let's go find out." The sheriff rose and went out through the outer office, with his two assistants close behind. The hallway was filled with news reporters and minicams. There was a liberal sprinkling of national news people now on the scene as the story had captured national attention. The noise was suddenly deafening as they competed in yelling questions at the sheriff. The three men ducked their heads, plowed through them without comment, and continued to the elevator. The men exited in the basement and turned left down the hall, which traveled underground to the row of interrogation rooms, ignoring friendly greetings from staff members as they marched on. Sanders was entering that mindset of cold anger that policemen get when they're closing in on their prey.

Tim Carter was standing in front of one of the rooms with a clipboard of information ready for his boss. To the casual eye, the rooms looked like they were connected, but a hallway on the other side allowed entry to a narrow room between each, which permitted sheriff's personnel to view and record what went on in the interrogation rooms through one-way mirrors. Sanders took the clipboard from Carter without comment and studied the facts regarding the prisoner, with Walker looking over his shoulder. Satisfied, he nodded to Carter, who opened the door, and they stepped into the small room. Inside sat a forty-one-year-old Caucasian male with blond hair, dressed casually. The man was clearly nervous and he looked anxiously from one man to the other.

"Mr. Terrance, I'm Sheriff Sanders. This is Captain Walker and Detective Blair. Have you had your rights explained to you and what the charges are against you?"

"Yeah. That man, Carter, went over it with me."

"Terrance, we really don't have an ax to grind with you. If you fully cooperate, we don't plan to file any charges against you at all."

"What do you mean, fully cooperate?"

"Tell us all you know about Stewart. Tell us where he is and agree to testify against him in trial. I want to know the full extent of Angel's involvement in this. That's what I mean by full cooperation."

"Would I have to testify against Angel, too?"

"Maybe. That depends on the circumstances and whether Angel cooperates."

"What if I don't agree to testify against Angel?"

"Then it's no deal. We'll gather evidence against you and prosecute to the full extent of the law. It wouldn't be fair if Angel cooperated and skated while you took the fall, would it?"

"Hell no, it wouldn't be fair. What do you want to know?"

"Start at the beginning on this Stewart affair. If I need to, I'll break in with questions."

"Stewart called us Wednesday afternoon and wanted a gun. We sold him one."

That was way too brief for the sheriff. "Who's we?"

"Me and Angel."

"Who sent him to you?"

"I don't know."

"Who did he talk to? You or Angel?"

"He talked to Angel."

"Did he say what the gun was for?"

"I don't know. I don't think so."

Blair broke in. "Why not?"

"Angel would never supply a gun to kill a judge."

"What kind of gun was it?"

"A .357 Magnum revolver."

"Where did you get it?"

"I bought it about a week ago from some guy I've seen around."

"What else did you sell him?"

"The ammo and a speed clip. Angel sold him a burglar tool, too."

"Where did you meet him to sell him this gun?"

"At a service station in Arlington."

"Was that when you and Angel agreed to hide him?"

"Maybe, I don't know for sure. I wasn't part of that conversation."

"When did you find out that you were going to hide Stewart?"

"He called back about two in the morning and talked to Angel again. I think that's when the deal was struck."

"What happened next?"

"We met him in Mansfield the next morning and drove him to Dallas."

"What time did you meet him and where?"

"About 9:30 at the country club."

"Where did you take him in Dallas?"

"To a house that we know about, over on Swiss Avenue."

Sanders took over again. "Do you know the address?"

"Not exactly, but I could take you to it."

"Does Angel own that house?"

"No. Some guy in Dallas owns it."

"Does he live there?"

"No. He just hides people there."

"Is Stewart still there?"

"As far as I know he is."

"Is he still armed?"

"I think so. Angel tried to get it back from him in the car while we were driving over there, but Stewart wouldn't give it to him. He said he paid for it and it was his."

Sanders looked at Fred. "Do you have anything else for him?"

Walker nodded. "How much did Stewart pay you to do this?"

"Two thousand. We got five hundred and we had to give the guy in Dallas fifteen hundred."

"How much time did this buy Stewart?"

"Two weeks, I think."

"Where was he going after that?"

"I don't know."

"Can we surprise Stewart at this house?"

"Probably not in daylight. After dark you probably can."

"Who else is in the house with Stewart?"

"I don't think there's anyone else."

"Are you sure?"

"No. I can't be positive."

"When were you there last?"

"Thursday, when we took him over there."

"Could the man in Dallas put somebody else in there with him?"

"It's possible, but not likely."

"Why not?"

"The man in Dallas told Angel that it was too dangerous. The less people that knew about Stewart the better."

The sheriff checked his watch. It would be dark in an hour. "Terrance, draw us a map of that house, with as much detail as you can. Fred, you and Larry stay with him. Figure out how many officers are needed to take the place and I'll call the Dallas sheriff. I'll meet you all in the sally port in twenty minutes. Tim, come with me."

The two men went down two doors and entered a room. Sanders looked down at a dark-complexioned man with mean eyes that sent shivers down his spine. He immediately disliked the man. "Angel, are you ready to talk?"

"How about the reward?"

"That deal's off. You screwed it up when you tried to run. I'll go to bat for you with the DA to go easy, but that's only if you spill all. I want names and locations of your total criminal involvement. Not only where Stewart is, but who sent him to you and who else is involved in hiding him. Are you prepared to cooperate?"

Angel turned those mean eyes on Sanders, stifling an urge to spit on him. "Up yours, Sheriff. You're going to rot in hell before you find out where Stewart is."

The sheriff nodded with a poker face and followed Carter outside.

"Tim, process him in. I'm going to nail his ass. Do you want to go with us to Dallas?"

"Yes sir. I want in on Stewart."

"Then be in my office in ten minutes." Sanders stalked away toward the elevator with that determined look still in his eyes. He was about to enter the exhilarating high of nailing somebody big. As he turned a corner, he almost bumped into Charles Rogers, who was escorting his prisoner down to the interrogation rooms. Sanders had forgotten about him. The sheriff looked into the eyes of the prisoner. He saw a calm, dark-complexioned face with eyes that coolly looked back into his. "Charles, something's come up and I have to leave. Take your prisoner back to intake, and I'll talk to him in the morning. You go on back to base and make sure that everything's okay. I'll talk to you in a couple of hours."

He continued on his way, up the elevator and down the hallway through the crowd of reporters. The furor rose again. Sanders decided to stop and give them two minutes. He held up his hands for silence as bulbs flashed and reporters crowded up for vantage points with their microphones.

"Folks, I'm really sorry that you had to wait so long, and I've little time now to go into details. We have had some significant arrests today and more to come. This case is very close to closure. We have evidence that there was a conspiracy to kill Judge Sterrett that has no connection to the original suspect. Two arrests have been made today, and one is an elected official in this county. Another is a police officer from Arlington. That's all I can tell you now. I may have more in a couple of hours for a more in-depth news conference. Thank you for your patience."

As he turned to go into his office, Betty Anderson, who was sticking her microphone in his face, blocked his way. Sanders managed a thin smile. Betty had been kind to him in his election campaign and he had a soft spot for her. "Sheriff, when you said the case was nearing closure, did you mean that the arrest of Billy Earl Stewart is imminent?"

"I can't comment on that right now, Betty. All I can tell you is be here in two hours." Sanders gave her a wink and escaped into his office, nodding to Baker who was on the phone.

Gary put his hand over the mouthpiece. "I've got the police chief from Joplin on the phone. Do you want to talk to him?"

"I can't right now, Gary. If we move quick, we get Stewart. He's in Dallas. Do you want to go with us?"

Baker smiled. "Yes sir. I sure do." He spoke back into the phone. "Chief, something's just come up. I'll have to call you back."

A relieved Buck Reed was escorted back to intake, where he was put into a cell with several other male prisoners, whom he ignored. His attention was fixed on a phone hanging on the far wall. He maintained his composure as he dialed Torrey's beeper number. The operator interrupted the call.

"This has to be a collect call, sir. I'll have to give your name to the other party to connect you."

Reed gritted his teeth. "I'm trying to call a beeper number, ma'am."

"They cannot return your call, sir. This is an outgoing number only."

"If I give you a credit card number, can I call this beeper number?"

"I guess so. I've never done it before, but I guess it would work. The phone company don't care as long as we get paid."

"Very good. I have an AT&T calling card. The number is 444-36-2939. The pin number is 6420."

"Thank you, sir. Please hold while I verify." Reed searched his memory for Torrey's office number and remembered as the operator came back on the line. "Your billing number is confirmed. Please dial your number again. Reed dialed Torrey's beeper number. When he got the receiving beep, he punched in Torrey's office number and then 911-30. He hoped Torrey was bright enough to figure it out.

Reed sat down to wait as he checked the wall clock. It was amazing how he had been caught. After all these years, he had stumbled into a roadblock like an amateur. He had to concede one thing to the sheriff's deputies. They were good, but they didn't have a damn thing on him. His story would hold up in Joplin for a few days if they didn't force the name of a workplace out of him. Reed had never set one up. His picture and fingerprints were on file for the first time. This seemed like an ideal time to quit.

That is, if he could get out of here. If he did quit, there were details to clean up. What would he do with his farms? The additional acreage was now a liability. It could take too long to sell. Where would he go? The Caymans would be the starting place. That was where his money was, but where after that? His passports were home in Oklahoma. What name should he travel under? Once he decided on a destination, could he buy property under his real name? Reed figured not. The farms could be sold without his being there. That was simple enough, but would it be safe to transfer the money out of the country? If he was patient, the farms would bring over a million. That was too much to leave behind. Or was it? It wasn't needed now anyway. Reed checked the clock again. It was time to call, but someone else was on the phone. He ambled over and tapped the prisoner on the shoulder.

"I need to use the phone. Now."

The young black prisoner whirled and faced him without hanging up. "Get outta here, whitey. I'll get off this friggin' phone when I get ready."

Reed smiled at the irate inmate. "I can make it worth your while."

"How you going to do that, man?"

"I'll pay for your lawyer. What are you charged with?"

"Theft."

"How much do you have to pay a lawyer for that?"

"Probably $500."

"Done. Just give me the phone."

The prisoner eyed him suspiciously. "Hold on, honky. You jivin' me?"

"No. I'm calling my lawyer. You can talk to him when I'm through."

"Who's your mouthpiece, man?"

"Leonard Torrey. Do you know him?"

"I've heard of him."

"Do we have a deal?"

"What if he ain't there?"

"Then I'll give the phone right back to you. You lose nothing. If he's there, he'll verify the deal to you when I'm through."

"This phone means that much to you, man?"

"Yeah."

"Okay." The prisoner turned back to the phone. "I'll call you back in a few minutes. Something just came up." Without further ado, he hung up the phone and handed it to Reed. "You better not be jivin' me, man, or I'll whip your white ass right here."

Reed grabbed the phone without bothering to reply. After he dialed Torrey's number, the operator came on.

"Who is calling, please?"

"Just tell him a friend from Tulsa. He'll accept the call."

"Please hold on, sir." After a moment, Reed sighed with relief.

"Torrey here."

"Thank God you understood my emergency message."

"What's wrong?"

"I'm in jail under the name of William Wilson. I need you to get down here right away."

"What charges are they holding you on?"

"Nothing really. Suspicion is what they call it."

"Suspicion of what?"

"That's what I asked them. They didn't have an answer for me."

"What happened?"

"I'll tell you when you get down here. Just come quick. The whole deal can fall through if you don't move fast."

"Okay. I'll be there in ten minutes."

"There's one more thing."

"What is it?"

"I had to bribe another prisoner to get off the phone. I promised I would pay the first $500 for you to represent him. You'll need to verify that with him."

"Are you going to pay me the $500?"

"Yes, dammit."

"Okay. Put him on."

Reed handed the phone over to the prisoner and sat down to wait.

Sanders and his crew met the Dallas County sheriff on a side street just off Gaston Avenue, about two blocks from the suspected hideaway. With him was the Dallas city police chief, complete with a twenty-man SWAT team. A low current of excitement was running through the entire group. Sanders could feel it and understood. The feeling was the same within his own group.

The Dallas County sheriff smiled and extended his hand. "Hello, Lee. It's good to see you."

"Same here, Sheriff. I really appreciate the quick support."

"That's quite all right. This is Police Chief Carraway. He commands the SWAT team over here."

The two men shook hands, and Sanders looked into a strong face lined with wrinkles. The eyes showed a warmth that belied the tough features. "Nice to meet you, Chief. Thanks for your help."

"That's all right, Sheriff. Do you know which house it is?"

"No, sir. But I have a snitch with me who does. He's also made a sketch of the property."

"Good! Can we put him in an unmarked unit with one of our officers and identify the house while we're looking at the sketch?"

"Certainly." Sanders turned and motioned his men out of their units. "Fred, take Terrance and go with some of the Dallas boys to locate the house. We need an exact address. Larry, bring that sketch over here."

The deputies hurried to their assignments as the two sheriffs and the police chief bent over the hood of a car to examine the crude map. The SWAT leader soon joined them. Blair became the tour guide. "Gentlemen, this house sits in the middle of a block facing west. It has a large porch with two windows in the front. There's a hallway running down the center of the house, with rooms off to both sides. Each room has a window, so there are many ways to escape. The garage is separate from the house. It's located at the end of the driveway. There's a side entrance to it from the back yard. We don't know whether it's locked or not. Any questions?"

The SWAT team leader leaned over for a closer look. "Is it a one-story house?"

"Yes sir."

"How close are the adjacent houses?"

"Real close."

"Are they occupied?"

"I don't know, but I assume that they are."

The leader looked at his chief. "Should we evacuate those houses?"

Carraway looked off into space. "I don't know yet. Let's wait until the scout team comes back. Can you cover those side windows in the dark?"

"Yes sir. That's no problem." Bob looked over to Sanders and Blair. "Did you bring mug shots of the suspect?"

"Yes sir. We brought about thirty copies," answered Blair proudly. He reached into his shirt and handed a stack to the team leader. The leader kept one and handed the others to an assistant, who headed back to the team with them. Bob turned back to Blair.

"What was he wearing when last seen?"

"When he drove over here, he was wearing a dark blue water department uniform, but he brought two suitcases. We assume he had extra clothes."

"What kind of armament?"

"A .357 Magnum pistol with a four-inch barrel."

"Will he fight?"

"Probably."

Chief Carraway broke in. "We better evacuate those neighbors."

Bob looked down at the ground and slowly shook his head. "Chief, there's another danger here. These old homes are on flophouse row. We could stumble into anything in the houses next door. We could end up rousting druggies. They could make enough noise to wake the dead."

Carraway bent over the map and studied it closely. There were a lot of rooms in these old houses. There was no way of telling which one Stewart was in until they got there. There was another way. He turned back to Bob. "Call dispatch and get Leah out here. She can scout the neighbors and Stewart, too, for that matter. We'll try to get him to the front door."

"The lost kid diversion?"

"Yeah."

"I'll get right on it."

The scout unit drove up, and Walker and a Dallas officer disembarked with excited grins. Walker was the one with the announcement. "We've spotted the house, and there's a light on toward the back of the house."

"Which room?"

Fred pointed to the last one toward the back. "That one."

"What about the houses next door?"

"The one closest to the lit room is dark. There's lights on in the house on the other side."

"Are there any kids playing in the street?"

"No, sir. Things are quiet."

Carraway checked his watch. It was 8:40 and getting dark fast. "We'll move in fifteen minutes. I have a female undercover officer on the way to evacuate the house next door and ring Stewart's doorbell. She won't spook anybody. When she gets here, we'll move."

At 8:55, Lee Sanders and his group slowly drove their unmarked units down the old street and parked four houses down from the hideaway. Sanders focused his binoculars on the house and strained to see any movement. There was none. The room with a light on was on the other side of the house. Two minutes later, he could see a woman approach the house next door on foot, a stack of leaflets clutched in her left hand. Beyond her, Sanders could now see other shadowy figures moving quickly down the side of the house, with weapons at high port. Sanders eased out of his car and nodded at Fred in the car behind him. The two of them, along with Larry Blair and Baker, slowly approached the neighbor's house as the woman rang the doorbell. The four of them found dark recesses as the front door opened. An old woman in tattered clothing appeared. "Yes? What do you want?"

"Ma'am, I hope you can help me. My friend's child is missing. Please look at this picture and see if you might have seen her."

"How long has she been missing?"

"Since about four o'clock yesterday afternoon."

The woman held the leaflet up to the light and took a long look. "No. I don't think so. I'm sorry."

"Could you ask your family to come to the door and check this?"

"I don't think it will help. My husband's sick. He hasn't been out of the house in several days."

"How about your children?"

"Sorry. The children have all grown and gone."

"Is there anyone else living here?"

"No ma'am. I'm sorry."

"I'm sorry about your husband. What's wrong with him?"

"Diabetes, mostly."

"What is your name, please?"

"Why? What difference does that make?"

Leah flipped out her badge. "Lady, I'm Leah Barnett with the Dallas police department. I'm sorry for the inconvenience, but I need you and your husband to leave your house for a few minutes. It's a very important security matter. It won't take too long."

The woman started to close the door. "I thought you said you were looking for a lost child."

"Please, ma'am. You could be in danger here."

"What the hell are you talking about?"

"All I can tell you is that the police are moving on the house next door. If shots are fired, you or your husband could be hit."

"Why didn't you say that in the first place?"

"I couldn't, ma'am. Not until I knew who was here in this house. Please hurry."

Sanders listened to fading footsteps, and a few moments later the old couple was escorted away. The sheriff's excitement grew as Leah walked briskly up to the suspect house and pushed the doorbell. Sanders watched two men quietly close in on the front of the house. The Tarrant County group moved in closer, hiding under the high porch as Leah pounded on the door. Things stayed quiet for about two minutes. Obviously, Stewart wasn't foolish enough to answer the door.

Leah motioned her two team members up on the porch with her. Sanders leaped over the decrepit banister to join them, with his deputies following suit. From the back of the house, they heard glass breaking. One of the team members broke out one of the front windows and slid into the house, with Larry Bair right behind him. Rapid footsteps could now be heard at the back of the house. The other front window was broken. Sanders, Walker, and Baker followed the team member inside, inching down the hallway, checking each room.

"Police officers! All occupants get on the floor with your arms spread! Do it now!"

Sanders thought quickly. "Check the closets! He likes to hide there!" The officers checked every nook and cranny of the house. Sanders heard steps behind him, and he whirled with his pistol at the ready. Blair was holding a dirty blue uniform. Sanders snatched it and checked the logo. Stewart was stitched on it just below the words "Arlington Water Department." The sheriff looked up at Larry, who was slowly shaking his head.

"This is all there is. We missed him, boss. He's gone."

Chapter Twenty-Three

Torrey checked his watch impatiently as he paced the visitor's floor. Finally, a tall deputy motioned him toward the elevator. Without conversation, they rode upstairs and turned left. The deputy turned on his radio. "Open unit E." A lock clanged, opening the small green and cream colored cubicle. Torrey entered and faced a relaxed-looking Reed, sitting there in jailhouse greens. Reed picked up his telephone and waited for Torrey to remove his raincoat. Finally, they sat looking face to face.

"I thought you said ten minutes. I've been waiting two hours. What the hell's going on?"

"Torrey, is this line secure?"

"Yeah. They can't listen in."

"You can't have visitors while you're in intake. You have to be assigned a cell before you can have visitors."

"What happened?"

"Are you positive this line isn't being tapped?"

"Yeah. I've used them often. It's illegal to tap these phones. They'd lose every case they've got if they did. They're not that stupid."

"Okay. I was trailing Sterrett's head clerk. They caught me in a trap."

"What did they catch you with?"

"A pair of binoculars."

"Were you on a public street?"

"Yes."

"What did you tell them?"

"I have a driver's license from Joplin Missouri showing the name of William Wilson. I told them I was here watching the Ranger-Royals games this weekend, and I came down to sell somebody an insurance policy."

"Will that story stand up to scrutiny?"

"Part of it will. The address belongs to an old lady named Wilson. She's never there anymore. They can call up there until the cows come home. The insurance story won't hold up, though. You should be able to get me out on a writ. They don't have anything to charge me on."

Torrey broke out laughing. "There isn't a judge in Texas that would issue a writ this weekend especially if I asked for it."

"I don't understand."

"That's how I got Stewart out. The judge is catching hell for it."

"Oh. Then how can I get out?"

"I guess when they let you out. They can't hold you long. How did they catch you trailing the girl? I thought you were too good for that."

"I had to follow them too long. I got spotted."

"You couldn't get away?"

"No. They trapped me before I had time to react. I couldn't move."

"What do you want me to do?"

"Several things. First, I need you to go to the Holiday Inn at I-20 and Cooper. There's pickup with a lawn mower in the back. There's a key to room 173 under the floor mat on the passenger side. I want you to clear the room. I've got a pistol in there and a Genie garage door opener. Throw the gun away and hold on tight to the garage door opener. Take my shaving kit and clothes to the Holiday Inn at I-20 and Park Springs Boulevard. Get a key from the front desk for room 249. I'm registered there under this name. Put the clothes and shaving kit in the room like they were being used there. Next, call the number you gave me, 555-3139, at 7:30 in the morning. Tell our client where I am and that I'll need his help to finish the job."

"Wait a minute. What if I can't get in the room at the Holiday Inn?"

"Just tell the clerk that you're William Wilson and that you lost your key. Can't you figure out how to do a simple thing like that?"

"I'm not in your kind of business, man. What's with the door opener?"

"That's the trigger for the job. I've got an explosive wired in Sterrett's bedroom. When you're sure he's in bed, drive two blocks away and press the Genie. Presto, the judge is gone."

"How do we know when he's in bed?"

"There's a key in the glove compartment of the pickup that fits the lockbox of a vacant house across the street from Sterrett's. From the second floor you can see the reflection of his bedroom light off the stockade fence in his back yard. Wait thirty minutes after his bedroom light goes off, drive off, and trigger it. It's that simple."

"If you think I'm going to kill him, you're nuts."

"That's between you and our client. I don't care who does it."

"Is Sterrett home now?"

"No. The sheriff's hiding him, I think. That's why I got nailed."

"So the client has to wait until Stewart goes home, is that it?"

"That's the best I can do under the circumstances."

"What if my client wants a refund?"

"The way I figure it, he owes me another $15,000. Triggering the Genie is the easy part of the job. Anybody can do it."

"Will the whole house blow up?"

"No. Only Sterrett's bedroom. There's no danger to the kids. Too many walls are between them and the bomb. Tell our client that."

"Do you want me to do anything with the pickup?"

"No. It's fine right where it is."

"What else do you need me to do?"

"Find a way to get me out of here."

"They'll have to release you soon. You can finish this job yourself."

"No. I can't risk it. Not with my picture and prints on file here. When I get out, I'm leaving town."

"What about the rest of your money?"

"You get $500 of it to defend that turkey you talked to. I don't care about the rest."

"Anything else?"

"Yeah. When you get through at the hotels, put both keys back under the floor mat of the pickup."

"Anything else?"

"Nothing. Just get moving on it as soon as you leave here."

"Okay. I'll get right on it."

Torrey headed toward Arlington again. By the time he finished the hotel assignments, the sun was peeking over the east horizon.

A new Buick Park Avenue crawled north on Highway 75 from Dallas as the bottom of a red sun escaped the east horizon. The dark-complexioned driver scrupulously adhered to the seventy miles per hour speed limit. A routine traffic stop would spell disaster. Sitting immediately behind the driver was a corpulent man in his late fifties, with a large cup of coffee in one hand and a chewed-on cigar in the other. His clothes were casual but expensive, with dark colors to soften his obesity. His hair was dyed dark to match his complexion and his sunglasses hid shrewd, unkind eyes. He was Harvey Kearns, and everyone in the Dallas underworld knew who he was.

Kearns had built a fortune on other people's crimes, specializing in fencing stolen goods. He avoided a criminal record by never going near his criminal operations. Kearns wasn't in good spirits this morning, having to personally oversee an operation. He had to transfer some cargo to his brother's boat that sat on Lake Texoma. His brother was very touchy about his boat. Kearns had to promise that the cargo would cause no damage. Sitting on the far side of the back seat was the cargo, Billy Earl Stewart.

Stewart was sipping coffee, trying to wake up after a bad night in a cheap hotel. There hadn't been much talking for the last sixty miles. His host had not been gracious. Jerked out of his haven on two minutes notice, he was driven to the cheap dive with no explanation from Hassan. Stewart leaned back against the leather seat to touch his pistol for a small measure of comfort. When he finished his coffee, he dropped the cup into the floorboard. That finally got a response from his Capone-like host.

"Pick that cup and hold it, kid. I just bought this damn car and I don't want you spilling coffee on it."

Stewart thoughtfully picked it up, broke the lid, and looked inside. *I guess he's right. If I had a car this nice, I'd be the same way.* "I'm sorry. I thought you were asleep, as quiet as you've been. How about telling me what's going on. Why am I being moved?"

"Because Angel got arrested yesterday. It was too dangerous to leave you where Angel dropped you off."

"Do you think Angel would have ratted on me?"

"The police hit the house ten minutes after you left there."

Stewart's eyes widened. "No shit?"

"That's right, kid."

"How did you know to come get me?"

"The idiot press let it slip. They said your arrest was imminent."

"Well, thanks for saving my ass."

"Don't flatter yourself, kid. I have a reputation to protect."

"What do you mean?"

"I mean that nobody I ever hid got caught while under my protection. If you had got nabbed at one of my hiding places, my business would go to shit."

"I thought that was Angel's place."

"Nope. Angel's places are in Tarrant County. Mine are in Dallas."

"I see. So you guys swap people back and forth."

"That's right, kid. You catch on fast."

"Where are you taking me?"

"My brother has a houseboat at a marina on Lake Texoma. I'm going to put you up there until Thursday night. Then I'll have to find someplace else for the rest of the contract."

"Why don't you just put me some other place in Dallas?"

"Several reasons. You're too hot. The reward's too big. I'd have to keep you in a house alone, and my other places are too crowded right now."

"But I wasn't noticed at the other house. I never went outside."

"All you have to do is turn the lights on to get noticed, kid. If somebody stays at a house and doesn't come out, that gets noticed, too."

"Well, thanks just the same. When I paid Angel all that money, I thought I was getting screwed. But I can see that I'm a lot of trouble."

"You're right, kid. As hot as you are, the price is a bargain."

"I've never stayed on a houseboat before. Can I fish off it?"

"I doubt it. You would be seen. There's mechanics who work on the boats as well as marina security. You can't even play a radio up here."

"Can I turn on the lights at night?"

"Absolutely not. Not unless you want to get caught."

"I sure don't want that. My ass is fried if I get caught."

"That's right. Where are you going after you leave me?"

"I don't know. I might go to Mexico."

"Have you ever been to Mexico, kid? Do you speak Spanish?"

"No."

"Then take my advice and don't go there."

"Why?"

"They'll fleece your ass, and you'd stick out like a sore thumb."

"What would you suggest?"

"I know somebody in Miami. You could work there and your Southern accent wouldn't be so noticeable. And it's a long way from Texas."

"What kind of work would I be doing?"

"The guy I know runs everything from drugs to stolen merchandise. It would be up to him."

"How much would that cost me?"

"I don't know. You can't go by air. If I put you on a bus, you'd have to change your appearance. I'll check with my friend if you want me to."

"Yeah. Go ahead. See what you can do. I need to get out of here. Is there a phone on that boat?"

"Yeah, there's a phone. Just don't use it."

"I mean you could call me and let me know about Miami."

"Okay, kid. If I call, I'll ring twice and hang up and call right back again. That's the only time you answer that phone. You got it?"

"I got it. It wouldn't cost much to go to Miami by bus, would it?"

"The bus ticket wouldn't cost much. That's not the problem. The problem is getting to a bus route that don't go through Dallas."

"I see. Do you have a ballpark figure?"

"What's the matter? Are you broke?"

"No. I'll need some when I get where I need to go."

"Don't worry about it. My friend can advance you some money when you get down there. How much have you got left?"

"I've got a little under five hundred left," he lied.

"I see. That doesn't give me much room. I'll see what I can do."

"Thanks. How much further to the lake?"

"We're almost there."

The Buick topped a hill, revealing a large beautiful lake in the distance with the sun dancing off the clear water. Stewart could see islands large enough to camp on beyond the marina. As the car drew closer, he could see boats that were larger than any he had ever dreamed of. Fish were jumping between the boathouses. Birds of all sizes were flying around and chirping. Stewart immediately loved the place.

The car slowly circled to a boathouse on the far side of the slue. The men exited the car, retrieved Stewart's suitcases from the trunk, and walked across a bridge to a locked gate. Kearns unlocked the gate and led the way to the far end of the boathouse where a sixty-foot Holiday Mansion houseboat slowly rocked in a slip. It was secured by six large ropes to poles and had a rear entrance to a walkway that encircled the inside area. The outside of the boat was dirty and had many spider webs hanging on it. Stewart couldn't help but admire the improvements on the slip, which included a 4 × 8 storeroom. A double sink, surrounded by cabinets above and below, rested between marble counters. The storeroom and cabinets were made of T-111 siding and stained a natural wood color. There was a white plastic table bolted to the floor of the slip. He wondered if there were any fishing poles in the storeroom when he noticed that it had no lock. Off to his left, he could look over the water and see a marina store with gas pumps. A clerk sat with his back to them, reading a newspaper. Stearns unlocked the houseboat and motioned Stewart inside as they heard the gate opening behind them. Stearns looked back to see the security guard walking toward them.

"Hide under the bed, damn it," he whispered loudly to Stewart. After quickly shutting the door, he and Hassan walked toward the security guard as casually as they could. "Good morning, Officer."

"Good morning. Who are you guys?"

"I'm Harvey Kearns. My brother, Johnny, owns the end houseboat."

"Are you staying here this week, Mr. Kearns?"

"No. Johnny wanted me to check on it. We're coming down this weekend and wanted to make sure everything was okay."

"Is everything okay?"

"Yes sir. Everything looks fine."

"Are you leaving now, Mr. Kearns?"

"Yes. I have to get back to Dallas."

"Then have a good day, sir."

Kearns nodded and followed Hassan to the Buick. He watched the security guard lock the gate by the bridge as they drove away.

Stewart waited under the bed for a half hour or so. It was dirty and hot under there. Finally, he crawled out and checked through a window to see if anyone was about. Satisfied that the boathouse area was empty, he started exploring the boat. The inside was dank but was remarkably clean for a boat seldom used. The bedroom was large, with a double bed and a small closet on one side. On the other side of the bed was a door leading to a tiny bathroom, which contained a showerhead and a commode. Checking under the sink, he discovered there was no toilet paper. Below a mirror there was a sign that said not to put toilet paper in the head. Stewart laughed to himself. There's no chance of that. I wonder where the damn corncobs are?

Stewart went past the bedroom to a larger living room area, which had sofas on two sides of the room below windows looking out on the lake. To the left was the captain's area, with a steering wheel and various levers. Just above the steering wheel was a radio. The rich sure knew how to live. The kitchen looked as modern as one you would find in a mobile home, complete with a double sink and cabinets. A refrigerator stood off to one side. A quick inspection of the cabinets and the refrigerator revealed a startling fact. There was no food or drink on the boat.

Ray Sterrett watched the rising sun through the bedroom window of a guesthouse on a ten-acre estate in Westlake. The cottage had two bedrooms, a small kitchen, two bathrooms, and a living room. The children were still sleeping in the other bedroom, and Cass was slowly stirring from her chaste location on the couch. Ray could see four security men in the adjacent woods and one near the front entrance gate. The officer near the gate was in plain clothes and stayed well back to avoid attention. Both the main house and the guesthouse sat well back from the road. Ray been told that he wouldn't meet the owner, another security precaution by the sheriff.

Cass had been distant to him after her arrival, but as usual, marvelous with the children. When it had been time to go to bed, she had camped on the sofa without comment. Ray turned his thoughts to Stewart and wondered where he could be after the disappointing raid in Dallas. Lee Sanders had called and explained the situation, trying to stay positive and upbeat, but Ray could hear the frustration in the sheriff's voice. It would take days to trace the owner of the house. It was like starting the search all over again. Sooner or later, Stewart would vanish. Perhaps he already had. Ray knew there had to be a limit to the time he could hide out and remain away from the office. If Stewart was not caught soon, risks would have to be taken. It was hard to imagine Stewart coming after him again. If it did happen, there wasn't much he could do about it. What would happen to his children? His parents were old, and his brother had too many children already. There was one thing he needed to do. It was time to make out a new will. That was a detail he had avoided since Doris had been killed. If only ...

Ray heard Cass get up and go into one of the bathrooms. Soon he saw her reappear, go into the kitchen, opening cabinets and rattling pans. Cass looked up from a Mr. Coffee pot with a wan smile as he entered the kitchen. She looked very domestic with her housecoat, light make up, and hair pulled up to reveal a sexy neck.

"Good morning, Cass."

"Good morning."

"Did you sleep well?"

"As well as can be expected."

"That couch didn't look too comfortable."

"It will have to do."

"If we stay here tonight, I'll sleep there and give you the bed."

"That's okay. I'll be fine there."

"Look, Cass. I'm really sorry about the other night. I hope you're not too disappointed in me."

"I'm not disappointed with you. I'm disappointed with me."

"Why?"

"I think you know."

"No. I don't. I don't think less of you because of what happened."

"Well, I do."

"That's ridiculous, Cass. Let's put this behind us."

"And pretend that it never happened?"

"No. I didn't say that."

"What are you saying?"

"I don't know. Let's just not be distant with one another. It doesn't feel right."

"What do you want me to do?"

"Just relax and be your natural self."

"I'll try, but I feel really awkward right now."

"Then why did you come back?"

"I didn't want to put you and the kids in danger. I understood when you explained it."

"Was that the only reason?"

"For the time being, yes."

Ray poured himself a cup of coffee and left the kitchen without another word. There was no use pursuing this right now. Before he could enter the shower, he was interrupted by a knock on the door.

"The sheriff's on the phone. He wants to talk to you."

"Okay. I'll be right out." Ray donned his robe and took the call on the bedroom phone, waiting for Cass to hang up the extension. "Hello, Lee."

"Hello, yourself. Is the guesthouse okay?"

"Yes, Lee. It's fine. Thank you. Anything new going on this morning?"

"Just one thing, Ray. I hate to bother you with this, but I have a very persistent young lady out here who's threatening to sit in my outer office all week if I don't let her talk to you."

"That sounds like it might be Marilyn Shaw."

"That's right. She says it's not a business call. Is that accurate?"

"Yes. That would be correct."

"Well, you devil. I had no idea that you were such a ladies' man."

"Don't joke, Lee. It's not very funny right now."

"I see. I suppose I can figure out why Cass left the other night."

"You're correct again. Did you tell her that Cass was out here?"

"Are you kidding, Ray. I'll let you have that honor."

"Well, put her on. I'll be happy to talk to her."

"Thanks, Ray. Hold on, and I'll have her pick up an extension."

Ray checked his bedroom door again, making sure it was closed.

"Hello Ray? Are you there?"

"Hello, Marilyn. I'm right here. How are you?"

"How am I? Forget me. How are you?"

"I'm okay."

"I couldn't believe it when I heard on the news that you'd been wounded. How bad are you hurt?"

"It's just a shoulder wound. I'll be fine in a few days."

"What the hell were you doing going out to do a wedding when you claimed it was too dangerous to let me see you?"

"We thought it would be safe. Obviously, we were wrong."

"How bad is your shoulder?"

"It'll be okay. Really, it's just a scratch."

"The sheriff said the wound went clear to the bone."

"Marilyn, I could fight again by Friday, if I had to. It's healing."

"I want to see you, today."

"We can't, Marilyn. It's too dangerous."

"Let's not go through that again."

"I'm not making this up. We had to move yesterday because our cover was blown. Besides, I don't want to put you in danger."

"I'll be fine. Where are you? I'm coming right now."

"Marilyn, you can't. Somebody could follow you out here."

"Aren't you and the sheriff being just a bit paranoid?"

"I thought so at first, but I don't anymore."

"I can't believe that redneck's doing all this."

"You haven't heard?"

"Heard what?"

"The redneck didn't hire those guys. Commissioner Wade and a rogue cop in Arlington did. Stewart didn't have anything to do with it."

"What? Wade, the county commissioner? Why?"

"I don't know for sure. You'd have to ask him. Sanders thinks they did it because Stewart would get the blame for it."

"That's crazy. What possible reason would Wade have for killing you?"

"According to the sheriff, he was convinced that I was going to run against him next year."

"That's absurd."

"I thought so, too. The sheriff says that I have to stay put until they catch Stewart."

"Did Wade confess to this?"

"No. I don't think so."

"Surely the sheriff could be wrong about this. What kind of proof does he have?"

"You'd have to get all the details from him. He got enough probable cause to arrest him and put a quarter million bond on him."

"Wow! I see now why you're being so careful. But I don't want to wait weeks and weeks until I see you, Ray. Can't something be worked out?"

"Let's wait a day or two and see. I want to see you, too. We have a lot to talk about."

"We sure do. I better go now. The secretaries are coming in and I'm losing my privacy. You better gets lots of rest between now and then because you're going to need it, big boy. Bye now."

Ray smiled a little as he hung up the phone. *Who would have believed it about straight-laced Marilyn? All that fire under her serene composure.*

"This is 555-3139."

"This is Leonard Torrey. We've got a problem."

"Why are you calling me here?"

"Our friend from Tulsa told me to."

"What's the problem?"

"Our man's in jail."

"He's not talking, is he?"

"No. Of course not."

"What happened?"

"He got caught trailing Sterrett's head clerk to where they were hiding Sterrett."

"Do they know who he is?"

"I don't think so."

"What did they charge the idiot with? Possession of a deadly weapon?"

"He may be a lot of things, but he's not an idiot. He had nothing on him but a pair of binoculars. He's been booked in on suspicion."

"Suspicion of what?"

"Just suspicion."

"Can they do that?"

"Yes. It's an investigation charge. But they can only hold him for a day. If they don't file charges, they have to release him."

"Can they find out who he is in that time?"

"He don't think so."

"Then we don't have much of a problem, do we?"

"Yes we do. He's not going to finish the job."

"Well, son of a bitch. This means we have to start all over. There may not be time for that."

"That's not quite accurate. He was almost finished. He said you could finish it."

"Give me the details."

"He's planted a small bomb in Sterrett's bedroom. It's triggered by a garage door opener, of all things. All you have to do is wait till he's asleep and pull the trigger."

"Does he still want his money?"

"He says the work's almost completed. He said you could deduct $10,000 for the new triggerman and forward the rest to him through me."

"I don't like it. I don't want to kill everybody in the house."

"He said that wouldn't happen. The only damage will be in the bedroom."

"I still don't like it. I can't go get a triggerman in the yellow pages. Where's the door opener?"

"I've got it."

"Well then, you go use it."

"Not me. I'm no killer."

"Then I'm not paying him another damn cent. This is bullshit!"

"I wouldn't recommend that."

"Why?"

"You're forgetting who he is. I wouldn't want him mad at me."

"To hell with him. He don't even know who I am."

"Do you want to take the chance that he can't find you? He's got to be good to get a bomb in the man's house so soon. Do you want to look over your shoulder for the rest of your life?"

"Are you threatening me, Torrey?"

"Of course not. I'm just citing some obvious facts, that's all."

"Did he threaten me if I didn't pay?"

"No. That kind of man wouldn't."

"I see. I still don't like this worth a shit."

"I understand. What do you want me to do?"

"I don't know yet. Hold onto the door opener. I'll call you at noon."

"Don't call me at the office anymore."

"Then you can call me back at this number. When I get to this phone, I'll beep you with a code of four fours. What's your beeper number?"

Rod Sample looked down on his huge marina domain from his office atop a sprawling blue building that housed the offices, a women's boutique, and a showroom for various yacht accessories. The yacht sales office and restaurant rested placidly by the water below. Beyond those stood the store and gas docks. Sample had stumbled on an investment of a lifetime a year before. The previous owner had fallen on bad times. Sample had the good luck to be in the right spot at the right time. Buying a going concern like this for forty cents on the dollar was beyond his wildest dreams. Over nine hundred yachts rested in the slips below, with an average rent of over two hundred dollars a month plus electricity. It took a crew of eleven to keep up with the boat repairs and his boat sales were flourishing. His profit from the restaurant and nightclub alone paid the nut for the whole year.

Sample enjoyed puttering around his lavish office. Some of his best marketing ideas had come to him while he viewed the water below. His new slogan—"A sample of heaven on earth"—graced his billboards, spaced all the way to North Dallas. That idea had come to him while he was standing on this very spot.

His gaze followed a fifty-five foot Chris Craft as it crawled slowly to the gas docks. "What's Walter doing here today? He can't take that boat out. We're not finished with the repairs on it."

After hesitating a moment, he hurried down to prevent his customer from burning up his engine. It was a two-minute journey. After a brief consultation with the boat owner, he invited him into the store for a cup of coffee. As they headed into the store howling over a joke, Sample pulled up short, looking at his clerk. There was a young man at the counter with his back turned to him who, in reaching for his wallet, exposed a pistol resting in his belt under a denim jacket. The clerk looked unconcerned, but Sample circled the counter for a look at this young man. He was just a kid and looked a little nervous. Sample relaxed when it was clear that he wasn't going to be held up. The kid, quietly balancing two large grocery bags, turned and walked out. Sample gave his attention back to Walter. As they talked over coffee, Sample watched the kid through the glass as he walked around the slue, shifting the full bags as he walked. The kid slowly wound his way to the houseboat at the end of house twenty-seven, only two hundred feet from where Sample was standing.

"Harry, what did that kid buy who was in here a minute ago?"

"I thought he was going to buy out the store, Mr. Sample. He bought food mostly. A little beer and some worms."

"What's he doing on the Kearns' boat?"

"I dunno."

"What did he say when he came in?"

"Nothin' much. I couldn't get him to talk."

"How much was his bill?"

"A little over forty-eight dollars."

"I didn't know our house boats needed bodyguards these days."

"What's that, Mr. Sample?"

"Nothing, Harry. Forget it."

Sample moseyed over to yacht sales, then to the parts department and repair shop. After stopping to chat with some tourists, he picked up his papers and mail before heading back to his office. The mail was scant and required little time, so he opened the *Dallas Morning News* to catch up on what was happening in the world. When he got to page three, he dropped the paper on the floor and called the Grayson County sheriff.

Lee Sanders' temper was mounting. Biting his lip, he softened his reprimand to Baker. "Sorry, Gary. The press is getting to me."

"I understand, boss. That cartoon in the *Star-Telegram* is a low blow. They're giving you hell in the *Dallas Morning News* about the raid, too."

"Are you making any progress with the house owner?"

"No. The house is registered to a dead man. The ad valorem taxes are paid by a Delaware corporation. The corporation is defunct, and the addresses of the corporate officers are no good. Terrance either can't or won't identify the owner of the house."

Sanders bit his lip again. "The trail is getting cold."

Baker nodded. "We'll get him. He can't stay lucky forever. When is Frances' funeral? I would like to go, if it's okay."

"It's in Houston tomorrow. Walker's whole department wants to go. Somebody's got to stay here. I'm sorry, Gary." Sanders' phone rang persistently. He considered letting it go and getting some rest. After four frantic days, he was getting weary. With his temperature rising, he picked the receiver up. "Yes?"

"Sheriff, this is Carter. I tried to reach the police chief in Joplin as you instructed. He left on vacation this morning."

"Well, shit. What else can go wrong? Were you able to talk to anyone else up there?"

"I talked to the assistant chief. He didn't know the woman at that address and seemed uninterested in checking her out. Since he didn't know them, he figured they were all right."

"Did you ask him to send a unit out to talk to the neighbors?"

"Yes sir. He said if they weren't too busy today, they'd get around to it."

"Did you tell him what this investigation was all about?"

"I sure did."

"It's probably a blind lead anyway."

"Should I turn the prisoner loose?"

"Not yet. Send him down to the interrogation room and I'll talk to him. I'm not very busy this morning."

"Yes sir. What about Terrance? Do you want to continue to hold him?"

Sanders sighed. "I guess not. Terrance did all we asked of him. Let the DA's staff interview him before he's processed out."

"Will do. Do you want me to call you when we get that other prisoner down to interrogation?"

"Yes. What's his name again?"

"Wilson, William Wilson."

"Okay. Call me when you're ready." Sanders hung up the phone and headed to the coffee station. After getting a refill, he spent several minutes returning calls. When he got the return call from Carter, he took the familiar elevator down to the basement. The interrogation rooms were busy. Carter was waiting outside the room on the far end. Sanders nodded and entered the room to face a dark, quiet, reserved man in his late fifties, who sat facing him with a poker face. The man failed to speak as the sheriff sat down and studied him without a word for several moments. The man had a receding hairline and grayish hair that contrasted with a rather dark complexion. Sanders couldn't tell what his national origin was, but his features were Caucasian. There was one thing that stood out about the man. He looked remarkably thin and fit for a man of fifty-eight.

"Mr. Wilson, you look mighty healthy this morning. The jail fare must agree with you."

"Oh, I'm quite content, thank you. It's a real pleasure sitting here and counting my money."

"Counting your money?"

"That's right. I was mad as hell when I got arrested but this is my lifetime opportunity. I can retire after I collect the judgment."

"What judgment is that?"

"The judgment I collect after I sue your ass for false imprisonment. I have a friend in Springfield who's the meanest lawyer you'll ever meet."

"That's fine, Mr. Wilson. We get sued every day. If you're lucky, you will come to trial in ten years. If you win, the appeals will take another five. Let's see, that would make you about seventy-three then."

"I doubt that. My friend specializes in federal lawsuits. You can cut that time by three-fourths."

"I've got some questions to ask you, Mr. Wilson. What were you doing following my squad car yesterday?"

"I've been through that with your officer. I was nice and cooperative and that don't seem to work around here. I've said all I'm going to say."

"I see. Your cooperation could expedite your release."

"That's okay. The longer I'm here, the larger the award. I'm in no hurry, and there's nothing pressing. Keep me here as long as you like."

"Won't your office be worried this morning? Would you like for me to call your boss and explain what's happened here?"

"Sheriff, whatever your name is, you're free to call anyone you like. It appears that I'm not."

"Captain Rogers failed to tell me that you were a hardcase."

"You'll see what hard is when I get you in a federal courtroom."

"Well, you can be as hard as you want. I'm getting a warrant to search you hotel room. I wonder what I'll find there."

Mr. Wilson smiled a mischievous smile. "Be sure to do a thorough search, Sheriff. If you tear into the walls, the hotel can sue you, too."

Sanders bit his lip to hide his frustration. Interrogation was never his strong suit. Questioning Blade Hawkins was more productive than this. "What are we going to find when we do a thorough search of your car?"

"A lawsuit from Avis, probably."

"You seem to have lawsuits on the brain this morning."

"You're right, but only to a point. I'm also thinking of how much fun I'm going to have at my next chamber of commerce meeting in Joplin."

"Are you a member there, Mr. Wilson?"

"I'm going to be the star by next week."

"Are you a member now?"

"Why don't you call up there and find out. I will admit this: I'm not a member of your chamber. Compared to what I've done, that may be a major felony here."

"Will you give us permission to search your hotel room, Mr. Wilson?"

"I really don't care what you do. I thought you were getting a warrant. Where I come from, you don't need permission if you have a warrant. Or is that different down here, too?"

"You're saying you don't care if we search your room?"

"What I said was, I don't care what you do."

"Is that permission?"

Mr. Wilson paused and reflected. "No, Sheriff, it's not. You could save yourself a lot of grief if you planted something in my room."

"I see. Then I'll have to get a warrant."

"May I make a request?"

"What is it?"

"I would like a hotel employee present when you search the room."

"If you give your permission, yes. Otherwise not. Are we agreed?"

"How will I know you did what I asked?"

"You put the permission in writing and phrase it any way you want to. We have to check with the management before we go in anyway."

"All right. We're agreed. What are you going to do when you find the room clean?"

"Release you, probably."

"Damn, Sheriff. Can't you keep me here about a week? My award won't be that much if you only keep me one day."

Sanders nodded to Carter who ducked out for a pencil and paper. He turned back to Mr. Wilson. "Is this the first time you've ever been arrested, Mr. Wilson?"

"Yes, but it's not as bad as I thought it would be. I've met some really interesting people. The treatment I've received here is better than I got out on the street yesterday. I've got some great stories to tell."

Carter returned with the writing implements and placed them in front of Mr. Wilson. The prisoner reflected a moment and then wrote: "The undersigned hereby authorizes the sheriff's department to search my room, which is room 249 at the Holiday Inn at I-20 and Park Springs Boulevard, provided that they permit two hotel employees to be present during the search. Bill Wilson." The prisoner handed the sheriff the paper. "Will that do?"

"Yes. That'll do fine. I'll get back to you. Tim, get somebody to take this prisoner back to his cell."

After arranging for the routine return, Carter returned to Sanders. "What do you think of this guy?"

"He don't act like a criminal. I think we have a lawsuit on our hands. What do you think?"

"That talk about keeping him here for a longer time was bullshit. He wouldn't have given permission to search if he didn't want out."

"Does wanting out make him guilty of involvement in this mess?"

"No, sir. Not necessarily."

"That's my sentiments exactly."

The children awoke in bad sorts that morning. Unfamiliar surroundings no longer agreed with them, and they remained cranky the whole morning. Robbie and Jan missed Anita, who had chosen to go home. The sheriff had consented since she didn't know where they were. The food supply was limited and the kids wanted something else. Ray's patience and humor deteriorated with each passing hour. Cass initially stayed out of the fracas, but by 11:00 am took charge. She dispatched a security man to the store for the children's favorite items, then sent another one to a mall for new toys and children's books. After preparing a tasty lunch, Cass assigned Robbie to paint a picture by numbers. That kept him absorbed, but he had to be continuously supervised to avoid making a mess. Cass sat on the sofa with Jan, reading her four books. The child was captivated with the stories and pictures, laughing and giggling constantly.

Ray busied himself by calling family members and associates to assure them that everything was all right. Between calls, he glanced in at the children, amazed at the transformation that Cass had wrought. His admiration for Cass grew by the hour as he watched her from a distance. After getting a soft drink from the refrigerator, he went back to his bedroom, pulled a chair by the window and watched an unfamiliar tranquil family scene. Anita could have never accomplished what Cass was doing. Ray knew that he didn't have that kind of touch either. There just wasn't enough kid left in him, and he reflected on the difference between a father's role and a mother's.

It was impossible to picture Marilyn sitting there with Jan and entertaining her for hours on end. Marilyn was an adult, just as he was. Feelings of guilt and selfishness slowly sank into his mind. The children needed someone even more than he did.

Ray thought back to when he and Cass had discovered common passion and affection. Could Marilyn be any better than that? Marilyn would make a wonderful companion for him; that was a given. But, this was a family of three. The hardest aspect of a second marriage was always acceptance by the children and the new parent. He realized for the first time that a relationship with Marilyn could never work. It would be no fun telling her that, though.

Jan finally nodded off to a dreamy nap. Cass put the book down and marched Robbie off to bed for a nap as well. By midafternoon, the guesthouse was quiet. As Cass tiptoed past the bedroom door, Ray motioned her inside. After a moment's hesitation, she came in and sat on the bed facing him as he remained in the chair. He began in a low voice. "You are an absolute marvel with the children."

"Thank you. It's not hard, really."

"You are an absolute marvel, period."

"You're full of compliments today. Is there going to be a but or however at the end of these compliments?"

"No, Cass. There are no buts."

"What are you saying?"

"I'm saying that I want you."

"What about Marilyn?"

"Marilyn who?"

"Don't joke."

"I'm saying that Marilyn has many fine attributes, but she doesn't come up to your knees. I've thought this out, Cass. You and me can work. Marilyn and me can't."

"Because of the children?"

"Yes, that's a big part of it, but not all of it. You're not just a good mother to my children; you kindled fires in me that I thought were gone. You don't have to back up to anybody. You're all I could hope for."

Cass fought back the tears as she looked back at Ray. "Are you absolutely sure of this?"

"I'm as sure as I can be."

"No looking back? No comparing me to that gorgeous reporter?"

"There's no looking back. You don't need to worry about comparisons either. Will you come home with us when this is all over?"

Cass slipped off the bed and into Ray's lap. Ray kissed her softly and drew back suddenly, feeling tears. "Cass, why are you crying?"

Cass smiled through her tears and returned his kiss lightly. "Don't you know when to shut up?"

Chapter Twenty-Four

Billy Earl Stewart watched the slow-paced activities at the marina all day from the window of the houseboat. The beauty, tranquility, and the vastness of the marina mesmerized him. This was a world he'd never seen. Some of the yachts were huge, with crews scrubbing them down and tinkering with the engines. There were racing boats with engines that sounded like the dragsters that he had seen at Ennis last year. Stewart could see two men fishing off the end of a boathouse down the row. One was fishing with live bait while the other was constantly casting an artificial lure. Every now and then, one would snag a fish and Stewart watched the struggle. If the fish was very large, the rod would bend almost double as the men struggled to get them in. Their laughter and jokes could be heard drifting across the water. They were having a great time.

About two o'clock, Stewart went to the back of the boat and carefully studied his boathouse. The gate remained closed and no one was around. Carefully, he stepped out of the houseboat and opened the storeroom door. Inside to the left was a row of rod and reels. There was a small one with a weird double-hook apparatus. Stewart went back inside the houseboat to get his worms and returned to a shady area to give this fishing a try. A school of perch swam by, and Stewart raised his bait to their depth and waited. The largest perch chased the others away and circled the worm, eyeing it suspiciously. Unable to resist it further, the fish grabbed the bait and swam away. Stewart jerked on the line and lost the fish. Undaunted, he tried again with the same result. This went on for twenty minutes as Stewart's bait supply dwindled. The fish were winning every battle.

"Are you catching any of those perch, young man?"

Startled, Stewart looked up at the two fishermen standing right behind him. So immersed in what he was doing, he'd paid no attention to the men coming into his boathouse. One of them held a stringer of at least a dozen fish. The other carried the two rods. They were older guys, but seemed friendly enough with amused smiles on their faces. "No, sir. I can't catch a damn thing. These little fish are too fast for me, I guess. I can't get the hang of it."

"Pull up your line and let me look at it."

Stewart pulled in his line and held it out for their inspection. "Son, you're using too big a hook. You're fishing with a crappie rig."

"Oh. Thanks. I don't have any smaller hooks, though."

The men laid down their equipment. "Harold, give him a perch hook."

The man pulled a plastic box out of his pocket and extracted two tiny hooks. "Here, son. Give me your line." After changing the two hooks, he handed the rig back to Stewart. "Here. Put some worms on those and try it."

Stewart smiled his thanks and threw the line back in the water. In less than twenty seconds, he had one of the frisky perch hooked and started reeling it in with a glow of satisfaction. The fish was almost in when he felt something hard press against the back of his head and a hand deftly removing the pistol out of the back of his belt.

"Freeze, Mr. Stewart. You're under arrest."

Stewart threw the fishing pole down on the deck and raised his hands. "Put your left hand behind you real slow."

Stewart felt the gun move slightly from behind his head as the man reached for his cuffs. With desperate speed, Stewart shoved one man into the other, dove into the water, and disappeared.

Lee Sanders looked up as Gary Baker walked in to his office. "Have you heard from your undercover boys from Dallas on Chief Parker?"

"Yes sir. I had a report on my desk when I got in. Parker's never been tied to any criminal activity, but he has a reputation for defending his officers, even when they're wrong. His last chief's job was in Temple about ten years ago. The newspapers down there had three stories where he refused to suspend officers until they were convicted. The newspapers gave him hell over one of them where a patrolman damn near beat his wife to death. He was quoted as saying that it was a family matter and the woman would drop all charges. He was right about that, she did. But the newspapers showed some gruesome pictures of her injuries. Shortly after that, the City of Arlington hired him as the assistant chief."

"Did the undercover guys get the feeling that he felt that his officers could do no wrong?"

"That's my impression."

The phone rang and the sheriff picked it up. "Yes?"

"Sheriff, this is Scroggins. We searched this room in Arlington."

"Did you find anything?"

"No, sir. Just a few changes of clothes and a shaving kit."

"Did he have any business cards or insurance brochures?"

"No, sir. Nothing like that."

"Hmm. What about ticket stubs to Rangers games?"

"No, sir."

"Did he leave anything in the hotel safe?"

"No, sir."

"Did he have any dirty clothes?"

"Some were dirty, some were clean. The dirty ones were sweated down pretty good."

"I wonder why that would be?"

"I guess it's pretty hot at the Rangers games, sir."

"What address did he put on the register?"

"The same one you gave me."

"Did he put a home phone number on the register?"

"No, sir."

One of the other lines starting ringing insistently, so Baker moved over to the conference table and picked it up. "Boss, Sheriff Little from Grayson County is on the line. He says it's urgent."

Sanders nodded. "Bob, it looks like this guy is clean. Take off and get some sleep. I'll call if anything comes up. I've got to go now. Thanks." Sanders punched in the other line. "Hello?"

"Is this Sheriff Sanders?"

"Yes, it is."

"This is Sheriff Austin Little from Grayson County. I've got some great news for you."

"I could use some today. Go ahead."

"I've got your boy Stewart up here."

Sanders feet came off his desk and he stood abruptly. Baker looked up expectantly as his boss spoke. "You have him in custody?"

"I sure do."

"Where was he?"

"Hiding on a houseboat at Sample's Marina on Lake Texoma."

"Did you arrest him personally?"

"Well, yes and no. Let's just say I was there. He got away from me. Sample captured him himself."

Sanders cupped the phone. "Gary, gather the troops. They got Stewart."

Sanders turned his attention back to Sheriff Little. "I take it that he didn't give up easy."

"No, sir, he didn't. We had him in the boathouse, but he dove in the water. He swam over to the gas docks, and the marina owner fished him out. He was too tired to give him any fight by then."

"Are you certain it's him?"

"The prints match and he's admitted who he is."

"That's great! How did you find out where he was?"

"Mr. Sample called me. He saw him at his store this morning."

"Well, you tell Mr. Sample that he has a handsome reward coming."

"He knows about the reward, but he won't take it."

"He's certainly entitled to it."

"If I know Mr. Sample, he might give it to some charities."

"That will be fine. Listen, Sheriff, I can be up there in an hour or so. Can I pick up this prisoner today?"

"Certainly. I'll have him ready for you."

"You've read him his rights?"

"Of course."

"What's his attitude?"

"Scared."

"Is he talking?"

"He's singing like a bird."

"Good. See what you can find out from him on how he got up there and when. I'll deal with him on matters down here. And sheriff?"

"Yes?"

"Would you ask Mr. Sample to be at the jail when I get there? I want to thank him personally."

"I sure will."

"Are you in Sherman?"

"Yes."

"We'll be on the road in fifteen minutes. When we get in range, we'll call you for specific directions to your jail. Thanks again, Sheriff. I owe you a steak dinner at the convention for this one."

"I'll look forward to it. I'll see you in an hour and a half."

Sanders paced the floor, his excitement tempered by disappointment. It would have been much better to have captured Stewart himself, but at this stage he was happy just to have avoided his ultimate escape. The press could squawk all they wanted, but he still got his man. If Stewart would talk, Sanders could clear up everything by midnight and still make the funeral with his whole team. It would mean a lot to the Mendez family. He remembered one more detail and picked up the phone. "This is the security base."

"Let me talk to Charles."

"Yes sir. I'll get him for you, sir."

"This is Rogers."

"This is Lee. I've got some great news. Stewart's been caught."

"Where was he?"

"At Lake Texoma."

"When will you have him?"

"As soon as we can get there. About an hour and a half, I reckon."

"Is he talking?"

"I'm told that he is."

"What do you want to do about Sterrett?"

"I don't want to do anything until I talk to Stewart."

"I agree. What about that man we caught following our unit?"

"We still have him but he looks clean. He's clammed up and threatening to sue."

"Have you verified him in Joplin?"

"No. We've had all kinds of problems up there."

"Then you still don't know for sure who he is."

"No. That's right. He did consent to a search of his room. There's nothing there that looks suspicious. There's a phone under the Wilson name at the address he gave, but it's unlisted."

"What about the police in Joplin? "

"We can't get their attention. That's what I meant by problems."

"How much longer can you hold him?"

"Not long, I'm afraid. If Stewart connects him, we're okay. Otherwise ..."

"I understand, but my gut tells me he's dirty."

"Charles, I'm doing the best I can. Part of the problem with Joplin was that I couldn't talk to them last night. This Stewart thing in Dallas was breaking loose at the same time. Their chief left on vacation this morning, and we can't get jackshit out of the assistant."

"I'm sorry, Sheriff. I didn't mean anything. I just hope you don't have to release him too soon. That's all. What do you want me to tell Ray?"

"You can put them on standby to go home."

"Will Stewart tell you if he put out a contract on the judge?"

"I won't know until I talk to him. I'm taking Fred with me. Between us, we should be able to get it out of him."

"Good luck. Maybe this guy was working for the other bunch."

"You mean Agnew and Wade?"

"Yes sir."

"Could be. They're not talking and we're making no deals. Besides, they'd been caught several hours before we caught Wilson."

"That's true, sir. But he might not have known that they were caught. They were the guys that were hiring someone else to do it, not Stewart."

"I see what you mean, Charles. If that's the case, we'd never be able to prove it. What are the odds of them hiring this guy and getting him here fourteen hours after their first attempt failed?"

"There's a way to check that. Call the airlines and find out when he made his reservation."

"That's a good idea. I'll have somebody check on it. I'm leaving now for Texoma. I'll get back to you when I know something more."

Sanders hung up the phone to face his excited investigative team. Scroggins was the only one absent. "Where's Bob?"

"He's on his way. We caught him on the way home from Arlington."

"How soon can he get here?"

"Three or four minutes."

"Then we'll wait. Gary, check on Wilson's flight schedule. I need to know where he flew in from and what time he made the reservation."

Baker moved with alacrity as the rest sat down to await Scroggins. Blair pushed back his Western hat and looked at Sanders. "Sheriff, have you decided on who gets to go to the funeral?"

"If we can wrap this thing up tonight, we'll all go."

Fred Walker's mind was on other things. Getting Stewart was foremost on his mind. "How many units do you want to take to Grayson County?"

"Two should be enough. I want you with me and Stewart on the way back. Bring your tape recorder, too."

Fred nodded in appreciation to his unasked question. "How long will it take us to get there?"

"Gary tells me that we can take a shortcut on Highway 289 through Frisco. We can be there in about an hour and ten minutes if we go with lights and sirens."

"This is 555-3139."

"Where have you been? I've called three times, starting at noon."

The muffled voice came back with force. "Let's keep this straight, Torrey. I'm the employer. You're the employee. You don't chew my ass out. I told you I might not be able to keep that schedule and I beeped you when I could. Now quit the damn whinin'. Is our boy out yet?"

"I don't know."

"What do you mean you don't know? That $2,500 I sent you wasn't just for you to file your nails."

Torrey clenched his teeth to keep from exploding. Who did this asshole think he was? "In case you missed it before, there was no reason to maintain contact with our friend. If and when he gets out, he's splitting. Except for what he figured was owed him, he's severed the relationship."

"Well, I don't figure it that way. If he can't finish the job, he gets nothing."

"Suit yourself. It's your funeral."

"No it's not. It might be your funeral, but not mine. If he comes after me, I'll tell him I gave you the money and he'll come after you."

Torrey forced a laugh. "You think that you'll get to talk to this guy before he nails you? You obviously don't know him very well."

"And I don't intend to. He knows only you, remember?"

"If you think I'm going to take the fall for you, you're crazy."

"There's nothing you can do about it, Torrey."

"There you go, underestimating people again."

"What the hell does that mean?"

"It means that I followed your courier, you son of a bitch." Torrey grinned as he visualized the prick squirming on the other end of the line.

"You're gonna play hardball, huh?"

"That's what it sounds like from your end. I can play hardball, too."

"Well, you're betting against a much stronger hand. That courier couldn't trace it back to me, even if he wanted to."

"That's not my problem. Our friend has succeeded before with less information than that."

"I'm going to lay it out for you, Torrey. I'm not doing this on my own. I represent a group and they're pissed when they lay out thirty-five grand up front and don't get what they paid for. And furthermore—"

"Thirty-five grand? I thought he only charged twenty-five."

"That's what we thought, too. But he charges double for elected officials and ten grand for expenses. That was all up front."

Torrey whistled. "That's a hefty chunk of change."

"You're damned right it is, and all we've got is his word that he has a firecracker in Sterrett's house that might get him."

"Where does that leave us?"

"The group isn't paying out another dime until Sterrett's dead. After that, we'll pay as agreed. That's the bottom line. There's only one way out of this, from my view."

"And what is that?"

"You haven't figured it out?"

"No."

"Then I'll draw you a picture. You figure out how to complete the job and everybody's happy. You get ten grand, our friend gets fifteen, and we're blessed with a completed job. Otherwise nobody's happy. Capisce?"

"Yeah. I understand, but you've got the wrong boy."

"We think different."

"How's that?"

"There are some people in our group who are so pissed over the money that they're blaming you."

"What kind of threat is that?"

"It means that some little bird might whisper in Sanders' ear that you're the one that brought in Reed."

Torrey gritted his teeth again. The bastard might be right. That law firm could be just the courier. If that was the case, his hand was weak. "You bastards are really something. Maybe I can't find a triggerman."

"In case you haven't figured it out, we checked our program, and our team is fresh out of reserves. That's when your name came up."

Ray looked down at Cass, who was peacefully napping under the covers, with her luxuriant auburn hair spilling over the pillows. After brushing some of the hair aside, he slowly nuzzled her ear.

"Umm. What time is it?"

"Three forty-five."

"Do I need to get up?"

"Yeah. Something's happened."

Cass jerked up with concern. "Oh my God! What's happened now?"

"It's okay. Nothing bad. They caught Stewart."

"Really?"

"Yes, honey. I wouldn't kid about a thing like that."

"Can we go home?"

"Probably."

"Why not for certain?"

"The sheriff's worried about that guy that followed you."

"Isn't he still in jail?"

"For the moment. But they don't have much to hold him on. They're going to question Stewart and see if he hired this guy. If not, he'll probably be released."

"What if he's connected to Commissioner Wade?"

"They can't prove it if he is. If he's guilty of anything, it's just helping someone else. Sanders thinks he's just somebody's flunky, if anything. I think we'll be okay."

"When is the sheriff going to talk to Stewart?"

"They're on the way to pick him up now."

"Then we might be able to go to your place tonight?"

"Our place, Cass."

Cass raised herself up from the sheets and hugged Ray in a long embrace. "That sounds wonderful. Do you know what we ought to do?"

"Yeah."

Cass giggled softly. "No. Not that. Next summer, we should take the kids out West for a vacation. Have they ever been to Yellowstone?"

"No."

"It's beautiful. They would go nuts over seeing all the wildlife."

Ray chuckled with amusement. "I guess I'll have to start calling you Mama Cass. You look a lot better than the original, though."

Cass smiled and pecked him on the lips. "No more wooing, Romeo. The kids will be up soon."

Ray leaned back on the bed and rested. Things were going to get a lot better. It would be nice to get back to a normal life.

Lee Sanders marched into the Grayson County sheriff's office, followed by five grim deputies. The jail and sheriff's office was small and unpretentious by big-city standards. The group waited impatiently as they looked through a glass partition at Sheriff Little holding a television interview. Sanders grudgingly conceded that Little was entitled to all the press he could get. Little finally looked out the glass and saw the Tarrant County contingent. After completing a comment, he waved Sanders in and greeted him warmly while the two minicams were rolling. Lee played along and answered a few questions, being careful to praise Little's quick decisive action. Little quietly basked in the limelight for a few moments and then terminated the interview, leaving several disappointed reporters with unanswered questions. The local TV station had grabbed the whole interview. After casting unappreciative glances at the Tarrant County sheriff and his deputies for their untimely arrival, they moved outside to photo the exit of the suddenly famous prisoner.

Sheriff Little beckoned Sanders to sit down and invited his deputies in for introductions all around. Little brought in his chief deputy and available personnel for further glad-handing as Sanders quelled his impatience. Finally the others drifted toward the Coke machines so the two sheriffs could get down to business. "How big is your staff, Sheriff Sanders?"

"We currently have 1,379 employees."

"I can't even imagine that. I have a staff of eleven. I wouldn't know what to do with all those people."

"You would if you had my crime rate. I envy the tranquility that you enjoy here."

"It's not a vacation. I do a lot of patrolling myself. Although we're a much smaller community, there's enough trouble here to keep us hopping."

"I'm sure there is. How's our prisoner?"

"He's fine. We fed him and talked to him."

"Is he still talking?"

"I think so. I've got a deputy in there with him now. He seems to respond to women more than men in the questioning."

"That's good to know. I don't have any lady deputies with me. I lost my best one two days ago."

"That's what I heard. I'm sorry. I can send you a copy of my deputy's report if you like."

"I would appreciate that. Thank you. Do you think he will talk to us on the way back?"

"Probably. We tried the good guy–bad guy approach with him. The bad guy didn't work at all. We only got him to talk when we acted sympathetic."

"I don't think there's any good guy in us after what that son of a bitch did. How much money did he have on him when you got him?"

"We found his billfold inside the boat. It had $847 in it."

"That's good."

"Why do you say that?"

"I was afraid he might have hired somebody to finish the job."

"I don't think so."

"Did you talk about that?"

"No. Not directly. He told me he got so sick over what he did, he wouldn't even kill a fly again. I don't see him doing anything like that."

"That's good. Have you had time to arraign him? I don't think we can transport him until that happens."

"That's the first thing I did. There's a justice of the peace in Pottsboro. We stopped there on the way in."

"Good! Did the judge set a bond?"

"Bond was denied. That's a good judge over there."

Sanders nodded in approval. "I'll need a copy of the paperwork."

"Of course. I have it for you. Stewart's pistol, too. We may be small, but we're not amateurs."

"I can see that. I'm impressed. What about Mr. Sample? Is he here?"

"No, he couldn't make it. He had a hot yacht prospect show up. You know how that is."

"I'll call him later, then. Did you ask him about the reward?"

"No. That's a waste of time."

"Then, pass along my thanks. I guess we better get back. If I can ever return this favor, don't hesitate to call."

"Thanks, Sheriff. I will. I better take you back there and ease this kid into this. He can be pretty jumpy."

"That sounds good. May I get Walker with one of your men for the paperwork and his personal effects?"

"Sure. No problem. That'll only take a minute."

"Thanks. We're anxious to get started. We have a long night ahead."

Sheriff Little led them outside, motioning to his chief deputy to help Walker. The two sheriffs walked into the back area to a narrow hall with three cells. In the cell farthest away sat a young lady in uniform across from a subdued young man dressed in dark blue, who looked at the two approaching men with fear in his eyes. Sanders followed Little into the cell as Stewart rose as if greeting the hangman. Little motioned with his right hand back toward Sanders.

"Mr. Stewart, this is Sheriff Sanders from Tarrant County. He's here to transport you back there. Don't be nervous, he's not going to hurt you."

Sanders removed his Western hat and nodded to the nervous prisoner with a look of forced nonchalance. "I'm going to have to handcuff you, son. Stand up and put your hands behind you."

Stewart nodded and complied, his head drooping. Sanders cuffed him tight, taking satisfaction in Stewart's grimace.

"When we get outside, there's going to be a bunch of people with cameras. They may shout a lot of questions. If that happens, don't say anything. Just move quickly to the car. Do you understand that, Stewart?"

"Yes sir. Who are those people out there? Will they try to shoot me?"

"Most of them are just press people. They won't hurt you, and I've got men outside to make sure."

"Yes sir."

"Let's get started then." Sheriff Little walked out in front with Stewart directly behind him. Sanders took Stewart's right arm, leading the trembling prisoner through the outer office. The deputies had formed a double line from the door to halfway to the waiting squad cars, and Blair was forcing the reporters out of the way. Carter was sitting in the driver's seat of the first car and Walker in the second. Blair plowed through the growing group of onlookers. After opening a four-foot path through the group, Blair opened the back door of Walker's unit and nodded at Little. Little glanced back at Sanders.

"I'll keep the crowd out of the way; just move quickly." With that, he surged out the door toward the group that he estimated at seventy people. The first fifteen steps were easy, but as they neared the group, the reporters began shouting questions, and the crowd started shouting angry insults at Stewart. Sanders saw a bottle sailing toward them and jerked Stewart out of the way just in time. The trailing deputies came forward and reopened a small path to the second car. Sanders pulled the frightened Stewart to the door and pushed him in. As Sanders followed him into the back seat, Scroggins circled the car and got in on the other side. As soon as the doors closed, both cars shot forward with their lights on. Several people barely got out of the way. Sanders breathed a sigh of relief. An ugly crowd had not been expected.

"Fred, radio ahead. I want officers in riot gear on the street outside the sally port. I don't want another circus when we get home."

Walker dived for the radio as Sanders looked over his sweating prisoner. Stewart was shaking like a leaf and had sweat beading on his forehead. "There must be a lot of people mad at me. Are you mad at me?"

"Whether I get mad at you or not depends on how much you cooperate. If you don't, I can be difficult and ugly. You don't want that, do you?"

"No, sir."

"Good. I need some answers right away. Are you gonna talk to me?"

"Yes sir."

Sanders nodded to Scroggins, who leaned over the front seat and turned on the tape recorder. Sanders pitched his hat into the front seat. "Your name is Billy Earl Stewart, is that right?"

"Yes sir."

"Did that judge in Pottsboro explain your rights to you?"

"Yes sir."

"Did you break into the subcourthouse the night before the shooting?"

"Yes sir."

"How much cash did you get?"

"About $2,800."

"Did you have any other money at the time?"

"Not much."

"Did you give two thousand of that to Angel?"

"Yeah. How did you know that?"

"We've been busy. Did you talk to anyone about killing Judge Sterrett after the shootings?"

"I don't understand what you mean."

"I mean did you hire anybody to finish the job?"

"No, sir."

Sanders fished out a mug shot out of his pocket. "I'm going to show you a picture of a man called Wilson. Have you ever seen this man before?"

"No, sir."

"Are you sure?"

"I'm positive. Can I have a Coke, please? My mouth's really dry."

"Sorry, Stewart. We don't have one in the car."

"Can we stop somewhere and get one?"

"Maybe later. Did you talk to anyone else who wanted Sterrett dead?"

"No, sir."

"Do you know a police officer named Agnew?"

"No, sir."

"How about Jim Wade? He's a county commissioner."

"No, sir."

"You've never talked to any of these people?"

"No, sir. I've never heard of them."

"Did Angel ever say anything about wanting Sterrett dead? Did he give you any encouragement before the fact?"

"No, sir. Can I ask a question?"

"Sure. What is it?"

"What's going to happen to me?"

"You're going to stand trial for capital murder."

"Will they execute me?"

"I don't know."

"I want something to drink. I'm thirsty."

Sanders looked at the scared kid, with no pity. In the old West Texas days, Sanders would put trash like this out in a pasture with a mad bull and let him run awhile to learn what thirsty was. These were different times. "All right. We'll stop up ahead and get you a Coke. Fred, call Gary in the other unit and find out who he got to check on Wilson's flight reservation. I want to talk to him."

A few minutes later, the units stopped at a small convenience store in Prosper. Scroggins got some soft drinks while Sanders jumped into the front seat. His call was coming through.

"This is Blevins. Over."

"This is Sanders. Did you trace the flight reservations of this guy Wilson?"

"Yes sir. He arrived at DFW Saturday morning on American Airlines at 7:05 am from Tulsa. The reservation was made Friday at 1:37 pm."

"Call Charles out at the security base and release the family from protective custody. Keep a deputy with them for a couple of days as a precaution."

"What about the prisoner, Wilson?"

"Cut him loose, Blevins. He's innocent. Over and out."

Chapter Twenty-Five

A gratefully released Buck Reed pulled out of the pound in his rental car and pointed it toward Arlington. At the first red light, he turned on the radio, tuning it to a news station. Being careful in jail to show total indifference, he had read no newspapers and watched no television. The few prisoners that had displayed interest in him learned no more than the sheriff's deputies. Reed's attention was immediately drawn to the radio.

"Billy Earl Stewart was apprehended at Lake Texoma this afternoon, according to news sources in Grayson County. Sheriff Austin Little announced that he and his deputies responded to a tip from a local citizen. With the help of officers from Texas Parks and Wildlife, Stewart was apprehended at Sample's Marina. Details are still sketchy, but the news was confirmed by a spokesperson from Sheriff Lee Sanders' office in Tarrant County. According to the sheriff's office, Sheriff Sanders is now en route back with the prisoner.

In a related story, the brother of the late Judge Joe Chavez announced that he was going to Austin tomorrow to file a complaint against Judge Jake Eaves with the Judicial Conduct Committee. Mr. Chavez announced that he will ask the committee to remove Judge Eaves from office for criminal negligence. Judge Eaves could not—"

Reed turned off the radio and increased his speed about ten miles per hour. If Stewart was caught, the sheriff would let the judge out of seclusion. If his employer chose to, the bomb could be exploded as early as tonight. At least it would be late if his instructions were carried out, but Reed had no guarantee of that. Plus, the triggerman could get anxious and bungle the job. There was no time to waste.

Reed took the next exit off Highway 287 and turned northeast toward DFW airport. His watch showed 5:15. His mind raced as he fought going-home traffic. Going back to Tulsa was now out of the question. Getting out of the country had to be the first priority, but where and how? His passports were at the farm. At least one was needed to get a plane ticket. Reed reached Airport Freeway and turned right, racing toward the airport as a plan began forming in his mind.

After turning in his rental car, he called his assistant at the farm and had him Fed-Ex the passport, driver's license, and credit cards for a third identity to the Hilton Hotel outside the New Orleans airport. Reed caught the van to the American Airlines terminal and purchased a ticket to Los Angeles on the next plane out, using the Wilson credit card. Going through security didn't take much time, and Reed soon found himself at the departure gate.

Suffering through a fifteen-minute wait, he placed himself about tenth in line. After giving his pass to the agent, he walked about five steps, then abruptly reversed direction and walked past the busy agent. Discarding the boarding pass in a trashcan, he walked outside and hailed a cab to the second hotel room. After arriving there, he made sure that his truck was safe and in good order. The second set of identity papers was safe in the glove box. Reed threw away the Wilson driver's license and credit cards, retrieving the money in his "real estate papers" folder out of the safe before he headed for his room. Reed left a message on the car lot's voice mail, telling the dealer where to retrieve his truck in New Orleans. That would be better than the police finding it.

After making sure that Torrey had properly cleaned the room, he checked out, leaving instructions to the clerk to call the rental place for the edger and lawn mower. A sealed envelope with $200 was left with her for payment. The large tip should keep the rental place quiet. Reed hid most of his money under the seat of the pickup. Two blocks away was a Mobil service station, where he gassed up, checked the oil. He bought maps for Texas and Louisiana. Packaged cashews and a six-pack of sodas were bought for the road. The road through Shreveport was interstate all the way. That was the shortest route out of Texas, and he was already on I-20. Unless he hit trouble, he could easily make New Orleans by daylight.

As Reed was leaving town, Marilyn Shaw rang Ray's house for the fourth time. Slamming the phone down in frustration, she redialed her boss.

"Stanley here."

"This is Marilyn."

"How is the study going?"

"It's been difficult, but I'm making headway. In the last eight years, five hundred seventy prisoners have been released on writs."

"Has Eaves released all of those five hundred and seventy?"

"No, sir. About half is all. One other judge has issued several."

"How many were released without hearings?"

"It's impossible to tell."

"Who is the other judge?"

"Judge Lassiter."

"He died last year."

"I know. I've discovered something else. These cases have six attorneys showing up repeatedly."

"So?"

"So that's a pretty small group. I wonder if these attorneys are favorites of these two judges."

"Have you checked the judges' campaign reports? They could be heavy contributors."

"No, but that is a great idea. I will check that first thing in the morning. The county offices are closed by now."

"Okay. Let me know when you have something."

Marilyn signed off as one of her other lines lit up. That must be Ray. "Hello?"

"Marilyn?"

"Oh hello, Mother."

"You don't seem happy to hear from me."

"It's not that. I was just hoping that it was Ray. They caught that killer today."

"Have you seen him since you got back?"

"No. He's been in hiding. I hope to see him tonight. I thought he would be home by now."

"You seem sure he's the one. We are all so excited here. We thought you were going to die an old maid."

"Don't worry, Mother. I'm not going to let him get away. I've got it all figured out. The kids will require adjustments, but the housekeeper can be retained. That will give me more time with Ray."

"Are you going to quit work?"

"Of course not. I could never just stay at home. I would be bored to tears. Ray would never expect that."

"You know your father has always wanted a grandson. Would that be a possibility?"

"Sure."

"He is getting pretty old, you know. Could it be soon?"

"I think I'll start on that project tonight."

As Marilyn hung up, they were both laughing. She tried Ray's number again and then slammed down the unanswered phone, tossing her long black hair in irritation. *Where the hell was he? I think I'll go over to the jail and ask the sheriff if I can interview Stewart. Maybe he'll tell me where Ray is, now that the danger is over.* After checking her makeup, she grabbed her purse and headed for the jail. The trip turned out to be a waste of time. Stewart was still in interrogation and the sheriff was unavailable. Marilyn visited with a few of the many reporters that were hovering around and then headed for a restaurant alone. Dinner had been an afterthought. Marilyn needed the coffee more than the food. It could take past midnight to finish the digging and prepare the story, if the money connection worked out. That is, if she couldn't find Ray. It was going to be a long night.

"This is 555-3139."

"This is Torrey. I received your beeper message to call."

"Yes. Has our boy showed up at home yet?"

"Yes. He arrived twenty minutes ago. He also has a woman with him and one deputy sheriff."

"The kids, too?"

"Yes. What do you want to do?"

"Get on with it."

"What about the other people?"

"Who's the woman?"

"I don't know. I didn't get a good look at her."

"Don't worry about it. You've got him in your sights. Go."

"What about the deputy?"

"I said don't worry about it. What's the problem?"

"You said you didn't want anyone else hurt."

"Sterrett sleeps alone. The device will be contained to that room."

"So you want to go tonight?"

"Certainly. Has the bedroom light gone out?"

"Not yet."

"Let's see. It's 10:20. If the light goes out before 11:15, go at midnight. If it goes out later, go forty-five minutes later."

"What about my money?"

"What about it?"

"I want it tonight."

"That can't be done. It'll be delivered tomorrow."

"Delivered where?"

"Someone will find you with it. I promise you this: you won't be able to follow this courier. Don't even try."

"Is there a reason why you want this done at midnight?"

"Yeah."

"Why?"

"If I wanted you to know, I would've told you already."

"More games?"

"You don't need to worry about it. It has nothing to do with you."

"I still don't like the cop being there. There could be more. I could get caught."

"Just do it the way our boy told you. Leave the house and trigger it from two blocks away. You could do it at a red light with a cop parked next to you. It's that simple."

"What if some of the others get hurt?"

"They won't. If they do, it's tough shit."

Ray waited impatiently as Cass buzzed around the house. First, she had tucked in the children and then tore into the kitchen, throwing away bad milk and mildewed vegetables. A grocery list was drawn up and trash thrown out. Ray was thankful the neighbor had mowed the lawn or Cass would have been outside doing that. It was almost 11:00 pm and he was getting tired. At last, Cass breezed into the bedroom. Ray threw back the covers.

"Come here, Mama Cass."

"In just a few minutes. I need to shower and freshen up first. Ray watched her waltz into the bathroom and shut the door. Cabinets were opened and closed as she explored the unfamiliar territory. Ray listened as he imagined her finding the towels and stepping into the shower. For a moment, he was tempted to join her. But it was getting late and his fatigue was mounting. God, it was good to be home. The shower finally went off, and Ray heard her humming a tune as she dried off. At last, she appeared in a ravishing see-through nightie.

"It's a felony to look as beautiful as you do."

"Thank you. You're really sweet."

"I mean it."

Cass slipped into bed next to him and greeted him with a long searching kiss. Ray finally broke away.

"I didn't tell you about me coming from English nobility did I?"

"What do you mean?" This isn't time to talk about something like that."

"Yes it is. Once a king, always a king. But once a night is enough."

Cass giggled. "Aren't you clever? How's your shoulder?"

"It's okay."

"That's not the problem?"

"No, baby. I'm just worn out. Can you wait till tomorrow night?"

Cass smiled mischievously. "Maybe not. How would you like to be attacked in your office tomorrow?"

Ray smiled and pulled her close. "Sorry. It's got to be all business at the office. I'm going to bring Helen out tomorrow for an interview."

"The Helen from Judge Rhoads office?"

"That's right. Do you approve?"

"I don't know. That's kind of sudden."

"You told me a month ago that she was ready."

"I didn't think about her replacing me. Phyllis can't stand her."

"Phyllis probably needs to go anyway."

"Are you going to fire her?"

"I don't know."

"Why?"

"She has shown a lack of instinct for the job. Things happened out there Friday that I'm uneasy about."

"You mean about her telling Wade where you were going to be?"

"Not only that, she formed an alliance with him."

"Oh. You didn't tell me about that. I see what you mean."

"Will she quit if I hire Helen?"

"Probably."

"Good! Then that's the way to handle it."

Cass leaned against the pillow and stroked Ray's head as she talked. "My mean old boss. You never showed me this side of you before."

"I never had to. If I can't trust an employee, they have to go."

"How about me? It looks like I'm getting fired tomorrow, too."

"No, baby. You're getting promoted, if that's what you really want."

"Of course that's what I want. I've dreamed of having a man like you all my life." Cass rose up and looked at Ray with a serious look. "Is this what you really want?"

"Of course it is."

"Are you happy?"

"Happy isn't the word for it. I'm ecstatic."

"We'll both have to make a lot of adjustments."

"I know. That's part of it. Have you spotted something already?"

"Uh-huh."

"What do you want me to do?"

"First of all, I can't sleep on this side of the bed. I want to switch."

"But I've always slept on this side of the bed."

"So have I. Will you do that for me?"

"I suppose. But what if I can't go to sleep?"

Cass moved around the bed. After shutting the drapes, she eased in next to Ray. "Don't worry. I know how to put you to sleep every night."

Marilyn struggled with her story. The words just weren't flowing. It was impossible to write a story when you only had half the information. Without the facts about the campaign donations the story just wouldn't jell. The editors would be disappointed with her if she didn't have at least an outline for a story ready. There had to be a way to get more information. The night news manager might have some ideas.

Leaving her things, she took the elevator down to the fourth floor, to find a frantic pace at the night desk. Marilyn counted a staff of fourteen pounding away at their computers, while a frayed man in his fifties sat in a back office proofing a story. Thankfully, his name was stenciled on the glass outside his door.

"Mr. Stinson?"

The balding night manager looked up in irritation. "What is it?"

"I'm Marilyn Shaw, just transferred from the Arlington section. I need some help and advice with a story I'm running."

"What are you working on?"

"I'm doing an exposé on judges who have issued writs of habeas corpus without hearings."

"Is that a follow up on the courthouse shootings?"

"Yes sir."

"Well, get on with your question. Can't you see I'm busy here?"

"I need the campaign reports on two judges. Do we keep copies of those records here in the building?"

"Not that I know of. You can check with Douglas Harrison in the morning. He does most of the political work."

"I really need them tonight. Could they be in his files?"

"Who are the judges?"

"Eaves and Lassiter."

"I doubt that he would have something like that. It's been three years since they've had an election. Their campaign reports wouldn't be hot enough to keep ordinarily."

"Would it be all right if I checked?"

"I wouldn't recommend it. Harrison's damned touchy about his files. You better wait till morning."

Marilyn managed a dry smile. "Thank you, sir." As he returned to his copy, she walked slowly past the row of reporters. A young man near the end looked up and smiled, so Marilyn took a chance.

"Could you tell me where Douglas Harrison's office is?"

"Sure. It's up on the next floor. Who are you?"

"I'm Marilyn Shaw."

"Oh yeah. I read your article on Eaves last week. Nice goin'."

"Thanks. Who are you?"

"Harley Kent. Are you new around here?"

"Kind of. I was transferred in from Arlington last week."

"Well Marilyn, come by sometime and I'll take you to dinner."

"Thanks Harley. It's nice to meet you." Marilyn moved on past the young man before the hit became more serious.

The fifth floor was a line of dark cubicles on both sides of a wide aisle. Nametags on desks were rare, and no desk had a nametag with Harrison on it. Marilyn spied an employee directory on one of the desks and looked up Harrison's extension. After ringing his phone, she found his desk in one of the larger cubicles toward the back of the room. Harrison's work area was twice hers, but still without privacy as his cubicle could be entered from two directions and another desk was only ten feet away.

Marilyn flipped on a nearby light switch and the back office area was immediately illuminated. Next to Harrison's desk beckoned a four-drawer filing cabinet. Harrison's desk was a mess, but his files were tidy, and political names were in alphabetical order. Marilyn found Eaves folder in the second drawer. The folder was thicker than most, so Marilyn placed it on Harrison's desk and started flipping through it. On the top were some surveillance photos of Eaves and his flashy secretary sitting at a table looking at each other over highballs. The bottom photo showed them outside some motel room. Underneath were clippings of favorable articles on Eaves, written by Harrison. Underneath those was a year-old campaign report, which Marilyn grabbed and scanned. Contributions had continued to flow, even in off-election years. Marilyn counted thirty-four law firms that made up the contribution list, but the largest by far were those same six attorneys who were getting the writs. Her eyes widened as she noticed that the six attorneys had given multiple amounts, with dates closely corresponding to—the elevator opened and more lights came on at the far end of the hall. Marilyn could hear two male voices and footsteps rapidly approaching.

Her eyes widened more as she peeped around the corner and saw Harrison himself with someone she didn't know. Harrison was obviously drunk as he talked loudly with slurred speech. Hastily, she grabbed the file and stepped into the cubicle behind Harrison's as quietly as she could.

"—not drunk, I tell you. I can drive home myshelf."

"You're drunker than hell, and you're not driving home yourself. Let's find your car keys and get the hell out of here."

"I know where the keyeshar. They're in my drawer. Then we'll go have one more drink to shelibrate that that pieche of shit dyin'. We'll be shafe then."

"Shut up, you fool. Somebody might hear you."

"There'sh nobody here but ush chickens, and in about ten minutes everybody'sh gonna know that Schterrett's dead. He goesh to bed and Torrey pushes a button. Kaboom. Nighty-night, Schterrett."

Harrison's drunken laughter pervaded the whole floor as his companion rifled his desk and found his keys. They faded back toward the elevator, with Harrison's friend doing his best to quiet the drunk.

Marilyn stood perfectly still, with a pounding heart until the elevator doors closed. After snatching up the nearest phone, she remembered that she did not have Ray's number memorized. The high heels came off after only three steps as she raced wildly for the elevator. The elevator was still occupied. Thoughts moved wildly through her head. *My floor's only two up. I've got to make it.* "Oh my God, don't let him die!" she screamed as she raced up the stairs to her office, arriving frantically at her desk and digging for Ray's number.

"Please God, don't let him die!"

In her hurry, she dialed the wrong number. Then she carefully redialed as her panting subsided. The phone seemed to ring for an eternity. Finally, it picked up with a sleepy female voice answering.

"Hello?"

Who the hell was that?

"Hello?"

That voice was familiar. *Who could it be?*

"Hello?"

Marilyn remembered. It was Ray's head clerk. *What's she doing there?*

"Hello?"

Marilyn disconnected the line with a shaking hand. With her other, she hurled her purse against the plate glass window. **No! Oh my God! Noooooooooo!** The tears flowed as she numbly put her head in her hands.

"Oh God! Please no!"

Chapter Twenty-Six

Leonard Torrey watched Sterrett's back fence closely. The light had gone off at 11:16. Should he wait until midnight? That was still twelve minutes away, and Torrey couldn't find a reason why he should wait. What would keep these assholes from turning him in whenever they felt like it? Would they use this in the future against him whenever they wanted some dirty work done? On the other hand, there was the money. Twenty-five grand would solve a lot of his problems, and there might be more to come if Stewart used Torrey as his attorney. This trial would receive national attention. The evidence against Stewart was overwhelming, but there was always the possibility of getting him off on insanity. If he could find the right doctor, it was possible. He could become a nationally prominent attorney in a year. If he got big enough, those assholes might leave him alone.

Torrey's attention was brought back to the issue at hand when a car pulled onto Sterrett's street. The dark sedan eased past, turning into a driveway four houses down. While the driver got out and went inside his home, Torrey cleaned up the room and legged it downstairs. After making sure the coast was clear, he got into his car and drove slowly out of the quiet neighborhood. A convenience store parking lot situated two blocks away allowed him an unobstructed view of Sterrett's back fence. Torrey parked there and checked his watch, which showed 11:59. The store was empty, and the clerk had nothing better to do than stare at Torrey. Torrey stared back thoughtfully. He must be worried about me holding him up. I better go in and buy something. Two minutes later, he was back in his car with a Coke, but the clerk was still eyeballing him.

Torrey reached down and picked up the garage door opener and checked the clerk again, who returned his steady gaze. Torrey wheeled the car around slowly until he could see Sterrett's fence in his rearview mirror. After putting the car in drive and releasing the brake, he started easing out of the parking lot. The clerk's attention went elsewhere. Torrey's stare went from the clerk to the rearview mirror. "Good–bye, Sterrett, you arrogant bastard."

An explosion shuddered the ground and a fireball rose to the heavens as Torrey drove away.

"Unit thirty-two, this is dispatch. This is an emergency. I repeat, an emergency. Over."

"Unit thirty-two, do you read me? This is an emergency. Over."

A sleepy security officer reached over to the coffee table and picked up his radio. "This is unit thirty-two. Ov—"

"Get the family out of the house through the front door! There's a bomb about to go off in the bedroom! Do not acknowledge until the family has cleared the house! Move!"

The dispatcher waited impatiently and looked at his overhead clock as the seconds ticked by. Twenty-two seconds later, he heard a deafening explosion through the radio.

"Unit thirty-two, this is dispatch. Do you read? Over. Unit thirty-two, do you read me? Over. Unit thirty-two, acknowledge. Over." The dispatcher shook his head and dialed a number. "Sheriff?"

A sleepy voice acknowledged. "Yes. This is Sanders."

"This is dispatch. Somebody just bombed Sterrett's house, and I don't think I got them out in time."

"Oh God, no! Not after all this. What happened?"

"I got a call from a reporter who claimed she overheard a conversation where somebody named Harrison said that Sterrett was gonna get bombed at straight-up midnight. I called our security unit and warned him, but I think the bomb went off before he could evacuate the house."

"Do you have units dispatched to the scene?"

"No, sir. I called you first."

"Get some units out there fast. Dispatch three ambulances just in case. I'll be on the way in about two minutes. You can reach me by radio."

"Yes sir. I'll get on it."

"Call Walker too and get him out there."

"Yes sir. Anything else?"

"Not now. Move it." Sanders hung up the phone, cursing under his breath, jumped into his uniform, and dashed for his unit. With lights and siren on, he floor-boarded the car toward Sterrett's.

"Unit one to dispatch. Over."

"This is dispatch."

"I'm en route. ETA twelve minutes. How long will it take to get our units there?"

"The first unit is still five minutes away."

"Who was the reporter that called? Was it Marilyn Shaw?"

"Yes sir. I think so. I didn't take the time to write it down."

"You did the right thing. I'll deal with the call later. Are the ambulances on the way?"

"Yes sir."

"What's their ETA?"

"About ten minutes."

"Which of our units is approaching?"

"It's unit forty-six. Officer Cleary."

"Have him report as soon as he gets to the scene, and patch his report through to me while he gives it."

"Roger, sir."

"Over and out."

Sanders hit Loop 820 and punched his unit for all it had. The cars ahead pulled over for him as he raced south from the northeast part of the county toward south Arlington. There was still ten miles to go.

"Dispatch to unit one. Over."

"This is unit one. Go."

"I have the report coming through now, sir."

"Patch him through, dammit."

"—ty-six with an initial report. There's extensive damage to the house, and two children are staggering around in the front yard. There's a woman lying on the sidewalk about ten feet from the front door, and a man lying three feet behind her. They're either unconscious or dead."

"This is unit one, Cleary. What about our deputy? Is that him lying on the lawn?"

"Whoever it is does not have a uniform on, sir."

"Check on the adults and report right back. Leave the radio on."

"Roger."

Sanders stayed on the floorboard as he rounded Loop 820 and merged into I-20. *God, would this nightmare never end?*

"Unit one, this is forty-six. Over."

"Go forty-six."

"Their both alive, sir. There's blood coming out their ears, and they're in shock, but they're breathing."

"What about the deputy?"

"I found him just inside the door. I'm afraid he's dead."

"Is your backup unit there yet?"

"No, sir. But I hear them approaching."

"Secure the children, Cleary. I'll be there in about four minutes. Over and out. Unit one to dispatch. Over."

"This is dispatch, go ahead unit one."

"Get Charles Rogers on the phone and find out who he assigned to guard Sterrett tonight. Give him the bad news and tell him to come to the scene. Have you reached Walker yet?"

"Yes sir. He's en route. ETA twenty minutes."

"Good. Is he calling in his team?"

"Yes sir."

"Good. Call Arlington PD and tell them I want their fire chief out there. If he has a demolition expert, bring him, too."

"Roger. Anything else?"

"Just one thing. Keep Marilyn Shaw available."

"I took the liberty to do that already, sir."

"Good man. I'm arriving at the scene now. Over and out."

Sanders dashed out of his car into a war zone. The rear of the house was a smoldering ruin. Neighbors were wandering around, with one lady trying to console the children while one of the two officers was helping Cass into a sitting position and covering her with a blanket. The other officer was kneeling over Ray, just outside the front door. Sanders went there first.

"How is he?"

"He's stable, I think. His vitals are okay. I think the concussion just knocked him out. Getting outside saved him."

The sheriff stepped inside and looked at his deputy lying in the hallway, just inside the door. His eyes were protruding and blood was still seeping from his nose, mouth, and ears. Sanders put his hand on the man's chest, feeling nothing. Slowly shaking his head, he rose and went back to Ray. Eyes open, Ray looked around wildly, sweat pouring down his face. The sheriff turned to a concerned neighbor.

"Ma'am. Would you be kind enough to bring me some wet towels and dry blankets?"

The lady moved off to comply. Sanders went over to Cass, who was sitting up and stammering wildly to the officer. It was plain that she was disoriented, but reviving. The neighbor returned with the towels as ambulance sirens wailed in the distance. As the children were cleaned up, towels were applied, then blankets, to Ray to ward off shock.

Sanders watched the ambulances arrive, wondering why it had taken so long. When the lead driver jumped out, he summoned him over.

"I need a report on the injured man before you move him. Also, check on the man inside and see if there's any hope of reviving him."

The man raced off to do the sheriff's bidding and returned shortly. "The man outside is going to be okay. He probably has a concussion. There's no hope for the man inside. He died instantly, I'm afraid."

Sanders nodded sadly. "Is it critical that you take him to the nearest hospital, or can you take him to JPS?"

"We can take him to John Peter Smith Hospital. It's not critical."

"Good! Take the whole family there and have them checked out. Admit them as John and Jane Doe. That's very important. Do you understand?"

"Yes sir."

"I'm going to send one of my officers with them. Tell the doctors that my man's to stay with Sterrett every possible minute."

"Yes sir. I'll attend to it."

"Why did it take you so long to get here?"

"We were on another call, sir."

"All three units?"

"Yes sir. We had a bad accident on the west freeway."

"All right. Get moving."

Sanders motioned Cleary over. "Go with them to JPS. Make sure they're admitted under John Does, and stay with Sterrett every minute except when the doctors run you off. I'll send a full security team out there shortly."

"Yes sir." The officer helped Cass and the children into one of the ambulances. All three seemed to be numb and disoriented.

Sanders turned to see a frayed Fred Walker approaching. Walker did not immediately notice the sheriff, but instead walked into the shell of the house, examining the dead deputy briefly before walking to the bedroom. Sanders could see his flashlight flicking around the debris. After watching ambulance personnel remove the body, he joined his investigative chief.

"Did you know the deputy, Fred?"

"Yeah. His name was Hennessey, age forty, a wife and three kids."

"Damn. This just keeps getting worse. What's happening to us, Fred?"

"You got me, Sheriff. I've never seen anything like this."

"What do you see here?"

"A bomb planted behind Sterrett's bed."

"How can you tell?"

"Look at the hole in the wall right behind what is left of the bed. See the small holes in the opposite wall? Those were caused by some type of flying debris traveling from the direction of the bed."

"What about the damage to the window and the ceiling?"

"The blast caused that."

"If that's the case, what killed Hennessey?"

"The blast."

"Why didn't the blast kill the family?"

"Once they made it outside, the blast force would dissipate."

"How was it detonated?"

"I don't know. I assume there was a headboard on this bed. See the splintered area behind the mattress?"

"Yeah."

"The bomb was probably hidden behind it. If anyone had been in that bed, they wouldn't have had a chance."

"Who did this, Fred? Wade and Agnew?"

"It must have been. I guess they had a backup plan."

"That guy I cut loose yesterday?"

"Maybe. But I doubt it. If anything, he was just a spotter."

"Then this is a big organized operation we're dealing with?"

"That's how I see it."

"That reminds me. I need to talk to Marilyn Shaw. She's the one who tipped us on this."

"We knew about this ahead of time?"

"Yeah. About forty-five seconds before. If we'd had three more seconds, Hennessey would have made it out, too."

"Let's get her on the phone. I didn't know about this."

The two grim-faced men radioed in. "Unit one to dispatch. Over."

"This is dispatch."

"Where is Marilyn Shaw?"

"I've got her in the outer office, sir."

"Have her call me on the mobile phone. Over and out."

The sheriff's phone rang thirty seconds later. "Hello, Marilyn?"

"Yes."

"Tell me exactly what happened."

"I was digging some political information out of Harrison's files when he came up with some other guy. I hid behind a workstation nearby and heard them talking. Harrison was drunk and spouting off about Ray getting killed in ten minutes. When they left, I ran up to my office and called Ray, but I got a woman on the line instead. I got upset and hung up because I couldn't deal with it. I called your office after that."

"Why did you hide?"

"I ... I wasn't supposed to be looking in his files."

"Who was the man with him?"

"I don't know."

"My dispatcher said you told him there was a bomb in his bed. How did you know that?"

"Harrison was bragging about it."

"Did he say who put it there?"

"No. But he did say something about Torrey pushing the button and then kaboom."

"Torrey? Leonard Torrey?"

"Yes sir. I guess."

"What else did he say?"

"That's all I can remember? How's Ray?"

"He's all right. A concussion maybe. He barely got out of the house."

"And the children?"

"They'll be okay."

"Thank God. I was so scared. "

"He's gone to the hospital for treatment. I'll be back downtown in a few minutes. Would you mind sticking around for a while?"

"I'll be here."

"Okay. I'll talk to you in a few minutes." Sanders hung up the phone and stared at Fred.

"Harrison is up to his ears in this. Get somebody to arrest him as soon as you can locate him. Torrey, too."

"The attorney?"

"That's right. I think he triggered the bomb."

"Is that what Marilyn Shaw said?"

"Yeah. She overheard a conversation of Harrison's. This could've been a whole lot worse."

"Do you need me to stay here? I can put Blair and Carter on the arrests if you want me to. But, I don't see what I can accomplish here."

"Yeah. Go ahead, I can handle it. Get Jack Rhoads on the phone for emergency arraignments. If I'm not there yet, grill those bastards hard. When I get through with the fire chief, I'll be along."

"Yes sir. Do you want me to call Hennessey's wife?"

"That's a job I better do myself."

"I understand. I'll see you back at the office." Walker tucked his flashlight under his arm and headed for his unit.

Sanders poked around the debris for a while. Moving around was difficult without disturbing the wreckage. It was probably better to leave everything as it was until the fire marshal looked at it. The sheriff shook his head sadly. There was no point in stalling any longer. A phone call had to be made to Mrs. Hennessey.

An hour later, Walker had both of the new prisoners waiting in separate interrogation rooms. Before he decided which one to question first, he tiptoed into the small rooms with the one-way glass and studied the prisoners. Torrey was visibly nervous as he fought the shakes. Harrison was sitting, slumped over the table, fast asleep. Walker wondered if he was drunk. It made more sense for Harrison to be nervous since Torrey was familiar with the system. Questioning Torrey first was the obvious choice. Walker slipped out of the narrow observation room and nodded to Carter to follow him in as he opened the door to the interrogation room. He stared grimly at an anxious Torrey.

"You're in a hell of lot of trouble, counselor."

"Would you tell me why? Nobody's told me a damn thing except to read me my rights, which I already know."

"Yeah. I'll be glad to tell you. You're under arrest for capital murder. I've never been to an execution, but I'm going to make an exception in your case."

"Capital murder? You must be crazy. Who died?"

"Nobody special— just a police officer, a man with a family."

"I have no idea what you're talking about."

"I'm sure you don't. You can detonate a bomb from quite a distance. You wouldn't know or care who died."

Torrey tried to remain calm. "What makes you think I did something like that?"

"Somebody ratted on you. How else do you think we'd know who did it so soon after the fact?"

Torrey's eyes turned downward. That had to be true, but why? To get out of paying the money? What about Sterrett? This cop hadn't said anything about him. How can I find out without tipping my hand? "If that's true, somebody is trying to fool you. You grab the wrong man while the right one gets away. It's an old trick, Officer."

"Guess again, counselor. I've got him in the next room."

Torrey winced as the word counselor was spat out. He hated to be called that. "Where and when was it that I was supposed to have done this?"

"You know the answer to that. Don't try to get cute with me."

"No, I don't know the answer."

"Suit yourself, asshole. I don't need your confession. You're going down, and I'm going to watch you all the way."

Torrey raised his eyes and studied this iron-hard man, knowing not to give anything away. He could be bluffing, but he had hit home with the fact that he had Torrey so quickly. And who the hell was the other prisoner? There might be a way to tiptoe out of this. "I'm not admitting anything, you understand. But I have something that's vital to you on another matter."

"We're not interested in anything else, counselor."

"Yes, you are. You just don't know it."

Walker smiled inwardly. He had Torrey. "All right. Spit it out."

Torrey looked down again. "Not so fast. I want the details on what I'm being charged with. I can't bargain when I don't know the game."

"It's real easy to figure out, Torrey. When you tried to kill Sterrett tonight, you got our security guard instead."

"Kill who?"

"Judge Ray Sterrett."

"Why would I want to do something like that?"

"I don't know. You tell me."

"This is crazy, Officer. I'm an attorney. I don't go around killing people. Who told you that I did this?"

Walker shook his head no. "No dice, Torrey. You're giving me information, remember?"

"I'm not saying anything else until you answer my question."

"All right, counselor. I'll tell you this much. Your coconspirator shot his mouth off and somebody overheard him. They called in, and we were able to get everybody out of the house just in time, except the security guard. Harrison named you as the trigger man. I've got him and the witness. You're going down. You can talk if you want or not. I really don't care."

Torrey looked down again and thought it over. *It had to be true. Nothing else made any sense. I'm in deep shit.* "What do I get if I talk?"

"Not much, counselor. I'll tell the jury that you cooperated, that's all. I'm not going to cut a deal for no death penalty. Not with my deputy getting killed."

Torrey looked down again. That wasn't much, but it might be better than nothing. It would be smarter to wait and get another attorney to bargain for him, but if he waited for that, his bargaining chip would be gone. "That's not good enough. I want off the death penalty, and I want it in writing. Otherwise, no deal."

Walker looked down at the shabbily dressed lawyer with contempt. *I could pull the switch myself.* "That's what I hoped you'd say, counselor. I don't want to help you. I don't need you anyway." Walker turned to leave.

"Wait."

Walker turned back. "Wait for what?"

"Will you put it in writing that you will testify that I cooperated?"

"Maybe. What can you tell me that I can't get from the other guy?"

"I can get you the most famous killer in the Southwest."

The sun was rising to his left as Buck Reed pulled into New Orleans on I-10. A right turn on Highway 49 put the sun behind him as he drove cautiously toward the airport and the Hilton Hotel. The trip had been uneventful, but slow, as he had stopped for a leisurely dinner in Shreveport and drove the speed limit all the way. There was no hurry to get to New Orleans since his passports wouldn't arrive until mid morning. Reed had craved one more crawfish bisque dinner at Don's Seafood and Steakhouse. It would probably be his last one. As he followed the road into the airport, he rubbed the sleep away, feeling the overnight stubble of beard. After parking his truck, he made his way into the terminal and got in a short line at the American Airlines counter. Two counter people briskly handled the line, and soon Reed faced a pretty, bright, young thing.

"May I help you, sir?"

"Yes. What are your flight schedules to Grand Cayman?"

The young lady tapped her computer. "Let's see here. We have two flights there. They're both through Miami. The first departure is at 7:41 this morning and arrives in Grand Cayman at 1:55 this afternoon. Would you like me to book you on that one?"

"What about the other one? I don't think I can leave that soon."

"The other one leaves at 1:03 this afternoon and arrives in Grand Cayman at 5:57 this evening. Will that work for you?"

"That also is through Miami?"

"Yes sir. There's an hour and a half layover there."

"Is there plenty of space on that one?"

"Yes sir. It looks wide open to Miami, but there are only six seats left on the connecting flight. Shall I book that one for you?"

Reed hesitated. The identity he had with him couldn't be used. There was no passport under that name. But he couldn't wait until his documents got there to buy a ticket for today. "Yes ma'am. I should be ready to go by then. But I don't have my credit card with me. What should I do?"

"You could call in the reservation into our SABRE system by phone as soon as you get us your credit card details."

"I'll do that then. Thank you." Reed turned and left, a little irritated with himself. You couldn't purchase a plane ticket with cash unless you showed your ID. A slipup like that could get you remembered. It was a short trip across the highway to the Hilton Hotel. The lobby was deserted at 6:15 in the morning and a bored desk clerk awaited.

"Yes sir?"

"Do you have any rooms?"

"Yes, we do, but if you check in now you'll have to pay for last night and tonight, unless you check out by 1:00 pm."

"That's fine. I'll be out by one. I just need a little sleep. I'm expecting a package, Federal Express. When it comes in, keep it at the front desk for me, and give me a wake up call at noon."

"Sign in here please, and I need a credit card."

"Can I pay cash?"

"Yes sir. If it's in advance."

"That's fine. How much is it?"

"That will be $115.46, and I'll need an additional twenty-dollar deposit for room charges."

Reed fished out the money, got the key, and returned to his truck. After making sure that no one was watching, he removed the cash from under the seat and put it back in the "real estate" envelope. With the envelope tucked under his arm, he found the way to his room. The first call was to his farm, where he got the credit card information on the name that corresponded to the passport he planned on using. After leaving instructions to include the credit cards with the passports, he called American Airlines and made his reservation. A quick hot shower helped him into quick dreamless slumber.

The efficient hotel woke him at noon. Reed laughed as he washed his face and cleaned his teeth with a washcloth. Thirty-one grand in cash and no toilet articles. It had just been too risky to pick those up at the other hotel in Arlington. The mirror reflected a bewhiskered man with disheveled graying hair.

A quick visit to the hotel gift shop rewarded him with a set of extra clothing, toilet articles, a baseball cap to hide his tousled hair, a hanging suit bag, and a small satchel. After placing his "real estate papers" in the satchel, he went to the front desk, where he picked up his Federal Express package and checked out. After getting his sunglasses out of his truck and leaving the keys under the mat, he caught a cab to the airport across the street. It only took ten minutes to pick up his ticket and board the plane for an uneventful trip to Miami.

Reed deplaned in Miami with his baggage in tow and headed for the departure gate for Grand Cayman, many gates down. A few steps later, he almost stopped in surprise as he spied his mug shot plastered everywhere. It was the picture of his Tarrant County book-in. As he donned his sunglasses, he noticed that a uniformed police officer was standing at every gate. At the third gate, he caught a glimpse of a tough-looking man in a suit, talking with a uniformed officer. That looked like the FBI. Reed managed to stay in the middle of a crowd until he could leave the terminal. A waiting cab whisked him away.

"Where to, sir?"

Reed gathered his thoughts. "I want to go fishing. Where can I charter a boat?"

"There's some fishing boats working at the Miami Yacht Club off MacArthur Causeway."

"Good! Take me there."

The long ride ended at a row of fishing boats across from the Miami Port Authority. After paying the cab fare, he walked slowly along the docks.

A sleek thirty-two foot Bertram near the end of the dock caught his eye. The captain was on board supervising a cleaning detail. Reed quickened his pace until he reached them. "Ahoy there."

The captain looked up from the deck and squinted at the man standing on the dock. "Ahoy yourself. What do you want?"

"How's business?"

"Slow."

"Are you interested in booking a charter?"

"For when?"

"Right now."

"That's crazy, mister. You can't catch anything today. It's too late. Why don't you wait till morning?"

"I don't want to fish. I want you to take me to Freeport."

The captain eyed him suspiciously and then walked off the boat to get a better look. "What's the hurry?"

"I want to go now. What difference does it make?"

"If you're in that big a hurry, take a plane. It's cheaper."

"I don't care. I'm afraid of flying and I love the water."

"Don't shit me, man. You must be on the run."

"You don't need to worry about that. Do you have the fuel capacity to get me there?"

"Yeah. That's no problem. It's going to cost your ass, though."

"How much?"

"Five grand, cash."

"When can we leave?"

"As soon as I fill up the tanks. About ten minutes. I'll have to stay there overnight, so I'll need to take my hand with me."

"That's fine. Let's go."

"As they say in the movies, show me the money."

Reed took the money out of his billfold. "Here's half now and half when you get me there."

"You've got a deal, mister."

Ray opened his eyes, immediately aware of ringing ears and a headache. The light was bright, so he raised his right arm to shield his eyes and became aware of the stiffness in his back. There was an IV in his left arm. What happened? Where was he? Then he remembered. Slowly moving his wrist away from his eyes, he focused on the hospital room. Across the room sat Bob Scroggins and the security chief, Charles Rogers. Rogers was sound asleep, but Scroggins was eyeing him intently.

"How do you feel?"

"I'm okay, I guess. How long have I been out?"

"Just about all day."

"What time is it?"

"Six thirty in the evening."

"Where are the kids and Cass?"

"They're out at the security base."

"Are they okay?"

"Yeah. They're fine."

"Where's the security base?"

"It's in Westlake, where you were before."

"Where's the sheriff?"

"He's on the way back from a funeral in Houston."

"Did you find out who did the bombing? Was it Wade?"

"We're not sure who's in and who's out."

"Who is in for sure?"

"Harrison and Torrey."

"Torrey, the attorney?"

"Yeah."

"Who's Harrison?"

"Douglas Harrison, the political reporter."

Ray moved his wrist away from his eyes, withstanding the pain for a better look at Scroggins. Rogers was awake and stretching. Ray momentarily absorbed this without comment. What was a *Star-Telegram* reporter doing mixed up in this? "Are they in custody?"

"Yes and no. Torrey's in jail but Harrison made bail an hour ago."

"Are they talking?"

"Torrey is, but apparently he was controlled by somebody else. The only thing he helped with was the guy that followed Cass home on Sunday. That son of a bitch was none other than Buck Reed."

"*The* Buck Reed?"

"Yep."

"I knew that guy was dirty," chimed in Rogers.

"Why would Harrison want me dead?"

"We haven't figured that out yet. He might not even be in on it. He might have just known about it."

"And you let him out on bail?"

"We had no choice. The newspaper put up the bail."

"What about this Reed? He's still loose?"

"Probably not for long. We turned it over to the FBI. They've locked up the airports and borders tighter than a drum. They want him real bad."

"Torrey don't know who's behind this? He's got to be lying."

"Maybe not. He says that he was hired by telephone."

"When?"

"Last Friday, about noon."

"That sounds like Wade and Agnew."

"They already had a hit man. Pablo Cruz. Remember?"

Ray covered his eyes again. Then there was someone else that wanted him dead. *Why?* "Do you believe Torrey?"

"For the moment, we do. He told us he had a hunch on who it was. But we checked them out, and they're clean."

"Did Torrey know why whoever hired him wanted me dead?"

"No. He did say they did this because Stewart would get the blame."

"What does it cost to hire this Reed?"

"Twenty-five grand, I've heard."

"Jesus Christ. Somebody would pay that much to kill me? That doesn't make any sense."

"This whole damn thing don't make sense."

"Reed will know who hired him."

"I doubt it, if Torrey's telling the truth. They hired Torrey to hire Reed. They work strictly by public telephone and disguise their voices."

"How did Harrison know?"

"We don't know. He wouldn't talk. He invoked his right to counsel as soon as he sobered up. We didn't get a damn thing out of him."

"Who's his lawyer?"

"Lindsey."

"Then whoever hired this hit man is still out there."

"For the moment."

"Then my family and I aren't safe yet? Right?"

"That's how it looks to me."

Ray withdrew into silence as he thought things over. *How big was this and why? No court cases were big enough to cause this. If Harrison was involved, it has to be politics. Wade may have had a backup plan. That made more sense than anything else, but what is Wade's connection to Torrey? As far as I know, they don't even know each other. Harrison is no friend of Wade's. Harrison had blasted Wade in a newspaper column just a few weeks ago. What is Torrey's connection?*

"Who did Torrey name as a suspect?"

"He thought it was George Masters. He gave us a story about following Masters around when he was talking to a bunch of men about something, but it turned out to be just a lawsuit they were defending. Masters said he was there where Torrey followed him, but the subject was about something else."

George Masters! There was a guy that might benefit if I was dead. "Are you sure he's clean? Masters knows Wade pretty well."

"Yeah. We're sure of it. We checked the story out with the men he was meeting with and the court where the case is pending."

Ray closed his eyes again. A mixture of fear and anger slowly rose in his mind. These faceless people had tried to kill his children. That was his link to the future. *What kind of sickos would do something like that?* There was no ready answer, and the sheriff couldn't beat a confession out of the suspects.

Dr. Pulliam and a nurse walked into the room. The doctor checked Ray's chart at the foot of the bed for a moment, then approached him. After removing a small flashlight from his pocket, he opened Ray's left eye and studied it carefully. As he moved to the right one, he finally spoke. "How's your shoulder?"

"It's healing, Doctor. That seems to be the least of my problems."

"That appears to be so. Trouble seems to be finding you a lot these days. Look over to the wall to your right for me."

Rogers broke in. "How is he, Doctor?"

"He looks okay to me. There's not much chance of a serious concussion."

"Can we move him?"

"I suppose so, but I'd rather keep him here until tomorrow."

"That could be dangerous. The sheriff wants him moved as soon as you think it's possible. Our security's limited here."

The doctor bade Ray to sit up on the bed and checked his reflexes. "Stand up for me, please."

Ray stood. "Now extend your arms out, with your palms up. Keep your eyes closed and tilt your head back. Do you feel dizzy now?"

"No."

"Okay. I'll release him. Watch him close for aches in his eyes and head. Also watch for dizziness. If that happens, bring him back immediately."

"Yes sir. We will. Ray, get dressed. We're getting out of here."

"Get dressed in what? I wasn't wearing anything when I got here."

"Cass sent one of my men to buy you some clothes before she left. Here, I'll get them for you."

Scroggins waited until Ray was dressed and then extended his hand to Ray. "I'll keep you advised if anything else pops. I'm worn out. I'm going home for a little shut-eye."

Ray nodded as he tied his shoes. Declining a wheelchair, he followed Rogers out back to the waiting squad car, slowly working the kinks out of his muscles. Six blocks later, they approached a convenience store.

"Captain Rogers, could we stop for a Coke? I'm dry as a bone."

Rogers wheeled into the parking lot. "Don't take too long in there."

"Would you mind getting it for me? I don't have any money."

"That's right, you don't." Rogers switched off the engine and opened his door.

"Would you mind leaving the air conditioner on?"

"Sure. No problem." Rogers headed into the store. As soon as he disappeared, Ray moved over into the driver's seat as another car pulled up next to him. A young lady got out. Ray motioned her over.

"Miss, would you tell that guy inside with a blue shirt that I saw someone pass by that I must talk to? Tell him I'll be back in ten minutes."

"Sure. No problem."

"Thanks," said Ray as he reversed out of the space and tore out of the parking lot. The car hurtled west for a few blocks, until he found a restaurant. Ray ran inside and borrowed a phone book. Thankfully, Harrison had a listed phone number with his address. Ray wrote it down and went back to the car, frantically digging the Mapsco out of the back seat. It took only ten minutes to find Harrison's house. Ray drove carefully by and scouted the adjacent area. Harrison's garage door was open, and the surrounding houses looked quiet. After parking a few houses down, he stole cautiously into the garage and eased down the door. The garage was a smallish two-staller, with an empty space closest to the entrance to the house. Hanging on the walls were various garden tools, and there was a bench with tools sitting on it. Ray hurried to a blind spot next to the door as he heard footsteps approaching from inside the house. A big brute of a man appeared with a suitcase in each hand. He descended the two steps into the garage and stopped, noticing that the door had been pulled down. He dropped the suitcases as he spied Ray closing the distance to him. "What the—"

"You're going to tell me what I want to know, Harrison, or I'm going to break you up a piece at a time."

"You're Sterrett, aren't you?"

"Yeah. Who's trying to kill me?"

"Your mistake, Sterrett. I'm going to kick your ass! I used to box in the Golden Gloves. You've picked on the wrong man." Harrison swung at Ray with a roundhouse right. Ray sidestepped to his left and parried the punch with his right hand. With his left hand, Ray protruded his two prominent knuckles and punched Harrison with a left reverse to his right ribs, just below his collarbone. There was an audible crack as the ribs broke. Harrison staggered to his left, falling against the wall where the garden tools were. With his left hand, he reached up and grabbed a pair of garden shears and pointed them at Ray.

"You little bastard. I'm gonna cut your throat out for that."

"Your price just went up, Harrison."

Harrison lunged at Ray, snapping the shears at his throat. Ray easily ducked under the shears, sliding to his right. Raising his left leg up as far as it would go, Ray planted a roundhouse kick in Harrison's groin. Screaming in pain, he fell to his knees. As Ray kicked the shears away, Harrison rebounded to his feet and lunged for Ray with surprising speed, attempting a running tackle. Ray again slid to his left and caught him with a shin-to-shin sweep. Harrison cursed in pain as he fell to the concrete, landing on his face and hands.

Ray approached him cautiously as he had underestimated his strength and speed. "It takes special gutterslime to try to kill kids from a distance. When I get through with you, you won't be able to whip a five-year-old. You're nothing, Harrison. Nothing but slime at the bottom of a barrel. What's the matter, big boy? Has the fight gone out of you already? Two little broken ribs going to finish you?"

Harrison slowly rose to his feet, fear and hatred in his eyes. "When I get my hands on you, you little ass wipe, we'll see who can't whip a five-year-old." Assuming a boxer's stance, he aimed a left jab at Ray's jaw. Ray faded back, sliding his left foot past his right. Turning backwards to Harrison, he folded his right foot and sent a vicious side kick to Harrison's broken ribs. Harrison screamed as he went down flat. Ray withdrew his foot and backed away from the now panting Harrison.

"It's going to get worse, kid-killer. You're going to get acquainted with pain. Then you're going to beg to tell me what I want to know. But only when I'm ready."

Harrison slowly rose to his feet, holding his right arm in tight against his broken ribs. Feinting with his left, he swung a slow roundhouse right toward Ray, who blocked it with a rising left-forearm block. With his right hand, Ray extended his knuckles again and sent a knuckle strike to the inside of Harrison's right bicep. Harrison screamed again as he clutched his right arm. His forward motion carried him past Ray to the garden tool wall again. Ray smiled in amusement as he watched him grab a pitchfork off the wall.

"I let you do that, gutterslime. Is that what you use on ten-year-olds?"

Harrison lunged forward, the pitchfork extended with his left arm. Ray ducked down and aimed his right foot at Harrison's left knee. There was an audible crack as the knee snapped. Harrison screamed again as he slid down to his right, clutching his leg and supporting his body with his left arm. With sweat poring off his face, he looked up at Ray. The anger had faded. Now there was only fear.

"Don't quit now, scumbag. You've got too many good pieces left."

"What do you want, shitface?"

Ray snapped a kick at Harrison's left elbow, which cracked as loud as the knee had. This time Harrison screamed louder and longer. Sterrett leaned against the garden-tool wall and waited for the pain to subside. Harrison was wailing like a woman, with a high-pitched scream. Ray glanced out the window to see if the neighbors had been aroused. A front door was opening across the street. Ray moved quickly to Harrison's side and clamped his hand over his mouth. Harrison's screams subsided as he looked at Ray with fear radiating from every pore.

"Who's trying to kill me, sewer scum?"

"Screw you, Sterrett."

Ray grabbed Harrison's temples with his little fingers, extended his thumbs over Harrison's eyes, and pressed with medium pressure. Harrison screamed again. Ray took one hand off Harrison's eyes and clamped down on his mouth again.

"Want to try for blindness, too?"

"All right. All right. What do you want to know?"

"Who's trying to kill me?"

"Rachael Frank."

"Why?"

"I don't know."

Ray pressed down on the eyes again as he clamped Harrison's mouth. Harrison's strained against Ray's hand. "Why, Harrison?"

"The money, dammit."

"What money?"

"The money we're getting from the county suppliers. You were going to blow the lid on it when you asked for an investigation."

Ray stared at Harrison in disbelief. "That don't make any sense. I already turned that in to Commissioner Campbell. You had nothing to gain by killing me now."

"Rachael took care of Campbell this weekend."

"How?"

"She sent Brenda to compromise him. We've got pictures."

"Campbell would never fall for something like that."

"She set him up with a story that Rachael sent him bad figures and that she had the good ones. Once she got in the hotel room, she used her skill."

"You assholes tried to kill me and my family over a few measly bucks?"

"It's not measly. We're splitting a quarter of a million a year."

"Is that why the purchasing prices have been so high?"

"Yeah. Let me go."

"Who all is involved in this?"

"Rachael, me, and Gary Reynolds."

Ray heard a siren approaching. It sounded several blocks away. "How long has this been going on?"

"Several years."

"Where's Rachael right now?"

"I don't know. Probably at the Stagger Inn."

"Where's that?"

"Jacksboro Highway and University."

Ray reached back and coldcocked Harrison, whose head slumped back onto the concrete. That would gain him a little time. After seeing an ever-growing crowd of neighbors outside, he left out the back door and down the alley.

"This is Tarrant County Dispatch."

"This is Captain Charles Rogers. Is the sheriff back yet?"

"I don't think so, sir. Their flight's delayed out of Houston."

"Send me a unit to Rosedale and South Main. I'm stranded."

The dispatcher chuckled. "Did somebody steal your car?"

"As a matter of fact, he did. It was Judge Sterrett."

"Really? What in the hell for?"

"I don't know for sure, but I'm getting a sinking feeling that he's going after the bombers."

"Does he know who they are?"

"He knows enough. Transfer me to book in."

"Yes sir. Right away."

"Book in. This is Officer Stanley speaking."

"Stanley, this is Captain Rogers. We arrested a Douglas Harrison early this morning. I need his address pronto."

"Coming up, sir." Rogers heard computer keys being tapped. "906 Somerset Trail, Fort Worth."

"Thank you, Stanley." Rogers hung up as the sheriff's unit swung into the parking lot. The command to go was given as he swung inside.

"Where's your Mapsco?"

"It's in the back seat, sir."

Rogers grabbed the Mapsco and found the address. "Turn left and go the TCU area. Hit the lights and siren."

Five minutes later, they arrived and parked behind the Fort Worth police unit. After fighting through the crowd, they found the officers kneeling over a man who looked like he had just lost a war. The man was unconscious, with his left leg protruding out at a sickening angle. His breathing was labored.

Rogers abruptly turned back to his unit, his new assistant close behind. "What happened here, Captain?"

"Disaster. Total disaster."

After carefully slipping into the bar unnoticed, Ray spotted Rachael Frank and Gary Reynolds sitting together on the upper level. Quietly retreating to the parking lot, he waited for over an hour. Darkness was settling in when he spied the two exiting the club. Ray ducked down and barely beat them to Rachael's car. Approaching them from the rear, he turned Reynolds around and kicked him in the stomach before Reynolds knew what hit him. Ray whirled to Rachael, who hastily pulled a revolver from her purse and pointed at him.

"The jig's up, Rachael. We know everything."

"Then I don't have anything else to lose by killing you, do I?"

Ray pointed down at Reynolds. "Are you going to kill him, too? You'll never be safe with a witness."

Rachael Frank glanced down at Reynolds, as he knew she would. With his right foot, Ray sent a quick crescent kick to the gun. The gun swung away to the right but not out of her hand. As she swung it back toward Ray, he sent another kick to her right arm, sending the gun bouncing off the tire on the adjacent car. Between curses, she spat in his face. Wiping the spittle away, he slapped her with all his strength, sending her to her knees. After knocking the gun away from Reynolds, Ray reverse-kicked Rachael's legs out from under her as she attempted to rise. As she lay there sobbing, he turned his attention to Reynolds, who was regaining his breath. "How much more do you want, Reynolds?

Reynolds propped himself against the car, holding his stomach with both hands. "No more, Sterrett. Please. I'll do anything you say."

"Will you tell the sheriff everything you know about this? Including the theft scheme?"

Ray couldn't see Rachael crawling toward her revolver but Reynolds could. "Fat chance, Sterrett. I'll—" Ray turned out Reynold's lights with a kick to the chin. Watching his eyes roll back in his head would have been satisfying except for the clicking noise behind him. Ray whirled and chopped Rachael Frank in the throat as he felt his left chest and shoulder explode. The blast pushed him back against the car, and he slowly slipped to the ground as he fought for another breath. *Oh God! Don't let it end like this!* A shrill shriek pervaded his mind as he watched the blinding light coming at him from the kaleidoscopic sky. Brighter and brighter. *The kids, oh please! I can't stand this light!* "Cass—" Brighter and brighter.

Epilogue

A hush hung over the county offices the next morning. Employees read the newspaper in stunned silence. Legal counsel for the city of Arlington was calling for an investigation of Police Chief Parker. The FBI and the state comptroller's office were competing to do a countywide audit. Flags remained at half-mast. A few of the employees hovered around television sets, watching the special coverage. Newspaper reporters were scurrying everywhere trying to get quotes, but no one felt like talking.

Lee Sanders walked out to the top steps of the courthouse with Gary Baker and looked over his domain.

"Gary, I guess we're the laughing stock of the nation."

"It's a damn shame, boss."

"At least it's over."

"Yeah. A full night's sleep will be nice."

"Did you call the FBI to check on the manhunt for Reed?"

"Yes sir. No trace of him yet. I bet they get him by tomorrow. All the airports are covered, and the borders are shut tight, even Canada. They want him real bad."

"I really feel sorry for Ray."

"I know. He was damn lucky to get away with just a broken collarbone and punctured lung."

"I was with him when he came to. He thought he had died."

Baker turned toward the street. "How much legal trouble is he in?"

"Strictly self-defense as far as I'm concerned."

"Then why did you send the custody unit out to the hospital? Isn't he under arrest?"

"No. The custody unit was for Harrison. The newspaper rescinded their bond when they got the whole story this morning."

"What about beating the hell out of that reporter? You can't go around beating confessions out of people."

"I know. I know. But what would you do if somebody tried to kill your family, and the police couldn't get them to talk?"

"I'd do what he should have done and let the police handle it. I'd hide if necessary until they broke the case."

"That's easy to say. Hard to do."

"Will he lose his office?"

"Probably not. He'll have to face assault charges, but the DA told me that the grand jury won't even indict if he handles it right, and the DA knows how to handle it. He expects a no-bill."

"How long will Ray be in the hospital?"

"A few days."

"Did he say anything about marrying that clerk?"

"He said something about visiting his wife's grave."

Baker nodded. "I'm glad this is finally over. I bet he is, too."

"No matter what, he'll carry mental scars from this to his grave."

"Sheriff, this is a terrible thing with all the dead people."

"I know. There's one valuable lesson to be learned from this."

"What's that?"

"When violence takes over, everybody loses."

"Sheriff, there's one consolation, though."

"Yeah?"

"Some tranquility for awhile. I'm going to make a note on my calendar today. September 10, 2001. The first day of lasting peace in Tarrant County."

Acknowledgments

There were so many people who provided their knowledge and expertise that I can't begin to name them all. The ones listed below volunteered many hours helping with this work.

Don Andrews	North Richland Hills Fire Department	Explosives
Judge Roy Kurban	Precinct 7 Justice of the Peace	Karate
Barbara Davis	True crime writer	Book format and editing
Dr. Steve Weinberg	Doctor, lawyer, and good friend	General advice
Janice Eisen	My daughter	Editing
Dave Leiber	Fort Worth Star Telegram columnist	General advice
John Steinsiek	Retired chief deputy constable	Cover photography

Last and not least, my wonderful wife, Linda, who always gave me encouragement and was determined to see this book achieve success.

About the Author

Sandy Prindle was a Tarrant County justice of the peace for twenty-four years. He retired December 31, 2006. During his career, he served Texas by sitting on numerous boards, ,writing and passing laws to better the justice courts, and lecturing on the civil war and the Lincoln assassination. His positions of service included president of the Justices of the Peace and Constables Association of Texas (JPCA), vice president of Texas Association of Counties (TAC) and legislative chairman of JPCA three times. In addition, he taught law to the other judges through the Texas Justice Court Training Center from 1995 until retirement. His awards include JPCA Judge of the Year (2000), JPCA T. A. Vines award, and JPCA Lifetime Achievement Award.

He lives in Tarrant County with his wife, Linda. He has retired to write fiction full time.

Watch in the near future for *Neptune's Farewell, The Sins of Our Forefathers,* and *The Cleansing of the Sins.*

To order more copies of this book, read about his future novels, or provide input, please visit his website at prindlesnovels.com

BUY A SHARE OF THE FUTURE IN YOUR COMMUNITY

These certificates make great holiday, graduation and birthday gifts that can be personalized with the recipient's name. The cost of one S.H.A.R.E. or one square foot is $54.17. The personalized certificate is suitable for framing and will state the number of shares purchased and the amount of each share, as well as the recipient's name. The home that you participate in "building" will last for many years and will continue to grow in value.

Here is a sample SHARE certificate:

THIS CERTIFIES THAT

YOUR NAME HERE

HAS INVESTED IN A HOME FOR A DESERVING FAMILY

1985-2005

TWENTY YEARS OF BUILDING FUTURES IN OUR COMMUNITY ONE HOME AT A TIME

1200 SQUARE FOOT HOUSE @ $65,000 = $54.17 PER SQUARE FOOT
This certificate represents a tax deductible donation. It has no cash value.

YES, I WOULD LIKE TO HELP!

I support the work that Habitat for Humanity does and I want to be part of the excitement! As a donor, I will receive periodic updates on your construction activities but, more importantly, I know my gift will help a family in our community realize the dream of homeownership. **I would like to SHARE in your efforts against substandard housing in my community!** *(Please print below)*

PLEASE SEND ME _____ SHARES at $54.17 EACH = $ $_____

In Honor Of: _____

Occasion: (Circle One)   HOLIDAY   BIRTHDAY   ANNIVERSARY

     OTHER: _____

Address of Recipient: _____

Gift From: _____ *Donor Address:* _____

Donor Email: _____

I AM ENCLOSING A CHECK FOR $ $_____ PAYABLE TO HABITAT FOR HUMANITY <u>OR</u> PLEASE CHARGE MY VISA OR MASTERCARD *(CIRCLE ONE)*

Card Number _____ Expiration Date: _____

Name as it appears on Credit Card _____ Charge Amount $ _____

Signature _____

Billing Address _____

Telephone # Day _____ Eve _____

PLEASE NOTE: Your contribution is tax-deductible to the fullest extent allowed by law.
Habitat for Humanity • P.O. Box 1443 • Newport News, VA 23601 • 757-596-5553
www.HelpHabitatforHumanity.org